# SEE
# HER DIE

# ALSO BY MELINDA LEIGH

## BREE TAGGERT NOVELS

*Cross Her Heart*

## MORGAN DANE NOVELS

*Say You're Sorry*

*Her Last Goodbye*

*Bones Don't Lie*

*What I've Done*

*Secrets Never Die*

*Save Your Breath*

## SCARLET FALLS NOVELS

*Hour of Need*

*Minutes to Kill*

*Seconds to Live*

## SHE CAN SERIES

*She Can Run*

*She Can Tell*

*She Can Scream*

*She Can Hide*

*"He Can Fall"* (A Short Story)

*She Can Kill*

## Midnight Novels

*Midnight Exposure*

*Midnight Sacrifice*

*Midnight Betrayal*

*Midnight Obsession*

## The Rogue Series Novellas

*Gone to Her Grave* (Rogue River)

*Walking on Her Grave* (Rogue River)

*Tracks of Her Tears* (Rogue Winter)

*Burned by Her Devotion* (Rogue Vows)

*Twisted Truth* (Rogue Justice)

## The Widow's Island Novella Series

*A Bone to Pick*

*Whisper of Bones*

# SEE
# HER DIE

## MELINDA LEIGH

Published by Montlake, Seattle

www.apub.com

Amazon, the Amazon logo, and Montlake are trademarks of Amazon.com, Inc., or its affiliates.

ISBN-13: 9781542006965 (paperback)
ISBN-10: 1542006961 (paperback)

ISBN-13: 9781542006989 (hardcover)
ISBN-10: 1542006988 (hardcover)

Cover design by Shasti O'Leary Soudant

Printed in the United States of America

First edition

*For Charlie, Annie, and Tom*

# CHAPTER ONE

The scream faded, the sound muffled through the walls of the cabin. Alyssa blinked in the darkness. Outside, the March wind whistled through the trees. Inside, the quiet that hung in the air was almost as sharp as the bitter cold. Her heartbeat thrummed in her ears.

*An owl?*

Her instincts said no. The tone had been all wrong.

There were no lights to turn on. Electricity and running water to the cabin had been shut off. But then, they were trespassing in a campground that was closed for the season. She couldn't complain about the lack of facilities.

"Harper," she whispered. "Did you hear that?"

No one answered.

She glanced sideways, looking for the other sleeping bag stretched out in front of the fireplace, where her friend usually slept a few feet away. Overnight, the fire had died to glowing embers, and it took a few seconds for her vision to adjust to the predawn dimness. The floor was empty. Harper's sleeping bag was gone. So was her backpack.

Alyssa's pulse quickened, scrambling through her veins like a mouse scurrying for its hole. She bolted upright, the sleeping bag falling away from her shoulders. The chill and a rush of adrenaline swept away her grogginess like a freezing wave. Holding her breath, she stared at the empty space on the floor and listened hard. Harper had probably gone out back to pee. She could have startled an animal. Or an animal could have startled her.

*No.*

She almost groaned at her own stupidity. Harper wouldn't have taken her sleeping bag and backpack outside to pee.

She'd left.

But why? And how did she leave? Harper didn't have a vehicle.

*Shit!*

Alyssa grabbed for her own backpack at her feet. She unzipped the front compartment and shoved her hand inside. Her wallet was gone. She rooted deeper in the bag, but it wasn't there. Neither were her keys. Her wallet contained her driver's license and her last forty-three dollars, which had to last until Friday. Today was Monday. How was she going to buy food? How was she going to get to work with no transportation?

Her stomach cramped. She'd been played. Harper had made friends with her with the sole intention of stealing her money and truck. Forty-three dollars would top off the gas tank. Harper could get pretty far away. Alyssa thought about when she'd picked up Harper from work the night before. They'd stopped at a convenience store. Harper had said she'd gotten a tip. She'd splurged on the makings for s'mores. They'd toasted marshmallows over the fire and eaten every bite.

Had the celebration been Harper's way of saying goodbye?

Alyssa sprang out of her sleeping bag and scooped her parka off the floor. Standing, she shivered as she zipped her coat and shoved her feet into her boots. She'd worn her wool hat to bed.

She'd trusted Harper, but they'd met only the previous month at the homeless shelter. What did Alyssa really know about her?

*Only what she told you. And you believed her. Because you're naive and stupid.*

Alyssa ran for the front door and flung it open. She fished a flashlight from her pocket and shone it into the trees. Her breath whooshed from her lungs when she saw her old 4Runner parked where she'd left it. Harper hadn't taken her SUV. Alyssa sagged against the doorjamb. Snow had fallen the previous evening while she was at work, and there were no other new footprints in front of the cabin except her own. Harper hadn't gone out the front door. Alyssa closed the door and turned around.

So, where was Harper? And where were Alyssa's wallet and keys?

She returned to her backpack. Maybe she'd put her keys in a different pouch. She'd been tired after work. She inspected each section, then checked her coat pockets. No keys. No wallet. She took out her cell phone and turned it on. She could only charge it at work or in her car and tried to conserve the battery. Besides, she only used the phone to contact work or text Harper. When they were together, there was no reason to keep the phone on. The phone came to life, but she saw no texts or missed calls.

She shoved the phone into her pocket. She didn't want to believe that Harper had betrayed her. It had been Harper's idea that they travel as a pair. The whole point of sticking together was to have each other's backs. It didn't feel right that she would have left without saying a word. Alyssa replayed their last conversation in her mind. Harper had given no indication that she wanted to leave. She'd said the cabin was the best spot she'd slept in all winter. She'd gathered enough firewood to last for days. But there was no one else here who could have taken Alyssa's things.

Teary-eyed, she repacked her bag. She needed the key to her vehicle or she was stranded. Why had Harper taken the keys but left the 4Runner?

*What the actual fuck?*

It made no sense. Harper was street-smart. She wouldn't come up with such a dumb plan. Maybe the plan wasn't the issue. Maybe she hadn't left *yet*. Alyssa could possibly still catch her.

She set aside the pack and strode to the window overlooking the backyard. Fifty feet of ground separated the cabin from the surrounding woods. Alyssa squinted into the darkness at the area they'd designated as their bathroom, behind a group of fir trees. A figure moved at the edge of the trees.

*Harper?*

Anger blurred Alyssa's vision. She hurried to the back door.

*Think you can steal my stuff? Think again.*

Opening it quietly, she slipped outside and jogged across the snow to the woods. She peered around a tree trunk, looking for the figure. She spotted the dark shape emerging from the trees near the lake.

The figure wasn't carrying a backpack. Had Harper stashed it somewhere? What was she up to? Alyssa followed, keeping her distance, but also keeping the figure in sight. She'd walked maybe a hundred feet when the silhouette turned toward her.

The shape of the figure didn't feel like Harper. She was thin. This shape was too large, too wide—more masculine.

Panic welled in Alyssa's chest.

Could that be the campground owner, Phil? Someone could have seen smoke rising from the cabin's chimney and called him. The campground was closed. No one was supposed to be there. Maybe it was Phil, coming to chase them out of the cabin. That might be the reason Harper had run.

Bitterness tasted sour in the back of her throat. If that scenario was true, then Harper had saved her own ass and left Alyssa to face Phil alone. And she'd still stolen from Alyssa.

*Bitch.*

*Now what?*

If it was Phil . . . He was in pretty good shape, but he was old. She could probably outrun him.

He retraced his steps—heading right for her.

*Phil?*

The man's posture wasn't annoyed or angry. He moved with intention.

She ducked behind the tree and waited, holding her breath. A tiny sound croaked deep in her throat, as if something had broken. Pressing her back into the tree, she prayed he hadn't heard. The wind blew through the trees, kicking up snow dust. *Where is he?* Slowly, she peered around the tree trunk and froze. He was barely thirty feet away.

She withdrew. Tears ran down her cheeks, feeling as if they were freezing on her face.

*Please don't find me.*

A footstep crunched in the snow. Was he closer? She risked another peek from behind the tree trunk. Two blasts sounded over the snow— and fear paralyzed her. Her mouth opened. Slapping her hand across it, she stifled the scream before it left her mouth.

For a few precious seconds, her feet felt glued in place; then she shook off the shock, whirled, and ran.

# CHAPTER TWO

Sheriff Bree Taggert reached toward her nightstand and killed the ringer on her phone. Tilting the screen, she read the display. The call was from dispatch. She glanced at her eight-year-old niece, Kayla, pressed against her side, but the child hadn't stirred. A large white-and-black pointer mix, Ladybug, lifted her head from its resting spot on Bree's ankle. Vader, Bree's black cat, occupied the second pillow, as far away from the dog as he could get. The sprawling child and animals left Bree with approximately eight inches of mattress. Trying not to wake Kayla, Bree half slid, half fell out of bed. Clutching her phone, she scrambled for the bathroom before it rang again.

She closed the door and answered the call in a low voice. "Sheriff Taggert."

"We received a 911 call reporting multiple shots fired at Grey Lake Campground." The dispatcher gave the address.

Adrenaline blasted the grogginess from Bree's head. A few gunshots in the woods would not rate a dark o'clock phone call to the sheriff. "Casualties?"

"One victim reported, a female. The caller, also a female, was whispering and not speaking clearly."

"Is she still on the line?" Bree knew from personal experience that 911 operators tried to stay on the phone with callers until law enforcement arrived. She suppressed that memory before it interfered with her concentration. Her compartmentalizing skills had been working overtime since her sister had been murdered back in January.

"Negative," the dispatcher said. "She was worried the shooter would hear and hung up."

The banished memory resurfaced and soured Bree's empty stomach. "How many units are responding?"

"Three. ETA for the nearest car is twelve minutes."

*Too long.* They must be on the other side of the county.

The graveyard shift was bare bones in the upstate New York sheriff's department Bree had been appointed to lead just three weeks before. Day shift wasn't staffed much better. Her deputies were spread across the huge expanse of mostly rural Randolph County.

"I'm on my way." Bree ended the call, swigged mouthwash straight from the bottle, spit, and slipped out of the bathroom. She opened the closet. The dog watched as Bree changed from her flannel pajamas to dark-brown tactical cargo pants, a base layer tank top, and a tan uniform shirt. After tugging on wool socks, she opened the biometric gun safe she'd mounted on the top shelf. She strapped her baby Glock to her ankle, threaded her utility belt through the loops on her pants, and added her Glock 19 to its holster.

When she'd been a Philadelphia homicide detective, she'd worn only a gun and badge. As sheriff, she didn't need the full twenty-five pounds of standard patrol gear when she wouldn't even leave her office most days. But she carried a few small essentials in addition to her gun: handcuffs, pepper spray, an expandable baton, and a combat tourniquet.

Two months ago, she'd seen how quickly a person could bleed to death.

As Bree headed for the door, the dog jumped off the bed. The mattress shifted and dog tags jingled. Bree held her breath, but her niece continued to snore. Ladybug followed Bree downstairs. The sun was an hour from rising, but a light glowed in the kitchen. Bree smelled fresh coffee as she rushed into the room, trying not to trip over the dog, who was far too large to be underfoot.

Dana Romano, Bree's former partner at the Philadelphia PD, now retired, sat at the table reading a cookbook and drinking coffee. An early riser, she was already dressed, and her short, gray-streaked blonde hair was fashionably tousled. She lowered her coffee cup. "What's wrong?"

"There's been a shooting." Bree shoved her feet into a pair of boots sitting in the rubber tray by the back door. Ladybug pressed against Bree's legs, nearly buckling her knees. "You could give me some space," Bree said to the dog.

"She's really attached to you." Dana got to her feet.

"But why?" Two months after Bree had been masterfully manipulated into adopting the rescue, she was still disconcerted by the dog's presence. But she was pleased that the panic had ebbed. Ladybug was nothing like Bree's father's dogs. The chubby rescue would never maul a child. The scars on Bree's ankle and shoulder ached with the thirty-year-old memory. Thoughts of her father and his dogs automatically led to the night her father had shot her mother and then himself. Bree had hidden her two younger siblings under the porch. She forced the past from her mind. She was on her way to stop a shooter. She couldn't afford to be distracted.

"Maybe she knows you need her." Dana moved toward the fancy coffee machine she'd brought from her apartment in Philly. Bree's best friend had dropped her whole life to move to Grey's Hollow and help raise Bree's orphaned niece and nephew.

"No time for coffee." Bree slipped into her winter jacket.

As usual, Dana ignored her. She poured coffee into a travel mug.

"Kayla is in my bed. If she wakes alone . . ."

Dana screwed on the lid and fished a protein bar from a drawer. "I'll go sit with her."

"Thank you."

Dana handed the mug and bar to Bree and grabbed the dog's collar. "Be careful."

"Will do." Bree slipped out the back door. A horse neighed from the dark barn as Bree ran along the shoveled walkway to her county-issued SUV. In upstate New York, early March was still very much winter. She slipped into the driver's seat, shoved her coffee and protein bar into the console cup holders, and started the engine. She drove onto the main road and entered the address into the GPS. Her ETA was seven minutes. The campground wasn't far from her house. Five minutes had passed since she'd received the call. Lights flashing, she pressed the gas pedal and cut her drive from seven minutes to six.

Bree slowed her SUV as she approached the entrance to Grey Lake Campground. She turned off the cleared main road onto the snow-covered lane that led into the campground. The lights from her vehicle swirled in red, white, and blue on the snowy ground. Beyond, the woods were dark. She saw no sign of other sheriff vehicles.

Bree was first on scene.

She reached for her radio. "Sheriff Taggert, code eleven."

Dispatch answered, "Copy. Be advised ETA for Unit Twelve is one minute. Two additional units following in four."

"Copy," Bree said and let out the breath trapped in her lungs. Backup was right behind her, not that she would have waited. A possible active shooter needed to be stopped ASAP.

Her headlights illuminated tire tracks in the narrow, snow-covered lane. Did they belong to the shooter's vehicle?

The hairs on the back of her neck stood at attention, and a rush of adrenaline cranked up her pulse. Her SUV slid through a bend in the lane and fishtailed. She steered into the skid. As soon as the tires gained traction, she pressed the gas pedal again.

Wooden signs nailed to trees directed visitors to the numbered cabins. She followed the arrows for another few minutes, driving deeper into the woods, until she spotted a sign that read CABIN TWENTY. She stopped her SUV at the end of the lane and scanned the clearing for the shooter or the victim.

She saw no one. She reached behind her seat for her Kevlar vest marked SHERIFF. She wiggled out of her jacket and donned the vest over her uniform shirt. As she kept watch through the windshield, Bree slid her arms back into her jacket, leaving it open for easy access to her weapon.

A cabin occupied the center of a clearing roughly the size of a baseball diamond. Her gaze followed a set of tire tracks. Forty feet from the cabin, the rear bumper of a gray Toyota 4Runner poked out from behind a stand of trees. One set of footprints led from the 4Runner to the cabin's front door. There were no footprints heading back to the vehicle. Someone had gone inside.

*The victim? The caller?*

*The shooter?*

She reached for her door handle. Emergency lights pulsed in her rearview mirror. She glanced behind her. The lights of a patrol car cut through the predawn gloom. A few seconds later, the vehicle parked next to her SUV, and Deputy Jim Rogers emerged.

Bree stepped out into the cold and joined him behind his vehicle. Their breath steamed in the pale gray morning. Despite the temperature, sweat gathered under Bree's shirt and vest.

She drew her weapon.

Rogers did the same. "We're going in?"

"We are." Bree had a clear view of the north side of the cabin, but she couldn't see the south side or rear. "Have you been inside these cabins?"

"Yes." Rogers squinted at the cabin. "This looks like a one-bedroom." He picked up a stick, drew a rectangle in the snow, and used the stick as a pointer. "Main room. Bedroom. Bath."

"Let's check around back first." Bree led the way to the front corner of the cabin. They stuck close to the building. Bree stopped beneath a window too high for either one of them to see inside. She motioned for Rogers to give her a boost. He cupped his hands. Bree stepped into them and peered over the windowsill, ready to duck if someone pointed a gun at her face.

The shooter could be anywhere.

She could see into the main room, a combination kitchen and living area. A wood-framed couch and chair had been pulled away from the fireplace to make room for a sleeping bag. In the fireplace, embers glowed pale orange under a heavy layer of gray-and-black ash. A backpack stood nearby, zipped and ready to go.

Stepping down, she shook her head and whispered, "Empty, but someone is squatting here."

"Not the first time," said Rogers.

They continued around to the back of the cabin. Multiple sets of footprints led to and from the covered rear porch, across fifty feet of open ground, to the woods. Still, they saw no body, no blood, no shooter.

Bree rounded the next corner. The shore of Grey Lake lay approximately a hundred feet to the south of the cabin, and she could see the flat, opaque surface of the frozen water through the winter-bare trees.

They halted next to another window and repeated the leg-up procedure. The single bedroom also appeared empty.

She stepped down. In a low voice, she said, "There are two closed doors."

Rogers nodded. "Closet and bathroom."

A bird screeched, but the woods were otherwise silent.

Bree led the way back around toward the front of the cabin.

She stopped next to the porch steps and scanned the surrounding woods. "Where are they?"

Rogers lifted and dropped a tense shoulder. "The call could have been a prank."

"I don't like the setup." Goose bumps rippled up Bree's arms. Her instincts screamed that something was wrong. In her early patrol years, she and her partner had responded to an odd call. They'd been ambushed by a gang and had been lucky to escape without any extra holes. Now, possible ambush scenarios played through her mind. "Could also be a trap."

With a cool eye, Rogers acknowledged her point with another jerky shrug. Regardless of the danger, they were going in. They stepped onto the porch and flanked the door. Bree tried the knob. It turned, and the door opened with a squeal of rusty hinges.

Bree crossed the threshold first and swung to her left. Rogers angled to the right. Bree swept her weapon from corner to corner. Dust motes hung suspended in the pale light that poured in through the window. Her side of the room was empty. No large furniture or doors for anyone to hide behind.

"Clear," she said.

Rogers echoed, "Clear."

She returned to Rogers's side, and they approached the open bedroom door shoulder to shoulder. The room was empty. Bree crossed the rough plank floor to one of the two closed doors. She pulled a flashlight from her pocket. Standing to the side, she opened the door and shone her flashlight inside. There was no one in the small bathroom.

"Clear," she said.

Rogers crouched to check under the bed. "Clear."

One closed door remained.

Rogers was closest. He flung the door open and aimed his gun into the doorway. A scream split the air.

Bree's heart lurched. She pointed her flashlight into the closet. At the rear of the small space, a teenage girl stood clutching a short-handled ax in one hand and a cell phone in the other. She was pressed into the corner, and she looked as if she was trying to be as small as possible. In the eerie light, her face was as white as the snow outside, and tears streaked her face.

"Drop the ax!" Rogers shouted.

Sobbing, the girl opened her fingers and raised her hands in front of her face. She cringed. The ax and phone clattered to the floor.

"Push the ax away from you!" he commanded.

The girl obeyed, nudging the ax with her foot. Outside, sirens marked the arrival of additional deputies.

Rogers backed up. "Come out slowly! Keep your hands where I can see them."

The girl emerged from the small space, her movements uneven and shaky. She was tall, probably eighteen or nineteen years old, dressed in worn jeans, boots, and a dirty parka. Long dark hair tumbled in a thick tangle from under a knit cap, and she looked like it had been a while since she'd showered. She moved toward them. "Y-you have to help her. He shot her. He shot Harper."

"Stop right there!" Rogers angled off, aiming his gun at her.

She blinked at Rogers and then Bree. "Did you find Harper?"

"Who's Harper?" Bree asked.

"My friend." The girl wiped her eyes.

"Keep those hands visible," Rogers shouted again.

The girl raised them over her head. "No. You don't understand." Her voice rose and broke. "A man shot Harper."

Rogers rushed forward. He holstered his weapon, then jerked her hands behind her back and cuffed her. He spun her around so fast she almost went down. "Where's the shooter? Where's the victim?"

"I don't know!" the girl cried. "But Harper was shot. Why aren't you looking for her? Why are you arresting me?"

"Because you were carrying the ax," Rogers said.

She shook her head. "It was all I had to protect myself."

"From whom?" Bree asked.

"From the man who shot Harper." The girl's tone sharpened with frustration.

"Your friend Harper was staying here with you?" Bree asked.

"Yes," the girl said. As the female officer on scene, and not liking Rogers's rough handling of the girl, Bree moved in to search her pockets and person. She found a small folding multi-tool, but no weapons. For now, she'd bag the tool, the ax, and the girl's phone as evidence.

Opening the phone, Bree verified the girl was the 911 caller. "What's your name?"

"Alyssa Vincent," she said. Her face twisted in confusion and fear.

"And your friend's name?" Bree asked.

"Harper. Harper Scott."

Rogers yanked her toward the door. She resisted Rogers's attempt to move her. He pulled harder. The toe of her boot caught on a raised floorboard, and she stumbled and pitched forward. With no hands to block her fall, she hit the floor face-first.

Bree glanced at Rogers. He was breathing hard. His face was flushed, and sweat gleamed on his forehead. Adrenaline overload? Could he not handle the stress? He was an avid hunter, but deer didn't shoot back at you. The girl was unarmed, handcuffed, and clearly no longer a threat, but he didn't seem to register that information. Was something wrong with him? He seemed off. Bree had worked with him for only a few weeks. She didn't have enough personal experience with him to make a judgment on his behavior.

Bree motioned Rogers to back off, then helped the girl to her feet. "Where did the shooting happen?"

The girl led them back into the main room. Red-and-blue strobe lights pulsed through the window.

"Out there." Alyssa turned to the rear window and inclined her head toward the view. "On the ice. Behind the cabin next door. A scream woke me up. I couldn't find Harper. I went outside to look for her. That's when I saw him shoot her. She fell." The girl's words flowed over one another. "And she didn't get up. He saw me, and I ran."

"How many times did he fire his weapon?" Bree asked.

"Twice," Alyssa said with no hesitation.

"Describe him," Bree said.

Alyssa closed her eyes, as if trying to picture him in her mind. "Tall, dark pants, boots, dark coat. He was wearing a hat."

"Could you see the color of his hair or eyes?"

The girl shook her head. "The hat covered his hair, and it was too dark to see his eyes."

Two deputies came through the front door; one of them was Bree's second-in-command, Chief Deputy Todd Harvey.

Bree handed the girl over to the second deputy. "Put her in your vehicle and watch her."

She signaled to Rogers. "Let's check out the lake."

"Yes, ma'am." Rogers's words were clipped.

Bree scanned the snow. Somewhere in the forest, a victim was bleeding.

And a shooter was on the loose.

# CHAPTER THREE

"Let's go, Greta." Matt Flynn waved a hand, directing the pure-black German shepherd toward the next obstacle on the homemade agility course. The approaching dawn brightened the horizon. Snow flew from under the dog's feet.

Greta pricked her ears and sprinted for the plastic tunnel. Her body was lean and sleek as she zoomed across the snow. She raced through, emerging out the other side at top speed and looking to Matt for his next command.

He headed for the next obstacle, a crate pushed in front of a four-feet-tall section of wooden fence. Matt motioned for Greta to go over it. The dog leaped onto the crate and scaled the fence in one smooth motion. Matt called her back, and she repeated the jump from the other side. He dangled her tug toy, and she latched on to it.

"Good girl!" Matt swung her around in a circle. She held on. The dog landed, tail wagging, loving every minute of their game. Extreme tug was her favorite at the moment.

"I can't believe her transformation," a familiar voice called.

Matt turned toward the voice.

His sister, Cady, stood at the edge of the yard, her hands propped on her hips. The spotlight mounted on the back of Matt's house shone on her strawberry-blonde ponytail. "I'm amazed with what you've done with her. She was rejected by two families."

Cady operated a dog rescue organization. As a former K-9 handler with the sheriff's department, Matt was specially equipped to deal with her more challenging rescues, including Greta.

"People buy puppies because they're cute without any knowledge of the breed characteristics. Herding dogs are bred to work. They get bored easily." Matt commanded the dog to release the toy. When she dropped it, he stuffed it into the leg pocket of his cargo pants. "She is super smart."

*Probably smarter than the people who returned her.*

"Do you think she'll calm down?" Cady asked.

"Honestly, I don't know. She's a year old and still high maintenance." Matt looked down at the dog. Greta stood at attention, her huge black ears still pricked forward, her focus entirely fixed on Matt. She was ready for the next game. "I wouldn't call her excitable. *Driven* is a better word. I'm not sure it's a trait she'll outgrow."

A few seconds of unnatural silence passed. Matt's instincts went on alert. His sister was never quiet.

"I need to ask you a favor," Cady said.

"The last time you said that, you took over my kennel." Matt and his K-9 partner, Brody, had been caught in the cross fire between the sheriff's department and a drug dealer. Injuries had ended both of their careers. With his settlement from the county, Matt had bought the property and built a kennel to train K-9s. He'd intended to import dogs from Germany, but Cady had "temporarily" filled the kennel with overflows from her dog rescue. Three years later, the kennel was still full of homeless dogs, and Matt hadn't made any progress getting his business started.

Cady turned both palms up in a sorry-not-sorry gesture.

Matt snapped the leash onto Greta's collar. "What do you need?"

She gestured toward the kennel. Matt recognized the older woman standing next to Cady's minivan. In her seventies, with a head of fluffy white curls and a hearing aid, Mrs. Whitney fostered senior dogs for Cady's rescue. Since most of the animals Mrs. Whitney took in were unadoptable due to age and illness, Cady referred to her house as a small-dog hospice. Usually, she was energetic for her age. Today, her posture was stiff, and she was clenching her hands together.

"What's wrong with Mrs. Whitney?" he asked.

"She reported her grandson missing."

"Eli?" Matt had never met him, but Mrs. Whitney talked about him all the time, and there were about a thousand pictures of the university student in her house.

"Yes." Cady's brow furrowed. "She's really worried. Could you find out what's happening with the case? She can't hear well, and she gets confused."

"I don't work for the sheriff's department anymore."

Cady pursed her lips. "But you must still have friends in the department."

*Friends?*

Matt suppressed a snort. "You do remember I was shot by friendly fire."

Officially, the incident had been labeled an accident, but Matt's relationship with the sheriff's department was strained.

"But you're close to the new sheriff," Cady suggested.

"I haven't seen her since she became sheriff."

Matt and Bree were supposed to have dinner a few weeks ago, but she'd canceled. He hoped she was just busy.

Cady's eyes begged. "Please, just listen to Mrs. Whitney."

Matt sighed. "You know I will."

They walked over to Mrs. Whitney.

The wind kicked up across the yard, and Mrs. Whitney shivered. "Thank you so much for helping."

Matt held up a hand. "Come inside. I haven't had my coffee yet."

Greta needed exercise immediately upon being freed from her crate in the morning. Otherwise, she tormented Brody. Matt commanded her to heel in German, and they walked toward the house. Greta fell into step at his side, glancing up at Matt every few strides to look for a new direction.

Matt led the way into the kitchen. Brody sighed from his dog bed in the corner. Greta made a beeline for the older dog, dropped her shoulders to the ground, and wagged her butt in the air. When Brody ignored her, she nipped at him.

Matt commanded her to leave him alone.

Greta stopped and glanced back at Matt as if to check whether he was serious. He maintained eye contact. Her tail drooped. She gave Brody one last *killjoy* look, then veered off toward the water bowl. When she was finished drinking, she plucked a black KONG toy from a wooden box in the corner and tossed it in the air.

Matt brewed coffee.

Cady pulled out a chair for Mrs. Whitney, then sat down. Brody got to his feet, stretched, and walked over to greet Cady. She rubbed behind his ears. "That's my best boy. Does that youngster annoy you?"

Brody wagged. A traditional black-and-tan German shepherd, he had big brown eyes and excelled in looking pitiful. Today, he rested his head in Cady's lap and gave her a *woe is me* look that could have won an Oscar.

"Brody has traded early-morning training sessions for after-breakfast naps," Matt said.

Brody moved from Cady to greet Mrs. Whitney, sitting and lifting a paw with his best company manners. The older woman seemed to calm as she stroked the dog's head.

Matt brought three mugs to the table and sat across from Mrs. Whitney.

"Thanks for seeing me," she said. "I don't know who else to ask. I'm so worried about Eli."

"When did he go missing?" Matt rested his forearms on his kitchen table and gave Mrs. Whitney his full attention.

She pulled a tissue from her handbag and pressed it to her blotchy face. "Last night, he was supposed to come to my house for Sunday dinner. When he didn't show up, I called his friends."

Matt cleared his throat. "I don't want to be . . . um, indelicate, but maybe he's with someone. Does he have a girlfriend?"

Mrs. Whitney's parchment-colored cheeks flushed. "No. He doesn't have a girlfriend at the moment, and I'm well aware that a young man would rather spend a weekend with a young woman than visit his grandmother." She blew out a loud breath through her nostrils. "But if Eli was going to cancel, he would call. He might give me a ridiculous excuse, but he'd call. He knows I worry. I called him. I texted, but he hasn't responded. *That's* not like him either."

Matt asked, "What about other family? Brothers, sisters—"

"There's no one." Mrs. Whitney's voice dropped to almost a whisper. "Eli is an only child. My son and his wife were killed in an auto accident when Eli was sixteen. For the last six years, it's just been the two of us."

"I'm sorry." Matt swallowed a lump of empathy the size of a basketball.

She nodded. "His friends said he went to a party Saturday night. They asked around, and someone who was at the party saw Eli leave around one in the morning, but no one has seen him since. I called the police. An officer came and took a report, but he said what you did. Eli probably *hooked up*." She said the last two words as if they were unfamiliar.

"Did he drive to the party?" Matt asked.

"No. He always uses one of the apps to get a ride." Mrs. Whitney shook her head. "A drunk driver killed his parents. Eli would never drink and drive."

"Mrs. Whitney is worried the police aren't doing enough." Cady wrapped her arm around the older woman's shoulders.

Mrs. Whitney bowed her head and closed her eyes for a few seconds. Her pink scalp shone through her white hair.

Raising her chin, she opened her eyes and sniffed. "The officer kept saying, 'He's an adult. He doesn't need to check in with his grandmother.'" She paused for a long, shaky inhalation. "But I know my grandson. Something has happened to him. Please tell me you'll help find him."

"Where does he live?" Matt slid a sticky-note pad and a pen from the center of the table.

"Scarlet Falls." Mrs. Whitney gave an address in the neighboring town.

Matt wrote it down. "Which police department is handling the case? Scarlet Falls is under town, county, and state jurisdictions."

"I don't know." Mrs. Whitney's eyes creased. She stopped, stifling a sob with her tissue.

"Do you know the original officer's name?" Matt asked.

"No," Mrs. Whitney said. "I'm sorry. I can't always hear. He gave me a card, but I lost it." Mrs. Whitney patted the pockets of her jacket. "I'm so worried. I can't concentrate."

"No worries. I can call around and find out who's in charge of the case." Matt could not turn down this little old lady who, despite her own frailties, never said no to an animal in need.

"I was up all night. This morning I turned on the news, and I saw—" She inhaled, her breath shaky. "The reporters said the police were organizing a search of the riverbank this morning. They're looking for a missing university student." She stifled a sob. "It must be Eli."

"You don't know that." Cady touched Mrs. Whitney's forearm, then turned to Matt. "I went to Mrs. Whitney's house early to pick up a dog for a vet surgery appointment. She was in tears."

"Did the officer give you any more information when he took your report?" Matt asked.

Mrs. Whitney sniffed. "He said he would talk to Eli's friends and ask around the neighborhood where the party was held. He was going to find out if Eli used a rideshare app after the party too. But I haven't heard anything from him since. At the time, he didn't act very worried."

"Matt will find out what's happening with the investigation." Cady's eyes silently pleaded with her brother.

Mrs. Whitney blew her nose. "Please help me find him."

"I'll do what I can," Matt said.

Most missing persons turned up on their own. Cops didn't usually launch full-scale investigations for adults without signs of foul play or unusual circumstances.

A grateful tear slid down Mrs. Whitney's cheek. "Bless you."

"Can you give me a list of Eli's friends?" Matt asked. "And a picture of him."

"I'll text you a photo," Mrs. Whitney said. "His best friend is Christian Crone. They live with two other boys in an off-campus apartment." She opened her purse and took out a small notebook. She slid it across the table to Matt. "Here is the address and all their cell phone numbers. Eli made sure I could reach any of them in case I needed something and he wasn't available. They're good boys. They've all been to my house for Sunday dinner."

Unease nagged at Matt. Eli seemed like too good of a kid to let his grandma worry.

Cady stood and escorted Mrs. Whitney out the door. On the bright side, the case would give Matt a reason to call Bree again, one that didn't smell of desperation. He lifted his phone and checked the time. Six thirty. Too early to call her personal number. He reached for the remote and turned on the TV to check the local news. A meteorologist was giving the weather report.

He called the sheriff's department, but Bree wasn't in her office. He left her a message. As he debated who to call at the Scarlet Falls PD, he thought about all the things that could have happened to a drunk student in the middle of the night.

Eli could have stumbled into the park, slipped, and hit his head. He could have fallen into the river and drowned. If Eli was too responsible to stand up his grandma, then none of the remaining scenarios in Matt's head had good outcomes.

# Chapter Four

Bree studied the trees but saw no one. She turned to Todd. "Get your rifle and cover us."

When she'd first taken over the department, she'd reviewed all her deputies' files to get a sense of their skill sets. Todd was the top marksman with a long gun.

In order to reach the woods, they'd have to cross fifty feet of open ground. The morning sky had brightened to pale shades of pink and orange. A few evergreens clustered at the edge of the woods. The shooter could be hiding behind them. Todd brought his AR-15 from the trunk of his patrol vehicle and took up a position behind a boulder. He knelt and aimed his rifle across the top of the rock.

Bree and Rogers ran across the snow. Once they reached the trees, she pressed her shoulder to a tree, then peered around the trunk. She saw nothing but snow and woods. She met Rogers's gaze and circled her finger in the air. Rogers's flushed face had gone pale and clammy. They separated and went around the evergreens from opposite sides.

The snow was heavily trampled behind the pines, but no one was there.

Bree turned in a circle. She could see no additional hiding places in the stark woods, but the hairs on the back of her neck refused to relax. Though she'd been raised by a cousin in the city after the deaths of her parents, she'd been born in Grey's Hollow. Her family had owned a rural chunk of land. The first eight years of her life had been spent running half-wild in woods like these. But this morning, the forest was creeping her out.

She turned back to Rogers. He was studying the ground. Lines creased around his eyes as he concentrated. He was reportedly the best tracker in the department. Bree was all about letting people do what they did best. She kept one eye on the woods and watched him read the tracks.

Rogers cleared his throat and pointed to the snowy clearing. "Someone used this spot as a latrine."

"Makes sense," Bree said. "There's no water in the cabin, and the evergreens create privacy."

Back in his element, Rogers seemed to calm. "Most of the tracks just go back and forth to the cabin, except these." He gestured to footprints that led away from the latrine area and ran in a track parallel to the lake.

"Too bad the snow is too powdery to see any real imprints."

"Can't even tell the size of the boots," Rogers agreed.

Bree and Rogers followed the footprints along the shoreline. Behind the next cabin, number nineteen, the tracks led to the back porch. From there, the prints turned toward the lake and disappeared on the ice.

Todd left his position behind the boulder and followed them. His head swiveled as he scanned the woods while he walked.

Rogers said, "The wind blew the snow off the ice."

Bree brushed some snow dust from her jacket. "Any thoughts on which way the shooter went?"

"Are we sure there really *was* a shooter?" Rogers shook his head. "If somebody got shot, where's the body? Where's the blood?"

Bree stared out over Grey Lake. Long and narrow, it stretched out for miles. It was the beginning of March, and the lake was still frozen over.

Rogers cleared his throat. "There's also the possibility she's lying. Maybe she made up the whole story."

"Why would she do that?"

"Attention."

Bree raised a brow.

Rogers continued. "Think about it. She has nowhere to go, and it's fucking cold out. That cabin has no water, and the only source of heat is the fireplace. Surviving out here is rough. Just gathering dry wood every day would take a serious effort, especially for a girl."

Bree pictured the girl clutching her ax. Definitely not the helpless type.

"You think she invented a friend and gunshots?" Bree asked. "Seems like an elaborate plan. Why would she bother?"

Rogers shrugged. "I've had people commit crimes to get back into jail, especially in the winter."

"How does reporting a crime get her a place to stay? By calling us, she admitted to trespassing and lost access to her only shelter." Bree saw more motivation for Alyssa to remain silent.

"Maybe she didn't want to stay here," he said. "Maybe she isn't stable. Most homeless people are either drug addicts or have mental problems."

"Plenty of people are homeless for reasons beyond their control," Bree said.

Rogers scowled and swept an arm out. "I find it hard to believe someone was shot out here, and we haven't found a single drop of blood on all this white snow and ice. All I'm saying is that it's one possibility. We don't have any proof that a second girl exists, let alone a shooter."

Bree didn't know what to believe. She had a pretty accurate bullshit meter. The girl had seemed genuinely traumatized. But the circumstances *were* strange. "It's our job to figure out what happened."

The corner of Rogers's mouth twitched, as if he wanted to say something and was having a hard time holding back the words. A few seconds later, he couldn't restrain himself any longer. "All I'm saying is that we're already spread thin."

"So, you want to walk away from a citizen's report of a shooting because we're *busy*?"

He shifted his weight. "The citizen isn't very credible." He mashed his lips together for a second, but again, couldn't keep them that way. "Sheriff King wouldn't have wasted resources until he had real proof a crime was committed."

Bree ground her molars. Her predecessor's blatant corruption was public knowledge, and it was frustrating that he was still idolized by some people. "We will not walk away from a reported crime until we have conducted a thorough investigation. Is that understood, Deputy?"

"Yes, ma'am." Rogers's words were as tight as his lips.

As much as Bree hated to put him in his place, she had no choice, not if she wanted to keep the respect of all the people under her.

So many people.

As sheriff, her responsibilities entailed much more than supervising a patrol division. She ran the county jail too. In municipalities without their own PDs, the sheriff's department was the main law enforcement. They covered every crime from traffic tickets to murder. Her office also issued gun permits, served warrants, and transported prisoners. Hell, animal control was under her jurisdiction. Being sheriff was a massive responsibility.

She rubbed her forehead. The cold stung her face. She wanted to go somewhere warm. She wanted a cup of coffee, a giant breakfast, and eight hours of uninterrupted sleep. Instead, she was going to walk through the shooting.

Bree turned and started back toward the cabin. She stopped to talk to the chief deputy. "Todd, let's photograph the tracks in the snow. Then I want the girl to show us exactly how the shooter and victim were positioned. We'll do a second in-depth interview at the station. Also, get a warrant to search the two cabins."

They'd shifted from responding to a 911 call and looking for the shooter and victim to searching for evidence. The latter required a warrant.

"What about the scene?" Todd asked. "Do you want to expand the perimeter?"

"Secure the area but hold off on the foot search. If we can get a K-9 out here, extra bodies traipsing around could disturb the scent. Call the state police. See if we can borrow a K-9 unit."

"Yes, ma'am." Todd turned and strode toward his vehicle.

Despite her personal issues with canines, she valued their ability to sniff out everything from drugs, explosives, and lost kids to suspects.

Bree turned to Rogers. Resentment buttoned up his expression. She didn't like him challenging her authority. But she also didn't want to lose him. She was already shorthanded, and his skills as a tracker were valuable. Despite his negative attitude toward her, his job performance over the past three weeks had been solid. Her overall impression of Rogers's ability as a deputy was favorable. Was Rogers's poor attitude today a reflection of his dislike for her or a personal response to this particular case?

She studied him for a few seconds. Dark circles hovered beneath his crow's-feet. He'd been up all night. His shift had officially ended a while ago, and he'd dealt with a potentially dangerous situation running on nothing but adrenaline. To make matters worse, after he left the scene, he'd have to go back to the station and finish the night's reports.

Bree said in a low voice, "Look, Rogers. I hope you're right. I hope she did make the whole thing up. I hope we're all wasting our time. Because I'd rather be lied to than have a loose shooter or a lost victim potentially bleeding to death at this moment. I could never forgive myself if a young woman died because I didn't look hard enough for her. Or if other people became victims because I didn't try to find a killer. Or if I allowed myself to be prejudiced against a witness because she was homeless and discounted her story based on her circumstances rather than a thorough investigation of the case."

Rogers spoke through a locked jaw. "Yes, ma'am."

Frustrated, Bree took a deep breath. The truth was, while she had plenty of years as a cop to draw on, she had no leadership experience. She'd worked patrol in the beginning of her career, then progressed quickly to detective. She'd worked in cooperation with teams of people, but she'd never been the boss. Navigating the new role of leadership was like picking her way across a field of cow pies blindfolded. Everywhere she turned, there seemed to be a new pile of crap to step in.

She headed for the front of the cabin. Rogers fell into step beside her, and they walked in uncomfortable silence. By the time they reached the clearing, two more deputies had arrived.

She turned to Rogers. "There are enough uniforms here now. You can go off shift."

He moved away. Though he hadn't wanted to work on the investigation, his posture was stiff, as if he was irritated at her dismissal.

She could not win.

From what she'd learned of the previous sheriff, he would have fired anyone who challenged him on the spot. Bree couldn't afford to fire everyone who was difficult. The department had lost almost a third of its deputies. When she'd accepted the job, she'd known the department was in turmoil. She'd known she'd have to rebuild the whole unit, and that the transition process would be painful. Some people naturally resisted growth and change.

But the reality of transforming the sheriff's department was proving to be more frustrating than she'd anticipated, and she'd been at it for only three weeks.

*The hell with it.*

Bree stopped at her SUV for her coffee and took a few fortifying sips. She didn't have the time or energy to deal with attitudes and egos this morning. She had a shooting to investigate. Having a case to work was almost a relief.

For now, she would put aside her department's issues and do what she did best. She'd solve a crime. She headed for the vehicle that contained her witness.

Todd jogged toward her. "Sheriff?"

She stopped. The title still felt strange.

"State police K-9 units are tied up searching for a university student who went missing over the weekend. The earliest I can get a team out here is late afternoon."

Bree glanced at the sky. To the east, the sunrise reddened the morning sky, but thick clouds gathered on the western horizon. She pulled out her phone and checked the weather. "There's more snow on the way. It's forecast to start by early afternoon." She wasn't sure how new snow would affect a dog's ability to track, but it would cover any evidence on the ground.

"What about Matt and Brody?" Todd asked.

Matt had been tied to her sister's murder through his best friend, and he'd helped her solve the case. They'd made a good team, but Matt's history with the sheriff's department made her hesitate.

"Doesn't seem like I have any other options," Bree said.

"Is there a reason you don't want to call Matt?" Todd asked.

"It would be preferable to use an official team." Bree didn't voice her real concerns. One of the deputies who had shot Matt had left the department. The other was Rogers. The incident had officially been declared an accident, but Matt's interactions with Rogers and the other deputies were understandably awkward. Asking him to work for the sheriff's department felt like an imposition.

But she'd get to see him again. Despite the fact that she didn't have the time or energy for a personal commitment outside of her family—as evidenced by her failure to return his messages for the past few weeks—she'd missed him.

Bree massaged her temple. Matt came with departmental complications, but she trusted him. She couldn't say that about all the men under her command. It would be nice to know someone had her back.

"I'll call him." Pulling her phone out of her pocket, she surveyed the uniformed men moving around the scene. She felt confident in her chief deputy. Todd had been one of the people who'd convinced her to accept the position. Most of her deputies seemed glad to have new leadership, but a few resented her appointment to sheriff.

She stepped away for some privacy to make the call. The rising sun reflected off the frozen lake in shades of bloody red. With the exception of Todd, Matt didn't fully trust her deputies.

Could *she*?

# CHAPTER FIVE

Matt's phone vibrated. He pulled it from his pocket. *Bree.*

He might be thirty-five, but seeing her name on his phone screen gave him a rush. He tempered his enthusiasm and cleared his throat. "Hey, how are you?"

"Sorry," Bree said. She sounded stressed. "I know I should have answered your text weeks ago, but it's been crazy at work and home."

"Everything OK with the kids?" Matt worried about them—and her. The Taggert family had suffered more than its share of tragedy.

"Not really, but I don't have time to get into it now," she said. "I need to ask you for a favor. You and Brody."

He could hear wind and voices in the background. Someone yelled for the chief deputy. Disappointment poked him. She was at a scene. She wasn't calling him back for personal reasons. This was business.

"How can we help?" he asked.

"I have an unusual situation." She explained her current case, a shooting with little evidence other than a single, less-than-ideal witness. "I need to track the shooter. I can't get a K-9 team until late afternoon, and there's more snow on the way. I know it's asking a lot, but is there any way you and Brody could try?"

Matt reached down and rested his hand on Brody's head. The dog's ears came forward, as if he could hear Bree's voice and understood the conversation. Hell, it wouldn't surprise Matt if he could. Brody was the most intelligent animal he'd ever encountered. Energy vibrated off the big dog, and his tail began to sweep back and forth across the tile. Matt often wondered which one of them missed the work more.

"Brody says he'd love to help," Matt said. "I have something I'd like to talk to you about anyway." Considering Bree had been avoiding him, doing her a favor might make her more likely to cooperate with him. "Where are you?"

"Thank you." Her voice rang with relief as she gave him the location.

"We'll be there ASAP." He ended the call.

Brody whined.

"Yeah. We're going out," Matt assured him. He sent Greta into her crate and gathered his gear. Brody was waiting at the door when he was ready. They went out to his Suburban. Brody rode shotgun. Matt cracked the window, and the dog pressed his nose to the opening. The dog vibrated with excitement.

As if he knew they had work to do.

◆ ◆ ◆

Forty minutes after Bree's call, Matt parked his Suburban in the clearing behind three deputies' vehicles and the sheriff's SUV. He climbed out of his driver's seat and held the door for Brody. After he snapped the leash onto his dog's collar, the big dog jumped down from the vehicle and stumbled when his front paws hit the ground.

"You OK, buddy?" Matt knelt next to his dog. Normally, Brody was agile and sure-footed. Matt inspected the ground, which glittered with patches of ice.

*Damn it.*

Brody pulled toward the uniformed men gathered in front of a cabin.

"OK. We'll get on with it." Matt stood and brushed snow off his cargo pants.

The wind and dampness hit him square in the face, and the air smelled like snow. The dog was right. They'd better get moving. He opened the cargo hatch, took out his pack, and hefted it over one shoulder. Searches could be unpredictable. Matt liked to be prepared. He tugged on a hat and a pair of warm gloves.

Brody whined, spotting Chief Deputy Todd Harvey standing next to his cruiser twenty feet away. The dog's tail wagged in big sweeps. Matt let the dog pull him toward the deputy.

"Hey, Brody." Todd rubbed Brody's ears. "There's a good boy. How've ya been?"

Matt shook his head. "I don't rate a greeting?"

Still patting the dog, Todd looked up. "You're OK, but you're not Brody."

"Fair enough." Matt didn't mind. He preferred his dog over most people too.

Todd pointed to the cabin that sat in the middle of the clearing. "The sheriff is back there with the witness."

"Thanks." Matt turned and called Brody to heel. He led the dog around the side of the cabin. He spotted two women through the trees. Even at a distance, he recognized Bree by the way she moved: with purpose. She didn't waste energy. Every motion of her body was as focused as her mind. In a way, she reminded him of Brody. Once they locked onto a trail, they wouldn't stop until they'd reached the end.

Bree and the other woman were standing on the edge of Grey Lake. Matt and the dog made their way through the stark, snowy woods. Bree was dressed for the weather in boots and a winter uniform jacket, but she hunched against the wind gusting across the ice.

Winter felt never-ending this year.

She turned toward him as he approached. Her shoulder-length brown hair was tucked into a hat. She wore no makeup, but a clean face suited her. It was the intelligence in her hazel eyes that grabbed him every time.

Underneath her eyes, deep shadows lurked. She'd caught this case only a few hours ago. It wasn't responsible for any missed sleep. What was worrying her? Was it the same concern that prevented her from returning his text and had caused her to blow off their dinner a few weeks ago? With two orphaned kids, her own grief, and a hot mess of a new job to juggle, her stress level must be off the charts.

"Thanks for coming, Matt." Bree extended a hand.

"We'll do what we can." Matt shook it. The gesture felt oddly formal, considering all they'd been through together. Then Bree's gaze held his and her eyes smiled at him for an extra heartbeat before she shifted smoothly back into professional mode.

Matt relaxed, just a little.

"This is Alyssa Vincent." Bree gestured toward the young woman standing next to her. Alyssa's brown hair and big eyes peeked out from under a wool ski hat. A parka several sizes too large dwarfed her thin frame. From her sunken cheeks, he suspected she was malnourished and gangly under the coat. Her gaze kept darting away from his, and her posture was traumatized and wary in a way that reminded Matt of stray animals that no longer trusted humans for good reasons.

"Nice to meet you, Alyssa." Matt didn't reach out to shake her hand for fear of spooking her.

But Brody had no inhibitions. He whined and wagged at her. The girl crouched and stroked his fur. She perked up as she petted the dog. Unlike Bree, the teenager seemed to be calmed by the dog's presence.

"Alyssa saw a friend get shot here early this morning," Bree said.

The girl froze, her hand stopping on Brody's head for a few seconds. Brody bumped her wrist with his nose, and she resumed petting him.

Bree continued. "The friend and the shooter are now missing. I was hoping Brody might be able to track them. I hope you don't need a scent article."

She'd seen Brody track only once. She had no idea what his dog was capable of.

"No," Matt said. "It's not necessary. I'll take Brody to the place they were last seen. He should be able to pick up a scent from their footprints. *But* we won't know whose scent he's following."

"We'll take what we can get." Bree tucked a strand of hair under her knit hat. Her nose and cheeks were red from the cold.

"Sheriff Taggert?" a deputy called from the woods. "We found something."

"Excuse me for a minute." Bree strode off toward the deputy. A minute later, she called for Matt and Alyssa. They followed her voice. She was surveying an area of flattened snow. "Looks like someone stood behind that tree for a while."

"He was watching," Matt suggested. "Do you want Brody to follow the scent from here?"

"Yes. Let's try it." She instructed a deputy to take Alyssa to the sheriff's station and make her comfortable.

Matt scanned the expanse of ice.

"Is he ready?" She inclined her head toward Brody.

"Hold on." Matt knelt and removed his pack, setting it in the snow. He opened a side pouch and took out Brody's boots.

"Your dog has boots?" When Bree worked with K-9s, she kept her distance, but Matt could still see the frustration in her eyes as she fought her phobia. She did a hell of a job faking it. He would not have picked up on her small tells if he didn't already know she was terrified of dogs.

"Yes," Matt said. "The rubber bottoms will give him some grip, protect him from any sharp edges in the ice, and keep snow from accumulating between his pads."

Brody took three paw-shaking steps before he settled into the boots. He didn't love them, but he'd wear them because he wanted to work. Once he focused on the scent, he wouldn't even remember they were on his feet.

Brody led them across fifteen feet of ice. The thin ice at the edge of the lake cracked under their weight. The sound echoed across the lake.

Matt paused, but the ice held. It became thicker a few feet farther onto the water, but late-winter ice always made him nervous. The frozen lake surface wasn't completely smooth, and their boots found traction on ridges and other surface imperfections, but they moved slowly.

Bree gestured toward the ice at her feet. "Alyssa says the shooter was standing in this area."

Brody sniffed the ground, and Matt let the dog have some leash.

Brody sniffed in circles. He put his nose to the ground, then lifted his head to test the air. Within a few minutes, he was off, meandering at first. Then he picked up speed as he settled on the scent.

Matt slid as the dog pulled. He righted himself. "Be careful, Bree. It's slick."

Bree followed a few steps behind them. Their pace was slowed by the slippery footing. Brody led them in a path parallel to the shoreline, about twenty feet from solid ground.

"The shooter probably walked on the ice so he didn't leave footprints," Bree said.

"Brody doesn't need footprints. People constantly shed skin cells. They're as good as flags for the dog."

Matt controlled Brody's pace. He didn't want the dog slipping and hurting himself, especially after his stumble out of the SUV. They continued for twenty minutes, only covering about a quarter mile of frozen lake, before Brody stopped and circled again. Nose in the air, he angled toward the shore.

Flurries began to drift through the air.

"Will the snow hurt his ability to track?" Bree asked.

"It depends. Moisture in the air actually helps hold and trap scent close to the ground. That said, colder environments hold less scent in general. This isn't necessarily a bad thing. Since there's less scent confusion, it could help Brody find and stay on the trail."

"But?"

"But if the snow accumulates on top of the scent, it can obscure it." Matt glanced at the sky. "These flurries shouldn't affect Brody one way or the other."

"We're supposed to get several inches later today."

Matt shrugged. "We shouldn't waste time, but Brody is very good."

As if he heard the compliment, Brody pulled ahead, following the frozen shoreline. They walked in silence for a half hour, their progress halting as the dog stopped periodically to sniff and circle.

"Did you hear about the missing university student, Eli Whitney?" Matt asked.

"The one they're looking for on the riverbank?"

"That's him."

Bree nodded. "He's the reason I couldn't get a K-9 team this morning."

"How much do you know about the case?"

Bree glanced at him. "Just what I read on the BOLO alert. Why?"

Matt explained about Mrs. Whitney. "I promised her I'd look into it."

"The BOLO was issued by the Scarlet Falls PD."

"Do you know who's running the investigation?"

Bree nodded. "A Detective Dane."

"Thanks."

Brody began to limp.

Matt stopped him. "What's up, buddy?"

He checked the boots to make sure they weren't rubbing against his paws.

"Is he OK?" Bree stopped next to him and frowned.

"I don't know." Matt straightened. They hadn't gone far.

Brody turned his head and sniffed the air. He pulled forward, still limping.

"He doesn't want to quit." Bree sounded confused.

"He won't ever give up voluntarily."

Bree shielded her eyes and scanned the lakeshore. "The public park and boat ramp are just ahead."

In summer, the park was a popular spot for people to launch boats, kayaks, and Jet Skis into the water.

Matt watched the dog take a few more clearly painful steps. "He's done. I'm sorry."

"Nothing to be sorry about." Even from a distance, Bree could see footprints from the ramp to the parking area.

Matt went down on one knee and checked Brody's leg and foot again. When he palpated the dog's shoulder, Brody flinched.

Bree frowned. "Can he walk back?"

"I'll let him rest for a few minutes." Matt watched his dog. *Did Brody hurt himself jumping out of the SUV?*

She started to walk ahead, her steps quickening, her stride gaining an excited bounce. "I see tire tracks in the parking area too."

The dog moved to follow Bree.

"Easy, boy," Matt said.

But Brody had a different plan. His nose shot into the air, and he lunged into the leash.

*"Fuss!"* Matt commanded him to heel.

Brody ignored him. Instead, he sniffed the wind and stared ahead. He lurched forward, dragging Matt to the edge of the lake. Instead of resisting, Matt gave up and let Brody have his head. He'd learned early on that he was holding the dumb end of the leash. The dog knew what he was doing.

Limping, Brody stopped next to the boat ramp. The area around the concrete looked like frozen swamp. Empty water bottles and other pieces of litter were piled up against the ramp and embedded in the ice. Clearly, this was a downstream point that collected debris. Brody sat down and barked.

"What is it?" Bree was right behind him.

"I don't know." Matt crouched next to the dog. The thin ice at the edge of the lake cracked under his weight. The sound echoed, and Matt's waterproof boots broke through, sinking into a few inches of water. He brushed some drifted snow off the ice. Something thin and dark was suspended beneath it. *A branch?*

"What did he find?" Bree leaned over Matt's shoulder.

He moved more snow with his glove. The ice cracked further, breaking apart and shifting on the water. The thing underneath was no branch.

Exhaling, he straightened and caught Bree's eye.

Bree drew in a sharp intake of breath. Something bobbed to the surface between long, jagged sheets of ice.

A human hand.

# CHAPTER SIX

Bree lunged forward. At the very edge of the lake, her boots crunched through the ice, and water sloshed over her ankles. The hand looked male. Was it the shooter? Depending on how long the man had been underwater, there might be a chance he could be revived.

She grasped the body by one of the biceps. Matt gave Brody a command. The dog lay down, then Matt took the man's other arm. Together, he and Bree dragged the body onto the bank. *Definitely male.* He was dressed only in boxer shorts.

His skin was bluish-gray. Bree doubted he could be saved. But cold-water drowning victims had been resuscitated after being underwater for up to forty minutes. When she'd been a rookie patrol officer in Philadelphia, she'd pulled a kid out of the Delaware River. He'd been in the water for at least a half hour. It hadn't seemed possible that he had been alive. Not only had he been resuscitated, he'd survived.

Bree rolled the man onto his back and gasped. His face was destroyed, pulverized into a mess of broken bone and ragged flesh.

She jerked backward, then exhaled. "It takes a lot to surprise me."

Water soaked through her gloves and chilled her hands for two shallow breaths. There would be no euphoric feeling of saving a life today.

"I'll bet." Matt rocked back on his heels. He was an impressive figure. Snow dotted his short, reddish-brown beard. A broad-shouldered six foot three, with a corpse at his feet, he looked like a Viking warrior on a winter battlefield.

Wind whipped across the lake, empty, frozen, and desolate. Bree glanced down at the brutalized body, and a feeling of foreboding passed through her. The case was going to be freaky. She could feel it in her bones. She had two handguns strapped to her person, but she was still glad to have Matt by her side.

A few yards away, Brody whined.

Bree shook off her initial shock. There was no need to take the victim's pulse. No one could survive the injuries to his face and head. His brain was visible in several places.

Shivering, she leaned forward to inspect the corpse's hands. Some aquatic creatures had been nibbling on his fingers. "I shouldn't have disturbed the body. He's been in the water too long."

"No way to know that until we pulled him out and turned him over."

"True."

"The body looks young," Matt said. "Possibly older teen or twentysomething."

"Yes," Bree agreed. The corpse was lean in a way that suggested youth. The victim's hair was shorn close to the scalp but was too wet for her to determine color. Mud smeared the skin. Plant matter and other lake debris clung to the body. "Could it be the university student you're looking for?"

"I hope not." But Matt's jaw was clenched and his eyes grim. He didn't want this to be Eli.

"I'll call the lead detective," Bree said. "And let him know we have a body the approximate age of the missing man."

Other than the damage to this man's face, the corpse wasn't in bad shape. Cold water had delayed decomposition. A body on land for one week resembled one that had been in the water for two.

Bree stared down at the ruined face. The body had been freshly pulled from the lake, and the victim's wounds were oddly bloodless. "His whole face is bashed in. I can't imagine any accidental way that could have happened."

"Me neither. Nor do I see any other obviously fatal injuries." Matt exhaled hard. "It would take some serious rage to do *that* to another human being."

"It would." Bree stepped back. "I'll call the medical examiner." She pulled her phone out of her pocket. "I'll get you and Brody a ride back to the cabin too." She and Matt retreated back onto the frozen lake. She reported the death to the ME's office, then called Todd and gave him the news. "We'll need a forensics team over at the boat ramp." Then she glanced at Brody. The dog looked sad. "I also need a car for Matt and Brody. The parking area is part of the crime scene. Don't let anyone drive over the existing tire tracks."

"Yes, ma'am." Todd ended the call.

Bree turned to Matt. "How is he?" She motioned toward the dog. Brody had stretched out on the snow, resting as if he knew his job was done.

Matt's jaw tightened. "I'll take him to the vet today. Hopefully, it's nothing serious."

Bree wished Brody didn't freak her out. Her brain knew he wouldn't hurt her, but she was conditioned to fear him.

A few minutes later, a sheriff's department cruiser drove up from the opposite direction, stopping short of the parking area.

Bree gestured toward the vehicle. "The deputy will take you back to your vehicle. Thanks for your help, Matt."

"It was all Brody, but you're welcome." Matt called the dog, who rose painfully to his feet.

She watched Brody limp to the patrol car and gingerly climb into the back. Worry for the big dog tugged at her.

Matt climbed into the passenger seat, and they drove away. She instantly wished he could have stayed. Not that she couldn't handle being alone with a dead body. That was hardly a first for her. But she missed having a dependable partner, and Matt was solid.

Another sheriff's department cruiser appeared on the road above the parking lot. Her chief deputy climbed out and approached Bree. He avoided stepping on the tire tracks leading to and away from the boat ramp area.

Bree turned back toward the body. Todd fell into step beside her.

She retraced her own path back to the bank. "Try to stay on the tracks Matt and I left so we disturb the scene as little as possible."

"Holy . . ." Todd stopped cold. "What the hell happened to him?"

Bree shook her head. "Best not to make assumptions this early in the investigation. Let's wait for the ME."

"Is he the shooter?"

"Too early to say. We'll have to wait for the ME to ID the body and give us a time of death. I need you to secure the scene. Include the tire tracks and footprints in the parking area. Direct responding vehicles to park on the south side of the access road. Set up an area for the press. When in doubt, add distance to the crime scene perimeter. You can always make the area smaller. Harder to go back and expand it later."

Todd took a small notepad from his pocket and wrote in it. "Yes, ma'am."

"Let's get a forensic team down here." Bree pointed to a set of tire tracks. "These tire imprints look good enough to cast. Some of the footprints here are clearer than they were back at the cabin, maybe clear enough to get an impression. Get someone on that."

"Yes, ma'am."

"Assign a deputy to start a crime scene log ASAP. I'm going to need you."

Todd hurried back to his car. While he secured the scene, Bree called the SFPD and asked for Detective Dane. The desk sergeant put her through to the detective's voice mail, and Bree left a brief message.

She turned back to the body.

Could this be the shooter? If so, how did he end up in the lake? She scanned its frozen surface for a place where he could have gone through the ice but didn't see a hole. A human body was slightly heavier than fresh water. Bodies sank, and a lake wouldn't have much of a current. Drowning victims were typically found close to the place they went under. Where and when had this victim gone into the water? What had happened to his face?

Bree surveyed the area. Even if they'd found the shooter, they were still missing the victim.

# CHAPTER SEVEN

Two hours later, Bree watched the forensics tech shake a can of spray paint and crouch over a shoe print next to the vehicle tracks. He'd set a camera up on a tripod over the shoe print. Now he sprayed the print lightly with gray paint to create enough contrast and show the tread.

Shoe prints in snow, white on white, were difficult to photograph. The spray paint would also help prevent the casting material from running between the crystals of snow.

The tech snapped a photo. Then he added a scale, a black L-shaped ruler, pushing it into the snow until it was level with the shoe print. He snapped another picture using the ruler to show the size of the print.

A few feet away from her, a second tech was preparing to cast the tire tracks. He'd already photographed them with and without spray paint.

Holding a plastic bag of powdered dental stone, the tech squatted next to the print and added snow to a stainless-steel bottle of water. Once he added the water to the powdered dental stone, the chemical reaction would heat up the mixture. The snow would chill the water and help keep the mixture as cold as possible so that it didn't melt the snow before setting. He poured the water into the plastic bag, closed it, and then kneaded the bag until the mixture reached the right consistency. Slowly, he poured it into the tire track. "I'll work on the shoe prints now."

"How long before you can lift them?" she asked.

"I should be able to transport them within the hour, but they'll take twenty-four hours to dry completely."

Bree turned as the medical examiner's van bounced over the frozen grass and parked next to the forensic unit. Crime scene tape encircled the entire parking area. Dr. Serena Jones and her assistant got out of the van and opened the hatch at the back of the vehicle. They donned coveralls and knee-high rubber boots before trudging to the edge of the lake.

"Sheriff." Dr. Jones was a tall African American woman. Today, she wore a purple fleece hat over her closely cropped hair.

Bree's heart ached. The last time she had seen the medical examiner had been over her sister's dead body.

Dr. Jones's gaze went to the body on the shore.

"A K-9 found the body at approximately nine a.m." Bree turned and walked toward the lake beside the ME.

They stopped ten feet short of the body. Dr. Jones scanned the area. "Has anyone touched the body?"

"Yes." Bree described finding the body and pulling it from the water. "I thought resuscitation might be possible. Then we rolled him over." She didn't need to say any more.

Dr. Jones signaled her assistant, who moved forward with a camera. The assistant snapped long-range pics first, then spiraled toward the body to take progressively more close-up photographs. When she'd finished, Dr. Jones walked closer and squatted in the mud. "Some fingernails are broken."

"Possible defensive injuries," Bree said.

Dr. Jones tilted her head and wiped some mud off the wrist, exposing a red line. "Considering these are ligature marks, I'd say self-defense is a good bet." She moved to his feet. "There are ligature marks around his ankles as well."

The ME covered the hands with paper bags to preserve evidence lodged under the fingernails.

Bree stood back and let the medical examiner work. A shiver ran through her bones. She'd been out in the weather since before sunrise with nothing more than a few sips of coffee in her belly. Not that she was hungry, just running out of energy.

Dr. Jones recorded air and water temperatures. Then the ME and her assistant removed the ice from around the legs and feet, piece by piece.

"We'll need samples of the water and the mud under and around the body," Dr. Jones said.

Her assistant took the samples and carried them back toward the ME's van.

"I'm ready to move the body. Can I get a hand, Sheriff?" Dr. Jones asked.

"Sure." Bree positioned herself on the opposite side of the body. She donned fresh gloves. Then she and Dr. Jones each took an arm and hauled the body onto a black body bag unfolded on the bank. Dr. Jones moved her kit, a plastic box that could have been used for tackle, closer to the body. She used a scalpel to take the body's temperature via the liver. She read the thermometer, then did some calculations on her clipboard.

"How long has he been dead?" Bree asked.

Dr. Jones frowned at her calculations. "The cold water will make estimating the time of death challenging."

It was eleven thirty. The call about the shooting had come in at five thirty.

"Can you tell me if he's been dead more or less than six hours?" Bree asked.

Dr. Jones glanced down at the calculations on her clipboard. "Definitely more than six hours."

Bree stared down at the faceless corpse.

*So, he's not the shooter. Who is he?*

"Scarlet Falls PD is looking for a missing university student," Bree said. "Detective Dane is lead."

"Yes," Dr. Jones said. "The SFPD called earlier asking about John Does."

Bree saw her chief deputy walking toward her.

"We've searched the boat ramp and parking area," Todd said. "Didn't find much other than the prints. The tire tracks went directly to the main road, as we expected."

Bree nodded. "I'd like to know where he went into the water."

"Must be close to here," Todd said.

"I agree."

"So, what now?"

Bree pointed to the frozen trash and debris trapped in the ice. "We need to bag all of that litter. When the ME is finished, we need to search the lake bed around where the body was found. The water is shallow. No need to drag out the dive team. A deputy in tall boots should be sufficient. Mark off ten feet in each direction."

Bree stood and crossed her arms to stop her shivering. She hadn't been this cold in a long time. She surveyed her scene. The ME was in charge of the body. Forensics was covering casting the tire tracks and boot prints. Deputies were searching the woods. She'd given instructions for processing the remaining scene. There was nothing more she could do here.

"Todd, you and I will head back to the cabin." Bree spotted a news van on the road. She was surprised there was only one. A deputy was directing the news team away from the scene. Bree walked over. As much as she hated being in front of a camera, she would rather give a voluntary statement and cooperate than create animosity with the press. They were doing their jobs, just like she was.

The reporter, a tall blond man with a killer smile and a microphone, spotted her. "Sheriff? Can I have a minute?"

"Yes," Bree said.

"I'm Nick West." He held out a hand. Nick was young, probably in his late twenties.

Bree shook it. A cameraman swung his lens toward them.

The reporter spoke into his microphone. "This is Nick West of WSNY News talking to Randolph County Sheriff Bree Taggert. Sheriff, is it true you found a body in Grey Lake this morning?" He extended the mic toward her.

"Yes."

"Have you identified the deceased?" he asked. "Is this the missing university student?"

"We don't know."

A second cameraman lifted his camera and pointed it at the lake.

Bree stepped in front of the lens. "I'm going to ask you not to take any video until the body is placed in the bag. That is someone's loved one. I won't have the family learn of his death on TV. As soon as the remains are covered, you can roll film."

The cameraman frowned. "You can't—"

West held up a hand. "We'll wait."

The cameraman lowered his camera.

"Thank you for respecting the victim," Bree said.

West turned off the microphone. "What can you tell us off the record?"

"I'm sorry, Mr. West. I don't do off the record, but I also won't hold back information unless I have a good reason."

"OK." West turned the mic back on. "What *can* you tell us?"

"This morning at approximately nine o'clock, the deceased body of a man was found near the boat ramp in Grey Lake. There was no identification on the body. The sheriff's department will assist the medical examiner in any way to determine the identity of the deceased as quickly as possible."

"Do you know if the victim was murdered?"

"Cause of death will be determined by the medical examiner, but we are conducting a full investigation. I'll hold a press conference as soon as I have more information."

He pulled the mic back. "Is this body related to this morning's shooting at Grey Lake Campground?"

The mic was in Bree's face before she could think, but she took the time to choose her words carefully. "At this time, we have not officially established a connection between the two incidents."

"But you were investigating the shooting when you found the body?"

"Yes." Bree kept her expression neutral, but a small spark of anger fanned inside her. Nick would only know that information if someone in law enforcement had told him. She squelched her irritation. Leaks in her department were not the reporter's fault. Bree was responsible for the behavior of her team. "But, at this time, we do not know if the two incidents are connected or coincidental."

"Is it possible that the remains belong to the shooting victim?" West asked.

"No." Bree shook her head. "The remains have been in the lake too long."

"Is it true there's an eyewitness to this morning's shooting?"

Bree froze, and her poker face felt twitchy. "I can't comment on an active investigation."

*How did he know that?*

Her department leaked like a colander.

"Excuse me, I need to get back to work," she said.

"Thanks, Sheriff." West lowered his microphone.

Bree gave him a slight nod and returned to her scene. She found Todd, and he drove them back to the cabin. Once there, she stopped at her SUV and drank the cold dregs of her coffee with the protein bar she'd left in the center console. She needed the calories, but the food left her nauseated. She found a water bottle in her vehicle and took a few minutes to hydrate.

She found Todd talking to a deputy. She walked over for a status report on the scene.

The deputy pointed toward cabins nineteen and twenty. "We're almost finished with the outside areas. We'll do inside the cabins next."

With snow coming, they'd prioritized the outdoor portions of the scene.

"We'll do number twenty." Bree gestured to Todd, turned, and went up the steps into the cabin. Todd followed her into the main room. They tugged on gloves. Bree slid her camera from her pocket and began taking pictures of the sleeping bag and backpack in front of the fireplace. The fire had long since cooled to ashes.

"When that fireplace is blazing, this room is probably nice and warm," Todd said.

"There are worse places for a homeless person to sleep," Bree agreed.

Away from the fireplace, Bree detected a faint chemical smell. She circled the kitchen, opening drawers and doors, all empty except for some general cleaning products in a bag under the kitchen sink: paper towels, cleaning rags, spray cleaner, Comet, and dishwashing liquid. Bree lifted a rag with one finger and sniffed it, then she smelled the spray cleaner. Same odor. Squatters who cleaned were rare.

Next she checked the fridge. Nothing. No point in using it since the power was off. Except for the area in front of the fireplace, the cabin appeared undisturbed.

Bree wandered into the bedroom. "It seems they only used the one room."

Todd followed her. "There's only one fireplace."

"True."

"What are we looking for?" Todd asked.

"I don't know," Bree admitted. "Anything that looks out of place."

"Are we even sure a crime was committed here? The body could be unrelated."

"We have a witness who reported a shooting and a body discovered less than a mile away from the cabin. Something happened here."

*But what?*

There was no proof the body was related to the shooting at the cabin. Only Brody's sense of smell linked the two scenes. She needed to keep an open mind. Todd lifted the mattress and checked under it. Bree went to the other side of the bed, knelt, and checked underneath with her flashlight. Nothing but dust bunnies. Todd pulled the bed out and inspected behind the headboard.

Bree tapped her flashlight in her opposite palm.

Todd slid the bed back into place, stepped back, and surveyed the room. "Maybe there's nothing to find in the cabin."

"Maybe not," Bree agreed. "The girls are homeless and streetwise. They trespassed, broke into the cabin, and illegally occupied it. They wouldn't unpack and get comfortable. They'd keep their stuff handy."

"Ready to bolt at any time."

"Right."

"Let's get fingerprints." Bree turned in a circle. The cabin was small, and there wasn't much to search. "Maybe one of the girls will be in AFIS." The Automated Fingerprint Identification System would match found prints against a pool of fingerprint records. Bree opened the closet door. The narrow space inside was as empty as the rest of the cabin.

Bree headed for the door. "We need background checks on Alyssa Vincent and her friend, Harper Scott. Also check the contacts and activity on Alyssa's phone."

"Yes, ma'am."

"I'll need to call the owner of the campground."

"I have his number." Todd read it to her. "His name is Phil Dunlop."

Bree entered it into her phone. No one answered, and she left a message. Then she exited through the front door.

Another deputy was walking behind the cabin, looking for evidence on the ground. Bree had called in additional officers, but she was running out of personnel.

"How much ground have you covered?" Bree asked.

He shoved his hands into the pockets of his jacket. "We searched the area behind the cabins. We didn't find anything but the footprints you already saw. We photographed and mapped them. Starting on cabin nineteen now."

"Keep at it. Let the chief deputy know when you're done."

"Yes, ma'am."

Bree walked behind the cabins. She wanted one more look at the shooting scene in broad daylight. She strode across the snow past the cluster of evergreens to the frozen lake. The sun peeked through the clouds. Its rays glittered on the ice. Wait. That was more than ice. Bree hurried closer. The clouds passed in front of the sun again, but not before she spotted something shiny. Bree crouched and scanned the ice, spotting two small pieces of brass.

A deputy trudged over. "What did you find?"

"Shell casings." Bree took out her phone and photographed the casings and their relative positions. She recorded their GPS location with her phone. Finally, she used tweezers to put the casings in an evidence bag.

Straightening, she shoved the bag into her pocket. She had evidence that a gun was fired at the cabin. Now all she needed was a body and a shooter.

# Chapter Eight

Monday afternoon, Matt shook snow out of his eyes as he lifted the dog out of the SUV. "Easy, Brody. You sprained your shoulder. The vet said no more jumping down out of the truck."

Matt was going to need a ramp. The shepherd weighed ninety pounds, and he did not like being carried. Matt set him carefully on the driveway. Brody limped into the house.

As they entered the kitchen, Greta whined and dug at the door of her crate. After Brody was settled in his dog bed, Matt grabbed a leash and freed Greta. The black dog jumped on Matt and lunged for Brody.

*"Fuss."* Matt commanded her to heel, but she was too excited and full of energy to be obedient. He snapped the leash to her collar. "Brody can't play today."

He took her into the bedroom and changed into running clothes. When he turned around, Greta was chewing something.

"What do you have?" Matt pried open her mouth and extracted a chewed-up sock. "That was fast."

He opened the garbage can with the foot pedal and tossed the soggy mess into it. Then he grabbed a jacket, gloves, and a hat and led her from the house. Luckily, the snow wasn't yet accumulating on the roads, and a half-hour run settled her down.

For now.

Matt returned to the house, gave Greta a chew bone, and showered. He dressed and spent the next half hour reviewing Eli's social media history. He had accounts on both Facebook and Twitter. Eli's Facebook page saw little activity—a few pictures a week of Eli with friends, grinning selfies, an occasional random dog picture. The Facebook account was very tame.

Matt switched to Twitter. A few posts in, he double-checked to make sure he had the right Eli Whitney. The profile photo was the same person, but his Twitter account was completely different. Unlike the three-a-week, PG-rated Facebook posts, Eli posted to Twitter multiple times a day, more than enough to provide a sense of his daily activities. Matt scrolled through photos. Eli clearly liked to party. Matt sighed at a photo of Eli chugging a beer bong.

Didn't Eli know future employers would look at these pictures?

Matt scrolled to Eli's weekend activity. He made fun of a girl with crooked teeth and posted a pic of a guy with saggy pants bending over to pick up his backpack at a bus stop on campus. Eli captioned that photo ANOTHER EPISODE IN THE PHIL McCRACKEN FILES. In yet another picture, Eli mocked a homeless man sleeping in a doorway.

So, Eli was a good grandson, but he was also juvenile, and he could be an ass. Saturday evening, he posted a photo of himself doing shots, pregaming for a party at an address on Oak Street. Anyone who followed his Twitter feed knew where Eli had been going on Saturday night. Matt made a note to verify the location. Eli even posted when he called for a rideshare. No one needed to stalk Eli. He practically posted his agenda.

Matt's phone rang. The display read SCARLET FALLS PD.

He answered the call. "Matt Flynn here."

"This is Detective Stella Dane returning your call."

Matt had left her a message earlier. "Thank you. I wanted to talk to you about Eli Whitney."

"How do you know Eli?" she asked in a wary voice.

"His grandmother is a friend of the family. She asked me to look into the case," Matt said. "I used to be a sheriff's deputy with Randolph County." Local agencies often cooperated, but Matt didn't remember ever working with Detective Dane.

"I'm at the station now if you want to drop by," she said. "I'll be here for about an hour."

"I'll be there in fifteen." Matt returned a tired Greta to her crate. Brody was asleep on his dog bed, his pain meds clearly kicking in. "Be back soon," he said to the dogs on his way out. "Be good."

At the Scarlet Falls Police Station, the desk sergeant recognized Matt from his days at the sheriff's department. Matt flashed his ID, but the sergeant waved it away. "Go on in."

Matt passed a few empty cubicles. Detective Dane looked up from her computer as he approached. She was tall with black hair and assessing cop eyes. Despite her heavy sweater, she looked cold. She wrapped both hands around a steaming mug. A half-eaten deli sandwich sat on a plate in front of her.

He held out a hand and introduced himself. "Call me Matt. Thanks for agreeing to speak with me."

"Stella." She half stood to shake his hand. "I asked around. You check out." Sitting, she waved at her food. "Excuse me for eating."

"Please go ahead. Long day?"

She sighed. "Yes. I'd been working a string of residential burglaries nonstop before I caught the Whitney case."

"How did the search go this morning?"

Instead of answering, she asked, "What do you know about Eli's disappearance?" Then she took a bite of her sandwich and waited for him to respond.

Matt settled into the chair next to her desk. "That he left a party late Saturday night and never got home, and that he used a rideshare app."

She swallowed. "The rideshare driver he called after the party said he was a no-show."

"Was the party on Oak Street?"

"Yes." She gave him the house number, which matched the address Eli had given on Twitter. "The party was large enough that the street was clogged. When Eli left, he summoned his ride from a block away, according to the rideshare app GPS." She wiped her hands on a napkin, picked up her phone, and pulled up a map. "Here is the house." She moved the screen slightly. "Here's where he requested a ride." She moved the screen an additional two blocks. "And here's where his cell phone was found last night on the banks of the Scarlet River."

"That's why you had the dogs out this morning." Matt sat back.

"Yes." The detective drank her coffee. "The lake is frozen, but the river is only partially iced over. If he fell in . . ."

*Then he's probably dead.*

"Did you hear about the body found in Grey Lake today?" Matt asked.

"I did, but the ME removed the remains from the scene before I could get there." Stella zoomed out on her map. "The body's location is a fair distance from the riverbank where the cell phone was found. I don't see how the current could have carried the body that far. Then again, we didn't find anything at all. I had three dogs out there. If there was scent, they would have located it. Maybe the boy was never on the riverbank. Maybe the phone was stolen or dropped there."

"My K-9 found the body in Grey Lake."

Stella's gaze snapped up from her phone. "But you're not a deputy anymore."

"That's correct. I was just helping out."

Stella took in that bit of information with a slight lift of one brow. "Then you know the body can't be ID'd visually."

"Yes. He doesn't have a face. Does his grandmother know about the body?" Matt didn't want to think of Mrs. Whitney getting the news that her grandson had died, let alone learning about what had been done to the body.

"I don't know," Stella said. "I took over the case late last night, after the cell phone turned up. I tried to reach Mrs. Whitney early this morning, when we started the search, but she didn't answer her phone. I plan to drive to her house as soon as I hear from the ME. His family doctor is here in town, so Dr. Jones will have his medical records."

"If it's Eli, please let me make sure someone is there when you tell Mrs. Whitney. He's her only family."

"I will. Thank you."

"What other leads have you found?" Matt realized she'd had the case for less than twenty-four hours, but the first day of the investigation was critical.

"None. We canvassed the neighborhood of the party. No one remembers seeing him. Eli lives in an apartment on the north side of the university. Two of his roommates were home when I stopped by. Eli's best friend, Christian Crone, was sick in bed during the party. He has no alibi. Dustin Lock was with his girlfriend all night. The girlfriend verified his story, but she lives alone, and no one saw them at her place. So, take that for what it's worth. I didn't get any glaring sense that Christian, Dustin, or Dustin's girlfriend were lying, but you never know. The third roommate, Brian O'Neil, is visiting his mother. He hasn't been around all week. I called his cell number and left a message last night. He hasn't responded."

"What did you think of the roommates?" Matt asked.

"None have criminal records." The detective pursed her lips. "They're all good-looking, athletic, popular. They like girls and partying more than going to class."

"You've just described a quarter of the university population."

The detective snorted. "You're probably right."

"Have you searched Eli's phone?"

"Yes. I looked through his recent calls and texts. Didn't see anything abnormal. No threats or conflicts. He's a party boy and has a mean sense of humor. Yet he seems to be very attentive to his grandmother."

"No one is perfect," Matt said.

"Have you seen his social media accounts?"

"You mean Twitter?" Matt asked.

"Yeah." She frowned.

Matt shrugged. "Clearly, Eli can be an ass, but there's nothing violent there. I suspect he thinks he's hilarious."

Stella nodded. "Mostly he texts back and forth with his roommates. There's some communication with a young woman named Sariah Scott. From her texts with Eli, she doesn't seem as hung up on him as he is on her. She referred to him as 'cute but immature.' Eli invited her to go to the party with him, but she turned him down." Stella finished her sandwich and washed it down with the end of her coffee.

"How do you think his phone ended up on the riverbank?"

"I don't know." Stella shook her head. "But I've found no sign of foul play. I heard from multiple people that once Eli starts drinking, he doesn't know when to stop. I'm more concerned that he passed out somewhere in the cold or fell in the river."

Either way, Matt thought there was a fair chance that the body Brody had found was Eli.

# Chapter Nine

It was three in the afternoon before Bree headed back to the station. She turned on her wipers to clear the snowflakes falling on her windshield. She had questions for Alyssa. Lots of them. She made a mental game plan for her interview, but her head felt heavy. Having missed lunch and spent too many hours in the cold, she'd burned every calorie from her protein bar. The twenty-minute drive seemed longer. She parked behind the sheriff's station and went inside. Her administrative assistant, Marge, showed up in the doorway of her office before Bree even got her jacket off.

Marge was about sixty, with dyed brown hair and drawn-on eyebrows. In her cardigans and sensible shoes, she looked like everyone's grandma—a deceptive appearance. On the outside she might be soft all over, but inside, she was pure titanium.

Marge had a steaming bowl in her hands. "I assume you haven't eaten."

"You are correct." Bree took off her jacket and Kevlar vest and hung them on a peg.

"Sit." Marge set the bowl on her desk. She held up a hand. "I know you're in a rush to question that girl, but you'll be sharper if you take ten minutes to eat."

"I'm not going to protest." Bree sat behind her desk. "I'm starving. Thank you."

"You are very welcome." Marge reached into the pocket of her cardigan and produced three small packages of crackers. She handed them over. "Do you want coffee or water or both?"

"Both would be wonderful." Bree picked up the spoon and started on the soup, which was vegetable beef. She booted up her computer and ate while it chugged to life.

Bree opened a pack of crackers and crumbled them into her soup. "Where is Alyssa?"

"Interview room two," Marge said.

"Has she eaten?" Bree worried about the girl. She looked malnourished. Had Rogers been right? Was the girl a drug addict? She hadn't had any of the other physical signs: bad skin, rotted teeth, nervous tics. But homelessness and drugs often went together.

Marge raised an offended brow. "Of course I fed her. I gave her soup and a sandwich. She could also use a shower and clean clothes, but we don't have a locker room for women in this building."

"We need to fix that," Bree said between spoonfuls. She waved at a pile of folders containing job applications on the corner of her desk. "Some of the deputies I intend to hire will be female."

Marge smiled. "I don't know how you'll squeeze another locker room into this tiny building. We're already busting at the seams."

It was true. The men's locker room didn't even have room for all the men. The facilities hadn't been upgraded since avocado-colored carpet was trendy. The sheriff's station resembled the set of a 1970s cop show, all worn wood, cracked linoleum, and lopsided file cabinets.

Marge's face turned thoughtful. "Maybe that's how we'll get our building upgraded."

Bree opened a second pack of crackers. "I'm not following?" Bree's brain was fully engaged with her new case.

"We can't discriminate against female applicants, and we also can't deny them equal access to facilities."

"Marge, you're a genius. How do we make it happen?" Bree had no illusions. Her administrative assistant knew way more about local politics than she did.

"You need to hold more press conferences, especially when you have a big case. The voters need to see you."

"I hate politics almost as much as I hate being on TV."

"That's part of what makes you a good sheriff." Marge's gaze hardened. "But this county is still a man's world, and they will stick together. You need the public on your side to even out the power dynamic. You say you don't like politics, but keep in mind that you work for the people. They deserve to hear the truth from you before rumors get the information all wrong."

"Thanks for the reminder."

"Anytime. I'll also work on a list of people you need to schmooze to get the building renovated."

Bree groaned, and Marge chuckled on her way out of the office. By the time she returned a few minutes later, Bree had shoveled down the entire bowl of soup.

Marge set down a cup of coffee and a bottle of water. "What are you going to do with the girl after you question her?"

"I don't know. Any ideas?" Bree pulled out her keyboard tray. On her desktop computer, she accessed Alyssa Vincent's motor vehicle records. Her driver's license photo was a match, and her driving record was clean. She'd never received a single ticket. An old 4Runner was registered in her name.

Marge shook her head. "We don't have many homeless shelters nearby."

"There's one in Scarlet Falls." Bree stood and stretched her back. Now that she'd eaten, her head felt clearer.

"Do you want me to call and see if they have space?"

"No." Bree wanted to keep tabs on the girl. Alyssa was a witness, but she could also be a suspect. "I don't know what I want to do with her yet. Thanks for the food." Bree finished the water and took her coffee with her. She walked down the wood-paneled hallway toward the interview and conference rooms. She stopped in the break room and bought two packs of M&M's and a Coke from the vending machine. Carrying them, she opened the door to the second room and went inside.

Alyssa sat at the table, her head resting on her arms. Her parka hung on the back of her chair. She lifted her head and blinked at the light. A line creased the side of her face.

"I can't believe I fell asleep." She rubbed her eyes. "I went from shaking to passed out in a few minutes."

"The body releases stress hormones during a traumatic event. They rev you up enough to get through the event. But when it's over, and they're depleted, you crash."

Instead of sitting on the other side of the table, Bree sat next to her and faced her—so she could better read her body language. She put down her coffee and set the Coke on the table in front of Alyssa. "Do you want water, coffee, or tea instead?"

"No, this is fine. Thanks." Alyssa popped the top off the can.

Bree fished the M&M's out of her pocket. She slid one bag across the table to Alyssa and opened the other. They sat and ate candy for a minute. Bree took her time settling into the interview. Alyssa wanted to talk. Bree could sense something ready to burst out of her.

Alyssa spun the pack of M&M's around on the table in a slow circle.

"This interview will be recorded. That way I can go back and watch it for details I might have missed."

Alyssa sniffed, and her head bobbed in a short nod.

Bree reached back and flipped a switch near the door. "This is Sheriff Bree Taggert interviewing Alyssa Vincent." The video would be time-stamped.

"How long have you been homeless, Alyssa?" Bree asked.

"About a year." She played with the edge of the candy package. "We were doing OK, me and my dad. But then he got cancer." Her whole body sighed. "It was in his brain." She paused, thinking. "He started chemo. The doctors wanted to hit the tumor hard. The treatment made him really sick and didn't do anything for his cancer. It was like one day he was fine, and the next he was dying." Her eyes welled up and tears began to run down her cheeks.

"I'm sorry that happened to you." Bree got up, left the room, and got a box of tissues from the supply closet. "Where's your mom?"

"She died when I was a baby. I don't remember her." Alyssa plucked a tissue from the box and dried her eyes. "My college money and all Dad's savings went to pay his medical bills. We had insurance, but it didn't cover everything. By the time he died, we were already being evicted from our apartment."

"So, you lost your dad and your home."

Alyssa nodded. "I couch surfed for a few months. But my friends all went away to college, and their parents got tired of having me crash on their sofas. Once spring came, I rented spaces at campgrounds. My dad and I used to camp. I had the 4Runner, all the gear, a nice tent, and everything. But then the campgrounds all closed for the winter."

"When did you move into the cabin?"

"Three or four weeks ago. I don't remember exactly." Alyssa sipped her Coke. "I'd been sleeping in the 4Runner, but I'd have to wake up to start the engine every couple of hours because of the cold. I wasn't getting much sleep, and the gas was getting expensive. I work part-time at the laundromat, but it doesn't pay enough to rent anything bigger than a campsite. I've been trying to get a full-time job. No luck so far."

"How did you meet up with Harper?"

"It got really cold that one week in February. I couldn't stand it. I went to a shelter in Scarlet Falls. It's run by a church. That's where I met Harper. That was the first time I slept through the night in a month."

Her mouth flattened. "It was the day after payday, and someone stole all my money while I was asleep. I'll never go back to a shelter."

"That's terrible."

"That's when Harper said we were better off sticking together and staying away from the shelters. I'd told her about camping all summer. It was her idea to use one of the cabins. She said no one would know." Alyssa scratched her arm, picking at the skin. The sleeve of her sweater rode up an inch, exposing two pink scars that ran parallel to her veins. "It isn't luxurious, but as long as we keep the fire going, we stay warm. I have my job, and Harper cleans offices a couple of nights a week. She makes more money than I do. I drive her around, and she shares her food. The arrangement works—worked."

"Where does Harper work?"

"Different offices all over town," Alyssa said.

"Do you ever drop her off or pick her up from work?"

"Yeah. The main office is in that industrial complex on the corner of Route 51 and Evergreen Road."

Bree wrote down the address. "Can you describe Harper for me?"

"She's about five seven or eight. She's thin and has long brown hair."

That description would also fit Alyssa, Bree noted. "There were cleaning products in the cabin. Did Harper bring those from work?"

"No." Alyssa shook her head. "She bought them. Taking them from work would have gotten her fired."

"You're right," Bree said. "Did you both clean the cabin?"

"Mostly Harper. She's kind of particular. Maybe a little OCD."

"What happened this morning?"

Alyssa had already walked Bree through the shooting back at the cabin, but Bree would make her tell her story several more times to check for inconsistencies. Lying was hard.

"I woke up thinking I heard a scream." Alyssa took a long, steadying breath. "It was still dark. I didn't know what time it was. But I saw that Harper was gone—and all her stuff was gone too." Her voice changed, taking on an angry edge. "I didn't know where she would have gone. She doesn't have a car, and she picked one of the cabins farthest away from the office in case anyone stopped in there over the winter. No one would see us." Alyssa's eyes tightened. "I checked my backpack. My keys and wallet were gone. All my money was inside. It wasn't much, but it was all I had until payday. Anyway, I thought she'd stolen my truck too, but it was still parked out front. I looked through the window looking at the backyard and saw a shadow. So, I went looking for Harper."

She paused for a breath, but Bree remained silent. She didn't want to interrupt the girl's story now that it was rolling.

"I saw a figure in the trees. I thought it was Harper, and I followed. It wasn't her. It was a man. Then Harper was there too. He pulled out a gun and shot her." Alyssa swallowed and her face went sickly gray. She scratched her arm harder, her dirty fingernails digging into the skin, leaving pink trails. If she pushed any harder, she would draw blood, but she didn't seem to notice the pain.

Bree nudged the Coke toward her, hoping to get the girl to stop hurting herself. "Did you get a good look at the man?"

Alyssa took a sip of her soda. "I was about thirty feet away from him, but it was dark." Her eyeballs shifted away. "We already talked about this."

"I was hoping you might have remembered more," Bree said. "How old was he?"

"I already told you it was dark," Alyssa whined, frustration heavy in her voice. She set down the soda can and went back to raking her nails along the inside of her forearm. Did she need a mental health eval?

Bree eyed the parallel scars again. Her stomach twisted. Suicide attempt? "Would you recognize him if you saw him again?"

Alyssa brushed her hair away from her face. Her eyes looked haunted, and she refused to make eye contact. "I don't think so."

*There's a lie.*

"Is there anything else you remember about him? A limp? The way he stood? Could you see the color of his skin?"

"He was white." Alyssa's face creased as she concentrated. "The hand with the gun wasn't wearing a glove, and the moon shined on it. I saw a mark on his hand. It was big and shaped weird."

"Weird?"

"I don't know. Just weird."

"OK." Bree made a note. "Like a birthmark or tattoo?"

Alyssa nodded. "Something like that."

"Right hand or left?"

Alyssa closed her eyes. "His right."

"What about Harper's things? Did she have them with her when she was shot?"

"She carried all her stuff in a backpack, like me." Alyssa tilted her head as she thought about the question. "It wasn't in the cabin, so she must have taken it." Her brows lowered. "But she wasn't wearing it when he shot her, so I don't know where it went."

Bree noted *missing backpack*. "Can you describe Harper's backpack?"

"It's gray."

"Do you know the brand?"

"Osprey," Alyssa said.

"What happened after the man shot Harper?"

"I don't know. I didn't see." Her breaths came faster, and her face flushed bright red. "I panicked and ran into the cabin and called 911. Then I grabbed the ax and hid in the closet."

"Did he see you?" Bree asked.

"He looked right at me." Alyssa shuddered.

"Did he follow you?"

"I don't know. I think so. I didn't look back."

Why didn't he pursue and kill her? Why leave a witness? Maybe he didn't see where she ran.

Alyssa ripped at the skin inside her wrist.

Bree reached over and stilled her motions with her own hand. "You've hurt yourself before?"

The girl looked up. Humiliation, then fear, then resignation crossed over her face.

Bree pointed to the scars on the inside of her wrist.

Alyssa yanked her sleeve down over the scars. Her gaze dropped to the table. "When my dad was sick, I started cutting."

"That must have been awful for you."

Alyssa exhaled a shaky breath. "I didn't know what to do."

"There wasn't anything you could do."

"Yeah." Alyssa's eyes welled up, but she blinked away the tears. "That was the problem."

"I lost both of my parents when I was young." With Bree's past, it was easy to imagine being overwhelmed by helplessness and vulnerability and also not having the emotional maturity to cope with trauma.

Alyssa met Bree's gaze for one breath before glancing away. "The pain . . ." She tapped her chest. "When my dad died, I thought I was going to die too, like my heart was just going to stop. It hurt so much."

Empathy and grief swelled behind Bree's breastbone, the pressure increasing until it felt as if she couldn't breathe.

"It does." Bree had had siblings who'd experienced the same trauma. Alyssa had been all alone.

"How old were you?" Alyssa asked.

"Eight." Even at thirty-five, the memory filled Bree with a hollow pain. She placed her fist over her heart. "It still hurts."

For a moment, she was self-conscious of the camera running. Her chief deputy, other investigators, maybe the prosecutor and/or defense attorneys might eventually watch this interview, but Bree hadn't said anything that wasn't public. The whole world knew about her parents' murder-suicide.

And that Bree and her siblings had been there when it happened.

One quick shiver passed through, an involuntary reaction to the memory.

Sometimes developing a connection with a witness or suspect took sacrifice. Bree had no issues with inventing a backstory to attain that connection, but this time it wasn't necessary. The truth would work, though this interview would leave her raw.

Alyssa tugged up her shirtsleeve. Tiny pink scars crisscrossed the soft, pale flesh on the underside of her forearm. "Most of the cuts were really shallow." She pointed to the two longer ones near the veins. "Except these two." She swallowed. "I made these the day he died. I didn't want to leave him at the hospital, but they made me go. I didn't want to be at home alone either." She traced a scar over her vein. "They bled a lot. I wanted to die that day too."

"Did you go to the ER?" Bree asked in a gentle voice.

"No, I wrapped my arm, and the bleeding stopped eventually. The cuts weren't deep enough to kill me." Alyssa's voice sounded regretful. "I couldn't even do that right."

The girl had gotten no help after her father died, and she'd at least considered suicide. Was Rogers right about this too? Did Alyssa make up the whole story in a plea for attention? Was the discovery of the body at the boat ramp a totally unrelated coincidence?

But how could she explain the boot prints, tire tracks, and shell casings?

*No assumptions.*

The evidence would lead her investigation.

"When can I get my 4Runner?" Alyssa asked. "And my other stuff. I really need my phone. I have to call work. I have to *go* to work."

Alyssa's vehicle had been towed to the municipal garage.

"You can use the phone here. I'll get Marge to get you an outside line. You can have all of your stuff back as soon as the forensic techs have processed it," Bree said. "When are you scheduled to work next?"

"Wednesday, from noon to eight."

"OK. You should have your 4Runner back in a couple of days." Bree didn't mention that Alyssa didn't have a driver's license. She'd said that Harper stole her wallet. But it would be impossible to obtain a replacement license without proof of identity and residency. Since Alyssa was homeless, she would not be issued a new license. But this was not the time to bring that up, not when Bree needed her cooperation.

Bree was in no rush to release the vehicle. She suspected as soon as Alyssa had wheels, she'd disappear. As long as Bree was holding her vehicle, clothes, and phone, Alyssa would likely stay put.

"But I don't have anywhere to stay." Alyssa's voice rose. "Or anything to wear."

"I appreciate how inconvenient this is for you. How about I put you in a hotel tonight, and we see how much progress the techs have made in the morning?"

"I don't know." Alyssa picked at her forearm.

"It's just for a night or so." Bree had no ability to hold the girl against her will, but she also didn't want to lose touch with her only witness to a shooting, especially when she didn't know if Alyssa's case was related to the dead body at the boat ramp.

"OK, I guess," Alyssa said in a reluctant tone.

"Good." Bree also thought the girl could use a hot shower and a clean, warm bed. She hated to think of her out on the street again. "Speaking of your phone, could I have your access code?"

"Why? I hardly use it."

"It has GPS, right?"

"Yeah," Alyssa said. "But I use it as little as possible."

"Who do you call?"

"Mostly work. Lately, Harper too. That's about it. I don't really have anyone else *to* call."

"You said Harper had money."

"Yes. From her job." But the confidence had dimmed in Alyssa's voice. Was she thinking of aspects of Harper's behavior that didn't quite add up? "It's all my fault that Harper is missing."

"Why do you think that?"

"I didn't help her." The girl shifted in her chair, as if unable to get comfortable—with her body or her actions. "I saw him shoot her, and I hid. Like a coward."

Maybe she ran before the shooter saw her. Maybe she just didn't want to admit she'd abandoned her friend that quickly.

"You called 911," Bree said.

"But I should have *done* something." She inhaled a long, quivering breath.

"Like?"

Alyssa's brows lowered in a troubled look. "I don't know."

"What do you think would have happened if the man who shot Harper caught you?"

"He would have shot me too."

"And then who would have called for help?" Bree pointed out.

"No one." Alyssa's voice sounded as small as Kayla's.

"That's right. So, no one would be looking for Harper right now. You and she would both just have vanished."

But Alyssa didn't seem reassured that she'd done the right thing.

Bree understood. She knew what survivor's guilt felt like because she felt it every day. Bree hadn't even been there when her sister died, but she should have been. Now Bree was alive, and her sister wasn't.

She said a silent prayer that Harper hadn't met the same fate, and that Alyssa would have an opportunity to alleviate her guilt with a long conversation with her friend.

"I have some other news for you," Bree said.

Alyssa's forehead creased.

"You know we used a K-9 to follow the shooter's trail?"

The girl nodded.

Bree continued. "We found a body. Not Harper's. A man's."

"The man who shot her?" Alyssa asked, eyes wide.

"No. This man was dead before you called in the shooting."

Alyssa's forehead furrowed. "Then who is he?"

"We don't know—yet." Bree watched her closely but saw no signs of deception. The girl looked genuinely confused. "You don't know anything about another man who might be missing?"

Alyssa shook her head.

"OK. I don't have any more questions right now. I'm going to leave you here while I find you a hotel room and finish up some paperwork. Are you hungry?"

"No, but why are you being so nice to me?" The girl's expression became guarded.

Bree gambled with the truth. "I want you available to answer more questions. As our investigation proceeds, I'm going to need your help." Bree hoped she'd find Harper alive, but if not, she might eventually need the girl to identify the shooter.

"OK." But Alyssa's eyes grew worried, as if she had seen the shooter more clearly than she'd admitted.

She was the sole witness to a murder, and thanks to reporter Nick West, everyone knew, which made Alyssa a potential target.

# Chapter Ten

By the time Matt walked into the sheriff's station, it was nearly dinnertime. "Hey, Marge."

Marge left her desk and approached the reception counter. "Where's Brody?"

"Home."

"I heard he was limping today."

"Yeah." Matt hadn't realized how accustomed he'd become to having the big dog with him most of the time. "Nothing's broken. He's on painkillers and seems to be resting comfortably." But Matt would still worry. Brody was a huge part of his life. "The vet is concerned about arthritis, though, in the shoulder where he took the bullet."

"Poor boy." Marge's eyes went soft. "I'll bake him some homemade biscuits. He's a hero."

"He is," Matt agreed. "I'm here to see the sheriff."

Bree had left a message asking him to stop by ASAP.

"Go on back. She's expecting you." Marge stepped back and buzzed him through the door that separated the lobby from the rest of the station. Like everything else about the department, building security was outdated. If someone really wanted to get in, all they had to do was vault over the counter.

He walked past the main room, where Jim Rogers was working on a computer. His eyes narrowed as Matt approached. Before Matt reached his desk, Rogers got up and strode away, heading for the rear exit.

*Jackass.*

You'd think Matt was the one who had shot Rogers, not the other way around.

Matt knocked on Bree's office door.

"Yes," she answered.

Matt opened the door.

She looked away from her computer. "Matt, thank you for coming."

Matt eased into a chair facing her huge desk.

"How is Brody?" Bree asked.

"OK. Home resting."

"But you look worried."

"He's not getting younger," Matt admitted to himself as much as to Bree.

"I'm sorry."

"Did the ME ID the body yet?" Matt settled into the cushion. Part of him wanted the answer to his question. The other definitely did not. He dreaded the thought of telling Mrs. Whitney that her grandson was dead. He wanted to find the boy alive. But Bree hadn't asked him to come to the station for a social visit, as much as he wished she had.

"No. I'm still waiting."

He breathed but knew the reprieve wouldn't last. Eli's medical records should have some means of identifying the body. Matt pushed it out of his mind. There was no point obsessing over something that hadn't happened yet. "You didn't answer my question earlier. Is everything at home all right?"

She sighed. "The kids are having trouble adjusting to life without their mother. I'm also sorry I blew off our dinner."

"I understand. The kids come first. Let me know if I can help." Matt knew the real reason Bree had moved to Grey's Hollow was to raise her sister's kids. She'd made it clear months ago that she didn't have the time for anything beyond a casual relationship. Matt had been the one to push. He respected her priorities, but he wasn't sure he could do casual—not with her.

Bree rested her elbows on the desk and rubbed her temples. "I need to clone myself." She looked up, and her expression softened. "I really wanted to go to dinner with you."

His gaze locked on hers. The green in her eyes intensified, and a flash of heat passed between them.

Suddenly warm, Matt unzipped his jacket. "We can reschedule when this is all over."

"I'd like that." She almost smiled, then looked down at her cluttered desk. Her expression sobered. "What I really need is ten more deputies and an experienced investigator or two."

"But?"

"Guess what happened to the sheriff's department budget after Sheriff King didn't replace lost staff and multiple budget cycles passed? The allowance for their salaries disappeared. Poof. Now, the county board of supervisors is convinced the sheriff's department doesn't need those deputies or an investigator. At this time, I'm down a dozen deputies, but I only have the funds to replace the five who quit during the last fiscal year. Those salaries are in the existing budget. If I want to expand to hire additional personnel, I have to make the request for the next budget cycle, but the county budget supervisor says don't bother. All increases will be denied. The county is operating in a deficit. I have to hire five deputies before the budget cycle ends or I'll likely lose those funds too."

"That sucks," he said.

"It surely does."

"The former sheriff saved time by only investigating the crimes he thought were important, and he didn't mind arresting people and pressuring them to confess instead of conducting a full investigation."

"Whether they were guilty or not?"

"I don't believe he looked at it that way. He saw himself as infallible." Matt had seen the old sheriff abusing his power—and Matt had been demoted from investigator to K-9 patrol, then shot in the line of duty when the sheriff sent him in the wrong door. Coincidence? Matt thought about Deputy Jim Rogers leaving the squad room the second Matt entered. He'd always wondered if Jim had been in on the old sheriff's plan. He acted weird every time Matt saw him. "Sheriff King bullied his way through budget meetings. If he didn't get his way, he'd stop patrols through county officials' neighborhoods, and response times in those areas would slow. If the board of supervisors wanted to be served by the sheriff's office, they did what King said."

Bree shook her head. "No, thanks. I've no desire to play dirty. No matter how good your intentions or how careful you try to be, the dirt eventually rubs off on you." Bree dropped her hand to the only clear space on her leather desk pad. "I won't work that way."

Matt had seen her interview witnesses and suspects. She was very good at getting people to talk to her—at getting what she wanted from them. She'd never allow her ego to take over. She'd find a way to work within the system.

"I am unable to hire a full-time investigator." Her eyes brightened. "But I found a workaround—actually, Marge found the loophole, because she knows everything."

Matt raised a brow.

"Sheriff King liked to hire consultants."

"He liked to channel money to his buddies," Matt corrected.

"The point is, there's money in the budget for that, and I want to hire you."

Shocked, Matt froze. Had he misheard her? "You want to hire me?"

"Yes. If I don't use the fund allocated for consultants, I'll lose that too." She raised one hand in a stop gesture. "This wouldn't be a full-time gig. I'd bring you in when we had a big case. You'd still have time to work with your K-9s." She frowned at him. "You don't seem excited."

"Honestly, I don't know how I feel. I assumed that part of my life was over." Matt's feelings were definitely mixed on several levels.

For the first two years after he'd been shot, he'd done everything possible to regain the dexterity in his right hand. But the nerve damage was permanent. It had taken a long time for him to come to terms with never working in law enforcement again. If this arrangement with Bree didn't work out, would he have to go through that all over again? But he'd loved being an investigator, and her offer sounded like a legitimate way for him to get back into the game.

Matt lifted his bum hand, flexed his fingers, and felt the familiar pull of scar tissue. He could shoot at very close range with his off hand, but his marksmanship with a handgun would never be what it once was. Therefore, he could never be a real law enforcement officer again. His aim was too unreliable.

Her gaze flickered to his raised hand. "I've seen you shoot left-handed. You're damned good with a long gun, and your pistol accuracy is better than you believe. I think you could qualify to carry." By federal law, former law enforcement officers who met certain criteria could carry a handgun if they passed a qualification test.

"Qualifying isn't the issue. Shooting at the range is different from using your weapon in a high-stress, dynamic situation." Frustrated, he held up his left hand. "The gun has to feel natural in my hand. It doesn't."

"I get it. You'd be a civilian. You wouldn't be required to carry." She sat back. His lack of a quick yes seemed to take her by surprise. "I appreciate you informally helping me this morning, but it would be better if you had credentials."

"That *would* help," he admitted.

Her chair swiveled a quarter turn. She studied him for a few seconds. The intensity of her gaze was like radiating heat on his face. "Is everything all right with you? Are you suffering any aftereffects from the shooting in January?"

Two months before, he'd helped her stop an active shooter. It had been the first time he'd been under fire since his own shooting. He'd had some nightmares, but he'd seen his old counselor a few times. He was working through his issues.

"No. That's not it," Matt said.

"Justin?" she guessed.

"No. He's still in rehab." Matt's best friend, the one who had been married to Bree's sister, was fighting depression and drug addiction.

"I'm sorry to hear that." Bree's eyes misted. "Erin's murder left marks on everyone who loved her."

Understatement of the decade. The emotional damage from a murder radiated from the victim into ever-enlarging circles of relatives and friends, like concentric rings of water expanding from a single raindrop. Justin had been depressed and battling substance abuse before his estranged wife had been murdered. Her death had devastated him. Afterward, his downward spiral had accelerated into a nosedive.

"It did." Matt sighed.

"Let me know if there's anything I can do."

"Thanks," Matt said. "But you have enough on your plate, and there's nothing to be done while he's still an inpatient." He lowered his voice. "Do you think any of your deputies would have an issue working with me?"

"You mean Jim Rogers?" Bree asked. No bullshitting with her. She got right to the point.

Matt nodded.

"I don't know." She went quiet for a few seconds. "I've only been in the job a few weeks. I haven't gotten to know any of the men very well yet, except Todd."

Matt read between the lines. She didn't trust her men.

"Problems?"

"Most of the deputies are ready for the department to be rebuilt."

"But some are resistant to change?" he asked. The old-school guard would hold on to the past with their fingernails.

"If they are, they'll have to adjust. But it's unfair for me to ask you to work here."

Matt had helped Bree when she was investigating on her own. Her new investigations came with all the baggage of the Randolph County Sheriff's Department. Matt didn't owe any favors to the sheriff's department, and he'd already promised Eli's grandmother he'd find her grandson.

Deputy Jim Rogers had fired the shots that ended Matt's career and could have cost him his life. Even worse, Rogers had shot Brody. Matt didn't want to think that Rogers had been in on the plan with the old sheriff. But nothing about Rogers's current behavior was giving Matt any warm or fuzzy feelings. How could he work with a man he couldn't trust?

Then again, how could he not?

Saying no would leave Bree to work with the very untrustworthy person who almost killed Matt, without Matt to watch her back.

If any other sheriff had asked him to return to the department, his answer would have been a resounding no. But this wasn't any sheriff. This was Bree.

The hell with it, and the hell with Rogers too. If he had an issue with Matt, he should step up and say so like a man. Damned if Matt would let Bree down because of him.

Matt also shouldn't let one incident affect the rest of his life. He stood. "Look, I promised Mrs. Whitney I'd look for Eli, so I'll have to juggle cases. I gave her my word. I can't back out of that. But other than that concession, I'm in. Sign me up."

"Great. Marge has the paperwork." Bree smiled. It was an expression he didn't see very often on her face, and it made him stupidly happy that he was the one who'd put it there.

Maybe he could find out if the shooting had been accidental or intentional. Maybe this would be the way to finally make peace with his past.

# CHAPTER ELEVEN

Bree gripped the steering wheel hard. She was relieved to have Matt on the case, but she wished she could have him full-time today. She respected his insistence on keeping his word to an elderly woman. She couldn't fault him for having integrity. It was one of the reasons she wanted him on her side.

How would Rogers respond? Having Matt on the team would most certainly shake things up. She considered Rogers's odd and insubordinate behavior. Maybe a shake-up was exactly what was needed.

She turned into the parking lot of Walmart. She didn't think she'd ever been this tired in her entire life, not even when she'd been working a case for forty-eight hours straight. This was an exhaustion that ran deep into her soul, one that was born of two months of stress and lack of sleep, of grief and hopelessness and floundering through raising two orphans while never knowing if she was doing the right thing.

It was after six. She should have been home by now, eating dinner with the kids. But here she was at Walmart.

"Why are we stopping?" Alyssa asked from the back seat of the SUV.

"The lab hasn't finished processing your backpack. You need clothes."

"You're going to buy me clothes?" Surprise lifted Alyssa's voice.

"It seems like the least I can do. You could have run from the scene this morning, but you didn't. You stuck by your friend. As long as you cooperate with my investigation, I'll do the same for you."

Alyssa's forehead wrinkled, and she said, "OK," in a hesitant voice, as if it had been a while since someone had been honest with her. If her story was legitimate, even her "friend" Harper had stolen her money and keys before getting shot. Her father might have been the last person to treat her well, and he'd been dead for a year.

Bree climbed out of the SUV and let Alyssa out of the back. Inside the store, she let her pick out two pairs of jeans, sweatpants, two sweatshirts, underwear, socks, and a pair of pajamas.

"The motel will have basic toiletries. Do you need anything else?"

"A hairbrush," Alyssa said.

Bree led her toward the front of the store. "Grab a toothbrush and toothpaste. If you need feminine products, get those too." She pushed the cart while the girl tossed essentials into the basket.

"I need deodorant and a razor." Looking almost excited, Alyssa abandoned the cart and darted down the aisle. She rounded the corner and disappeared. Bree grabbed the cart and followed her. Before she could catch up, a scream ripped through the store, followed by the sound of objects clattering to the floor.

"Sheriff!" Alyssa shouted.

"Alyssa!" Ditching the cart, Bree raced around the corner. She collided with Alyssa. Bree fell backward and crashed into a display. Pain zinged through her shoulder, and deodorants slid across the floor like marbles. She rolled to her hands and knees. Heart sprinting, she scrambled to her feet.

A few feet away, Alyssa was sprawled on top of a broken cardboard display of razors. Shaving products were piled around her. The girl's face was white in the fluorescent lighting.

"What happened?" Bree looked up and down the aisle. She saw no one.

"I saw him." Alyssa panted.

"Who?" Bree helped the girl to her feet.

"Him." Alyssa's eyes went wide. "The man who shot Harper."

Bree ran to the end of the aisle and looked down the main corridor that led to the cash registers. The only people she saw were an elderly couple and a young mom pushing a stroller. No man.

Bree hustled the girl out of the aisle and headed for the front of the store. While they hurried, she used her cell phone to summon a deputy. She wanted to check the exits and parking lot, but she couldn't chase the man and protect Alyssa.

She found the manager, and they went to the security office. Inside, she stood in front of the bank of monitors, showed her badge, and explained the situation.

"Show me the exits and parking lot." Bree watched the screens. "Alyssa, do you see him?"

Alyssa scanned the monitors. "No."

"Go back five minutes," Bree said.

The security officer tapped on the keyboard and played the video.

"There he is." Alyssa pointed to the last monitor. "The man in the baseball cap."

A man in jeans and a black coat crossed the parking lot. He wore a baseball cap with the brim pulled low. The collar of his jacket was turned up, his shoulders hunched, and his head was bowed.

"Damn. Can't see his face at all." Bree leaned closer. "We'll get his license plate when he gets into his car."

But he walked out of the parking lot, turned the corner, and disappeared down the side street.

Bree turned to the security officer. "Can you track his movements through the store? He has to show his face at some point."

"Yes, ma'am." The officer turned to his computer. A minute later, he pointed to a monitor. "He entered the store here, lapped the main aisles once, then stopped in the health-and-beauty area."

Bree watched the man walk into the aisle with Alyssa. She screamed, and he turned around and hurried away. He kept his face tilted downward, and the baseball cap brim shielded his face from camera view.

"Stop there." Bree squinted at the screen. The man rushed away from the personal products section of the store. "I can see the lower part of his face there."

"Yes, ma'am." The security officer clicked away on his keyboard.

"Can you rewind this?" she asked.

"Yes," he said.

The video replayed on the screen.

"Where are we at this moment?" Bree gestured to the monitor as the man approached the deodorant aisle.

"Here." The security officer pulled up another feed on a different monitor. "In the next aisle."

Bree straightened. The man's head turned as he passed each aisle. Had he been looking for a product?

Or Alyssa?

On the screen, Alyssa spotted the man and startled. She jumped backward, spun around, and ran straight into Bree. They both went sprawling into displays, while the man hurried away.

Why did he run? Because Alyssa had yelled, *Sheriff*?

Bree was wearing her uniform shirt—and her gun. Had he been following them? Why?

Throughout their encounter, he kept the rim of his ballcap over his face. The head position seemed unnatural. It couldn't be a coincidence. Could it?

Alyssa could have been mistaken. She could be hypersensitive after witnessing violence. This man could be just an ordinary citizen, spooked by a screaming girl.

But how many Walmart shoppers don't park in the lot?

"Wait." Bree pointed to the second monitor. There was a mark on the back of his hand. "Is that a tattoo?" She squinted at the image. "Can you enlarge that?"

The security officer zoomed in on the back of the man's hand. The mark's edges were irregular. "I don't think it's a tattoo."

The dark patch was roughly shaped like the state of Texas.

"It's a scar or a birthmark." Bree leaned in. "Could you copy all the videos with that man in them, the clip of this encounter"—Bree pointed to a screen—"and the parking-lot films for thirty minutes before and after?"

One of Bree's deputies arrived. She assigned him to wait for the videos while Bree and Alyssa retrieved the shopping cart. After paying at the register, Bree drove Alyssa to the Evergreen Motel. It was dark when she parked and called for another deputy.

"Wait here." Bree locked Alyssa in the back of the vehicle while she checked her into a second-floor room. Then Bree drove around to park in a spot facing the room. Deputy Rogers pulled up next to her SUV. She stepped out of her vehicle and approached his window.

"Did you get some sleep?" she asked.

"Yes, ma'am." Rogers's eyes were still shadowed, but he'd been off duty for twelve hours. He wasn't her first choice, but she would rotate the deputies on security detail throughout the night to keep their attention sharp. Solo surveillance was boring. It was too easy to lose focus or fall asleep.

"A suspicious man was following Alyssa in the Walmart. I need you to stay sharp."

"Yes, ma'am." His jaw tightened, and his face flushed.

"I also need to know you're going to treat her with respect."

He blinked, his gaze darting away. "I'm sorry about this morning. I was out of line."

Was he being sincere? He wouldn't look at her.

"OK, then." Bree scanned the empty parking lot. "She's in the first room on the second floor. There are enough vacancies that the manager agreed not to assign the room next to hers. I'll have another deputy switch with you in a couple of hours."

"Yes, ma'am."

Bree scanned the parking lot, then led Alyssa inside. The room wasn't fancy, but it was clean. Two double beds took up most of the space, and a wide window overlooked the parking lot. She checked in the closet, under the bed, and in the bathroom. There was one small window in the bathroom that no adult man could squeeze through. She returned to the living room and looked out the window. The deputy outside had a clear visual of the door and the cement stairs leading to the second-floor walkway. No one could approach Alyssa's room without being seen. This was the best Bree could do.

"All you have to do is look out these curtains and you'll see a deputy outside." Bree closed the curtains.

"What if he leaves?"

"Then another will take his place."

"What if I look out and no one's there?"

Bree pulled a business card from her wallet. "Here's my cell number. Call me anytime."

Alyssa stood in the middle of the room, clutching her Walmart bags and looking lost. "I haven't slept in a real bed in a long time, and I don't remember the last time I stayed in a motel."

"Why don't you take a hot shower? Are you hungry?"

Alyssa didn't answer. She didn't seem interested in food.

"Pizza OK?" Bree didn't like to miss dinner with the kids, but Alyssa seemed too nervous to leave alone.

She sat in the desk chair and called for pizza delivery. Alyssa went into the bathroom. Water rushed through pipes as the shower turned on. The pizza arrived before Alyssa emerged. Clean and dressed in the plaid flannel pajamas they'd bought at Walmart, she looked much younger than nineteen.

Bree had ordered bottled water and Coke with the pizza. "I didn't know what you wanted to drink."

Alyssa took the Coke and ate a slice.

"There's a mini fridge in the dresser." Bree opened the door and stashed the water inside. "Try to get some sleep. I'll see you in the morning."

Alyssa grabbed Bree's arm. "What if he comes back?"

"That's why Deputy Rogers is outside."

"He doesn't like me." Alyssa hugged her arms.

"He *will* protect you." Bree thought about staying, but as sheriff, she *had* to delegate tasks. Her own family needed to come first. "Lock the door after I leave. It'll be OK."

But Alyssa looked like a child as Bree left the room. Torn, Bree walked past Rogers's patrol vehicle.

Alyssa would be fine. She'd be watched all night long.

Bree slid into her SUV. Guilt followed her all the way home. While she drove, she reviewed the case in her head. Was Alyssa really in danger? Had she seen a murder? Alyssa was either lying, mentally ill, or a murderer had actually been following her.

A young man was dead. Alyssa's story had led her to his body. Those two things might not even be related. But Bree didn't like coincidences. She preferred logic.

She parked next to the house. It felt like days had passed since she'd left that morning. It was after eight o'clock when she slipped in the back door.

Kayla and Ladybug were waiting for her. The dog beelined for Bree's knees. Bree caught her and gave her an awkward rub behind the ears. Despite Bree's discomfort, the dog wanted her attention.

The little girl carried her stuffed pig under one arm. "You're late."

Bree kissed the top of her head. "I know. I'm sorry."

She hung up her jacket and kicked off her boots. She didn't know whether she wanted to eat or shower first.

"Dana left your dinner in the oven." Kayla stood as close as the dog. Bree gently nudged them so she could move.

"What is it?" Bree hung her messenger bag on a hook by the door. Moving into the kitchen, she set her phone on the kitchen island. After washing her hands, she opened the oven. The smell of chicken sent her stomach rumbling into overtime.

"Chicken marsala." Kayla pronounced the word slowly, as if she'd practiced. "I helped make it."

Bree grabbed a pot holder and used it to carry the dish to the table. The dog sank to the floor and rested her head on her paws, but her eyes followed the plate of food. Kayla sat her pig in a chair, then filled a glass with water and brought it to Bree, along with utensils.

"Thank you." Bree sliced off a chunk of chicken. "This is really good."

Kayla giggled as she sat across from Bree and rested her elbows on the table. "It has *wine* in it."

"The alcohol cooks off."

"That's what Dana said." Kayla sounded disappointed.

Kayla talked nonstop while Bree ate her chicken and potatoes. The little girl still suffered from nightmares and separation anxiety, but during the last few weeks she'd also had happy moments. Bree was grateful for each and every one. By the time Bree had finished her dinner, she knew every detail of Kayla's day, right down to what her teacher had worn.

"I'm glad you had a good day." Bree pushed back her plate. The child's company had soothed her raw nerves.

"Can we read another chapter of Harry Potter tonight?" Kayla pulled her pig into her lap and stroked its head.

"Of course. Go brush your teeth and get into bed. I'll be up in five minutes."

Kayla scrambled out of the chair and left the room.

Wrapped in a thick blue robe, Dana walked into the kitchen. "Tea?"

"Not now, but thanks."

"Ah, bedtime story?"

"Yep."

"I'm glad you made it home in time." Dana filled a mug with water and stuck it in the microwave.

"I try," Bree said. "Kayla seems to have had a good day. How is Luke?"

Dana sighed. "I don't know. He's been doing homework since he got home from baseball practice. It's crazy they're starting already. It's still winter."

"They practice inside until the weather breaks." Bree had been the same age as Kayla when she'd lost her parents. She remembered exactly how it had felt: the crushing confusion and loneliness, the sense of being completely alone even in a classroom full of other kids. She didn't want either Luke or Kayla to feel that isolated. She wanted to be there for them, but Luke seemed resistant.

Bree stood. "Kayla will at least talk to me. With Luke, I'm hitting a wall."

Dana nodded. "Same."

"I'll talk to him after I read to Kayla." Bree went upstairs. Luke's door was closed.

Kayla was in her bed. She had lined up her stuffed animals on either side of her for story time. The pig was on her lap. He always got the best seat. Bree sat on the edge of the bed and opened the book. They were halfway through. At first, Bree had been concerned that Harry Potter was too dark, but Kayla loved the story. Maybe she needed to read about another orphan whose life was as full of darkness as her own.

"Do you think Mommy would have liked Harry Potter?" Kayla asked.

The question took Bree by surprise. Grief clogged her throat, and her eyes blurred with tears. Erin should be alive to share these moments with her daughter. "I think your mommy would have loved him."

"Me too." Kayla smiled.

Bree read for a half hour, until the little girl's eyes closed and her breathing evened out. Bree left the lights on as she exited the room. She knocked softly on Luke's door, but he didn't answer. Light seeped beneath the crack under his door. It was only nine o'clock. Was he asleep?

She hesitated, her hand a few inches from the doorknob. Should she open the door or not? He was sixteen. Privacy was important to him, and she respected that, but she also wanted to keep tabs on him.

An image of Alyssa's scarred wrists flashed into her mind. She'd had no one to check on her after her dad had died, and her grief and loneliness had driven her to consider—maybe even half-heartedly attempt—suicide. Bree didn't want to see similarities between Alyssa and Luke, but she couldn't help it.

Bree knocked one more time.

To her relief, Luke responded with a sleepy, "Yeah."

Bree opened Luke's door a few inches. He lay on his side, writing in a spiral notebook. Brown, tousled hair fell over his forehead.

Bree went into his room, turned his desk chair around, and sat facing him. "How was your day?"

"It was OK." He was naturally lean, but his cheekbones looked more prominent. Had he lost weight?

She gestured toward his notebook. "What are you working on?"

"Big Algebra II test tomorrow."

What Bree remembered about algebra would fit on a postage stamp. "Anything important happen today?"

"Not really." Luke tapped on his notebook. "I really need to finish these review problems and get to sleep."

"Baseball practice again tomorrow?"

"Yeah."

"If you're tired, I can take over feeding the horses in the morning," Bree offered.

He shook his head. "I like doing it."

"OK." Frustrated, Bree stood and pushed the chair under the desk. "I'll let you finish up. Don't worry about the horses tonight. I'll do barn check."

"Thanks." He went back to his math problem.

Downstairs, she made a cup of tea and sat across from Dana. "He's been going to bed really early lately. Is that normal?"

"He gets up at dawn to feed the horses, has a full day of school, then goes to baseball practice. When he comes home, he cleans the barn and does homework." Dana got up and went to the pantry. "He has plenty of reasons to be tired."

Dana brought a bakery box to the table. She opened the lid to reveal chocolate croissants. "These were going to be for breakfast, but you look like you could use one now."

"Definitely." Bree took a napkin from the holder in the center of the table and selected a pastry. "He likes to be busy."

"And avoid dealing with his problems. Sounds like someone else I know." Dana had been her partner for years. No one knew Bree better.

"Guilty," Bree admitted. "How do I get him to talk to me?"

"I don't know. I haven't been very successful."

"Maybe he needs to talk to another man." Bree bit into the pastry. "I'll call Adam tomorrow. With my new case, I'm unfortunately going to be working overtime." Bree's brother lived close by, but he was an artist who tended to get lost in his work for long periods of time.

Dana wiped her hands on a napkin. "If he won't talk to Adam, maybe he'd see a therapist. It might be easier to talk to a stranger."

"Maybe." But Bree had her doubts about that. She wasn't fond of therapy, and Dana's spot-on assessment of Bree pointed out how similar she and Luke were. Bree's parents had been acutely—fatally—dysfunctional. Bree's sister had had significant attachment issues. Bree had never had a relationship that was marriage material. Were all the Taggerts flawed? Deep inside, she hoped her family wasn't simply destined to repeat their loop of violence and tragedy.

# CHAPTER TWELVE

He almost missed the turn in the dark. Half-covered with overgrown evergreens, the opening was barely visible. He stomped on the brake and jerked the wheel. His vehicle fishtailed. The tires spun, shooting snow and gravel behind his vehicle. He eased off the gas pedal and straightened the car.

*Relax!*

He couldn't panic now. He still had work to do.

Trees bowed overhead, making the narrow lane even darker. He let the car roll forward, maintaining a slow and steady speed on the frozen, rutted lane.

He drove around the main building and parked in front of a large garage. He got out of his car and opened the overhead door. The rusty metal mechanisms squeaked. He pulled his car inside. He stood in the dark, staring at the two bundles wrapped in black tarps and propped in the corner. Sweat ran down his back, chilling him.

Going to the Walmart had been a close call.

Following the sheriff had been risky, but he'd learned what he'd needed to know. The girl had definitely recognized him.

She had to die.

But first things first. The weather forecast called for a warmer spell next week. Dead bodies would smell once the temperature rose above freezing.

He reached for the sack of tools on a workbench, then went outside and walked down the slope. The lake gleamed black in the darkness. His boots slid on the icy ground as he scrambled onto the dock. He walked out over the water, taking care to avoid rotten boards. He'd considered dumping the body at the dam, where the water still flowed, but the area was too public. He needed seclusion. No one ever came here.

Halfway down the dock, he surveyed his surroundings. He couldn't have anyone watching him. He'd brought ice-fishing equipment as a cover just in case he encountered company, but there was no one.

The ice held as he shuffled to where the water would be deep enough. Then he dropped to his knees and took the chisel and hammer out of his bag. When he tapped on the chisel, a small piece of dried blood fell to the ice. It turned from dark crimson to bright red as it rehydrated. He wiped the hammer on the ice. It left a red trail. He needed to clean his tools better.

With every strike of the hammer, the chisel bit into the ice. He remembered the last time he'd used the hammer. He hadn't been so restrained or gentle. He smiled with the memory. He couldn't wait to do that again.

*Payback is a bitch.*

When the hole was large enough to accommodate his hacksaw, he switched tools. The ice wasn't too thick, and it only took him a few minutes to enlarge the opening. Murky lake water swirled in the opening. He climbed to his feet, turned in a circle, and checked his surroundings again.

He saw nothing but ice and trees and darkness.

Perfect.

Most people didn't like the darkness, but night was his favorite time. He could do anything in the dark. Anything he wanted. No one would see.

He shuffled back to the garage. After setting down the bag of tools, he wrangled the first black tarp out of the corner. Dead bodies were fucking heavy. By the time he'd dragged it out the door, his back ached. He wiped his forehead with a glove, then grabbed the edges of the tarp and pulled the body toward the lake. It slid easily downhill on the snow. When he'd reached the lake, the tarp slipped down the embankment onto the ice with little effort.

At the edge of the hole, he removed the duct tape from the tarp. It opened, revealing the bloody ruin of a face.

*Not so pretty now, are you?*

He gave the body a kick and watched it roll off the tarp. The naked limbs flopped, limp and useless, onto the ice. Satisfaction filled him as he shoved the body into the hole. It slid beneath the surface, one gray-tinged hand turned in a circle, almost like a wave goodbye, before it sank. The fingers slid beneath the surface and disappeared.

*See ya.*

Pride surged inside him. A certain someone would never fuck another woman.

Two pricks down, plenty more to go.

Would the body sink and stay put? Ideally, no one would find it until spring. But even if they did, it didn't matter. He'd never been arrested. No one had ever taken his fingerprints. His DNA wasn't on file anywhere. There was nothing that could tie him to the murders.

He turned away from the hole and collected his tarp. He was going to need it again.

# CHAPTER THIRTEEN

Tuesday morning, Matt and Greta finished their run before sunrise. He showered, then fed himself and the dogs and checked the morning news report. The coverage of the body found in the lake was superficial. No news on Eli's disappearance, other than the search hadn't turned up any clues. Bree had given a brief statement the day before at the boat ramp. The news channels replayed it.

Matt was drinking his second cup of coffee when his phone rang. Bree.

He answered the call.

"I'm headed to the ME's office. Thought you might want to come along."

Matt set his cup in the sink. "Has Dr. Jones ID'd the body?"

"Not yet, but she's doing the autopsy this morning."

As much as Matt hated observing autopsies, he felt as if this one was important. "OK. Do you want me to meet you there?"

"Sure. I'll see you soon." Bree ended the call.

Matt crated Greta and left the house. The ME's office was in the municipal complex, not far from the sheriff's station. Bree's official SUV was already parked out front when he drove up. He found her suiting up outside the autopsy suite. Her face was as pale as the mask she was tying around her head.

"You OK?" He stepped into coveralls and booties and grabbed a mask.

"Yep," she said through clenched teeth.

She paused at the entrance, one hand on the door. "I haven't been here since I viewed Erin's body."

"Do you *need* to go in? Dr. Jones will give you a report." Matt had stood with her that day two months before. He would stand with her today. He walked closer, took her hand, and squeezed it.

Her fingers twined with his. "Yes. I do. This is my first homicide since I've taken office. Besides, I have to take this step at some point. Might as well be today." She drew in a deep breath, released his hand, and opened the door. Bree would never take the easy way out.

Matt followed her inside. The main autopsy bay held a stainless-steel table, cabinets, and scales. For Matt, it wasn't the sights and smells that got to him, but his imagination. His years as an investigator had shown him countless horrors that could be inflicted on the human body. The second the smell of formalin hit his nose, those cases came back in a flood of bloody images that nearly gagged him.

Dr. Jones was deep into the autopsy. She was bent over the corpse's face and dictating her findings for her report.

She looked up. Her gaze went from Bree to Matt and back again.

"Sheriff." Dr. Jones straightened and pointed her scalpel at Matt. "I know you."

"Yes." Matt opened his mouth to tell her they'd met when Bree identified her sister's body, but Bree cut him off.

"This is Matt Flynn," she said. "It was Matt's K-9 that found the body yesterday. He will be assisting me as a criminal investigator."

The ME appeared to think over the explanation for his presence for a few minutes, as if not entirely satisfied. Then she pointed at Bree. "OK, but he's your responsibility. He faints and smacks his head, it's on you."

Slightly insulted, Matt wanted to say *I don't faint*. But he knew the second he expressed his manliness, he'd probably face-plant.

"Understood," Bree agreed.

Dr. Jones addressed Matt. "The information gathered during this autopsy is confidential. This man is my patient, and he has rights to his privacy just like any living person."

"Yes, ma'am. I was previously an investigator with the sheriff's department," Matt said.

She was not impressed.

The body lay on its back, its chest flayed open. The Y-incision had been made, the breastbone cut out, and the internal organs removed for examination and weighing.

Dr. Jones gestured to the body with her scalpel. "Here we have the body of a white male." She pointed to a monitor on a side-table computer. On it, X-rays of the chest and shoulder were visible. "The long bones have rounded ends called epiphyses that fuse as the body matures. This medial clavicular epiphysis is fully fused. In males, this occurs generally around the age of twenty, give or take a couple of years." She moved back to the body and pointed at the ribs, then the removed breastplate. "The sternal end of the fourth rib is another good indicator of age. The sternal end starts out round but becomes more irregular and pitted over time." She stepped back and scanned the body. "The general condition of the body is excellent. This young man was in good health and well muscled. I estimate him to be between eighteen and thirty years of age."

"What about time of death?" Bree asked.

"That's tricky with bodies that have been in cold water." The ME set down her scalpel. "I believe he went into the water shortly after death." She pointed to the victim's hands, which were a purplish color. "In a body floating in water, lividity is concentrated in the hands and feet because bodies float facedown underwater. Once the heart stops, blood pools in the lowest parts. In this victim, lividity is fully fixed, and rigor has come and gone. Normally, this would mean the victim had been dead more than thirty-six hours, but the cold water would delay the onset of both lividity and rigor mortis."

Her gaze swept over the body. "You can see some discoloration of the torso from the onset of decomposition in the internal organs, but it's not advanced."

Matt had seen bodies that were twice their normal size due to bloating.

The ME referred to her computer. "The best estimate I can give is a time since death of two to five days."

Bree propped a hand on her hip. "Today is Tuesday. So, he died between Thursday and Sunday."

"Correct," Dr. Jones said.

Matt couldn't wait any longer. "Do you know if this is Eli Whitney?"

Dr. Jones motioned toward the ruined face. "This man's teeth and jaw are too badly damaged to use them for identification or aging purposes. But we know from medical records that Eli Whitney broke his arm at the age of eight. He also has a birthmark the size of a playing card on the back of his shoulder. This body has no such birthmark. Nor do the X-rays show a healed break of the ulna. Based on those factors, I do not believe this body to be Mr. Whitney."

Matt exhaled. While relieved, he was acutely aware that this young man was someone's loved one. "How did he die?"

"At first, I considered blunt trauma." Dr. Jones moved to the head of the table. "The most obvious injury is to the face, but upon closer examination of his facial wounds, I found that he'd been shot."

"Someone shot him, *then* bashed his face in?" Matt clarified.

"Yes. I recovered two bullets from his skull." Dr. Jones gestured to a stainless-steel dish. "9mm."

Matt felt his eyebrows shoot up.

A moment of silence crept by as Matt and Bree digested the strange news. Then Bree cleared her throat. "Can you tell what kind of instrument was used to inflict the damage to his face?"

"I found tiny metal pieces in the wounds, and the implement used was heavy and round." Dr. Jones made a small circle with her thumb and forefinger, like an OK sign. "The striking end was about that big."

Matt knew instantly what had been used. "A hammer."

"That's the most likely object," the ME agreed. She motioned toward the body. "I also see bruising on the forearms that look like defensive injuries, and there *was* tissue deep under his fingernails."

"So, whoever killed him probably has some scratches," Bree said.

"Another odd thing we noticed is that the head is shorn." The ME pointed to the head. Next to it sat a bone saw. Dr. Jones had not yet opened the skull to remove the brain. Considering the damage, it would be an even messier job than usual. Matt wasn't squeamish, but he sincerely hoped he could leave before that happened.

"Lots of men shave their heads." Bree moved closer.

"Once we washed the body, we could see that the hair wasn't shaved down to the skin but buzzed very close to the scalp. There are small tufts of hair remaining in random places," Dr. Jones said. "We also found scrapes where the clippers or shears scratched the scalp."

"So, maybe the victim struggled while his head was being buzzed," Matt said.

"Possibly," the ME agreed. "As mentioned at the scene, his hands and ankles were bound at one point. From the width of the wounds, I'd guess plastic zip ties." The ME paused, then pointed to a pair of red marks on the victim's arm. "In addition, these small burns could be from a stun gun."

Bree leaned back. "That would explain how the killer incapacitated his victim."

The ME continued. "A few additional observations that might aid in identifying the victim. He died within an hour of eating pizza. The

X-rays show a previously broken and healed tibia, and he has a small tattoo of a shamrock on the back of his shoulder blade." She clicked on her mouse and brought up a photo of the tattoo.

"It's lopsided," Matt said.

"The color saturation is uneven, and the lines aren't smooth," Bree added. "This is the kind of tat a drunk gets and regrets in the morning. Can you forward me the picture of the tattoo?"

"Yes." The ME clicked a few buttons on her computer, then returned to her autopsy. She was donning fresh gloves and reaching for her bone saw when Matt and Bree left the suite to remove their personal protective equipment.

Ten minutes later, Matt and Bree exited the ME's office. They stood on the sidewalk. Matt breathed the fresh air deep into his lungs, but he knew he'd be smelling formalin and decomp for the rest of the day.

Bree turned her face to the sun and closed her eyes. At nine a.m., its rays were still weak. But the air was crisp, the sky a brilliant shade of blue that only seemed to occur on a cold winter day.

"Are you OK?" he asked her.

"Yep," she said without opening her eyes. "You?"

"Yeah."

She opened her eyes and turned away from the sun. "I need to review the case with Todd and make a game plan for the investigation. Can you come?"

"I wish I could, but I promised Mrs. Whitney I'd interview Eli's roommates and check out the area where he was last seen. You know the first forty-eight hours are critical to a missing-person investigation."

"Fair enough," Bree agreed, but she didn't look pleased.

He jerked a thumb over his shoulder at the ME's office. "I need to run down the obvious leads. Since that wasn't Eli, he could still be alive."

"I understand. You gave your word. I wouldn't want you to bail on a promise. True missing-person cases are tough," Bree admitted. "So many go unsolved."

Matt wondered how long the police chief of Scarlet Falls would let Detective Dane stay on Eli's case. If Stella didn't come up with some leads, the case would go cold, and her chief would pull her off.

"If I run across anything that links to your cases, I'll call you."

"Thank you. I'll do the same." Bree turned away from him. "Can we catch up afterward?"

"Yes." Matt thought of her investigating a murder—and finding a murderer—alone, without him at her side, and his bones went cold. "Bree?"

She glanced over her shoulder.

"Watch your back."

# Chapter Fourteen

Bree parked in front of Alyssa's motel.

She wished Matt hadn't been pulled away by Eli's disappearance, though she respected his decision to help the family. When adults went missing, barring any clear indications of a crime, most police departments didn't spend much time looking for them. Often, the family was on their own.

Bree would manage, but she hadn't realized how much she'd missed working with him. Matt saw connections she overlooked. He was smart and didn't bullshit her.

But she couldn't deny that her feelings went beyond their professional partnership. Her heart beat a little faster every time she saw him. She trusted him, an honor bestowed on very few people. His sense of humor and easy smile didn't hurt either.

But she didn't have the energy to start a relationship, right?

Matt had made it clear he was interested, but she'd put him off. He wouldn't wait forever. A bitchy internal voice told her she'd be sorry. This type of indecision was not like her. It wasn't as if she'd never had a relationship before, though she'd never been attached enough to any man to be devastated by their breakup. She hadn't even dated Matt, and already she was missing him.

Thankfully, she had an overwhelming amount of work to distract her. She needed to draw a firm line between their professional and personal relationships. All Bree's lines were blurring when she preferred them crystal clear.

She climbed out of her car. A patrol vehicle was parked in front of Alyssa's room. Bree checked in with the deputy, then went to the door. It swung open before Bree had the chance to knock.

"I was waiting for you." Alyssa wore Walmart jeans, a sweatshirt, and sneakers. Washed and dried, her hair was a rich, shiny shade of dark brown. But the circles under her eyes hadn't faded, and she had fresh scratches on her arms.

"I'm sorry. I had to make a stop on the way here." Bree stepped into the room and closed the door behind her. One look at Alyssa's dirty coat draped over the back of the chair made her wish she'd bought her a new one or taken that one home to wash it. "You can either stay here at the motel today with a deputy parked out front, or you can come to the station and hang out there."

"Will you be at the station?"

"Some of the time. Marge will be there all day."

"OK. I'll go there." Alyssa grabbed her dirty coat. "When can I get my backpack and 4Runner back?"

Bree had completely forgotten about the vehicle. Not that she was ready to let Alyssa go just yet, but without evidence to implicate her in a crime, she couldn't make her stay.

"I'll call forensics and see where they stand on processing it," Bree said, stalling.

The vague answer seemed to satisfy Alyssa. She put on her coat and went out the door without looking back.

Bree deposited Alyssa in the back seat of her SUV and climbed behind the wheel. "Are you hungry?"

"Not really."

Bree glanced at Alyssa in the rearview mirror. "You can order food from the diner. They'll deliver. Anything you want. Pancakes. Waffles. Eggs. A burger."

"OK." Either Alyssa didn't care, or she wasn't used to eating three times a day.

At the station, Bree left Alyssa in the conference room with a menu and went into her office.

Marge walked in and set a cup of coffee on the desk. "Good morning."

"Morning. Order Alyssa whatever she wants for breakfast." Bree sat and reached for the coffee. "What are we going to do with her all day?"

"I'll set her up with my iPad and she can stream movies for today, but you can't keep her forever."

"I know, but I can't just let her go. Either she's a witness and potentially in danger, or she's mentally ill. Either way, where would she go? It's barely thirty degrees outside."

Marge toyed with the reading glasses that hung around her neck. "What about employment opportunities at the university? Maybe there's a work-study program we could help her get into."

"That's a great idea. She needs something that comes with a place to stay. It's almost impossible to get a job without an address."

"Yes, and when her current driver's license expires, she won't be able to get a new one."

"You need an ID to get an ID," Bree said.

"Some of the homeless shelters will let their residents receive mail and use their addresses."

"Alyssa told me she won't go back to a shelter."

Marge frowned. "I'll think on it. Meanwhile, I'll feed her."

"Thank you," Bree said as her admin left the office.

Marge had been with the sheriff's department longer than anyone else in the station. If there was a way around a problem, Marge would find it.

Todd passed Marge on his way in, a file tucked under his arm.

"Got a few minutes?" he asked Bree.

"Yes." She gestured toward the door.

Todd pushed it closed and dropped into a chair. "I ran the background check on Alyssa. Her past address, her father's death, her eviction, all verified." He flipped through a few pages. "Her fingerprints were in the system, so her identity is also confirmed."

Surprised, Bree asked, "She has a record?"

"One arrest for shoplifting last summer. The charges were dropped, and she was released."

"What did she steal?"

Todd checked his papers. "Peanut butter and bread."

Bree sighed. "Is that her only arrest?"

"Yes." He looked up. "No drug offenses. Also, she has no active social media accounts. Two years ago, she posted regularly on Instagram. But then I guess not having Wi-Fi, a computer, or electricity would hinder posting."

"What about her phone?"

"She only used it to communicate with work and one other number. She said that was Harper's. That number also appears to be a prepaid account."

"What is the number?" Bree picked up her phone and dialed the number Todd gave her. The call went immediately to voice mail. "The greeting is the automated one that comes with the account. I hoped to hear a female voice to at least support the existence of Harper Scott."

"About her. I could not find her anywhere." Todd turned to the back of his folder. "I found a fifty-year-old doctor, a forty-two-year-old singer, and a male accountant with that name, but no nineteen-year-old Caucasian females. I tried motor vehicle records in New York, Pennsylvania, and New Jersey. There are no criminal records for Harper Scott in the tristate area."

Bree sat back. Her new chair squeaked.

Todd continued. "There is a commercial cleaning company, Master Clean, based in the Meadows Industrial Complex at the intersection of Route 51 and Evergreen Road. They do not employ anyone by the name of Harper Scott or anyone who meets her general description. The office manager said they don't have a single employee under the age of thirty. I called other local commercial cleaning companies. None of those employ a Harper Scott either."

"Did you search missing persons?" Bree asked.

"I searched both wanted and missing persons records by name and physical description, in case Harper Scott isn't her real name. I didn't find her." Todd paused for a breath and examined his ugly black uniform shoes. "Some of the other deputies think Alyssa made her up, that there was no shooting."

*Rogers?*

Bree didn't ask for names. She appreciated that Todd was being straight with her. Forcing him to rat out specific men would not encourage him to continue.

"How do they explain the shell casings?"

"They could have been planted there." He lifted a shoulder.

"What do you think?" Bree asked.

"I think it's too early to make a judgment."

"Good call," Bree said. "We are still in the evidence-gathering stage. We need more facts before we start formulating real theories. Do we have anything from forensics yet?"

"The evidence log." Todd pulled a sheet out of his folder and handed it to Bree.

She skimmed it.

"There were no usable fingerprints on the bullet casings," Todd said.

"Damn," Bree said. "I knew it was a long shot." Pulling prints from spent casings was challenging due to the friction and heat applied to the bullet during the firing process. "I was hoping we'd get some luck."

"They didn't have much luck pulling prints from the cabin's interior either. Many of the prints they did recover were not good quality. Lots of smearing. They're processing what they have, but many of the surfaces were very clean, too clean under the circumstances. The tech thought maybe they'd been wiped down with a strong cleanser."

The majority of fingerprints pulled from crime scenes were low quality, so this wasn't shocking. But squatters don't normally clean, so that was odd.

Bree pictured the cabin's kitchen. "There were some basic cleaning products under the sink. The cleaning rags were damp and smelled like the spray cleaner."

"Did the girls like cleanliness or intentionally remove their fingerprints?"

"According to Alyssa, Harper cleans often, but we don't know why. Please follow up with forensics." Outdoor scenes resulted in a plethora of evidence to sort through, and Randolph County had limited resources. The techs were already overwhelmed with two large scenes to process.

"Yes, ma'am." Todd rose to his feet. "What about the dead guy?"

Bree relayed the initial information from the medical examiner. "Whoever killed the victim had a lot of rage, which usually means the murder was personal. Until the ME identifies the victim, finding his killer will be difficult."

"Now what?" Todd asked.

"See if there have been any like crimes in the area."

"Shouldn't take long to find out if other victims have been shot in the face, then pulverized with a hammer," Todd said.

The heat turned on and hot air swept over her. Usually, Bree froze in her office, but today, she felt clammy and hot. She was hungry, thirsty, and tired. Because of her trip to the ME's office, she'd skipped breakfast. Sweat broke out between her shoulder blades. The stacks of papers on her desk felt claustrophobic. Her throat tightened, as if the responsibility were suddenly choking her.

She'd lived by herself since she graduated from the police academy. Now, she lived with two children and Dana. She loved them all, but the change was a huge adjustment. Someone was *always* talking to her. And with Kayla crawling into her bed every night, Bree didn't even get those hours to recharge. On top of that, her office saw a constant stream of county employees.

She needed to be alone for ten minutes, preferably out of the office in a quiet place where she could think. Her phone buzzed with an email. The owner of Grey Lake Campground was at the site. She returned his email, saying she was on the way.

Bree got up and put on her jacket. "Let me know if anything comes in."

There wasn't anything she could do about her exhaustion, but she could grab food and water on the way. The fresh air wouldn't hurt either.

"Where will you be?" Todd asked.

"Grey Lake Campground." Bree headed for her door. "I want to look over the cabin and boat ramp scenes again."

She couldn't suppress the feeling that she'd missed something.

# Chapter Fifteen

Matt spent two hours on Oak Street, knocking on doors and asking people if they remembered the party the previous Saturday. He showed neighborhood residents Eli's picture, but no one recognized him.

He drove to the other side of campus to the house Eli shared with his roommates. Like the rest of the area, the building was typical student housing: old, beaten, and maintained to the absolute bare-minimum standards. He parked at the curb and went up the front walk. A few red plastic cups littered the snow-covered lawn. Matt climbed the front steps onto the porch. Spindles were missing on the railing, and an upholstered couch sat under a window in the corner.

The big old house had been broken down into three apartments, one on each floor. Eli and his pals lived in the downstairs unit. Matt knocked on the door. No one answered, but he heard music within the building. He knocked again, louder.

"I'm coming." A blond guy in sweatpants and sporting a serious bed head opened the door.

Matt introduced himself. "I'm looking for Eli. I'm a friend of his grandmother."

"Shit. Yeah. Come in." The blond guy stepped back. "I'm Christian."

The front door opened into a small living room. The finish was worn off the wood floors, and everything needed painting. Christian led the way into a cramped kitchen. Other than a stack of pizza boxes, the surfaces were mostly cleared. A large water stain blotched the floor on the other side of the room, and the cabinets were peeling. But it was nicer than where Matt had lived in college.

"I have tea but no coffee." Christian filled a kettle and lit the burner under it.

"I'm OK." Matt turned and leaned against the counter. "I'm here because Mrs. Whitney is worried about Eli."

"Yeah. She's called us a few times."

"You don't seem worried."

Christian lifted one shoulder. "It's only been a couple of days."

"Where do you think he is?"

"With a girl, I hope." Christian laughed. "Seriously, I love Mrs. Whitney. She's a real nice old lady, but she's also a little paranoid regarding Eli."

"She's lost most of her family."

"I know, and that's why me and the other guys go see her sometimes. Well, that and her pot roast."

"His grandmother says he would have called her if he was going to miss Sunday dinner."

"Maybe he did. If she takes out her hearing aid, she can't hear shit."

Matt wondered if that was how Mrs. Whitney had missed Detective Dane's call as well.

"Can I look in Eli's room?" Matt asked.

Christian frowned. "I don't think I can let you in there without his permission."

"But he's missing," Matt said.

"Maybe."

"What if I get Mrs. Whitney to call you?"

"Sorry, man." Christian shook his head. "I'll tell you the same thing I told the lady detective. If Eli is hooking up somewhere, he'd be pissed that I let some random dude search his room."

"You didn't let the detective in?" Matt understood not letting *him* in. He didn't have a badge. One of the problems with not being a cop was not having any authority. The sooner Bree gave him credentials, the better. But a police detective was a whole different matter, and Christian's refusal to cooperate set off Matt's suspicions.

"She didn't have a warrant or anything." Christian's shoulder lifted and dropped. "I opened the door so she could see Eli wasn't in there. It's a small room. But I didn't let her go through his stuff."

Without a clear indication of foul play, the detective would have a hard time convincing a judge that she needed a search warrant. Not calling one's grandmother wasn't enough. But Matt still found Christian's attitude perplexing. Was he protecting his friend's interests? Or his own? Did Christian have something to do with Eli's disappearance?

Matt let it go. For now. "Tell me about Saturday night. What time did Eli leave?"

"I already went over all this with the detective." Christian pulled a box of tea bags from the cabinet. "Somewhere around ten. He took a rideshare, so there should be a record of the pickup. The detective has his phone." Christian frowned. "We were supposed to go together, but I was sick all week. The last thing I wanted to do was party."

"So, he went alone. Is that typical for him?"

Christian tossed a tea bag into a mug. "Eli's not shy, and he's been interested in a girl. Sariah Scott. She shot him down. He needed to blow off some steam."

Christian's story was consistent with what he'd told Stella Dane, but Matt still thought something was off about the roommate. If one of Matt's buddies had been out of contact for days, he'd be worried.

Another student shuffled into the kitchen. He wore flannel pajamas, a university sweatshirt, and sheepskin slippers with holes. His brown hair stood up on one side of his head.

Christian jerked a thumb at him and introduced Matt. "He's a friend of Mrs. Whitney's, looking for Eli. This is Dustin."

"Hey." Dustin did not seem worried about Eli either.

"Hey," Matt said. "Did you see Eli on Saturday night?"

"I saw him earlier." Dustin went to the cabinet for a box of cereal. He filled a bowl and crossed the room to the fridge. "But I stayed at my girlfriend's place that night."

"Do you stay with her often?" Matt asked.

He pointed at the water stain. "Since our water heater sprung a leak a week ago, I do. Fucking landlord had it disconnected but hasn't replaced it. Cheap ass."

"You have another roommate, right?" Matt glanced around.

"Yeah. Brian." Dustin poured almond milk on his cereal. "He went to see his mom for her birthday."

"When did he leave?" Matt asked.

"I dunno." Dustin took a spoon out of a drawer. "Last Tuesday, maybe?"

"I think that's right," Christian agreed.

"Isn't he missing classes?" Matt asked.

"Yeah, but his mom lives close. He could commute if he wanted."

Matt pushed harder. He couldn't believe these guys weren't concerned about Eli, let alone Brian. "Has Brian ever done that?"

"No," Christian admitted. "But we've never had to take cold showers either."

Dustin and Christian shared a *should we tell him* look that lifted the hairs on the back of Matt's neck.

Matt let them stare at each other for a few seconds. Most people don't like silence and will talk to fill it. The teakettle whistled, the noise seeming to break the moment.

Christian poured hot water into his mug. "Eli and Brian had a fight last week. Brian said he needed some space."

Matt wondered if the boys had withheld this information from Detective Dane or if she had kept it from him. "But he's been gone for a week. Have you heard from him?"

"No." Dustin shook his head, then scooped cereal into his mouth. "But Brian went kind of squirrelly after the fight."

"What did they fight over?" Matt asked.

Dustin swallowed. "Brian likes Sariah too."

How cliché. They fought over a girl.

Matt sighed. "Who does Sariah like?"

"I dunno." Christian's tone suggested he hadn't really thought about it.

"Has she dated either one of them?" Matt asked.

"No." Dustin set his spoon in his bowl. "Eli really likes her, but Brian has a better shot with her. Eli said Brian was being a dick about it."

Matt crossed his arms. "Why does Brian have a better chance?"

"Because he's Brian," Christian said as if this was a no-brainer. "He gets laid more than the rest of us combined."

Matt kept digging. "Have you tried to reach him?"

"Nope. He was pissed at us too. I figured he'd be back when he cooled off." Dustin finished his cereal, washed his bowl, and set it on the drainboard. The kitchen didn't have a dishwasher.

Matt had Brian's number from Mrs. Whitney. He called it. The line went directly to voice mail. "This is Brian. Leave a message. Better yet, just text me." Matt ended the call. Then he turned back to Dustin and Christian. "Why was Brian mad at you two?"

Christian dropped his tea bag in the garbage can. "We agreed that he was being a dick, and he should leave Sariah to Eli."

Matt thought Sariah should be the one to decide who she dated, but he kept his opinion to himself. "Do you have phone numbers for Brian's parents?"

"It's just his mom, but yeah. She lives in Scarlet Falls. That's where Brian's from." Christian picked up a phone from the counter and read off the number.

"Does he have other family?" Matt asked.

"Not that he's ever mentioned. He doesn't talk to his dad, and he doesn't have any brothers or sisters."

Matt entered Ms. O'Neil's number into his phone. "Is there anything else that might help me find Eli?"

Both boys shook their heads.

"He'll turn up," Christian said.

Dustin nodded.

"Do you have a picture of Brian?" Matt asked.

"Sure. I'll AirDrop it to you." Christian pressed a button on his phone.

Matt opened his photos and accepted the picture. Brian O'Neil was athletic-looking with dark blond hair and perfect teeth.

"Thanks. If you think of anything, please call me." Matt gave Christian his contact information. "Thanks for your help."

"No problem." Christian walked him to the door.

Back in his SUV, Matt called Brian's mother. The call went to voice mail, and Matt left a message. "Hello, Ms. O'Neil. I'm a friend of Eli Whitney, one of your son's roommates. I'm trying to get in touch with Brian. Please call me back." Matt left his name and number.

He'd barely ended the call when the phone rang in his hand. Ms. O'Neil's number popped up on the screen.

"Hello," he answered.

"Yes. This is Sandra O'Neil. How can I help you?"

"I'm looking for Brian. I'm hoping he can help me find his roommate Eli Whitney. Eli has gone missing."

"Oh, no," Ms. O'Neil said.

"Christian and Dustin said Brian was with you."

Two heartbeats of silence passed, then Ms. O'Neil said, "Brian was here last week, but he went back to school on Friday."

Matt's blood chilled. No one had talked to Brian since Friday. That was four days ago. Where was he? "Have you talked to him since?"

"No, but I'm going to call him right now." Fear tightened her voice. "This had better not be some sort of scam."

"No, ma'am," Matt assured her. "After you've called Brian's number, you can call Detective Stella Dane at the Scarlet Falls Police Department."

The line went dead. Ms. O'Neil would inform Detective Dane that Brian was missing. Matt called Bree. Her line flipped to voice mail. Frustrated, he left a message.

He started the engine. He needed to find Bree. When she didn't answer her cell, he didn't leave a second message. Matt wanted to see her in person.

Face it, he just wanted to see her. He dialed the sheriff's station. Marge would know where Bree was.

It could not be a coincidence that both Eli and Brian were missing, and a body had turned up. According to Christian and Dustin, Brian and Eli were angry with each other. Did Brian have something to do with Eli's disappearance?

Then again, Matt thought Christian and Dustin were oddly unconcerned. Maybe they were the ones who were lying.

# CHAPTER SIXTEEN

Bree turned into the entrance for Grey Lake Campground. The lake appeared around a bend in the lane. She stopped, stepped out of the SUV, and took fifteen minutes to eat a grilled veggie wrap for lunch and watch the sun shimmer on the ice. With some food in her belly, she drove to the campground office.

A man opened the door. "I'm Phil Dunlop." He held an ACE-bandaged hand against his chest, as if he was protecting it. "Sorry. I can't shake." He stepped back and held the door open wider. "Please. Come in, Sheriff."

Phil wore jeans and a plaid flannel over a thermal shirt. Gray chest hair poked out the top of the crew neck, and beard scruff covered his cheeks. He was about fifty and fit, with a permanent tan that suggested he spent time outdoors all year-round. His hiking boots had plenty of miles on them.

"What happened?" Bree stared at his hand. Was it a coincidence that he'd injured the same hand that was marked on the shooter?

"Slipped on the ice this morning and landed on my hand."

"Did you see a doctor?" Bree couldn't help but wonder if he was actually hurt or if he was using the bandage to cover the mark.

"No. I don't think it's broken."

Bree scanned the cabin. The tiny building was configured like cabin number twenty. A registration desk occupied what was supposed to be the living room. But the kitchen was fitted out, and through an open doorway, she could see a double bed.

"Does someone live here?" she asked.

"Only in the summer," Phil said. "Unlike the rest of the cabins, this one has heat and water in the winter. The manager moves in before the campground opens to the public and stays to close it down in the fall. But it isn't worth the money to pay someone to babysit an empty campground all winter." He shook his head. "At least it didn't make sense before. Maybe having someone on hand would discourage vagrants and shootings."

"Do you live here in the season?"

"No. I usually hire a kid. I have a place down the lake, but I'm here every day when the campground is open."

Bree showed him Alyssa's driver's license photo on her phone. "Do you recognize her?"

He squinted at the image. "She looks familiar. I think she rented a campsite last summer. Not a cabin, but a tent site. Is she the person who was trespassing in cabin twenty?"

"Yes. Do you remember any issues with her when she stayed here?"

"No." He went to the desk, sat, and opened a slim laptop. Still cradling one hand, he touched a key and woke his computer. "I brought my records just in case you needed them."

"Thank you."

"What is her name?" His hand poised over the keyboard.

"Alyssa Vincent."

He tapped on his touchpad a few times, then scrolled. "Here she is. She rented a site for the whole season. Paid cash at the beginning of every week."

"She is the woman who reported the shooting early Monday morning."

"Do you know who got shot yet?" Phil asked.

"No. We haven't found the shooter or the victim," Bree said.

"That's weird." He scratched his belly and closed the laptop.

Next Bree showed him two images copied from the surveillance tape at Walmart. The first one showed the jawline of the man Alyssa claimed was the shooter. Bree compared the photo to Phil, but his facial hair obscured his jawline. The second picture was a close-up of the mark on his hand. "Does this man look familiar?"

He got up from his chair, moved closer, and leaned over her phone. "I don't know. You can't see his face."

"What about this?" Bree pointed to the Texas-shaped red mark on the man's hand. "Have you seen it before?"

Phil shook his head. "I'm sorry. No."

"You said you live on the lake. Did you hear a gunshot yesterday morning before dawn?"

"No." He lowered his bandaged hand to his side. "When will you take that crime scene tape off the cabins?"

"Did you need to get into them for some reason?"

"No." He picked at the edge of his bandage. "I wanted to check for damage. This isn't the first time we've had squatters. Sometimes they leave a pretty nasty mess."

"No," Bree said. "The girls were actually very clean; there's nothing more than some residual fingerprint powder in the cabin."

"You're sure?" he asked. "Because if there's damage, I'll need time to fix it before the season opens."

"I'm going to give the cabins another look now," Bree said. "We'll try to have the scenes released in a day or so."

"Thank you." But he didn't look happy.

"Is there something wrong, Mr. Dunlop?"

His gaze dropped and he studied his hand for a few seconds. "I just hope the news about the shooting on my property and that body found so close doesn't impact business. The camping season is short. I can't afford to lose occupancy."

"You still have a few months." Bree wanted to fault him for caring more about money than a man's death, but she didn't know how much income the campground generated. Was Phil in financial trouble?

"Yeah." But he didn't look convinced. He tugged the ACE bandage lower on his knuckles.

"Thank you for your time." Bree left the office. In her vehicle, she confirmed that the F-150 parked behind the cabin was the only vehicle registered to Phil.

Then she drove back to cabin twenty. She sat in her vehicle drinking the last of her coffee and scanning the surroundings. The sun glittered on the snow, and she could see the lake shining through the trees. Nice and quiet, like Phil said. Maybe she needed to start camping.

Phil. She didn't know what to make of him. The bandage on his hand seemed like a big coincidence, and he'd seemed awfully worried about a pair of cabins he normally didn't visit all winter, even after Bree told him there was no damage.

She sent Todd a text asking him to do a full background check on Phil Dunlop.

She stepped out of her vehicle. The air wasn't as cold today, and the snow was beginning to melt in a few sunny patches of grass. She walked to the front door and went inside. Standing at the window that overlooked the back porch, she imagined Alyssa in this very place, in the dark, seeing a shadow on the snow and thinking it was the girl who'd stolen her wallet and vehicle key.

She went out the back door, down the steps, and across the open yard. When she hit the trees, she stopped where Alyssa had watched the shooting. The man had been in the trees, about twenty-five feet away. He'd been in profile to Alyssa. He'd raised his arm and fired.

Bree flinched as if she were hearing the shot in the present. Maybe her imagination was too good. She moved to where Alyssa said Harper had been standing when she'd gone down. Yet they'd found no blood in the snow.

In her mind's eye, Bree watched Alyssa run away. Why had the shooter not chased her? Maybe he removed the body instead. It was almost impossible to prove a murder took place without a body. Bree imagined the shooter hauling Harper's limp body over his shoulders and carrying her down the frozen lake to the boat ramp, where he put her in his vehicle and drove away.

Was she alive or dead?

Did he somehow clean up any blood? Maybe her winter coat absorbed it.

Bree turned, deep in thought. Her mental reenactment placed her behind cabin nineteen. Something shifted in the window. Bree watched to see if the motion was repeated, but all she saw was the reflection of the trees blowing in the wind. She strode toward the cabin and went up the back steps onto the porch.

Standing to one side, she tried the knob. It turned in her hand. The back of her neck prickled.

*It should be locked, right?*

She opened her jacket and drew her weapon as she pushed the door. It swung open. Bree listened, but heard nothing. She could see one half of the living area through the gap. The inside looked almost exactly like cabin twenty. Seeing no one, Bree stepped across the threshold.

Something banged. The door flew back at her, knocking her backward. Her gun soared from her hand into the snow. A large body came at her. She automatically registered his appearance as she prepared to defend herself. Male, about six feet tall, wearing a dark coat, a ski mask, and winter gloves.

Lowering his head, he charged her like a bull. His hands swept out, trying to catch her knees. Bree sidestepped out of reach. His shoulder rammed into her ribs, but her hands landed on his upper back. She put all her weight into them. With his weight forward and his arms splayed out, he had no leverage and went down on his face.

Bree reached for the handcuffs on her belt. Before she could snap them over his wrists, he snagged her ankle and yanked. Her feet went in the air, and she landed flat on her back. Her lungs emptied with a painful *whoosh*. Something stabbed the back of her shoulder, and her head hit the ground with a force that left the bare tree branches overhead spinning.

He shed his gloves and jumped on top of her, straddling her chest. He wrapped his hands around her throat and squeezed. The pressure cut off her air. Dots swam in front of Bree's eyes, and she grew instantly light-headed. Fear cut through the haze. Her vision and hearing dimmed. She was seconds from passing out and being at his complete mercy.

Her sight tunneled. In one last, desperate move, she pried one of his fingers off her neck and bent it backward. He released his grip before his finger broke. She grabbed his sleeve, yanked him sideways, and tried to buck him off her. He spread his arms out on either side of her body for balance. His face was closer to her. Pulling her arms in tight to her body, Bree jabbed at his throat. Her fist struck his windpipe, and he made a choking sound. The ski mask twisted, and she opened her hand to drag her fingernails through the soft skin at the base of his neck. As he coughed and gagged, Bree took hold of his sleeve, bucked, and rolled him off her. The last thing she saw before he levered to his feet was a large red patch on the back of his hand.

It was shaped like the state of Texas.

An engine sounded. His head turned. Then he scooped up his gloves and bolted for the trees, disappearing as she blinked her vision clear.

Still light-headed, she floundered on the ground like a dying fish, her hand sweeping the wet snow. She needed to stop him. Where was her gun? She flung her body into a sitting position and almost threw up. She turned onto her side and breathed the cold air in and out of her lungs for a few deep breaths until the nausea faded. Minutes passed. She couldn't keep track of how many.

"Bree!"

*Matt? What's he doing here?*

The sight of him sent a wave of relief through her. She hoisted herself onto one elbow. Matt was running toward her from cabin twenty.

"Are you all right?"

She waved toward the trees. "Someone jumped me. He went that way." Her sense of time had been hazy, but she suspected too much time had lapsed. Matt would never catch him.

Matt changed course and veered for the trees. A few minutes later, he jogged back into the clearing. "I didn't see anyone, but his footprints led to the road."

Bree sat up slowly. The wooziness was passing.

"What happened?"

She tugged on her jacket collar and described the attack. "When I tried to get up, I almost passed out."

"Instead of trying to get up immediately, you *should* have elevated your feet to restore blood flow to your brain."

"I wasn't thinking clearly." Bree fought her hazy brain to focus on the job. She touched her empty holster, and a stab of panic speared her.

*Where's my gun?*

She spotted an indentation in the snow and retrieved her weapon. After wiping the moisture from it, she shoved it into the holster on her hip. Feeling better with her gun in its rightful place, she pulled out her phone. "I'll call for backup. We'll send out a BOLO with his general description. The sun has softened the snow here. These boot prints look castable." She made her calls, then slipped the phone back into her pocket. Dusting some wet snow off her pants, she rose to her feet. "What are you doing here anyway?"

"I called to talk to you, and Marge said you were here," Matt said.

"I interviewed the owner of the campground, then I wanted to walk the scene again," she said. She summed up her interview with Phil Dunlop. "If the injury to his hand is fake, then it could have been him. I sat in my vehicle for a while before I drove here. He could have beat me on foot."

"Motivation?"

"I have to think about that." Bree rubbed her neck.

Matt moved her collar and examined her neck. "You'll have a bruise."

"Not my first." She assessed her condition. The good news was that her hearing and vision had almost returned to normal. Her stomach had settled, and she no longer felt like she was going to face-plant. The bad news was—Alyssa had not imagined the stalker.

Matt pointed to his own neck. "You just smeared blood on your neck. Are you bleeding?"

Bree examined her fingertips. She'd forgotten. "Not my blood." She raised her hand and showed him the blood and skin under her fingernails. "I got the bastard's DNA." Which had been the whole point of the scratch. Gross, but effective.

"Nice going."

"He's marked now. Unfortunately, the scratches are at the base of his neck and pretty easy to cover up in the winter." Bree's shoulder ached. She'd landed on something hard. She was going to have a mark there as well.

Holding her right hand away from her body to preserve the evidence, Bree turned toward cabin nineteen. "He came back for something. We need to find out what he wanted."

"Weren't these cabins searched?"

"Yes. But they clearly need to be searched again. He was wearing gloves while he was inside the cabin. No point in looking for prints. Guess what I saw when he took them off to choke me?"

"What?"

"A big red mark on the back of his hand shaped like the state of Texas." Bree paced the ground behind cabin nineteen as she waited for backup. "What did you drive out here to tell me?"

"Eli Whitney's roommate, Brian O'Neil, is missing." Matt summed up his conversation with Eli's roommates. "Brian's mother said he went back to school, but his roommates haven't seen him."

"What does it mean?" Bree asked.

"I don't know. I gave Brian's mother Stella's number."

"Stella will probably call the medical examiner," Bree said. "But I'll call as well. What does Brian look like?"

Matt showed her Brian's picture.

Bree squinted at the screen. "He's about the same height and weight as the victim. The hair color looks right too."

"It does, but that description is so vague, it could apply to two hundred university students."

As soon as Todd arrived, Bree had him scrape under her fingernails to collect the biological evidence. "Let's get that to the lab. Maybe we'll get lucky and the scumbag's DNA is already in CODIS."

The Combined DNA Index System was the FBI's national DNA database.

When Todd was finished, Bree used a dozen hand wipes and what felt like a gallon of hand sanitizer to clean under her fingernails. Then she headed for cabin nineteen. Matt and Todd were right behind her. She snapped on a pair of nitrile gloves and pulled a flashlight out of her pocket. "Todd, why don't you take the kitchen area. Matt, the living area is all yours. I'll handle the bedroom and bath."

Bree went through the bedroom doorway and stopped. The obvious places had already been searched. She shone her flashlight into the corners, then moved it slowly along the floorboards, looking for gaps. She took out a pen and crawled along the floor, testing each board to see if it was loose. A half hour later, she stood, rubbed her knees, and stretched a kink out of her back.

Then she moved the bed and checked the wood floor beneath it. Sounds of furniture being moved on the other side of the wall indicated Matt and Todd were in nook-and-cranny mode as well. Bree removed the drawers from the dresser and nightstand, then examined the backs and sides. She checked behind and under each piece of furniture, lifted the mattress, and inspected the seams. Tile floors made her search of the bathroom short. Missing or cracked grout would be easy to spot. After more than an hour of searching, she'd found nothing.

Exiting back into the bedroom, she beelined for the closet. Opening the door, she felt along the walls, pushing and knocking on the panels to test for hollow spaces. Nothing.

She walked out of the room. "Anything?"

Matt shook his head.

"No," Todd said.

Bree scanned the cabin. She could feel it in her bones that something was here. She considered the close proximity of cabins nineteen and twenty. Had Harper hidden something? On impulse, she pulled out her cell phone and dialed the phone number Alyssa had said was Harper's. Tinny, muffled music played.

"What's that?" Todd asked.

"Harper's phone." Bree followed the sound back to the closet. It was coming from the floor.

She aimed her flashlight beam down but saw nothing. She dropped into a crouch and crawled halfway into the closet. At the back corner, Bree spotted a small, light scrape on the otherwise dark wood flooring. Scratches marred the edges. The marks looked fresh, as if they hadn't had time to darken with age. She tried to pry up the board with her fingers. The board shifted a millimeter, but she couldn't get her nails under it.

She took a pen from her pocket, but it wasn't thin enough to fit between the boards. She looked up at Matt and Todd. "Do either of you have a knife?"

"I do." Matt pulled a folded knife from his pocket. He handed it to Bree. "Find something?"

"Not yet." She went back to the closet and used the tip of the blade as a lever to pull up the floorboard. Inside, a gray backpack had been stuffed into the space beneath the floor. The surrounding boards were loose too, and Bree removed them.

"Bingo." Bree snapped a few pictures. The brand was Osprey.

"What did you find?" Matt said over her shoulder.

"This looks like Harper's missing backpack." She hauled the bag out of the hole. It was surprisingly heavy, but then, it contained all Harper's personal possessions. Bree opened the front pouch and pointed her flashlight at the contents. Inside were a brown wallet and a Toyota key chain. She lifted out the wallet with two fingers and opened it. Alyssa's driver's license photo stared back at her. Bree snapped a picture, then opened the main pouch of the backpack.

Todd whistled over her shoulder.

On top of neatly folded clothes and a toiletry bag, a gallon-size plastic bag full of jewelry glittered in the beam of her flashlight. There were rings, necklaces, and bracelets in gold and silver with colored and clear stones.

Behind her, Todd asked, "Think those are real?"

One piece had been separated from the rest and stored in its own sandwich bag. A stunning bracelet in clear and red stones. The clear gems had a silvery richness that didn't look like Bree's cubic zirconia earrings, and the red stones looked equally expensive.

*Diamonds and rubies?*

"I think they are." Bree sat back on her heels and stared at the bag. "I don't own much jewelry. But why would anyone carry fakes around? It's heavy, and if this backpack contains everything Harper owns, the space in it is valuable."

"Some of it has to be real," Matt said over her shoulder. "No one would return to the scene of a crime for fake jewelry." He scratched his jaw. His reddish-brown beard had filled into what Bree already thought of as full Viking. "When I talked to Detective Dane, she mentioned she'd been working on a series of residential burglaries."

"Then I need to call Detective Dane." Bree positioned her cell phone over the backpack and took a photo of the contents. "Let's get that DNA sample and this backpack to forensics. Ask for a rush on the fingerprints."

"Maybe Harper is a thief," Matt suggested.

"Maybe they both are," Todd added. "I wonder how much that jewelry is worth."

Bree thought of her original call to a shooting.

*Enough to kill for.*

# CHAPTER SEVENTEEN

Matt looked over Bree's shoulder into the backpack. In his opinion, two homeless girls with a bag full of jewelry did not suggest they were law-abiding citizens. He saw an old, yellowed box of matches. The logo looked familiar. "Can you read that matchbox?"

"Yes." Bree turned her head and squinted. "It says Grey Lake Inn. Where is that?"

"Other side of the lake," Matt said. "It's been closed for years."

They shared a glance.

"How far is it from the boat ramp?"

Matt thought about the distance. "The road meanders, but it's not far."

"Then let's check it out." Bree stood and issued a few instructions to Todd regarding the backpack and casting of her assailant's footprints. Then she led the way out of cabin nineteen. "Do you know where we're going?"

Matt crooked a finger. "Follow me."

He climbed into his big SUV and rolled out of the campground, checking his rearview mirror to make sure Bree was behind his vehicle. They drove out to the main road and passed the park with the boat ramp. The road twisted and turned away from the lake before finding its way back toward the water. He slowed his SUV and looked for the entrance to the resort. He almost drove past the opening. Weeds and trees were reclaiming the gravel lane. If he hadn't been looking for the driveway, he would have missed it. But several sets of tire tracks turned off the road and through the snow. He made the turn, and the Suburban bounced through a deep, frozen rut in the private access road.

The lane ended in a circular driveway in front of the dilapidated, two-story lodge house. Matt pulled over and parked, not disturbing the tire tracks in front of the resort in case they needed to be cast as well. He parked his SUV and climbed out. He met Bree behind their vehicles. They stared at the old building. The original white paint had peeled to gray, and the wooden porch looked rotted.

Bree scanned the tire tracks. "Someone has been here since the snow fell."

"Either several people or the same person multiple times," Matt said. "Inside or outside first?"

Bree frowned at the decaying structure. "It's cold. I would think anyone who came here would seek shelter. We'll look inside first." She walked toward the front entrance.

The front door was broken. She pushed it open and stepped inside. Matt stayed close. The air smelled like mold and must. Black stains splotched the carpet runners and wallpaper like a 3D inkblot test.

"This place used to be beautiful." He skirted the remains of a dead rodent in the lobby. "When I was a kid, my family used to come here in the summertime. My dad knew the owner and he'd let me and my brother and sister use the little sunfish sailboats they kept for guests. My parents would sit on the dock and watch. We'd all have dinner at the restaurant afterward."

"Must have been fun."

"It was." Matt wondered if Bree had any good family memories. Probably not. How was she not bitter about her past?

She turned in a circle, her hands on her hips. "Do you know how many rooms are in this building?"

"The lodge has twenty-four rooms, but there are a few outbuildings."

"I'd love to call deputies to assist in the search. But I can't justify the overtime unless we find something. My staff is stretched to its limit."

"We can manage," Matt said.

"You know the layout. How do you want to proceed?"

"Basically, the main building is a rectangle, with the lobby and reception desk in the center. Rooms are on both floors on this side." He gestured to a long hallway that opened off the lobby. "On the other side, there's a game room downstairs, and a restaurant on the second level."

"One wing at a time then."

"Let's see if there's a master key anywhere." Matt headed for the registration desk. "The resort prided itself on its old-fashioned charm. Real keys. Not electronic locks."

"I haven't seen a real hotel key in . . ." Bree's voice trailed off. "Actually, I've never seen one."

Matt went behind the counter. The detailed mahogany still looked solid. A thick layer of dust and debris covered every surface. He rooted through the drawers, then went into the back office. He found the master key in a filing cabinet drawer and returned to Bree.

"We'll start upstairs."

Bree gestured for him to lead the way.

A curving staircase led to the second floor. Matt stopped at the top. A long hallway stretched out on either side of the landing, with a row of doors on one side.

"All the rooms face the lake?" Bree asked.

"Yes." Matt counted the doors. "The owner used to say there wasn't a bad view in the house."

The first door sagged open.

"Someone kicked in this door at some point." Bree went in first, one hand on her weapon. She glanced into the bathroom on her way in.

Matt followed her into the empty room. "Looks like the furniture and fixtures were sold off." Which would make the search go faster.

"How did the property become abandoned?"

"The owner died. Turned out he'd been in massive debt. He'd been sick his last ten years. The resort was pretty run-down. Seems like the bank has given up on selling it."

Bree stepped over an empty vodka bottle on her way out of the room. "There's no shortage of lakefront land up here."

"Right. The property value doesn't support knocking the buildings down for an alternative use."

"Nor is it worth the money it would take to fix it up." Bree gave a used condom on the carpet a wide berth. "People are gross."

They worked their way down the hall. With no furnishings, a few glances cleared each room on the second floor. What had once been a beautiful restaurant with outdoor seating on an expansive deck and a stunning view of the sunset over the water was a dirty, depressing space. They cleared the guest and game rooms on the first floor. The vacant lodge had clearly been used for drinking, drugs, and sex. They found more liquor bottles, beer cans, condoms, needles, a crack pipe, and other assorted trash.

Back in the lobby, Matt headed for the doors that led to the rear of the resort. He opened the french doors and walked outside onto the wooden deck. Three steps led down to the recreational area. The pool held several feet of frozen water. Trash and leaves dotted the ice. Closer to the lake, rows of broken and half-rotted Adirondack chairs were lined up facing the waterfront. Tall weeds poked out of the snow. A dock extended fifty feet onto the lake. On the left side of the property, tucked under the trees, was a long, low garage. A large storage shed sat on the right, closer to the dock.

Bree stopped on the bottom step. "More footprints."

The tracks crisscrossed the rear lawn back and forth between the outbuildings, the dock, and the lodge.

Bree veered toward the storage building and dock. Matt followed her tracks, so they minimized the disturbance to the existing footprints.

The roof had caved in, and the door was missing. Matt glanced inside. "They used to store everything in there, from fishing rods and kayaks to ice skates." But now it was a big, empty space.

They left the storage building and walked out onto the dock.

"I didn't realize how close we are to the boat ramp. You can see it from here." Bree pointed. "And the campground is just across the water. From here it's easier to see how close they are to each other."

"Maybe the killer has a connection to the lake. Maybe he lives on it or spent a lot of time on it."

Bree shielded her eyes with one gloved hand. "Someone could have cut a hole in the ice and slipped the body into the lake. The hole would have refrozen by now."

Matt scanned the lake. "There's no one out here to see."

"Except the two girls illegally living at the campground."

"Harper had the matchbox for the inn," Matt said. "Maybe she's the killer. She could have faked being shot and planted the shell casings."

"It would explain why there's no blood at the cabin," Bree agreed.

"What about the man who just attacked you?"

"She could have a partner."

They turned and walked back to land. Matt set out toward the garage with Bree close behind him. All four overhead doors were down. Tire tracks led into the first bay. Matt stooped, grabbed the handle, and lifted the door manually. The hairs on the back of his neck lifted. "That went up awfully smoothly."

Bree drew her gun. "Should be a rusty mess after all these years."

Matt sniffed. "I smell oil."

The garage was one big, open space with a solid concrete floor. Fifteen feet away, a chair stood near the rear wall. On the floor around it were cut pieces of rope and used strips of duct tape. The floor next to the chair was splattered with a dark substance, with a clear area roughly the size of a human in the middle.

Matt froze. Next to him, Bree inhaled sharply. They walked closer.

"Someone was tied to the chair." Bree stopped a few feet away from the dark substance on the concrete. "Looks like blood, brain matter, maybe even some bone." She glanced up at the cinder block wall. "Cast-off spatter."

Dark blobs of congealed blood and gore dotted the wall.

"So, maybe this is where our victim was killed."

"Could be." Bree straightened and turned to face the chair again. "The killer could have tied him to the chair and shot him."

"Then he laid him on the floor and bashed him with the hammer." Matt considered her theory. "It's weird."

"The whole case is bizarre. It's the definition of *overkill*." Bree pulled her phone out of her pocket. She called for a forensics team and a few deputies. "The first step is to analyze the substance on the walls and make sure it's what we think it is."

"It is." Matt had seen enough crime scenes. "I guess the blood *could* be paint or rust, but those spots are definitely brain matter and bone fragments."

"The county needs to add forensics techs." Bree glanced back at the stained concrete. "Next we'll see if the tire tracks and footprints match the ones from the boat ramp and campground, and have the DNA of the victim matched to the biological evidence at this scene."

Bree and Matt used their camera phones to take pictures of the garage. Two deputies arrived to secure the scene. The CSI unit parked behind the deputies' cruisers. The forensics techs started with a Rapid Stain Identification kit and confirmed the dark red substance was human blood.

"Then we assume this is a murder scene." Bree instructed her men to start a crime scene log.

The techs unloaded cameras and equipment and got to work.

Bree left the garage. "The techs know their job. They don't need me hanging over their shoulders. I've seen what I need to see."

"Where are you going?" Matt quickened his pace to keep up with her. She was a head shorter than him but moved quickly when she was focused.

"To the station. Are you going to keep looking for Eli?"

"Yes. But I'm out of leads." Matt had no access to Eli's phone or room or bank accounts. "And I keep trying to figure out how the shooting Alyssa called in might be related to the dead body, and the possibility that the body is Brian O'Neil."

"So far, the only link is Grey Lake." Bree climbed into her vehicle, leaving the door open. "You're welcome to observe my interview with Alyssa."

Matt stood next to her vehicle. "Thanks."

"You're welcome." Instead of starting the engine, she turned toward him. "I like working together."

"Yeah. Me too," Matt said. In two cases, they'd achieved the working rhythm of long-term partners.

Bree rubbed her eye. When she lowered her hand, her expression was bleak and lonely. Matt wanted to step closer, to touch her, to let her know with a physical connection that she wasn't alone. But he couldn't do that here. Frustrated, he curled his hand into a fist.

"Follow me back to the station?" she asked.

"Anywhere," he said in a voice too low for anyone else to hear.

Her gaze jerked up to meet his. Her mouth didn't move, but her eyes smiled.

Matt stepped back. "I'll see you there."

He drove his own SUV back to the sheriff's station. He parked next to her SUV behind the building, and they entered through the back door.

Once in her office, Bree took off her jacket and hung it on the coat-tree in the corner. "I called Detective Dane on the way over here. She agrees we need to meet."

"Does she want to keep Eli's case?"

"She didn't say. I think we can work together."

The sheriff could demand to take it over. Eli's disappearance was likely related to her murder case. But that wasn't Bree's style. She was a team player.

Bree gathered a notebook and pen from her desk. "I'm going to talk to Alyssa. I'd like you to watch from the monitoring room with Todd. I want your take on her."

"All right." Matt went into the hall. Bree was a few steps behind him. He headed for the monitoring room.

Yelling sounded from the back hallway. A few seconds and wall thumps later, Deputies Oscar and Rogers wrestled a huge man through the door. Six four and three hundred pounds, he was dressed in a studded leather jacket, ripped black jeans, and biker boots.

"Asshole!" he yelled at Rogers. "These cuffs are cutting off my circulation."

"Sit." Rogers pointed to the restraint bench.

"Fuck you!" the man spat in his face.

"We need the monster cuffs." Deputy Oscar stepped closer. He yanked the biker's handcuffed wrists higher behind his back, chicken-winging his arms and forcing him onto his toes.

Rogers wiped his face with his sleeve. His cheeks were flushed bright red, and a vein throbbed on the side of his neck. His hand went to the Taser on his duty belt.

The biker caught the movement and settled down, but his molars clamped tight and he glared at the deputies with resentment.

Oscar maneuvered the biker toward the bench. Bolted into the floor, the metal bench had rings to secure arrestees' handcuffs. One second the biker's ass was halfway to the bench, the next he was roaring to his feet and tossing deputies aside like the Hulk. One handcuff swung from his wrist. The other hand was loose.

He slammed his shoulder into Oscar and knocked him on his butt. Rogers lunged for an arm. The biker threw a punch. Rogers ducked, but the dangling handcuff struck him in the face. Blood spurted from the cut, and he stumbled backward.

Matt automatically moved toward the melee, but Bree had been closer. She was already beelining for the fight. He saw the confrontation coming but knew it would be over before he could intervene. He held his breath. Bree and the biker were going to collide.

She whipped her expandable baton from her belt. With a quick flick of her wrist, she opened it parallel to her leg, then raised it vertically in front of her face. Leading with the baton, her hands assumed a ready position just in front of her chin, elbows tucked close to her body.

The biker zeroed in on the movement and charged her like a bull. When she kept coming at him, surprise filled his face. He tried to stop, bailing on their game of chicken. But it was too late. His momentum carried him forward.

And Bree was ready.

She angled away from his line of movement. She pivoted on the ball of her foot and twisted at the hip. The baton snapped forward, striking the outside of the biker's upper arm, then back and down to sweep his legs out from under his body. The two blows happened in rapid-fire succession. The giant biker went down like the spring arm of a mousetrap. He rolled to his side and vomited on the floor. The smell of sour beer filled the room.

"Cuff him!" Bree said.

"Yes, ma'am." Rogers stepped forward with a pair of extra-large handcuffs. He snapped the new cuffs onto the biker's wrists, then removed the smaller pair. "Get up." The man groaned and retched again. Rogers kicked him in the thigh. "I said, get up."

Bree nearly vibrated with anger, but her voice was measured. "What is this man being arrested for?"

"Drunk and disorderly," Rogers said.

Bree snapped out commands like a seasoned drill sergeant. She directed two gawking deputies to transfer the suspect to the county jail. "We can't safely detain him here. He can wait for his arraignment in a concrete cell."

The sheriff's station had only two small holding cells.

Bree pinned Oscar with a piercing glare. "Get that cleaned up."

"I'm not the fucking janitor," Oscar grumbled.

Bree turned to Oscar and spoke in a very quiet, yet perfectly enunciated voice. "My office. Now." She pointed at Rogers. "You're next."

# Chapter Eighteen

Bree felt like a high school principal, with one troublesome student in her office and another waiting outside the door. She sat behind her desk. Deputy Oscar glared at her from a guest chair. Bree said nothing.

Oscar squirmed within the first thirty seconds. By the minute marker, he couldn't keep his mouth shut any longer. His jaw shot forward. "I'm not the janitor." His tone was still petulant, but more whiny than white-hot angry now.

"Clearly not." Bree held his gaze with unflinching attention. "The janitor didn't lose control of his prisoner."

The rage slowly drained from his face. Oscar swallowed, as if he knew he'd pushed the line.

"There will be no outbursts like that ever again. Nor do I ever want to see another sloppy restraint technique. We have procedures for a reason. You will register for the next defensive tactics refresher class."

He opened his mouth to argue.

Bree cut him off before he made the situation worse for himself. "Your other option is a written reprimand *and* a defensive tactics refresher class."

His mouth snapped shut. They both knew he was behind on his required continued training hours.

"Yes. Ma'am," Oscar said through clenched molars.

"Get to work cleaning up that vomit. Send in Rogers on your way out."

He rushed from her office. Rogers entered and began to walk back and forth in front of her desk. Oscar had been sullen, but Rogers was agitated.

"What was that about?" Not wanting to be at a height disadvantage, Bree got up and perched on the corner of her desk.

Rogers paced the area in front of her. "What?"

"You kicked the suspect while he was down."

Rogers's shoulder did a jerky shrug. "He was out of control. I subdued him."

"He had already been subdued." Bree reached deep for patience. "*And* restrained. He was on the floor, properly handcuffed, throwing up. The threat had passed except the risk of getting vomit on your shoes."

"You hit him with a baton!" Rogers's adrenaline was still flowing.

"I hope you know the difference between stopping an immediate threat and using unnecessary force."

"It's Oscar's fault. He let him out of the cuffs. Why didn't you yell at him?"

"I'm not yelling at anyone," Bree said. "I've already dealt with Oscar. We're discussing your actions."

Bree studied him. Rogers was more than angry. Leadership might be new to her, but her instincts told her there was something else going on here. "You had the same reaction when we took Alyssa into custody."

"She had an ax." Rogers turned and stomped across the small room again.

"Which she'd already dropped."

Rogers didn't respond. Maybe he needed training? The previous sheriff—Bree was beginning to think of him as Voldemort—had been old-school. She had no doubt he'd set an example of rationalizing, maybe even encouraging, the use of excessive force in a *teach them a lesson* way. "Enroll in the next use of force training class."

The department had been shorthanded for a long time, and ongoing training hours had been one of the sacrifices made to keep patrol shifts staffed. A deputy couldn't be in training and on the street at the same time. But a good law enforcement team needed regular training.

"I don't need a class."

"This isn't multiple choice." Bree lifted an eyebrow. "What I saw out there was a pissed-off deputy. You can't stop feeling emotions, but you can stop *acting* on them. Or worse even yet—reacting. We are supposed to be the professionals. If we can't keep control of ourselves, we lose control of the situation. We need to keep a clear head. Sometimes that is damned hard, especially when some scumbag spits in your face or urinates in the back of your patrol car." Yep, that had happened to Bree. She lowered her voice even further. "Or when your heart is hammering so hard all you can hear is the echo of your own pulse."

Rogers paused and looked at her, as if he was seeing her as a cop for the first time.

"But we are in a position of authority, and that comes with the responsibility to never abuse it."

*Well, that sounds lecturey.*

But Bree meant every word. She'd spent her childhood living with someone who not only acted on his anger every day but reveled in the fear he generated. It had been a horrible way to live and the reason she strove to maintain control of her emotions. But Rogers looked to be beyond exercise or yoga.

He blinked and resumed his pacing. He was too agitated for anything to sink in.

"I want you to take the rest of the day off," she said. "Go home. Cool down. We'll talk tomorrow."

"What? You're sending me home? But you're shorthanded."

How could he be surprised?

"Yes." Bree stood. "You are having issues. You need to deal with them. Do you have a counselor or therapist?"

"No." Resentment narrowed Rogers's eyes and his jaw jutted forward. "Sheriff King—"

"Is no longer here," Bree interrupted in a calm, firm voice. "*I* am the sheriff now. I will not run the department the same way. You need to get on board. Or get off. Your choice." She took a breath. "Go home, Rogers. Get yourself together."

Clearly, he was not thinking straight. If he said what was on his mind, she had no doubt he would regret it.

Red-faced, he spun and stormed out.

Bree took three deep breaths before leaving her office. She needed a hundred hours of hot yoga to decompress from today.

She found Matt in the break room. He'd helped himself to a cup of coffee. He lifted the pot and shook it in offering.

"Yes, please."

He handed her the cup. "Well, you can't say your job is ever boring."

"Boring would be fine with me."

Marge stuck her head in the room. "Detective Dane is here. I put her in the conference room and gave her coffee."

"Thanks, Marge."

Bree carried her coffee and grabbed a pack of Peanut M&M's from the vending machine. Matt followed her into the conference room. Detective Dane was draping her coat over the back of a chair. A cup of steaming coffee and a manila folder sat in front of her.

Matt introduced Bree to the detective.

"Thank you for seeing me, Sheriff," Detective Dane said. "Please call me Stella."

Bree lifted her candy. "We have vending machines in the break room."

"No, thank you," Stella said.

They dropped into seats. Stella opened the folder she'd brought with her. "We've had over a dozen residential burglaries in Scarlet Falls in the past six months."

Bree opened her phone and pulled up the photos of the jewelry in Harper's bag. "The backpack is in the forensics lab. I didn't unpack it for fear of smudging fingerprints. As soon as the fingerprint examiner is done, you can have access to it. Take a look at this jewelry." She handed the phone to Stella.

Stella enlarged the image. "The bracelet looks like one stolen from a house on Scarlet River Drive two weeks ago."

"Is that on the north side of the river?" Matt asked.

"Yes." Stella pointed to the bracelet. "That particular piece was a family heirloom. The homeowner was devastated to lose it." She slid a photo out of her folder. "Here is a picture of the owner wearing it."

Bree compared the two pictures. "Looks like the same piece, but we'll need to have a jeweler assess it."

Matt glanced at the photo. "Was it locked in a safe?"

"No." Stella shook her head. "It was kept in a box in the woman's lingerie drawer."

Matt stroked his beard. "That's not a very original hiding place."

"No," Stella agreed.

"Tell me about the burglaries." Bree sat back and sipped her coffee.

"Houses were hit between midnight and five a.m.," Stella began. "We think she must case neighborhoods looking for people on vacation or working the graveyard shift. That bracelet belongs to a nurse who worked nights in the ER."

"She?" Bree asked. "You're sure the burglar is a woman?"

"We have an image of her from a security camera at another residence in the area. This house is four doors from the house that was burglarized." Stella slid a photo from her folder. The black-and-white image showed a woman hurrying down the street. "Her body shape appears female. She is wearing black yoga pants, a tight black jacket, a hat, and a black bandanna tied around her face."

Bree studied the photo. "Definitely female." The thief's hair and face were covered, but she was tall and slim. Bree passed the picture to Matt.

He studied it for a few seconds and frowned. "She hasn't left any fingerprints behind?"

"No," Stella said. "She's careful. In other stills you can see she is wearing black gloves. Nothing large is taken. Cash, jewelry, gift cards, etc. She's in and out in a few minutes. She goes right to where the valuables are kept as if she can smell them. Then she's out. Usually, she snatches a few thousand in cash and jewelry from each house." Stella motioned toward the image of the bracelet. "But she hit the mother lode on Scarlet River Drive. That bracelet alone is worth over eighty thousand dollars."

"Do any of her victims have security systems?" Bree asked.

"No." Stella tapped the photo of the thief. "But she doesn't hit expensive homes. She ignores electronics and credit cards."

"Anything that can be traced." Matt's chair squealed as he leaned back.

"Sounds like she already has information before she goes in," Bree said.

"We suspect she might have an accomplice. Someone who cases the houses ahead of time."

"Makes sense," Matt agreed. "What kind of people walk through houses?"

"Real estate agents. Insurance agents. Repairmen." Stella shook her head. "We're cross-referencing companies that have worked on multiple homes that have been burglarized and real estate agents who have had homes for sale in the different neighborhoods."

"Any luck so far?" Matt asked.

"No," Stella said. "But the original officers only asked about 'recent services' performed in the homes. I'm sending officers out to reinterview the victims and get service records for several months preceding the burglaries. The thief or thieves are highly organized."

"What about strange vehicles in the neighborhood?" Bree asked.

"A second security camera farther down the street caught this image." Stella set another picture on the table and showed it to Bree. In it, the burglar climbed into a Toyota 4Runner and drove away.

Bree's hunger vanished. Her gaze snapped back to the photo of the burglar. Could that be Alyssa? She set aside her M&M's and dragged both hands down her face.

"What is it?" Stella asked.

"Alyssa Vincent drives a 4Runner." Bree was alarmed at how much she didn't want to share the information with the SFPD detective. Had she let herself get personally attached to Alyssa? "It's sitting in the municipal garage right now. We were supposed to return it to Alyssa tomorrow."

"Can you hang on to it and her?"

"I can try." Bree gave Stella a summary of Alyssa's original 911 call. "But her wallet and keys in the bag of stolen jewelry might buy me a couple of days—unless she lawyers up." Bree might be able to talk Alyssa into staying, but any competent attorney would advise the girl to walk.

"I'm surprised she hasn't asked for an attorney," Matt said. "Either she's innocent and naive or guilty and overconfident."

"Then who is the man who followed her at Walmart and was in cabin nineteen today?" Bree rubbed an eye.

"Her partner?" Matt suggested.

Bree lowered her hand and stared at the photo of the thief. She did not want to find out that Alyssa was a burglar, that she'd been playing Bree all along. It wasn't because Bree needed to be right. She'd been wrong plenty of times. Fact: people were weird. Years ago, she'd arrested a guy who stabbed his brother for eating all the garlic knots, and she'd worked a case where a little old lady bludgeoned her husband to death with a brick for not picking up his socks. Bree hadn't seen that coming. She'd wasted two days interviewing every employee of his accounting firm until the fingerprint match had come in. So, Bree could be wrong. But Alyssa as a criminal just didn't feel right.

Stella's jaw went tight. "How do you want to handle the case?"

Part of Bree wanted to take over the whole thing. Admittedly, she wanted to protect Alyssa, but she couldn't start her relationship off with the Scarlet Falls PD by taking a case after their detective had put months of hard hours into it. "The stolen jewelry is your case, but there's a good chance it's related to my homicide. I think we should cooperate."

"Sounds like a good idea." The tension eased from Stella's jawline. "I need to interview Alyssa."

"Yes, of course. She's here at the station now. But we need to make a plan for the interview."

Stella's eyes narrowed. "A plan?"

"Yes," Bree said. "Do you have enough evidence to charge Alyssa with burglary?"

"No."

"I am treating her like a witness. Since she's homeless, I put her up in a motel last night, but she is jumpy. If we pressure her too hard, I'm afraid she'll bolt, and we have no legal grounds to hold her." Bree had been manipulating the girl into staying, something she wasn't proud of. "Alyssa has no ties to this area. If you spook her, that might be the last we see of her."

"So, you want to soft-pedal the interview?" Stella didn't look happy. But then, she'd been chasing a serial burglar for months. She wanted to close her case.

"The goal should be to glean information from Alyssa and keep her, not to get a confession."

Stella considered her statement for a few seconds. "That makes sense. If she yells for a lawyer, we're screwed."

"Which is why I'm not going to mention the fact that the matchbox in Harper's backpack links her to a murder scene."

"OK." Stella tucked her folder under her arm and followed Bree into the interview room.

"This is Detective Dane." Bree took the chair next to Alyssa.

The detective sat across from her.

Alyssa's gaze jumped back and forth between them. "Why is she here?"

"We think you might have some information about a burglary case she's working."

Alyssa's head tilted. "Why would you think that?"

"Before we start, I need to read you a statement about your rights." Bree read from the script, then slid the paper and a pen to Alyssa. "I just need you to sign that you understand."

"OK." Alyssa's hand shook as she picked up the pen. "But why are you reading me my rights? Don't you do that when you arrest someone? Are you arresting me?"

"No," Bree said, glossing over the fact that Alyssa's role had shifted from witness to potential suspect when her possessions were found with stolen property. Witnesses didn't require Miranda warnings. "But I have to read you this by law. I also need to tell you that we're being recorded. Just like last time we talked. I don't want to remember anything wrong."

"OK." Alyssa's thumb went to her mouth, and she bit at the cuticle.

Bree showed her the first photo of the backpack.

"That's Harper's! Where did you find it?" Alyssa reached out as if she could touch the actual backpack.

"In the cabin next to the one you were staying in," Bree said.

Relief smoothed Alyssa's features. "Now you know I'm telling the truth about Harper."

Bree pulled up the next photo. "What do you see here?"

"My wallet! My keys!" Alyssa smiled, but the smile didn't last. Her face sobered. "I can't believe it."

"What?" Bree asked.

"See that blue zippered pouch?" Alyssa pointed to the phone.

Bree enlarged the image. "This one?"

"Yeah." Alyssa sat back and folded her hands in her lap. "Remember when I told you that me and Harper started hanging together because my money got stolen at the shelter?"

"Yes," Bree said.

Alyssa picked at the skin on her wrist. "My money was in that pouch. Harper must have been the one who stole it. Why would she do that?" The pain in her voice sounded genuine, and it tugged at Bree's heart.

Bree shook her head. "I don't know. Why do you think she did it?"

"She wanted more money from me, I guess." Alyssa looked away. A tear ran down her cheek. "Every time she bought me food, she was using my own money. I'm so stupid. I drove her to work and other places. I thought she was my friend, but she was just using me."

"Where does Harper work again?" Bree asked.

"Route 51 and Evergreen Road," Alyssa answered with no hesitation.

Bree shook her head. "We called Master Clean. That's the name of the company. No one named Harper Scott works there."

Alyssa's mouth opened a half inch. "I don't understand."

"Where did Harper say she was from?" Bree asked.

"Scarlet Falls." Alyssa sounded unsure.

Bree leaned closer. "We found no one named Harper Scott living in Scarlet Falls or all of Randolph County."

Alyssa just stared. "So, she lied about *everything*?"

Bree tapped her phone awake and showed Alyssa the contents of the backpack again. "Do you see the plastic bags?"

Alyssa glanced down. "Uh-huh."

"Do you know what's in them?" Bree angled her head, trying to see Alyssa's eyes.

"Looks like jewelry." Alyssa looked up.

Bree sat back and glanced at Stella.

The detective leaned forward and rested her elbows on the table. "Alyssa, did Harper ever borrow your vehicle?"

"No." Alyssa's answer was immediate. "That was my dad's truck. I would never loan it out."

"Do you know anyone who lives on Scarlet River Drive?" Stella ran a finger down the edge of her folder.

"No." With a fearful eye on the folder, Alyssa began to scratch at her scar on her arm.

Stella pulled out the picture of the bracelet. "Do you recognize this?"

Alyssa shook her head, then stopped. "That bracelet was in the picture of the backpack."

"It was stolen from a house on Scarlet River Drive two weeks ago." The detective moved the photo a little closer to Alyssa.

Alyssa studied it for a few seconds, then looked at the detective. "Harper had that bracelet in her backpack?"

"Yes." Stella sat back. "And other stolen jewelry as well."

"That makes sense, I guess." Alyssa picked at a scar until it bled. "She stole from me."

As much as Bree wanted answers, watching the girl struggle was hard.

*You're going soft.*

Bree didn't want to admit it, but helping her sister's kids work through their grief had changed her.

Stella didn't miss a beat. She slid the picture of the burglar climbing into the 4Runner across the table. "This is a doorbell camera picture of the thief leaving the scene of the crime."

Alyssa stared. "Is that my 4Runner?"

Stella shifted forward in her chair and pointed to the black-clad thief. "Do you recognize this person?"

Alyssa's voice rose. "It looks like Harper."

The woman also looked like Alyssa.

Alyssa's brows knitted. "If I had anything worth selling, I wouldn't have been sleeping in a freezing cold cabin with no water or electricity."

"Did you ever see Harper with jewelry?" Bree asked.

"No." Alyssa shook her head, but behind her denial, her brain was working. She pointed toward the picture of the 4Runner. "When was that picture taken?"

Stella tapped the photo. "Two weeks ago."

"You can't see the license plate," Alyssa said. "You can't even tell what color it is. How can you be sure it's mine?"

"It would be a pretty big coincidence, considering the person who drove this vehicle stole a bracelet that was found in a backpack in the cabin next to yours."

Alyssa stared at the scratches on her arm. "Harper must have taken my vehicle while I was sleeping."

"Are you a heavy sleeper?" Stella asked.

"I dunno." Alyssa's shoulder lifted and fell. Her shoulders slumped. She looked defeated. "I'm really tired. Can I go back to the motel now?"

"Yeah. I'll have a deputy drive you back."

Alyssa sighed. "OK."

Bree herded Alyssa out of the interview room.

"Sheriff, what's going to happen to me?" she asked.

"What do you mean?" Bree wanted to stall this conversation.

"That detective wants to arrest me."

"She wants to arrest the burglar," Bree said.

Alyssa sighed. "I feel like everything is out of my control. Like I'm on a roller coaster, and it's gone off the tracks. All I can do is hold on."

*And hope it doesn't crash.*

# CHAPTER NINETEEN

Matt watched Bree conclude her interview. In his opinion, Alyssa was holding out, but the girl didn't exactly act guilty either. They were clearly still missing information. Sitting next to Matt, Todd scribbled notes.

They both stood as Bree walked into the monitoring room.

"What did you think?" she asked them.

"She seemed surprised and angry that Harper stole from her," Matt said.

"I thought so too," Todd agreed.

"But I also think there's more to her story than she's saying," Matt added.

"Probably." Bree turned to Todd. "Any developments?"

"The search on like crimes in the NCIC yielded no open cases of victims who had been shot in the face, then bludgeoned." Todd pushed his empty chair under the table. The National Crime Information Center was a searchable clearinghouse of crime data. "The background check on Phil Dunlop is done. No criminal record. Taxes are paid up on the campground and his personal residence."

"Damn," Bree said. "Anything else?"

"I owe Mrs. Whitney an update," Matt said.

Bree shoved her phone back into her pocket. "I need to talk to Mrs. Whitney too."

"I can do that tonight," Matt said. "I already know her."

"I feel like I should see her personally." Bree's mouth pursed.

Frustration ran through Matt. "I understand your dedication and commitment, but if you still feel the need to control all aspects of the investigation, then why did you hire me?"

"I hired you because I trust you." Bree sighed and pressed a palm to her forehead.

"Then you also need to have faith in my ability to do the job."

"I do, and you're right. I need to delegate." She pulled out her phone. "I can still make it home to have dinner with the kids, but I am available later this evening if you need me."

"I could go with Matt," Todd volunteered.

"Are you sure?" Bree assessed him. "You've been working almost nonstop since yesterday morning."

"I'm sure. Those months I served as acting sheriff, I felt like I was in over my head. I need the investigative experience." Todd seemed determined to prove himself.

"OK. That would be helpful since Matt has no credentials yet, but make sure you eat and sleep. I need you in top form tomorrow."

Todd looked pleased. "Yes, ma'am."

Bree headed for her office, and Todd and Matt left the station.

"I'll drive," Todd said. "Best to have all the bells and whistles with us in case we need them."

"OK." Matt slid into the passenger seat of the patrol cruiser. The car was fitted out for a lone driver, and the space was tight. The dashboard computer intruded on Matt's side.

Todd drove to Mrs. Whitney's address. She lived in a one-story house near the train station in Grey's Hollow. Todd parked, and they stepped out of the vehicle.

Matt stopped on the sidewalk. "You like dogs, right?"

"Sure. I used to have a Lab."

Matt led the way to the front door. "These are little dogs."

"Ugh."

He rang the bell and yapping exploded on the other side of the door. A minute later, the door cracked an inch, and Mrs. Whitney peered out through the gap. "Matt."

"Mrs. Whitney." Matt raised his voice over the high-pitched barking and gestured to Todd. "This is Chief Deputy Todd Harvey. We'd like to give you an update and ask you a few questions."

"Yes. Of course. Hugo, move back. Larry, stop that growling." Mrs. Whitney leaned down and picked up a bristling, one-eyed pug mix. As she opened the door, she pushed a Chihuahua back with her foot. Her black slacks were coated in dog fur. She wore a cardigan layered over a sweater, and reading glasses on a chain around her neck.

Matt and Todd slid inside. Hugo the Chihuahua sniffed at their shoes. Each time they took a step, he sprang backward and barked. Larry continued to grumble from Mrs. Whitney's arms. "Let me put these two in the other room. Then we can talk."

The house was crammed full of furniture and dog beds. Several held elderly white-muzzled mutts. Toys littered the carpet. Framed snapshots covered every surface. Ninety percent of them were pictures of Eli from his infancy to the present. She took both dogs with her into a back bedroom and returned a minute later. Matt counted six dogs, including Hugo and Larry. The house smelled faintly of old dog, urine, and carpet cleaner.

"Sit down." She perched on a faded wing chair and motioned to a couch covered with blankets. "Do you have any news about Eli?" Mrs. Whitney asked.

"I'm sorry. Not yet, ma'am," Matt said. "Tell me more about Eli's friends."

She picked at a loose thread on her chair. "He has his roommates."

"Did he ever mention having arguments with them?" Matt asked.

"Not really," she said. "Nothing important anyway. He gets annoyed if Christian eats his leftovers, that sort of thing."

Matt wondered how much he didn't tell his grandmother. "Did he have any other friends?"

"His roommates are the main ones." She dropped the thread and folded her hands in her lap.

Todd shifted forward. "How about a girl?"

"He doesn't have a girlfriend—wait." She brightened. "There was a girl he brought to dinner about three weeks ago. What was her name?" she asked herself. "It sounded biblical. She didn't talk much. Samantha. No. Sariah, that's it."

Todd took a small notepad from his pocket and wrote the name down. "Can you describe Sariah?"

Mrs. Whitney's face turned thoughtful. "She's tall for a girl, and slim. She has dark hair. I have a picture. Let me find it." She stood and went to a secretary's desk against the wall and selected a framed photo. "Here she is." She showed it to Matt and Todd.

The young woman sat next to Eli on that same couch. She had dark hair pulled back into a ponytail. Eli had his arm slung around her shoulders, but she was leaning slightly away. This was the girl Eli and Brian had argued over.

"May I take this picture?" Matt tapped on the frame with one finger. "I promise to return it."

"You can have that one. I can print another." Mrs. Whitney pointed to a small, snapshot-size printer on the desk. "Eli bought that for me a couple of Christmases ago. I can print right from my phone. He knows how much I love pictures," she said with pride. She opened the frame, took out the photo, and handed it to Matt.

"Did you ever see her again?" Matt held the photo by the edges.

"No." She set the empty frame on the desk. "He only brought her once. He mentioned her a few more times, but I suspect she dumped him. Not a big loss, in my opinion. She didn't like dogs."

"Is there anything else you can tell us about Eli's life?" Todd asked. "Is he struggling in school? Did he seem normal last time you saw him?"

"He seemed perfectly normal." She traced the desk's edge with a finger. "He ate a pound of pot roast." Her voice choked up just a little.

Empathy swelled in Matt's chest. "I'll keep looking for him."

"I know you will." She sniffed back a tear.

"If you think of anything, give one of us a call." Todd handed her his business card.

She stuffed the card in the pocket of her cardigan and showed them to the door.

Matt and Todd went outside. The air smelled fresh after the old-dog smell in Mrs. Whitney's house. They climbed into the patrol car.

"What now?" Todd asked as he started the engine.

"I'd like to drive through the neighborhood where Eli was last seen again. Someone might have a security or doorbell camera."

"Good idea. We can knock on doors too. Sometimes the old-fashioned legwork gets the job done." Todd drove to the university campus.

As they cruised through the neighborhood, Matt checked the house numbers. A few students walked down the sidewalk, carrying backpacks.

Matt pointed to a big, beaten old Colonial. "This is the house that hosted the party. Stella said the street was clogged. Drive around the block."

Todd cruised around two corners. "This is where he requested his ride." He parked at the curb. "Look for security cameras. These houses are very close to the sidewalk. A camera on the porch might show the street."

They got out of the vehicle.

"Divide and conquer?" Todd asked.

"Yep."

Todd walked up the sidewalk, while Matt crossed the blacktop diagonally to start at the first house on the opposite side. Students occupied most of the housing in this area, so he doubted they were in bed at eight o'clock in the evening. There was no response to his knock at the first three houses. At house four, he pressed the doorbell, and a male student in sweatpants and a university zip-up jacket answered. His feet were bare.

"Hey. I'm Matt Flynn. I'm assisting the sheriff's department in an investigation." He pointed to Todd across the street.

"I'm Brandon Stone." Brandon was average height and build, with overgrown dark hair, a scruffy beard, and skin the color of someone who spent no time outside.

"Brandon, were you home last Saturday night?"

"Sorry. I went to a party." He blew long bangs out of his eyes.

"The one around the block?"

"Yeah. How'd you know?"

"I heard it was big. Did you see this guy?" Matt showed him a picture of Eli.

Brandon leaned in. "Yeah. He was at the party. I don't know his name, though."

"What time did you leave?"

"I dunno. One, two. Something like that." Brandon pointed to Matt's phone. "He left before me."

"Was he drunk?"

"Wasted." Brandon shuffled his bare feet. "I'm not judging or anything. I've had my nights." He grinned.

"But not last weekend?"

"I had a big paper to work on. I can't fuck up. I'm a senior." Brandon sounded depressed.

"Did you see him on the street when you left?"

"Nope," Brandon said.

"How about your roommates? Are they around?"

"They're not here, but they both went home for the weekend. It was just me here."

Matt was about to thank him and leave when he looked closer at the doorbell. "Is that one of those camera doorbells?"

"Yeah." Brandon pointed to it. "We had some packages stolen last month, so we installed that."

"Does it work?"

Brandon shook hair out of his eyes. "It's OK. It's a little too sensitive. It picks up everybody who walks down the sidewalk. I shut off my motion notifications. It was going off all day while I was in class."

"Doesn't turning it off defeat the purpose of having it?" Matt asked.

"I left the ringer notifications on. So, my phone rings if someone actually presses the doorbell. The app still tracks motion events. If we're missing a package, we can review the history. But the app just doesn't go off on my phone every time someone walks by."

This house was right in the middle of the block, and in the general area where Eli had summoned his rideshare.

Matt crossed his fingers. "Would you check your app and see if you had any reported motion on Saturday night, say between midnight and two a.m.?"

"Sure." He stepped back. "Hold on. Let me get my phone." He left the door ajar and returned a minute later, already scrolling on his screen. "I have a bunch of events recorded around that time."

He opened the first, and they watched three girls giggling as they walked past the house. The second video showed a couple walking arm in arm. The third was a sole young man. The clip was only about twenty seconds long. In the dark, it looked black and white, but Matt recognized Eli. He was dressed in jeans and a coat, but he wasn't wearing a hat. He stopped right in front of the house. Shoving his hands into his pockets, he turned his back to the camera and waited.

"He's waiting for his ride," Matt said.

A car pulled to the curb ten seconds later. On the dashboard, a lighted sign in bright purple letters announced the rideshare. The front license plate light was dark, but Matt recognized the vehicle make and model as a Dodge Charger.

"That's him," Matt said. "Can I have a copy of that?"

"Yeah." Brandon tapped on his screen. "I can text it to you. Give me your number."

A few seconds later, Matt's phone vibrated. "Got it. Thanks!"

Matt took Brandon's contact information. "The police might want a statement and access to your doorbell online account."

"No problem." Brandon rubbed his arms. "The online event history is only stored for sixty days."

"Great. Thanks." Matt turned and hurried down the walk. He finished knocking on doors on his side of the street. Two other residents were home. One young woman mentioned the party with an annoyed eye roll. But neither had seen Eli. Matt caught up with Todd and showed him the video.

"That's him all right." Todd gestured to his side of the street. "I got nothing. Should I text the sheriff?"

Matt thought of Bree home with the kids. "I don't want to bother her until we have something more concrete. Let's run a list of Dodge Chargers registered in the area first. *That* might give us a real lead."

# CHAPTER TWENTY

Bree parked her SUV next to her brother's ancient Bronco and turned off the engine. Adam was here. She stared at the house for a couple of minutes, decompressing, shifting gears from sheriffing to parenting. She was more comfortable with the former than the latter.

When Todd spoke of being in over his head as acting sheriff, Bree understood. That's exactly how she felt as the kids' guardian. Almost as if someone should have checked her references and denied her the job based on lack of experience.

Lights blazed in the kitchen windows, and Bree could see Dana at the stove. Kayla was setting the table for dinner, while Adam brought glasses down from an upper cabinet. Where was Luke? Bree glanced at the barn. The lights were on. Luke would be feeding the horses.

Two months after moving here, the house still felt more like Erin's than Bree's. She'd brought her own modern, sleek bedroom set from her apartment in Philly. She'd needed to make at least a small area of the house hers. But the rest of the house was all Erin—from her obsession with cows to family photos. Her sister's bedroom set had gone to a storage unit, and her clothes had been donated, except for a few pieces Kayla had asked to keep. Bree was afraid to get rid of anything in case the kids might want it someday. She didn't know what had become of her mother's things. No one had ever asked her if she wanted any of them. Bree's entire theory on child-rearing was based on knowing what didn't work.

Not quite ready to go inside, Bree picked up her phone and pressed a button.

The sound of her sister's voice brought tears to the corners of her eyes. "Bree? I'm in trouble. I don't know what to do. I don't want to give you the details in a message, but I need your help. Please call me back as soon as you get this."

Bree played the message twice more. It had been the last time she'd heard from her sister. Then she curled her fingers around the phone and listened to her own heartbeat in the quiet vehicle. She hadn't gotten back to Grey's Hollow in time to help Erin. The pressure in her chest swelled. When she was busy working, she could put her grief out of her mind, but the quiet moments hurt.

She stepped out of the SUV and went into the barn. The horses were chomping feed. Luke was in Riot's stall. The big bay gelding bobbed his head at Bree. She rewarded him with a rub on his forehead.

Then she leaned on the half door. "How was your day?"

Luke looked up from brushing his horse's foreleg. Dark circles hovered beneath his eyes. "OK."

"I'm always available to talk. You know that, right? About anything."

"Yes, Aunt Bree." Luke sighed, his tone irritated.

"I don't want to nag. I just worry."

"I know." He returned to grooming his horse.

Bree gave up. She remembered enough about being a teenager to know pushing harder might make him less likely to talk.

"I'll see you inside." Bree left the barn and headed for the house.

The back door opened, and Adam walked onto the back porch. Buttoning his coat, he ambled across the yard. At twenty-eight, he was tall, lanky, and loose-limbed. At a distance, he could pass for a teenager. Only his eyes showed his pain.

Bree smiled in the dark. Adam was an introvert and artist. He could spend weeks alone with his work and never notice the lack of human companionship. But he'd promised to help with the kids. Bree had had her doubts. He had trouble making emotional connections. But he'd stepped up since Erin died. He hadn't missed a single weekly family dinner, and here he was, going out to talk to Luke, just as Bree had asked.

As Adam passed her, he greeted her with a one-armed hug and a kiss on the cheek.

"Thanks for coming to dinner," she said.

"Dana bribes me with leftovers. She cooked enough to feed me all week." He continued to the barn.

Bree laughed as she jogged up the porch steps and went into the house. The kitchen was bright and busy. Ladybug and Kayla raced to meet Bree. She braced herself for the impact. Kayla hit her waist high with an aggressive hug. The dog slid on the tile and nearly took Bree out at the knees.

"Ladybug!" Dana called.

"It's OK." Though still nervous, Bree no longer panicked when the large, ungainly animal charged her. "I don't understand why she does this every single time I enter the house, even if I've only been to the mailbox or barn."

"It's a dog thing. She missed you."

Bree kissed the child's head and scratched behind the dog's ear. The kitchen smelled like garlic.

Kayla and the dog bounced back to the table. Kayla carefully folded napkins and placed them under forks while the dog watched.

"What's for dinner?" Bree toed off her boots, hung up her jacket, and set her phone on the kitchen island.

"Tortellini primavera." Dana opened the oven and peered inside. The garlic smell intensified.

"Dana made garlic bread." Kayla beamed. "I helped."

"Kayla likes butter." Dana transferred a baking sheet from the oven to the stovetop. "I think we're ready to eat as soon as Luke and Adam come in."

Bree went to the fridge and selected a can of lime seltzer. Dana poured herself a small glass of red wine. Vader jumped onto the island. He tapped Bree's phone with a paw.

"Vader," Bree warned in a low voice. "Don't do it."

She set down the can and moved toward the cat.

Without blinking or breaking eye contact, he pushed her phone off the edge. Bree jumped as it hit the floor. She picked up the phone and checked for cracks in the screen. None, and it still worked. She stroked the cat. "This is why we can't have nice things."

"It's your fault." Dana stirred something in a saucepan. "You pet the dog before him."

"I should know better than to upset the hierarchy." Bree rolled her eyes and scratched the cat behind the ears. He walked back and forth on the counter, rubbing on her.

"See?" Dana pointed with her wooden spoon. "He's marking you as his possession."

"Why do you have to be such a cat?" Bree scratched his favorite spot under his chin. He purred and drooled on her hand until he suddenly turned away, jumped off the counter, and left the kitchen. She washed her hands. Typical Vader. When he was done with you, he was done.

The back door opened. Bree marveled at the resemblance between Adam and Luke. Side by side, they looked like brothers. The Taggert genes ran strong in their lean bodies, disheveled brown hair, and tragic hazel eyes.

"Seltzer?" Bree asked.

"Sure," Adam said.

Bree had no taste for alcohol. But then, she'd grown up knowing that the smell of liquor on an angry man's breath meant someone was going to get a beating.

Luke and Adam washed up, and they all sat at the table. Bree let the conversation float around her.

Luke described the latest version of *Call of Duty*. Since they'd started the family dinner ritual, he and Adam had begun a weekly challenge. "Do you want to play, Aunt Bree?"

"You just want someone to kill over and over again," Bree joked.

Luke grinned. "You'd get better if you played more."

Kayla chattered about an upcoming math test. "Can you quiz me later, Aunt Bree? I have to know my times tables up to six times twelve."

"Sure," Bree said. "We can do that after dinner."

The conversation flowed, and Bree felt the tension ease inside her. In her previous life, Bree would have grabbed takeout or eaten scrambled eggs standing over the sink. Then she would have opened the file of whatever case had been most urgent, and she would have worked. No break. No family. She looked down. Ladybug rested her head on Bree's foot. No dog.

Maybe Dana was right, and Bree would grow to like the big mutt. Stranger things had happened.

By the time dinner was over and the table cleared, food and family had recharged her. Bree tested Kayla on her math facts and supervised the bedtime routine. She returned downstairs to find Luke gone and Adam putting on his coat.

"Luke went to finish his homework." Adam led the way back to the kitchen.

"I'll walk you out." Bree stepped into her boots and followed him to his rusty vehicle. "You need a new SUV."

The hinges squealed as he opened the door. "I don't go out much."

"Thanks for coming to dinner. It means a lot to the kids—and me."

Adam turned to face her. "It means a lot to me too. Thanks for nagging me about it every week."

Bree grinned. "You're welcome."

He put one foot in the vehicle, then paused. "Bree?"

"Yeah."

"Do you ever think what would have happened to us—all three of us—if someone had kept us together after Mom and Dad . . ."

"All the time, Adam." Sometimes, like at three in the morning, Bree could think of little else.

"I'm glad we can help Luke and Kayla."

"Yeah. Me too." And maybe Bree and Adam could help each other along the way. Their relationship had already changed, and Bree felt a connection with her brother she hadn't expected to develop after all these years. "Did you talk to Luke?"

Adam nodded. "He doesn't want to talk about it. All he said was he wants to be normal for a while."

"I can understand that, but I worry. Our family history isn't full of the most stable people."

"Everybody deals with their grief in their own way. I paint." After this discussion, Adam would probably go home and work until dawn. He'd leave his raw grief in broad strokes on a canvas. "He's not a little kid. We need to respect what he wants."

"That makes sense. So much of his life has spiraled out of his control lately," Bree said. "But do you think he's OK?"

Adam snorted. "I don't know. Are any of us OK?"

"Good point. He seemed to have fun tonight." But Bree wished Luke would open up to someone.

Adam's head cocked. "Have you ever been back to the house?"

The question surprised Bree. "Our old house?"

Adam nodded.

"No." She could do without those memories. "You?"

"A couple of times," he said in a vague tone. "It's still vacant."

"Not a shock." Shivering, Bree hugged her arms. "There's lots of land out here, and the property was run-down back then." If Bree's memories were correct, it had practically been a junkyard.

Besides, who wanted a house that had hosted a murder-suicide? Unless property values went through the roof, that acreage was going to sit.

"It should probably be condemned now," Adam said.

"I don't even know who owns it."

"I do."

"What?" Shock filled Bree. "You know who owns it or you own it?"

"It was up for auction, and I bought it." Adam took no interest in clothes or his vehicle or anything else that wealthy people seemed to value. It was easy to forget his talent and that his paintings sold at very high prices. He'd bought the farm for Erin, and he'd helped Erin pay her bills for years.

She forgot about the cold. "Why?"

"I'm not sure." Adam's gaze drifted to the night sky. "Sometimes I just . . ." He seemed to struggle for words. "I wonder how it all happened. How he could have done it. And why. I know you and Erin told me how mean he was, but"—he let out a breath—"I don't have any memories of that time. Nothing. It's all a big void. But I feel something when I walk around the old property."

"What do you feel?"

"I'm not sure. Not peace and happiness." He shuddered. "But there's a connection. Maybe my subconscious recognizes the place." He took a long breath. "I don't remember them. Not at all. I can't picture my own mother's face."

Bree had always envied Adam, with no memories of that horrible night. Even Erin's recall had been spotty, but Bree remembered every second in high-def and surround sound. She'd been terrorized by nightmares throughout her childhood. Those nightmares were paying her fresh visits since her sister died.

The wind gusted, and a blast of arctic air swept over her. It had been cold that night when Bree had taken her little sister and baby brother under the back porch to hide from their father. Twenty-seven years later, she could feel the frigid air blowing through her pajamas. She could feel the cold dirt under her bare feet and smell the damp earth.

Hear the gunshots.

Her entire life she'd thought Adam had been the lucky one, to have been too young to remember. Now she realized instead of a tragic memory, Adam had a hollow space. Was that what his art did for him? Fill the void?

She should have helped him fill that space. She'd had no control over being separated from her siblings after their parents died. Adam and Erin had been raised by their grandmother. Bree, the more difficult child, had been farmed out to a cousin in Philadelphia. But she'd been an adult for a long time, and she could not excuse decisions she'd made over the past twenty years. She should have done more than occasionally reach out to Adam. She should have done what she was doing now: demand a place in his life. Maybe he wasn't a loner because of his innate personality. Maybe he just didn't know how else to be.

She touched his arm. "I'm sorry if I haven't been a very good sister over the years. I'll do better."

"Bree, you literally saved my life."

"You were a baby."

"You could have run away. You didn't. You took me and Erin, and you kept us safe."

"I wish we hadn't been separated after that." As a child, Bree had longed for their connection. Whenever she'd had a nightmare, she'd wanted to hold tight to her brother and sister, the way she had under the porch that horrible night. But she'd been alone—isolated.

"Yeah, me too."

"We can't change the past, Adam, but we can make a new path forward, one of *our* choosing. We can learn from those mistakes and make sure we don't make the same ones with Erin's kids."

Adam paused, then asked, "Would you go to the house with me one day, when you have time?"

The cold sank into Bree's bones, and her smile was stiff. "Sure. Of course I will."

"Thanks. I know you don't want to."

"Maybe it will be good for me. You know, confront the past and all that." Bree had been avoiding her past all her life. She smiled and cupped his face. "We'll go together. Thank you for asking me."

"I know you don't mean that, but I appreciate you agreeing anyway." He gave her a quick hug. "You're freezing. Go inside."

Bree stepped back. He closed his door, and she watched him drive away. Their conversation replayed in her head. She'd thought she knew her brother, but she'd been wrong about so many things. She jogged to the barn and tucked the horses in for the night. Then she ran back to the porch and went into the warm house.

Dana was in the living room, reading a cookbook and drinking tea. She looked at Bree over her reading glasses. "Is everything all right?"

"Yes." Bree had a lot to digest. She wasn't ready to share Adam's request with anyone just yet, not even her best friend, not even herself. "I'm going to read to Kayla now."

Dana got up and turned off the light. "I'm going to bed too."

In Kayla's room, Bree opened Harry Potter and read for a half hour. She had to admit, she was loving the story as much as Kayla. Maybe she needed to escape into a fantasy world too. She kissed Kayla good night and went into her own room to put on her pajamas. She washed her face, brushed her teeth, and climbed into bed. Fifteen minutes later, a light went on in the hallway. Kayla, Ladybug, and Vader paraded into the room and climbed into bed. The dog and child pressed against Bree.

They both needed physical contact with her while they slept. The cat claimed the second pillow.

Despite her exhaustion, Bree stared at the ceiling while her bedmates breathed deeply, and the dog snored. Her conversation with Adam had brought too many memories flooding back. When she finally dozed off, she dreamed of angry men, gunshots, and a faceless corpse who turned out to be her.

She woke in the dark with a thumping heart, covered in sweat, and shivering. It took her a few seconds to orient herself to the bedroom.

Kayla and the dog both raised their heads.

"Did you have a bad dream?" Kayla asked in a sleepy voice from what sounded like six inches from Bree's face. The three of them were squeezed onto three feet of mattress. The cat sighed and curled tighter on the other pillow, as if trying to ignore them all was a chore. The entire rest of the bed was empty. Bree thought about sliding out and going around to the other side.

"Yes." Bree's voice was raspy.

"It's over now. You're safe." Kayla repeated Bree's words back to her. The little girl shifted closer and flung one skinny arm over Bree's waist. The dog rolled until her back was pressed against Bree's leg.

Bree rested her head against Kayla's, but she didn't go back to sleep. It wasn't worth a repeat of her nightmare. Eventually, the warmth of the extra bodies stopped Bree's shivering. Maybe living in a crowded house was better than being alone.

# CHAPTER TWENTY-ONE

He slowed his car as he passed a bed-and-breakfast. If the sheriff had stashed a homeless witness somewhere, the options in Grey's Hollow were limited to a few motels and B and Bs. The closest chain hotel was out near the interstate. But a witness would need protection, right? There should be an official vehicle there.

Two vehicles were parked in the tiny gravel lot: a minivan and a large SUV. No sheriff's car. Bright exterior lights left no dark areas to conceal a vehicle. So, probably no witness. Pressing the gas pedal, he moved on. He picked up a marker and crossed off the B and B. Next up was the Tall Tree Inn. To be efficient, he'd mapped all the local motels and B and Bs. Tonight, he'd check every possibility.

He'd find her.

The Tall Tree Inn was an old, two-story farmhouse with a wraparound porch. The parking lot was full. He eased off the gas pedal as he cruised down the road. None of the vehicles belonged to the sheriff's department. What were the chances the sheriff wasn't actively protecting the witness?

What if he couldn't find her? She could identify him. His fingerprints and DNA weren't on file. She could be the only thing to link him to the murders. A stupid girl could take him down.

He gripped the steering wheel. Anger tightened his fingers until his knuckles ached. He forced them to loosen, making fists and stretching his fingers to relieve the tension.

Worry knotted his insides like a noose.

It would be OK. No woman would bring him down, not the girl and not the sheriff either. He'd watched a clip of the new sheriff talking on the news. She looked like a rule follower. She wouldn't take chances with a witness's life. She would act predictably.

But he felt like he was wasting time. The anger built until he could barely breathe.

He fought the impulse to skip the silencing of the witness and get back to the one thing that released his rage. He replayed the last killing in his mind. He felt the pull of the trigger, and the strikes of the hammer. The so-called athletes had been arrogant. And for what? Playing sports? Being born with good looks? How had that worked out for them in the end? They hadn't done so well in a real contest of physical and mental superiority. The ease with which he'd overcome them had been the most satisfying thing of all.

When they'd died, they'd known he was their superior. He was the *real* alpha dog.

He pictured their battered corpses sliding under the ice of Grey Lake.

The steering wheel jerked. He blinked. The dark road reappeared through his windshield. His vehicle drifted off the shoulder and bounced. He yanked the wheel, and the car swerved back onto the highway. His pulse thudded in his head, his lungs burned, and he fought the panic building inside him.

*You're losing control. You're going to ruin everything.*

*Kill the girl; then you can get back to work.*

He checked the location of the next place on his list, the Evergreen Motel. He entered the address into the GPS on his phone, then followed the audible directions.

A vacancy sign flashed in front of the Evergreen. Three two-story buildings formed a U shape, with the parking lot in the middle. A sheriff's cruiser was parked on the left-hand side.

Excitement buzzed through him.

She was probably in one of the rooms facing the deputy's car.

*This is it.*

This was where the sheriff was keeping her witness.

Relief stomped his earlier fears.

He drove by the motel. A few miles up the road, he turned around and passed it again. Slowing the car, he raised his phone and took a video. How could he get to her with a deputy outside her room? There had to be a way. He'd need to analyze the property to make a plan.

He went home and uploaded the video to his computer. Then he entered the address in Google Maps. Behind the motel sat a strip of woods and a rural road that ran through it. Could he park his car back there and approach the motel from the rear? That was risky. He'd be too far from the car, and the deputy would see him anyway.

He had to think of something else, but it wasn't going to be easy.

As soon as he took care of her, he could get back to his real work. Back to his list of people he *wanted* to kill.

The ones who *needed* to die.

# CHAPTER TWENTY-TWO

Wednesday morning, lack of sleep drove Bree to her darkest sunglasses. The rising sun gleamed on the hood of her vehicle. She parked behind the sheriff's station and went in through the back door.

She was hanging up her jacket when Todd appeared in her office doorway. His face was flushed.

"You look like things have happened already." She checked her phone. It was seven o'clock.

"Yes. Several things. Matt's in the conference room."

*Already?*

"I'll be right in. Give me two minutes to check in with Marge." Rounding her desk, she planted her butt in her chair.

Todd all but bounced out of the room.

Marge walked in with a vat-size mug of coffee in her hand.

Bree waved a hand toward the doorway. "Is he always this obnoxiously bright-eyed this early in the morning?"

"Yes, but you're also unusually grumpy." Marge set the coffee on the desk. "You look like you need this."

"Bless you, Marge." Bree inhaled the steam, then took a long swallow. "I need a bigger mug."

"That would be the whole pot. Where is Alyssa?" Marge asked.

"The motel," Bree said. "I'll call her in an hour or so."

"OK. Let me know if you need me to arrange her breakfast," Marge said on her way out.

Bree took a few more deep swallows of her coffee, then rose and went into the conference room. Matt sat at the table drinking coffee and writing notes.

Todd was too excited to sit. "Alyssa's prints were found on her keys and wallet. But not on any of the jewelry."

Bree exhaled, aware that she shouldn't be so relieved. She should be objective.

Todd leaned both fists on the table, his eyes gleaming. "I'm not done. The footprints and tire tracks from the vacant inn matched the ones at the boat ramp and the cabin. The boot is a common brand and size." He rattled off a string of numbers that represented a tire size.

Bree wasn't a car buff. The numbers didn't mean much to her. "Is that a common tire?"

"Unfortunately, it is. But if we find a vehicle, we can confirm if it was at the scenes. Same with the boots," Todd continued. "Next, forensics got a match on prints from the stolen jewelry."

Bree set down her coffee. There was nothing like a solid lead to perk her up.

Todd slid into the chair, opened the file, and scanned the page. "Fingerprints found on the jewelry belong to Sara Harper of Scarlet Falls. Sara is a twenty-one-year-old with an arrest record."

Bree leaned over to see the file.

Todd tapped on a page. "She's been arrested three times for petty theft, and once each for shoplifting and prostitution."

"Did she go to jail?" Bree asked.

Todd shook his head. "The charges were dropped twice. The other cases were plea-bargained down to probation and community service. One of the larceny charges involved Sara calling elderly people and posing as their granddaughter and trying to get them to send her money."

"So, Harper Scott is an alias, and she's a scam artist."

"Yep. There were four burner phones in the backpack. One is the number that communicated with Alyssa's phone. Three were brand new, still in their packaging."

"Busy girl," Bree said. "Assign a deputy to research activity on the used phone. I want to know who she called and texted in the days leading up to the alleged shooting Monday morning."

"The phone is passcode protected," Todd said.

"Get a warrant for the cell provider records." Which would take time.

Todd nodded. "We need a specialist to assess the jewelry, but by appearance alone, the ruby-and-diamond bracelet matches photos of the stolen one. There were some other nice pieces in the bag too."

"Now we need to identify the guy who followed Alyssa in Walmart and assaulted me in cabin nineteen. Is there any mention of an accomplice in Sara's file?"

"No," Todd said. "But I will look deeper."

"Find out who lives at her last known address and get background records on them. Look for family members or an old boyfriend."

"Yes, ma'am." Todd turned to Matt. "Your turn."

"I'll start with this photo of Eli and his girlfriend, Sariah." Matt slid it across the table.

Bree looked at the photo, then compared it to the mug shot from Todd's file. It was Sara Harper. "So, Sara Harper is Sariah Scott *and* Harper Scott?"

"Seems like it," Matt said.

Bree leaned back in her chair. She was going to have to let that news settle. Her brain needed time to sort through the jumble of implications. "Sara Harper is the center of this investigation. I want to know everything about her. She's only twenty-one years old. I'll get Marge to request a yearbook from Grey's Hollow High School for 2016. Maybe she still has the same friends."

"There's more," Matt said. "After we talked to Mrs. Whitney last night, Todd and I canvassed the neighborhood. We found a doorbell video feed of Eli getting into a fake rideshare. We've already checked with the rideshare company and confirmed the car that picked him up was not the correct vehicle. Someone was pretending to be his rideshare."

"Do you have a copy?" Bree asked.

"I do, and Todd has already requested a copy directly from the company." Matt slid his phone across the table.

Bree picked it up.

"That's Eli," Matt said.

Bree watched the entire clip. "We have a fake rideshare driver in what looks like a Dodge Charger."

"Yes," Matt agreed. "He even has a light-up dashboard sign."

"Eli never even looked for the license plate." Bree set the phone aside. "The license plate isn't visible."

"No," Todd said. "I ran a search for Dodge Chargers in Randolph County and the neighboring counties."

Bree watched the clip again. The image of the auto was fuzzy. A doorbell camera was designed to capture images close to the house. The optics weren't optimized for distance.

Todd shuffled his papers. "This body design has been used since 2011. There are pages upon pages of them in the search area."

Bree rubbed a temple. "Would the size of the tire in the tracks at the cabin, boat ramp, and inn fit a Dodge Charger?"

Todd opened his phone and tapped on it with his thumbs. A minute later, he looked up. "Yes. It would."

"As much as I hate being on camera, I want to schedule a press conference in an hour. I want people on the lookout for the Charger and fake rideshares." Bree handed the phone back to Matt. "But why would anyone kidnap Eli?"

Matt set his phone on the table. "He doesn't have any rich relatives, so it's not money."

"Could it have been a prank, and something went wrong?" Todd asked.

"None of this makes sense," Bree said. "How would the kidnapper know Eli called a rideshare?"

Matt sighed. "Eli posted it on Twitter."

Bree exhaled. "Have someone sort through that list of Dodge Charger owners. See how many have criminal records."

"Yes, ma'am." Todd stood.

"There's one more thing." Matt's voice suggested it was important.

Bree's phone vibrated. She slid it out of her pocket and glanced at the screen. The ME was calling. "I have to take this. Excuse me."

In the hallway, she lifted the phone to her ear. "Sheriff Taggert here."

"This is Dr. Jones. The Grey Lake victim is Brian O'Neil."

"You're sure?"

"Yes, his mother was here late yesterday. We received his medical records early this morning and confirmed."

*Oh, my god.* That poor woman.

Bree had identified her sister's body. Erin had been shot in the chest. Dr. Jones had made sure her wounds were not visible to Bree. Erin had looked perfect. Bree remembered standing next to the gurney. Grief had ripped a hole through her that had felt as big as Erin's gunshot wound. She didn't think she would have been able to cope if Erin's face had been destroyed. No chance for visible confirmation. No chance to say goodbye.

"How did she identify him?" Bree asked.

"I sure as hell didn't let her *see* him," Dr. Jones said in a rare slip of her professional mask. She cleared her throat. "She described the shamrock tattoo, a small scar on his knee, and the previously broken tibia. Medical records from his family doctor confirmed the identification."

"Thank you for the call, Dr. Jones."

"You're welcome." The line went dead.

Bree squeezed her eyes shut for a few seconds, then opened them and returned to the conference room. Matt and Todd looked up as she entered.

"The ME just officially identified the body from the lake as Brian O'Neil," she said.

"So, it seems Eli's missing persons case officially rolls into our homicide," Todd said.

"Yes. We need to find him ASAP." Bree could feel that case was going to break open with enough digging.

Matt got to his feet. "Brian went missing on Friday. His body turned up Monday, three days later. Eli disappeared early morning on Sunday."

Bree finished his thought. "Today is Wednesday. Three days later."

"How are these cases connected?" Matt asked.

Bree threw up her hands. "We need Brian's financial and phone records. When I've finished talking to Ms. O'Neil, I'll need to interview the roommates. Is Brian's legal residence at the university or at his mother's home?"

Matt said, "The university." He'd done a little legwork on all four of the roommates.

Bree turned to Todd. "Then we need a search warrant for that address. Make sure Eli Whitney's room is also covered. Get a rush on it. Also get a deputy to do full background checks on Brian O'Neil, Eli Whitney, Dustin Lock, and Christian Crone. I know Stella Dane already did them, but we need to do our own due diligence. She might have missed something. As soon as we have the warrant, we'll bring the roommates in for questioning. Ideally, we'll interview them while the search is being conducted. That way, if we find evidence, we can use it as leverage during the interrogation."

"I'll get the warrant process started." Todd made a list in his note-pad. "Now that we have a victim, it shouldn't take long." Todd turned away.

Search warrants for homicide victims' residences weren't technically required, but multiple people lived at Brian's address. Bree wouldn't risk having evidence thrown out of court due to lack of paperwork. She also wouldn't risk holding the roommates at the station for any length of time. The longer they sat waiting, the greater the chance they'd call an attorney. Any decent lawyer would tell them they didn't have to answer questions.

"I don't want them tipped off ahead of time. If either or both of them are involved in the murders, they might destroy evidence if they think they're suspects."

"Yes, ma'am." Todd left the room.

Matt stood and went into the hallway.

Bree followed him. "I'm going to talk to Ms. O'Neil as soon as the press conference is over. What are you doing?"

"I still need to find Eli, but I don't have any leads." Matt had nothing.

"Come with me, then. Brian's murder and Eli's disappearance are related. We just don't know how yet."

Matt's head tilted, as if he was turning the idea over in his mind. "I feel like the motivation must be personal."

"I agree. Brian's murder was pure rage."

# Chapter
# Twenty-Three

Matt watched Bree's press conference from the sidelines. Standing on the sidewalk outside the sheriff's station, she gave some basic information on Brian's murder and Eli's kidnapping. The surveillance video of the suspect was released, as was the photo of the mark on the back of his hand and the fact that Eli was abducted by a fake rideshare driver.

"He was driving a Dodge Charger, but he could have access to other vehicles. Please be careful when using rideshare apps," Bree said as she concluded the conference. "Verify the license plate. If you have any doubts, do not get into the vehicle."

For the next ten minutes, Bree patiently answered reporters' questions, only holding back on details that might hamper the investigation or hurt the families of the victims. Then she excused herself and shut down the event.

Matt followed her back inside the station.

"I'm sorry that took so long." She tugged at her uniform shirt collar. "I do not like being on TV."

"You fooled everyone. The press likes you."

"I guess that's better than having them hate me." She rubbed her eye. "It's just part of the job I will never get used to, but the public has a right to know what's going on. If I don't give them the facts, they'll start theorizing. Curiosity starts rumors."

On the way to Ms. O'Neil's place, Bree fielded a call from Kayla. Her eyes were locked on the windshield, but her face softened as she talked to her niece. "Of course I'll come. Put it on the calendar." Bree almost smiled. "I love you too." She ended the call and glanced at Matt. "Career Day at school. Kayla wants me to talk to her class."

"Sounds like fun, right?"

"If you asked me that last year, I would have said no. Not that I didn't like kids, but my entire focus was my job. But now . . ." She paused. "I've only lived with them for two months, but I already can't imagine living alone."

"Kids grow on you. How have they adjusted to your new job and long hours?" Matt asked.

"Before this case came along, I was shielding them from my work schedule as much as possible." Bree frowned. "I usually go home for dinner, then work in the home office after they go to bed. Luke will be glad I'm busy this week. He's been avoiding me."

"What's up with Luke?"

"I don't know. He won't talk to me or Dana. Even Adam struck out. Luke has been throwing himself into baseball and homework and barn chores. He seems to not want a minute of downtime."

"Some people like exercise to relieve stress."

"If I knew that's what he was doing, I would respect it." She stopped for a red light. "For now, I guess I'm just going to worry."

Matt thought Bree's brother was too flaky to be very useful. "How much has Adam been around since you moved in?"

"He's come to dinner once a week," Bree said. "More importantly, he's been present." She seemed to search for the right words. "Emotionally. I don't know how else to describe it, but we had a discussion last night. A real one." Her brows lowered in a troubled expression.

Matt waited, but Bree didn't elaborate. She and her nephew were very alike. Bree used work the same way Luke used homework and baseball.

"What about Kayla?" he asked.

"She's been clingy and having nightmares."

"Clingy sounds normal after what she's been through."

"She still sleeps with me or Dana," Bree said. "But her guidance counselor says that's to be expected. She's afraid of losing us too. Ironically, I feel better about her mental state. She talks to me and Dana about her mom all the time. I know what's going on in her head. She's younger than Luke. She seems less resistant to accepting help."

"Being a teenager is rough enough without losing your mother to a violent crime."

"I know." The light turned green, and Bree pressed on the gas pedal. "Why don't you come to dinner as soon as this is over? The kids would love to see you. Dana will cook something awesome."

"I don't want to impose." But the invitation pleased him.

"You won't. I'm sorry if I made you feel that way," Bree said. "I'm overwhelmed right now. Handling the kids and the job are both harder than I expected. But the kids like you, and I like you. Can we leave it there for the moment? When this case is over, I'm going to figure out how to squeeze a personal life into my responsibility load."

"You like me?"

She sighed and rolled her eyes. "You know I like you."

"I didn't assume, but the confirmation is nice." Her admission meant more to him than he'd expected.

She gave him a small smile, and his heart did a double take.

*She* meant more to him than he'd expected.

There was no one else in the vehicle, so he reached across the console to take her hand. "Do you remember the first time we met?"

She looked down at their joined hands and lifted an eyebrow.

He'd surprised her. *Good.*

"I do." She didn't pull her hand away. "Erin's wedding. I remember being surprised that you were such a good dancer."

"My mother made me learn." As a teenager, he'd hated those lessons.

Bree smiled again. Her fingers squeezed his. "I'm glad."

Matt made a mental note to send his mom flowers.

Bree disentangled her hand to use the blinker and make a turn.

"I'd love to come to dinner." But Matt also vowed to take her dancing again.

It was nine o'clock when Bree turned into the long driveway of a lakefront home. A Mercedes SUV was parked at the end of a brick walkway that led to the front door. Bree used her dashboard computer to search the vehicle's license plate. "It's Ms. O'Neil's."

Matt climbed out of the SUV. Sunlight glittered off the water. The house had a million-dollar view of the lake. It was a big, rambling structure with plenty of wood, glass, and greenery.

Bree led the way to the front step. Matt's boots crunched on rock salt as he stopped beside her, facing the double doors of the huge house. Bree knocked on the door, her breath steaming in the morning light. Neither one of them spoke. Without speaking, Matt knew Bree was dreading the interview with the mutilated young man's mother as much as he was.

No one answered.

"I'm worried." Bree glanced back at the Mercedes. "She's home."

She knocked louder. When the house remained silent, Bree tried the knob. It was unlocked. She turned it. A dog barked, and a weight struck the other side of the door. Bree sprang back. Matt looked through the narrow glass panel alongside the door. A big fluffy dog barked and wagged at him, its big body wiggling and excited. Matt turned to Bree. The color had drained from her face.

"It's OK. It's just a golden retriever."

Bree took a deep breath, but her feet did not move toward the house. Her entire body was as stiff as a block of granite.

"I'm serious," Matt said. "Goldens are greeters, not guard dogs."

Humiliation flushed her pale face. "I'm sorry. I just can't."

"I'll go in and restrain the dog." Matt eased open the door. The dog barked once and greeted Matt with tail wags and sloppy kisses.

"Some watchdog you are." Matt scratched the boxy head. "Who's a good boy?"

The dog, a young male, panted, his tongue lolling out the side of his mouth.

Matt held the dog by the collar and waved Bree inside. She opened the door and slipped through, keeping her back against the wall and eyeing the dog like it was a hungry grizzly. The dog whined and tried to pull away.

"I promise this dog will not hurt you," he said. "This is a golden retriever. He has a scary bark because he's big, but he would let anyone into the house. For a belly rub, he'd help the thieves carry the valuables to their getaway car."

"Uh-huh." She didn't look convinced.

"I'm bringing the dog past you."

"Why?" Bree pressed harder against the wall.

Matt had seen her face an armed shooter and her own sister's dead body, but a golden retriever terrified her into near paralysis. "He seems agitated. He wants to show us something."

Bree raised an eyebrow.

"Trust me."

"I do." Her voice sharpened.

"Then stand behind me."

She moved into position.

He took her hand, gave it a reassuring squeeze, and released the dog. "Go find Mommy."

The golden raced out of the foyer, his feathery tail pluming behind him.

"You really expect him to understand you?" Bree's voice was skeptical.

"No." Matt started after the dog. "But he wants us to follow him, hopefully to his owner."

"Ms. O'Neil?" Bree called as they followed the dog. "It's Sheriff Taggert."

The foyer opened into a two-story great room with a view of the frozen lake. Huge glass doors lined the back wall. A massive stone fireplace faced the kitchen. Both were cold and empty. Matt caught a movement through the glass. The dog ran to one of the doors, barked, and pawed at the base of the door. Someone sat on the deck. Smoke plumed over the back of a tall Adirondack chair.

"She's outside." Matt went to the french doors and opened them. The dog pushed past Matt. Cold air swept off the lake as Matt stepped out onto the deck. A woman in her fifties stared over the lake. The only movement was the lift and fall of her cigarette. She wore a sweater and jeans. No coat or gloves or hat, even though the temperature was below freezing. Her hand reached automatically for her dog, who planted his huge head in her lap.

Bree edged past Matt. "Ms. O'Neil?"

She didn't respond. She didn't even register their presence. But then, she must be in shock.

With one eye on the dog, Bree moved to crouch in front of her. "Is there someone I can call for you?"

Ms. O'Neil's chin lifted. She stubbed out her cigarette in the ashtray next to her. "I quit two years ago. I found that pack in my office."

Her skin was waxy pale, her lips almost blue. How long had she been out here?

"Let's get you inside." Bree took one arm, Matt the other.

Ms. O'Neil didn't resist. They brought her into the great room. Bree eased her onto the sofa. Matt whipped an afghan off a chair and wrapped it around Ms. O'Neil's shoulders. The dog jumped onto the sofa and lay down with his body touching hers.

"The medical examiner didn't let me see him. She said they beat him, and I wouldn't recognize his face. But I would have. No matter what. I'd know my son."

Matt didn't comment. The ME had been kind when she'd used the word *beaten* to describe the injuries to Brian's face. He found a remote for the gas fireplace and turned it on. Flames surged, and warmth poured out instantly. "I'll make her some tea."

"He wasn't perfect, but he was a good man," Ms. O'Neil said in an absent voice. "Why would someone do that to him?"

"I don't know," Bree said.

Matt searched cabinets until he found tea bags and a mug. He used the instant hot water dispenser on the sink. After adding a heaping teaspoon of sugar, he brought the tea to Ms. O'Neil. She was shaking. Tea spilled over the rim of the cup. But she didn't react or seem to care.

Bree forced her to drink a few sips of the hot liquid. Ms. O'Neil pushed the tea aside. She set the cup down in the small puddle of liquid on the table. Then she rose on shaky legs and crossed the room to a bar cart. Trembling, she poured whiskey from a decanter into a tumbler. She lifted the whiskey with both hands and took a healthy swallow. After topping off her glass, she returned to the couch. "Can you find the person who did this to my son?"

Matt wanted to promise her, but that hadn't gone well with Mrs. Whitney, had it? But he had to say something. "We will do everything in our power to bring the person responsible to justice."

"All I want is a name. I can bring justice myself." Bitterness lowered her voice. She glanced back at them. "You're surprised? Don't be. Nothing is more dangerous than a mother. Nothing matters to me anymore. I don't have anything to lose. It all died with Brian."

Ms. O'Neil shouldn't be alone. She wasn't stable.

Matt cleared his throat. "Did Brian have any disagreements with anyone recently?"

"He and his friends were on the outs." Ms. O'Neil's voice was flat. "They were all a little jealous of Brian. He is—was—better looking than the rest of them. I guess that's not true now." She stopped. A choke led to a sob. She pressed her fist against her mouth. Two rings on her hand caught the light. One was a cluster of clear stones Matt guessed were diamonds. The second was a deep blue square the size of a marble. *Sapphire?* When she dropped her hand, she lifted her glass and drained it.

"By friends you mean his roommates," Bree clarified.

"Yes." Ms. O'Neil went back to the liquor cart and refilled her glass. At this rate, she wasn't going to be coherent for long. Matt didn't blame her one bit. The dog watched from the couch, his sad eyes following his mistress.

She crossed the room and stood. Her eyes were on the lake, but they weren't focusing on anything. "Brian and his roommates have been friends since freshman year. Christian, Dustin, and Eli come to the lake for a week in the summer."

"You said they were jealous. Do you think they could have hurt Brian?" Bree asked.

Ms. O'Neil fumbled and nearly dropped her tumbler. "I don't want to think that. But I also think no one ever shares all of themselves. Everyone holds something back. Who knows what that something is? I know they were all jealous of him. I spoiled him sometimes. Nice car. Nice clothes." Her smile was devastated. "Now I'm glad I did."

"How long have you lived here?" Matt asked.

"Since Brian was a baby. My husband and I bought the house to raise a big family. Then he left us." Her words were beginning to slur. She pressed a palm to her forehead. "Before you ask, I bought the house. My family has money. He's always broke, but I loved him. I didn't care. What a fool I was."

"When did you last see him?" Matt asked.

She shrugged. "I don't even know. Fifteen years, at least. He emailed weekly for the first few months, then every few weeks became holidays and birthdays. Then nothing."

"Why did he leave?" Bree asked.

"He couldn't handle the responsibility of being a parent," Ms. O'Neil said. "I know couples break up, but how do you walk away from your child? Brian was three when he left."

Matt had no answer. "Does Brian have a room here?"

"Yes." Ms. O'Neil tipped her head into her hand.

"We'd like to look at his room," Bree said.

"Go ahead." Ms. O'Neil gestured toward the staircase behind the fireplace.

Bree and Matt went up the steps. The two rooms that faced the road were guest rooms. Brian's bedroom was easy to find. University and high school pennants were pinned over the bed. Bree stopped and stared at a row of high school baseball trophies that lined a bookcase. She cleared her throat and took a pair of gloves from her pocket. She offered a pair to Matt. He took them and tugged them on.

"You want to take the closet?" She pulled out a dresser drawer.

"Sure." Matt opened the door. The closet was half-full. Matt went through the pockets of pants and jackets. He moved the sweaters on the top shelf. Two shoeboxes contained dress shoes. A third was full of baseball cards. Matt found nothing even remotely interesting.

"Nothing in the dresser." Bree turned.

"Same. Are we done?" Matt asked.

"Almost." Bree took pictures of the bedroom. "I didn't expect to find much here. He lived at school most of the time."

Matt motioned toward the closet. "Seems he uses his room here to store the stuff he doesn't need at school."

Bree returned her phone to her pocket. "OK. We'll say goodbye to Ms. O'Neil on the way out."

They went downstairs. Ms. O'Neil crossed the room to pour herself another drink. Her eyes were glassy, and her gait was unsteady. Yet she looked more coherent than she wanted to be.

Matt stopped to look at a row of framed snapshots. He spotted a photo of Brian with a dark-haired girl on the dock of a lake. It was Sara Harper. She and Brian were leaning into each other and grinning for the camera. Matt looked through the glass panels behind him and saw the dock in the photo. He took the picture off the shelf and showed it to Brian's mother. "When was this taken?"

Ms. O'Neil glanced at it. "A few weeks ago? Brian brought Sariah up here for the day." She drew in a shaky breath. "Does *she* know?"

Christian had said neither Brian nor Eli had dated Sariah. But it seemed like she'd actually dated both of them. Had the roommates lied, or had they been lied to?

"We're trying to contact her now," Bree said. "But we haven't been able to find her. Do you know where she is?"

Ms. O'Neil shook her head. "She only came here once. But I could tell Brian really liked her. He talks about her all the time—talked about her all the time." She closed her eyes for a second. When she opened them, they were filled with unshed tears. "They spent a lot of time together."

Matt turned the photo of Sara Harper and Brian so Bree could see it. She didn't look surprised. Ms. O'Neil pressed her fingertips to her eyes. Her rings caught Matt's attention again. "Ms. O'Neil, has any of your jewelry gone missing lately?"

She froze and lowered her hands. "Yes. How did you know?"

"There's been a series of residential robberies lately," he said.

"Do you think they're related to Brian's death?" she asked.

Matt looked to Bree. Did she want to give that possible connection away?

"We don't know if the crimes are related or coincidental," Bree said. "Can you tell me what went missing?"

Ms. O'Neil wiped a tear from her cheek. "I keep my valuable jewelry in a safe, but there were some smaller pieces in my jewelry box that I wore often—small diamond studs and a matching pendant."

"Can you estimate the value?" Bree asked.

"Roughly eight or nine thousand dollars." Ms. O'Neil acted like she'd said ten bucks.

"Did you call the police?" Matt asked.

"No." Ms. O'Neil shook her head. "I thought I'd simply misplaced them. The last time I was wearing them I'd been to a party. I'd had too much champagne."

Bree's eyebrows rose. "When did they disappear?"

"Two or three weeks ago." Ms. O'Neil lifted a shoulder.

Shortly after Sara's visit.

"Do you have any family nearby, Ms. O'Neil?"

"My sister."

"Let me call her for you," Bree said.

"Fine." Ms. O'Neil read a number off her phone. Only after Matt and Bree were sure the sister was on her way did they leave the house and return to Bree's vehicle.

In the passenger seat, Matt fastened his seat belt. "Sara Harper seems to be the center of everything."

Bree started the engine and turned the vehicle around. "She had been dating Eli and Brian. Neither one had told their roommates or each other. Was keeping their relationships secret her idea or the boys'?"

"I'm betting it was her idea. If she was targeting Brian for his mother's jewelry, she wouldn't have wanted anyone to know."

"That would also explain why she was less interested in Eli. His grandmother doesn't have any money."

"Could Sara Harper be behind Brian's death and Eli's disappearance?" Bree asked. "Why would she want Brian dead?"

"Maybe he figured out she stole his mother's jewelry and threatened to go to the police."

Bree turned the vehicle down the driveway. "So, she killed him to keep him quiet."

"With her record of four previous arrests and two convictions, I doubt she would get off with community service or probation. She'd likely spend some time in jail. But how does a slim girl move a dead body to dump it in the lake?"

"Wheelbarrow, hand truck, accomplice . . . There's always a way." Bree didn't look concerned by the logistics. "But if we believe Alyssa's story, then Sara Harper was shot Monday morning." She turned onto the main road. "Who killed her?"

Matt considered. "We know Sara Harper is a scammer. What if she staged the shooting to throw us off her track?"

"Let's see what Todd has turned up." Bree dialed Todd's number and put him on speakerphone. "Todd, do you have a last known address for Sara Harper?"

"Yes. 201 Mallard Lane."

Bree entered the address into her GPS. "What else can you tell us?"

"The property has belonged to Earl Harper, age forty-eight, for just over twenty years. Earl served five years in state prison for first-degree robbery. He beat a convenience store clerk with a baseball bat. Unfortunately, he copped a plea for a minimum sentence. He also has a list of other petty crimes on his rap sheet. Earl is currently self-employed." Todd paused for a breath. The shuffle of paper sounded over the connection. "Also living at that address is Rowdy Harper, age twenty-seven. Rowdy did eighteen months in prison for grand larceny. He also has a rap sheet of minor offenses. The only violent one is an arrest for sexual assault. But the woman dropped the charges before the case went to trial."

"Is that it?" Bree asked.

"Isn't that enough?" Todd snorted. "I handed you two more suspects. But yeah. That's it for now. I'll let you know what else I find."

"What kind of vehicles do Earl and Rowdy drive?"

Todd paused. "Earl has an old F-150. There's no vehicle registered to Rowdy."

"Thanks." Bree ended the call.

"Maybe Sara's family was in on the burglaries. Brian could have threatened to turn in Sara, which could have taken them all down. Sara went to Daddy or Big Brother and asked them to take care of the Brian problem."

"Fits with all of their previous histories of theft and violence. I wish one of them drove a Dodge Charger."

"That would be too easy."

Bree turned to Matt. "Ready to interview two violent felons?"

# CHAPTER TWENTY-FOUR

Checking the GPS map, Bree slowed the vehicle. On the right side of the road, she could see the sparkle of ice through the trees. "Sara Harper's father lives on Grey Lake?"

"Pretty stupid to dump the body so close to home," Matt said.

"But most criminals aren't that smart." She turned down the gravel driveway. The lane hadn't been graded in decades, and her SUV bounced and rolled all the way to the house. The Harpers lived in a run-down bungalow. Instead of landscaping, discarded household objects littered the grounds around the house. Bree parked between a kitchen sink and a mattress. The only similarity between the O'Neil residence and the Harpers' house was a water view.

"How do you want to handle the interview?" Matt asked. "Career criminals usually have a good handle on the law. They will scream lawyer the second they feel threatened."

"Good point. Let's approach them with concerns that Sara is missing and has possibly been shot. They might be more willing to talk about Sara instead of themselves."

"Worth a try."

"Let's see who's home." Bree slid out of the SUV. The clang of metal striking metal rang through the trees, an echo from her childhood. The memory turned her stomach. The Harper property reminded her of the old Taggert place: rural, weedy, and unkept. "Someone is splitting wood."

She paused to take pictures of the front of the property, making sure she caught the pickup truck parked in the driveway. Then Matt followed her to the front door. She pressed the doorbell but heard no sound. When no one answered, she knocked on the door. It opened, and a man in jeans, a quilted flannel jacket, gloves, and boots stood in the entrance. He was about twenty-five years old. His eyes were set too close together, and he hadn't shaved in a while. Unlike Matt's tight, trimmed beard, this guy's facial hair looked dirty. He scanned Bree from head to toe and back to her face again. His eyes went flat and hostile.

"What do you want?" he asked.

"I'm Sheriff Taggert." Bree introduced Matt. "We're trying to find Sara Harper."

"She ain't here." He moved to shut the door.

Bree stepped forward. "Have you seen her?"

"Not in a while." He scratched his head.

"Are you related to Sara?" Bree asked.

"I'm her brother." He had the same dark hair as Sara, though she had inherited all the good looks from their shared DNA.

"What is your name?" Bree asked.

He frowned and considered her question for a long minute, as if he were trying to think of a reason he shouldn't answer the question but couldn't. Not the brightest bulb on the Christmas tree. "Rowdy Harper."

"On Monday, a young woman was reportedly the victim of a shooting," Bree explained. "When we responded to the call, she was gone. We just learned the victim is your sister."

His face creased with confusion. "That's weird."

"We agree. We'd really like to find Sara. She could be hurt . . . or worse." Bree let her voice trail off. At this point, if Sara had survived the initial shooting, she could very well be dead. Or if the shooting had been staged for Alyssa's benefit, then Sara was likely involved in Brian's murder. At minimum, Sara was a thief, and the matchbox in her backpack tied her to the murder scene.

"What do you want from me?" he asked.

"Information on your sister," Bree said. "Her friends. Places she goes. Things she does. Last time you saw her, et cetera."

"Wait here." He closed the door in their faces. Thirty seconds later, the sound of wood being split ceased. Two more minutes passed until it resumed. The door opened. "Daddy's splitting wood out back. You can ask him your questions."

Bree stepped toward the open door.

He blocked her with his body, anger glittering in his eyes. "You can go around."

"Of course." Bree backed down the steps without turning her back on Rowdy.

Once they rounded the corner of the house, Bree fell into step beside Matt.

"I wish Brody was here," he said.

"Me too," Bree admitted. She'd seen criminals more frightened of a K-9 than a handgun pointed right in their faces, a reaction she totally understood.

The snow crunched under their boots as they walked around the house. As soon as they turned the corner, a huge pit bull began to bark. The big brown dog lunged at the end of the chain attached to a tree.

Bree jumped. Sweat broke out on her back. She breathed.

*Really? Another dog?*

She resumed walking, refusing to look in the dog's direction again, no matter how much it barked and howled. Outside, she hoped she portrayed a calm and authoritative officer of the law. But the dog, the junk-filled yard, the snowy ground, even the man splitting wood—all brought back memories of her childhood that she didn't have time to process right now. She was running out of mental compartments to stow all her baggage.

Matt bumped her shoulder with his, and the contact derailed her mental train wreck and brought her back to the moment.

A detached two-car garage built of concrete blocks sat behind the house, and a rickety dock extended out over the water. The garage doors were up. Junk was crammed into one bay. The second held a workbench and tools. On the other side of the yard, a long, low building stretched under the trees. Vines slithered up the cinder blocks toward the metal roof.

About twenty feet behind the house, a man swung a sledgehammer. It struck the metal wedge and split a thick log in two. An older version of Rowdy, Earl Harper looked up from his work with mean, close-set eyes. Like his son, he wore jeans, work boots, and a flannel shirt. He wore well-used leather work gloves. Sweat beaded on his brow, and a jacket was tossed onto the woodpile nearby. The dog continued to bark, the sound like sandpaper to Bree's nerve endings.

"Shut up, Rufus!" He picked up a stone from the ground and flung it at the dog. The rock fell short, but the dog still cowered and slunk into its house.

Anger surged in Bree's chest. Just because she was afraid of the dog didn't mean she wanted it abused. She glanced at Matt. His eyes narrowed, and his jaw went tight.

Earl let the head of his sledgehammer fall to the ground with a thud. "So, you're the new sheriff."

His gaze cruised her body. His attention felt like bugs crawling over her, but she didn't give him the satisfaction of seeing her response.

"Mr. Harper." Bree introduced Matt again. She glanced at the garage full of junk. "What is your business?"

"I fix things. People throw everything away. Take vacuum cleaners, for example. Most of the time, I replace a belt, and they work great. Five-dollar fix. People are stupid."

The back door opened, and Rowdy came out. He tugged on a knit hat and began collecting the logs his father split and adding them to a woodpile the size of a single-wide.

Earl leaned on the handle. "Rowdy says you're looking for Sara."

Bree repeated the abbreviated story of Sara's puzzling disappearance.

"That is strange." Earl's tone was unconcerned.

"You don't seem worried." Matt shifted his weight, angling his body to face both Earl and his son.

Earl chuckled. "My daughter is a piece of work. The last time she came here, she left with all my cash."

Bree watched for more breaks in his bravado but saw nothing. "What do you think happened to her?"

"I have no idea." Earl reached for another log. He positioned it onto the tree stump and inserted the wedge into a crack. "But Sara is a survivor. If someone was shot, my money would be on her doing the shooting, not being the victim."

"We have an eyewitness," Bree said.

He glanced at her, and something flashed in his eyes. Nervousness? Anxiety? It was gone before Bree could identify it, and his poker face returned. "If someone shot Sara, then why can't you find her?"

"That's what we'd like to know," Bree said.

"You have one eyewitness? That's it?" He scoffed. "People see what they want to see."

He had a valid point. Eyewitnesses were great for convincing juries, but their actual recall sucked. Twenty people could watch a crime being committed, and they'd all have varying accounts and different descriptions of the perpetrator.

But instead of responding, Bree simply held his gaze for a few seconds. She wanted him to wonder about what other evidence she might have. Emotion flickered in his eyes again. This time she caught it. Doubt. Worried about his daughter? It didn't last, though.

He sneered. "I'll tell you one more time. She's no victim. She's a predator. She's also a sneaky, scheming little bitch. I'll give her credit, though." Respect laced his tone. "She has bigger balls than Rowdy over there."

"Hey!" Rowdy protested.

Earl waved off his comment. "Sara would steal milk from a baby, then turn around and sell it back to the mother. She always has some little racket going, and she rarely gets caught." The last sentence came through with a ring of pride. He swung the sledgehammer, the motion sure and true. It struck the wedge dead-on. The log fell away in two pieces. "Nope, Sara ain't dead. More likely that she's up to something."

Bree pried deeper. "What can you tell me about her friends?"

"Sara doesn't have friends," Rowdy chimed in. "Just people she uses."

Earl agreed with a nod. "He's right."

"What about a boyfriend?" Matt asked.

Earl shrugged. "Not that I know of lately."

Bree tried again. "When was the last time you saw her?"

"More than a month ago. Six weeks, maybe." He set another log on the stump and positioned the wedge. "I'm not keeping track. I told her not to come back. Not after she stole from me."

"Did Sara leave any possessions here?" Bree asked.

"I don't know." Earl paused, his sledgehammer poised to heft. "Do you have a warrant?"

"No," Bree admitted. "But I can get one."

"Good luck with that." Earl turned his back on her and swung his sledgehammer again. "You got no evidence I done anything wrong."

"Where were you early Monday morning?" Bree asked.

"That's the kind of question I don't answer without a lawyer."

"What about you, Rowdy?" Bree faced the son. "Do you remember where *you* were early Monday morning?"

"Don't answer that," Earl said. "We don't have to answer any of the sheriff's questions. We are speaking with her now out of basic courtesy."

It was true. No one was obligated to speak to the police. Bree had no evidence to link Earl or Rowdy to the burglaries or Brian's murder.

Earl split another log, then turned back to face Bree and Matt. "We're done talking, Sheriff. It's time for you to leave." He never raised his voice, and his tone remained polite throughout the conversation, yet a threat came through his body language and his cold stare. Despite his outward calm, the potential for violence simmered just below the surface. His hostility was a palpable, kinetic energy that radiated from him like heat shimmered from summer pavement.

Bree wanted to drag him down to the station, but he was right. She had no probable cause, and a harassment suit could hinder her investigation going forward.

She tried one last question. "Would you please take off your gloves? Both of you?"

"No." Earl's brows lowered in a *what the fuck* expression.

She backed off and said in an equally polite tone, "Thank you for your time."

But as she said the words, she held his gaze for a few seconds. She didn't have the legal right to arrest him, but she was not intimidated. Not by him at least. The pit bull was her personal nightmare. The dog pulled her gaze. It paced the length of its chain, the links rattling.

Earl straightened to his full height and rested the sledgehammer over one shoulder, like Paul Bunyan. One eyebrow arched with arrogant challenge. He knew the dog upset her. She could not conceal her response well enough to put one past a guy like Earl. Can't scam a scammer.

Bree and Matt walked around the house to the driveway.

"Let's talk to the neighbors," she said.

"I feel bad for them," Matt said. "Can't imagine living next to the Harpers."

The house next door wasn't fancy, but it was well maintained. The property line was clear based on the lack of junk next door. Both the neighbor's detached garage and dock looked structurally sound. A man walked out of the house, grabbed a trash can, and rolled it past a plumber's van to the street.

Bree and Matt intercepted him in the driveway. He was in his early twenties, but his acne made him look younger.

His gaze darted between Bree's uniform and the Harpers' house. "What do you want?"

"I'm Sheriff Taggert, and this is my investigator, Matt Flynn. We'd like to ask you a few questions. What's your name?"

"I'm Joe Marcus." Joe wore a jacket and gloves, but his head was bare. "What's this about?"

"Your neighbor Earl." Bree motioned toward the Harper house. "How long have you known him?"

"All my life, unfortunately." Joe cocked his head. "What do you want to know?"

"Is he a problem neighbor?" Matt asked.

"Not really." Joe crossed his arms and hunched his shoulders as if he was cold. "That dog of his is always getting out. Couple of weeks back, it killed some chickens down the road."

Bree shuddered. Her father's dogs had killed everything they could catch: rabbits, squirrels, cats. Dad had liked to keep them hungry.

"Did you call the sheriff's department?" Bree asked.

"Me?" Joe pointed to his own chest, then shook his head. "Hell, no. They weren't my chickens. I don't have a problem with Earl."

Bree tried another angle. "What about the neighbor who lost his chickens?"

"That's none of my business." Joe raised both hands, palms out, a gesture of finality. Then he lowered his voice. "The Harpers keep to themselves most of the time, but they aren't the kind of people you want to fuck with, if you know what I mean."

"Are you afraid of him?" Matt crossed his arms. His head tipped back as he assessed Joe.

Joe's face flushed, the redness emphasizing his acne. "*Cautious* is a better word. I'm not stupid. Earl is volatile."

Matt motioned behind him by jerking a thumb over his shoulder. "Did you see if Earl was around this past weekend?"

"He was here at least some of the time," Joe said. "He's been working on that cord of wood for days."

"Do you remember any specific time you saw him here?" Bree asked.

"No," Joe answered, and his blunt tone said he wasn't giving up any info on Earl.

"How well do you know his daughter, Sara?" Bree would try a different subject. Maybe she could trick him into revealing something.

"Not that well." Joe crossed his arms again, this time looking stubborn rather than cold. "We went to school together. She was wild back in high school. I know she's gotten in some trouble since too. But she doesn't live there anymore."

"Do you know why she moved out?"

Joe hitched a shoulder. "She's an adult. That's reason enough."

"Does Sara have a good relationship with her father?" Bree jumped at a bark from the dog. *Damn it. The animal is chained. It isn't a threat.*

"No." Joe shook his head. "She and Earl don't get along at all. Rowdy is Earl's whipping boy, but not Sara. She's too much like her daddy. They butt heads."

"When was the last time you saw her?" Bree tried to focus on Joe, but the dog kept barking. Every woof made it harder for Bree to concentrate.

"I haven't talked to her in a long time, but I think I saw her over there last week." He looked upward. "Before you ask, I don't know any days or times. I was busy all weekend."

Or he was refusing to be any sort of witness against Earl.

The air went quiet for a few seconds. The dog broke into a howl. The sound raised goose bumps on Bree's arms. She forgot her next question. Inside her gloves, her hands went clammy.

With a quick glance at her, Matt jumped in with a question. "Doing what?"

"Minding my own business." Joe raised his voice.

*Focus!* Bree shook her head to clear it. "You're sure it was Sara you saw?"

Joe sniffed and swiped a gloved hand under his nose. "There is no way I could ever mistake Sara for her brother or father."

"Could it have been Earl's girlfriend you saw?" Matt asked.

"Earl doesn't have a girlfriend that I've ever seen." Joe's head swiveled at the sound of a loud engine. A delivery truck drove down the road.

A new round of barking erupted behind the Harper house. Bree swallowed, her stomach cramping, sweat breaking out at the small of her back.

Matt said, "Does Sara have a boyfriend?"

"I don't know who she's with these days." A car drove down the street, and Joe's gaze followed it past his house. "But Sara's good at making people—especially guys—do what she wants. Being hot helps, so does not caring much about other people." His eyes shifted back to the Harper house for a few seconds. "That's in her DNA, I guess."

"Is there anyone who might know where Sara is?" Matt rolled a hand in the air. "Does she have any close friends or an old boyfriend?"

"She went out with Zachary Baker senior year." Joe gave them another jerky shrug. "He lives with his mother down the road. The house with the chickens. Can't miss it." Joe took a whole step back toward his house. "I gotta go to work."

"Thank you for your time." Bree took his contact information. Then she and Matt walked back to her vehicle. Bree slid behind the wheel, exhausted. Trying to hold herself together had depleted her.

The dog had rattled her nerves. She seriously needed to get her fear under control. It had never affected her job to this degree before. She'd always been able to control her reaction to dogs—or at least conceal it. But today, she'd been compromised. "Thank you for taking over that interview."

"You're welcome."

Her hand curled into a fist on her thigh.

"No one is perfect, Bree," Matt said in a quiet voice.

"I know." But she was disappointed in herself. She brought the conversation back to the investigation. "Shall we go talk to Zachary Baker?"

"Let's do it."

Bree drove slowly down the road. As they approached the fourth mailbox, Matt pointed. "There it is."

The chicken coop that occupied the side yard was as big as a single-car garage. Attached to it, a rickety wood-and-wire structure enclosed an area the size of a basketball court.

Bree pulled into the driveway. The cottage-style house should belong to a little old lady in England. They got out of the car and started up the front walk. The sound of hinges squeaking caught their attention. Matt and Bree turned in unison to see a young man emerging from the chicken coop, a wire basket full of eggs in his hand. He wore a black parka and leather gloves.

Matt and Bree started toward him and met him in the side yard.

"I'm Sheriff Taggert." Bree gestured to her badge. "I'm looking for Zachary Baker."

"That's me," he said in a hesitant voice.

"I'd like to ask you about your neighbor Earl Harper," Bree began.

"I have nothing to say about him." Zachary shifted his weight. As he moved, he inched to the left, as if he were going to do an end run around Matt.

"We heard his dog killed some of your chickens." Out of the corner of her eye, Bree saw Matt take an identical half step, mirroring Zachary and subtly blocking his path.

"That was a long time ago." Zachary glanced over Matt's shoulder at his own house. He clearly did not want to talk to them.

"But it happened?" Bree asked.

Zachary met her eyes for a split second before averting his gaze. "Yeah. It happened. The dog busted through the fence and killed five of our chickens."

"How did Earl handle it?"

Zachary licked his lips. "He gave us fifty bucks and said that was fair."

"Was it fair?" Bree tried to catch his eye.

Zachary shifted his weight in the opposite direction. His eyes dropped to study the ground. "I guess."

"But you didn't ask him for more? Or call us?" Bree tried to catch his gaze with her own.

Zachary looked everywhere but at her. "Everybody around here remembers that Earl went to prison for beating a guy with a baseball bat. No one is going to talk against him."

"Do you know Sara Harper?"

Zachary sniffed. "Yeah. We went to school together."

"We heard you dated her."

"Just for part of senior year." His face reddened. "But I haven't seen her in a long time, not since she moved out of the neighborhood." A tight flash of anger lit his eyes, and his gaze settled on Bree's for a full two seconds before skittering away. "She needed help passing a couple of classes or she wasn't going to graduate. After I helped her, she dumped me." A muscle on the side of his jaw twitched, and his expression shifted back to longing. "Sara was a cheerleader in high school. She was way out of my league. I should've known that." He cleared his throat. "I have work to do. I'm done answering questions."

"We'd like to talk to your mother," Bree said.

"Her Parkinson's has gotten really bad. She doesn't want to see anyone. Excuse me." He straightened his shoulders, stepped around Bree, and headed for the house.

"Do you work?" Matt called after him.

Zachary stopped and answered without turning around. "I'm a freelance web designer. I work from home." He hurried toward the house and closed the door.

Bree turned toward her SUV.

Matt fell into step beside her. "He's a weird one. He couldn't look either one of us in the eye."

"Maybe he's an introvert." But Bree agreed. Zachary Baker's behavior had been odd.

"Or he's afraid that Earl will find out he talked to us about him. Neither Joe nor Zachary wanted to talk about Earl."

"Can't blame them."

"Not at all." Bree slid behind the wheel of her SUV. After Matt climbed into the vehicle, she said, "Also, I think Zachary got burned by Sara."

Matt agreed with a nod. They drove back the way they had come. Bree slowed the SUV as they passed Earl's property.

Matt glared out the windshield. "I feel bad for the dog."

"Nothing we can do about it." Bree glanced at him.

Matt's jaw went angry-tight. "You know the dog's aggression isn't his fault. He's tied up and frightened. Trapped animals get defensive."

Bree nodded. She didn't want to talk about the dog. She wanted to forget about it.

"Can you send animal control to pick him up?" Matt asked.

"You know I can't." Bree glanced in the rearview mirror. "There was food, water, and shelter. We didn't witness him injure the dog."

Matt crossed his arms. "We both know Earl's abusing that animal. The dog is thin."

"He didn't look like he was starving, and what we know and what we can prove are two entirely different things."

"Story of our lives, right?" Matt punched his knee, frustrated.

"Yep." Putting the dog out of her mind, Bree turned the dashboard computer toward Matt. "See if either Joe or Zachary drives a Dodge Charger."

Matt typed. "Nope."

"Criminal records?"

Matt worked the computer. "Nothing on Joe. Zachary has a couple of marijuana busts. He paid fines. The guy in the Charger could have borrowed or rented a car," Matt pointed out. "The vehicle doesn't have to belong to him."

"I know, but we have so little physical evidence. It would be great if we could get a lead on either the Charger or the birthmark."

"Too bad it isn't summer. No one would be wearing gloves."

"Yes." Bree's phone rang. She glanced at the screen. Todd. She answered the call. "What's going on?"

"We have another body," Todd said.

"Shit. Where?" Bree asked.

"Near the dock at the Grey Lake Inn."

# Chapter
# Twenty-Five

Matt followed Bree down the slope of the inn's back lawn to the edge of the lake. The sun shone from a cloudless sky. In places where the wind was blocked, the day felt almost warm. Patches of dormant grass showed through the melting snow.

Another body was the last thing they needed. They couldn't keep up with the killings.

Todd walked next to Bree and filled her in on the details of the new body.

"The forensics techs brought in lights and worked all night to process the evidence you found in the garage yesterday," Todd said. "Deputy Oscar arrived this afternoon to relieve the deputy who had been in charge. Oscar spotted a couple of kids out on the lake, watching. He went down there to run them off when he saw the body."

They walked along the bank for about a hundred feet until they reached a small culvert. Deputy Oscar stood on the bank. Freezing wind swept over the lake.

Matt shoved his injured hand into his coat pocket. Gloves weren't enough on days like this.

Oscar repeated his story. He hunched his shoulders against a sudden gust. "It was right under my feet. I was standing on top of it."

Matt didn't think the deputy's shivering had anything to do with the cold.

But Bree took pity on him. "Thank you, Deputy. If you need to warm up, go sit in your car for a while."

Oscar shook his head. "I'll stay."

They stared down at the ice where the ditch and drainpipe met the lake.

"Where is it?" Bree asked, scanning the area.

Todd pointed. They all looked down.

And Matt saw the back of a head, just barely visible through the opaque ice.

"Has the ME been notified?" Bree asked.

"Yes, ma'am," Todd said. "And the dive team is on the way."

Many of the Randolph County deputies served on special teams, including a dive team for underwater search and recovery.

Oscar crossed his arms and tucked his hands under his arms, as if the thought of going into the frigid water made him colder.

Matt scanned the lake. His gut twisted. Who was down there?

Ice crunched under boots. They all turned. The medical examiner and her assistant approached, each carrying a kit. Dr. Jones stopped next to Bree and motioned to the assistant behind her. "Let's get pictures. We'll map out which way the body is oriented to make sure we don't damage the remains while recovering them."

The ME waited for her assistant to photograph the remains from various angles and distances. Then Dr. Jones took a brush from her case and moved closer. She crouched and began brushing the ice. Removing the top layer of frost slightly improved the clarity. "Here's the neck. The back extends this way." She gestured. "I need to mark these locations."

"I have spray paint in my trunk." Todd turned and jogged back up the slope toward the inn. He returned a few minutes later with a can, which he handed to the ME.

She outlined a rough oval in dotted lines on the frozen surface to mark the location of the body. While they waited for the dive team, the ME and her assistant took samples, measurements, and temperature readings.

Four members of the dive team responded. They parked the truck and equipment trailer on the back lawn of the lodge. Two deputies set up the equipment while the other two donned dark-orange dry suits that would protect them from the frigid water. After the body was recovered, they would need to search the bottom of the lake for evidence, as they would in a crime scene on land.

Matt and Bree backed away while the men cut the ice away in chunks. It took thirty minutes to carve a rectangle large enough to allow the divers into the water with an underwater body bag made of heavy-duty, vinyl-coated mesh, which allowed water to drain when it was hauled ashore but kept forensic evidence inside. The tightly woven mesh would also protect the victim's privacy from onlookers as the body was removed from the lake. Floaters could be particularly nasty. Family members didn't need to see their loved one's bloated remains being dragged out of the water.

The ME consulted with the divers as they suited up. "The previous body had defense wounds and tissue under the nails. This is our first time working together, so I'm unsure of your procedures. I want to make sure any trace evidence that could be under the nails isn't dislodged during the removal."

The paper bags the ME used on land would not work underwater. The divers frowned.

The ME pulled ziplock bags from her kit. "These are women's nylon knee-high stockings. I rolled them so you can unroll them on the victim's hands and feet, like putting on a condom. The water drains, but the nylon should protect and preserve any evidence under the nails."

"That's a damned good idea." The diver took two bags and handed two to his partner.

The ME stepped back, satisfied.

The pair of divers donned tanks and helmets equipped with mini cameras. Matt stood a few feet from the team as they double-checked equipment that would monitor the men underwater.

The divers slipped into the lake. The recovery took nearly thirty minutes. They pulled the entire zipped body bag from the hole. Water drained from the bag as it lay on the ice, then it was loaded onto the ME's gurney and wheeled toward her van.

Matt went queasy as he and Bree followed the gurney to the parking lot in front of the inn. He and Bree exchanged a look.

*Was this Eli?*

Bree stopped the ME before she and the assistant loaded the body into the van. "Can you open it just a little? I need to see the body."

The ME glanced around the lot. The news crews were down by the water, watching the dive team. The divers would go back into the water and search the lake bottom for evidence. Dr. Jones opened a few feet of zipper. The corpse was a young male. He wore only boxer shorts, and his face was destroyed. His hair was shorn close to the scalp, like Brian's had been.

Matt lowered his voice. "Our missing person has a rectangular birthmark on the back of his shoulder."

The ME nodded. She'd already reviewed Eli's medical records once when she was trying to ID Brian's body. No doubt she remembered the birthmark. Matt braced himself as she lifted one of the corpse's shoulders. The mark was the size of a playing card.

*Eli.*

Matt instantly pictured Mrs. Whitney and felt sick at the pain Eli's death would bring to her.

Bree moved forward to stand next to Dr. Jones. She kept her voice low also. "Any estimate of how long he's been in the lake?"

But Dr. Jones had already zipped the bag. "Let me get him back to the morgue and do the calculations."

As with Brian O'Neil's body, determining time of death would be challenging, and the ME would only be able to give a window of time.

"I'll do his autopsy this afternoon," Dr. Jones said. "You'll have some answers by evening."

"Thank you," Bree said.

Then the victim was loaded into the van.

Bree and Matt returned to the rear yard. The inn had been designated a crime scene, but several news teams had ventured out onto the ice from the adjacent property to try to get a clear shot of the crime scene and the dive team at work.

A few minutes later, one of the divers emerged from the hole. He set his evidence bag on the ice next to him. He spit out his mouthpiece and removed his helmet. "Sheriff!" He motioned for her to come closer.

Bree hurried to his side and crouched low. Matt tuned in to hear.

The diver said, "There's another body down there."

Shock filled Matt. That was the last thing he'd expected to hear.

"We need another body bag." Bree glanced at the reporters. "And more of those nylons." She called for her chief deputy. "Todd, see if the ME is still here."

Dr. Jones was still in the parking lot. She returned with more nylons. The press sensed something was up and started filming.

A short while later, the second diver surfaced, and the other dive team members helped haul the second yellow mesh bag out of the water. The diver emerged from the hole, sat on the edge, and removed his helmet. Bree and the ME moved closer.

"Another male?" Bree asked.

The diver shook his head. "I'm not sure. It's dark down there, but the body has long hair and is still dressed."

Dr. Jones squatted next to the bag and discreetly opened the zipper enough to see the face. It was a woman with long dark hair. The collar of a coat was also visible. "Does she look familiar to anyone?"

"Yes." Bree whispered a name to the ME. "Her prints are probably in the system."

ID'ing her should be quick.

Matt breathed in Bree's ear. "Did you see her?"

Bree nodded. "She was fully dressed, and her face was intact. It looked like Sara Harper."

# CHAPTER TWENTY-SIX

Killing was addictive.

But he had to resist the temptation to rush. He needed to wait for the right opportunity, just like he'd planned. Poor timing could ruin everything, but it was getting harder to be patient. Since the press conference, he was almost afraid to use the Charger. But the vehicle was pretty common. It didn't really attract attention. He had removed the rideshare app sign. But the fact that the sheriff had a photo of the car made him unwilling to use his own vehicle. The Charger he could hide, but he couldn't afford to replace his regular vehicle.

He'd also been careful to wear gloves everywhere possible, and he'd used special makeup to cover the back of his hand. That bitch sheriff was trying to ruin everything. Maybe when he was finished with his current list, he'd make Bree Taggert a future target. The assholes he was currently hunting weren't so smart. The sheriff would present a whole new challenge.

Through his windshield, he watched pedestrians navigate a crosswalk. A few blocks off the main road through campus, parked vehicles clogged the street. The houses here were big and old. Most had been divided into apartments. The light turned green, and he let the car roll forward.

As he drove the next two blocks, the scenery changed from residences to university buildings. The student center was around the corner. He stopped at the light and scanned the sidewalks. He'd stalked his prey long enough on social media. The target usually went to the student center before his afternoon class.

He got lucky as he approached the student center. A car pulled away from the curb, and he slid into the spot and turned off the engine.

Three girls emerged from the building. They wore tight black pants and puffy jackets, backpacks slung over shoulders. Under knit caps, dark hair cascaded down their backs. One of the girls turned and said something to her friend. She was beautiful. The sort of woman who thought she was too good for him. The girl laughed, her perfect smile gnawing at him.

Bitterness burned deep in his belly. Seething, he slumped down in the seat, crossed his arms over his chest, and waited. Frustration burned inside him. It had to be today. He couldn't wait any longer. He curled his hand into a fist and punched his leg.

This street was too busy. The cold seeped into the car, but anger warmed him from the inside out. A half hour later, his target ambled out of the student center, late for class, as usual. He stared at his phone as he walked down the street. Instead of walking to the corner, he darted between two parked cars and jaywalked.

He wanted to kill him so badly that his fingers ached. His hands curled around the steering wheel, and his toe touched the gas pedal. He could just run him over right now. Easy. It would be done. One more down. He imagined his car striking the body, the boy flying into the air and flopping onto the street.

Anticipation buzzed in his veins. Would there be blood? Would the man die immediately? Too many uncertainties. He needed to be sure.

Plus, that's not how it was supposed to go down. Using the car was too quick, too remote. He wouldn't get to tell the fucker exactly why he was killing him. He wouldn't get to see the shock on his prey's face when he recognized him.

No. This death had to be as personal as the others.

He dimmed his excitement—for now. He would do this the right way. He would look the guy in the eyes as he pulled the trigger. It was vital that his victims knew exactly who was killing them and why. Otherwise, what was the point?

*He needs to be punished!*

No doubt this one knew what had happened to his friends and would be even more scared.

He rolled his shoulder and shifted into drive. He rolled away from the curb and followed his quarry.

The fucker looked over his shoulder. Could he sense the danger? Was he already nervous?

*I hope so.*

He cruised, keeping a hundred feet between him and his prey. The fucker turned onto the next street. He steered through the turn. This street was almost empty. The closest other students were a half block away. He waited for them to turn the corner, out of sight, then checked the road in both directions.

Clear. No moving cars. No people. But he had to hurry.

He pulled the ski mask down over his face. He'd smeared mud on his license plate. Even if his vehicle was caught on camera, the bitch sheriff wouldn't have any more evidence than she already did.

*Now.*

He punched the gas pedal. The car leaped forward, catching up to the target in a few seconds. The man veered toward the street. He was going to cross midblock.

Perfect.

He aimed just in front of his quarry, stopping just short of hitting him, as if he'd barely stopped in time by accident. The quick light of fear in the man's eyes was awesome.

"You asshole!" The jerk jumped back and dropped his phone. He slapped one hand on the hood of the car. "What the fuck is wrong with you?"

"Me? You ran in front of my car!" He checked the rearview mirror. The street was still clear.

He picked up his gun from the passenger seat and aimed it right at the guy's face. The asshole's eyes opened wide. He opened his car door and got out, keeping the gun steady. "Get in the back seat."

"No." Wide-eyed, the guy backed up. His face went white. He glanced at the phone at his feet.

"Don't touch it." Power surged through him. "I'll fucking shoot you right here."

The target moved on shaky legs to the rear door of the car, opened it, and stepped inside. He hesitated halfway in, as soon as he realized there was a divider between the front and rear seats. The car was an old police vehicle purchased at auction.

Scanning the street again, he slid behind the wheel and locked the doors. The man slid to the other side of the seat and grabbed for the door handle. Nothing happened. Because it was an old police car, the rear doors didn't open from the inside.

"There are handcuffs on the floor," he commanded. "Put them on."

This time, the guy didn't argue. He did as he was fucking told.

"Why are you doing this?" the asshole whined.

"Shut up." He straightened the car in the street. He had to get out of here. Then he ran over the phone. Excitement flushed his body. He'd done it. Nothing was better than a perfectly executed plan.

Except a perfect execution.

He took off his ski mask and tossed it onto the passenger seat. If anyone saw them now, they'd see a guy sitting in the back seat of a car. That's it. Nothing suspicious about that.

He left the campus and headed for the new place he'd picked out.

"I'll pay you to let me go," the guy begged.

He looked in the rearview mirror. "If you say one more word, I'm going to pull over and shoot you in the leg."

The rest of the drive went by in silence. He used the time to envision what he was going to do to the occupant of his back seat. He imagined it over and over in his head. Just like he would watch the video over and over after the killing.

But he had to be patient. The anticipation was part of the fun.

When they reached the destination, he got out of the car and opened the rear door. "Let's go."

Now that the sheriff had found the inn, he couldn't go back there.

His victim stepped out, lunged forward, and made a grab for his face with his bound hands.

He'd been expecting a final, panicked effort to escape. These assholes were so predictable. He pulled a stun gun from his pocket and pressed it to the man's forearm, holding it down for several seconds. The man's body jerked and shook, then he went limp and slid to the ground. That would keep him quiet for a few minutes. The electrical impulses emitted by a stun gun traveled through muscles. The bigger, beefier guys took a harder hit.

So easy.

Every one of these guys did the exact same thing. Mindless dummies, all of them. Yet they considered themselves the superior males of the species.

*Please.*

These college boys did nothing but screw around, drink, and waste their parents' money. Useless, every single one of them.

Fury blurred his vision. He blinked hard, inhaled, and held the air deep in his lungs. He couldn't wait to kill him.

The target stirred and groaned as if he felt the attention.

The threat.

He gave the man another short zap for good measure, not enough to completely incapacitate him again. This one was just for fun. He chuckled at the spasm of the guy's body.

Dancing like a puppet, and he held the strings.

He waited until the man came to. Then he rolled him to his back and slapped his cheeks.

His victim moaned. His eyes fluttered.

"That's it. Wake up. This won't be any fun unless you see it coming. Get up!"

The target sputtered and blinked, his eyes quickly focusing. Effects from the stun gun were short-lived. If he'd used drugs, his second option, the man wouldn't be ready for action for a long time. This way, the whole business was over and done in one night. Unlike the soon-to-be dead man, he didn't have time to screw around.

His victim's eyes were clear now. He tried to sit up. Confusion lowered his brows as he tugged at his bound hands.

"You're not going anywhere."

The man's gaze snapped up. Confusion shifted to fear. "What's going on?" His voice trembled.

*Who's the alpha male now, pretty boy?*

"Here's what's going to happen," he began. He gave him a step-by-step account of the upcoming evening. "Now get up and walk inside."

"What? No. You're crazy." The asshole's head was moving in a slow, disbelieving shake.

"You'll do it or die right now." He showed him the gun. "Or I'll zap you again and drag you inside. Your choice. Get up!"

"No." Belligerence lifted the target's chin.

He should really wait until the asshole was completely recovered. It would be more fun to have him alert and scared.

But his patience had run out. He wanted—needed—to start.

He lifted the pistol and stun gun and moved them up and down as if they were on a scale. "What's it going to be? Make your choice."

# CHAPTER TWENTY-SEVEN

It was dark before Bree was ready to leave the scene at the Grey Lake Inn. The medical examiner had taken both bodies back to the morgue. The dive team packed up their equipment. Bree, Matt, and two deputies had walked the bank of the lake, searching for any additional evidence in the tall weeds and ice. They'd collected every bit of trash they found. Every piece of evidence would be examined, but at this point, nothing appeared to be relevant to her case. They made their way back to the inn's parking lot.

"Where do we go from here?" Todd asked. "The search warrant for the house where the four boys lived came in."

"I want the roommates, Christian Crone and Dustin Lock, picked up and brought to the station for questioning immediately." Bree shivered. She hadn't been the one to go into the lake, but she was chilled down to the marrow of her bones. "I'll meet you there. We'll have deputies search the house while we're interviewing the subjects."

"Yes, ma'am." Todd walked away.

Bree and Matt hurried for her vehicle. She cranked the heater to full blast and headed down the private lane. "I have to call home."

Tonight would be a very late night.

She explained the situation to Dana, then talked to both kids. Matt made his own calls, asking his sister to look after his dogs. They set their phones down at the same time. .

"We think those bodies are Eli Whitney and Sara Harper, correct?" Bree asked.

"Yes," Matt agreed.

"That means we were wrong about everything. Neither Eli nor Sara killed anyone." She reached into her console, looking for an ibuprofen for the headache behind her eyes, but she came up empty. "Our entire case has changed. We no longer have a single, very personal homicide. We have a triple murder with a killer on the loose. Since we know the murder cases are related to the burglaries somehow, I need to call Detective Dane. I'd like to get her to work with us. I suppose I'll have to clear it with the Scarlet Falls police chief first."

Bree had made a point of introducing herself to the police chiefs in her jurisdiction soon after she took office. But she'd been so swept up in her own department's issues, she hadn't seen any of the chiefs since. She dialed Stella Dane first. After Stella agreed, Bree made the call to the SFPD chief.

Before she could put down her phone, it buzzed. "That's Dr. Jones."

"That's fast," Matt said.

"She promised to do the autopsies tonight, but they can't be complete." Bree checked her watch. It was six o'clock. The ME had left the scene several hours before, but each autopsy would take four hours. It was unlikely the autopsies would be finished before midnight. Everyone would be working overtime until the case was solved. A triple murder with a killer still at large took precedence over everything else. She answered the call. "Yes. Dr. Jones?"

"We have confirmed the identities of both victims. The male is Eli Whitney," Dr. Jones said. "I already had his medical files here, so the comparison didn't take long. As you suspected, the female's fingerprints matched those of Sara Harper. I'll get back to you as soon as I'm finished with the autopsies."

"Does Detective Dane already know about Eli Whitney?" Bree asked. "Eli's missing persons case belonged to the Scarlet Falls PD."

"Yes," Dr. Jones said. "She said she would do the death notification. Do you want to notify Sara Harper's family, or do you want me to do it?"

"I'll do it." Bree wanted to see Earl Harper's reaction in person.

"Thank you." Dr. Jones ended the call.

Bree set down her phone and glanced at Matt. "Did you hear?"

"I did. We have IDs."

She parked behind the station. Her phone buzzed. She read the text message aloud. "Stella says she'll be here after she performs the death notification. She wants to know who she can call for Mrs. Whitney."

Matt scrubbed a hand down his face. "My sister will know who to call, or she'll go there herself. Cady Flynn." He read off her phone number.

Bree texted it to Stella. "I'm probably going to work through the night."

"Same." Matt's eyes hardened. "This is going to break Mrs. Whitney. I will find out who killed Eli."

"Thank you. I appreciate the help." Bree climbed out of her vehicle. "I need to check in with Todd and Marge, then we'll go notify Earl Harper."

"OK."

They went into the station.

Marge followed them into Bree's office. "Alyssa is still at the motel, but she isn't happy about it. She saw the news about the bodies found at the Grey Lake Inn. She's upset."

"I'll call her. Three people are dead, and we're still not sure how Alyssa is mixed up in all this. I don't want anything to happen to her." Brian had been dead before Bree caught the case, but if Bree had done things differently, could she have saved Sara or Eli? Only the ME could say.

"You're going to have a long night." Marge frowned. "I'll order a platter of sandwiches. Anything else?"

"Hold on." Bree dialed Alyssa's motel room phone. When the girl answered, Bree said, "It's Sheriff Taggert. I need to give you some bad news. We found Harper's body today."

Alyssa gasped. "I knew it. When I saw the news footage, I just knew it was Harper."

"I know this has been hard on you," Bree said. "Her real name is Sara Harper."

The line was quiet for a few breaths, then Alyssa said, "I'm scared."

"I want to keep you safe, which is why I want you to stay put in your room with the deputy outside. Don't contact anyone."

"There's no one for me to call even if I had my phone." Alyssa sniffed. "I don't like it here. This room is claustrophobic. I feel trapped."

"We're doing everything we can to find this killer, Alyssa. Hang tight, OK?"

"OK." But Alyssa didn't sound convinced.

Bree pressed "End." She looked up at Marge. "After you order those sandwiches, check in with the deputy watching Alyssa every thirty minutes."

"Will do." Marge left the room. Matt didn't sit down. He walked the floor in front of her desk.

Bree sank into her chair, still wearing her coat. She couldn't get warm. She grabbed the case files. "I need ten minutes to review my notes on our previous interview with Earl before we go to the Harper place."

But she didn't want Earl to hear about his daughter's death on the news. The ME wouldn't release the names until next of kin had been notified, but these things had a way of leaking to the press.

Bree consulted her short list of suspects. The top two names were now confirmed dead. "In my mind, Earl Harper is now the most prominent suspect. He has a history of theft. He and his daughter didn't get along. He even said she stole from him."

Matt paced the length of the room. "He seemed angry about that, and the amount of facial damage makes these murders feel like rage crimes."

"But Sara's face wasn't damaged."

"Maybe he couldn't do that to his own daughter. That would explain why the bodies look different."

"But why would he have killed Eli and Brian?" Bree asked.

"They were both involved with Sara."

Bree rubbed her eyes. "He refused to take off his glove when I asked. So, we don't know if he has a mark on his hand."

Matt lifted a shoulder. "He wouldn't cooperate in any way. But he's a jerk. Hard to say if he's hiding something or just being himself."

"The brother didn't seem smart enough to mastermind a crime," Bree said. "Was that an act?"

"He felt genuinely stupid to me, but that doesn't rule him out in my opinion. These murders feel more brutal than genius. Plus, his criminal record means we need to keep him on the list."

"Rowdy was wearing gloves too. We couldn't see his hands."

"True." Matt stopped to stretch his back. "Could either he or Earl have been the man who jumped you at the cabin?"

Bree thought about his body type, and the way Earl had swung the sledgehammer. He was a hard man in emotional and physical terms. "He's certainly strong enough."

"Maybe it was a family project. Both Earl *and* Rowdy could be involved."

Someone knocked on the door, and Bree looked up. "Come in."

Todd entered the room. "A deputy picked up Dustin Lock. Christian Crone wasn't home."

"Where is he?" Bree's belly went cold.

"That's the thing," Todd said. "No one knows."

Bree stood and rounded the table. "Where's Dustin?"

"Interview room one." Todd moved aside as Bree walked past him into the room.

Dustin Lock looked like Todd had dragged him out of bed. He wore sweatpants and a university T-shirt. He'd shoved his bare feet into sneakers, and his hair was mussed. A winter jacket was draped over the back of his chair.

His expression was stunned as she entered the room. "I don't understand what's happening."

Bree introduced herself and turned the chair next to him around to face him. "Brian was murdered. We found another body in Grey Lake today. The medical examiner has identified the body as Eli. There was also the body of a woman in the lake near him."

Dustin's face paled. "Is it Sariah?"

"Yes," Bree said.

"Eli is dead?" His eyes were blank, as if he wasn't fully comprehending the situation.

"Yes."

"I don't understand." Dustin dropped his head into his hands. "What's happening?" His voice was high-pitched and panicky.

"That's what we're trying to find out," Bree said in a calm voice. "Where is Christian?"

Dustin lifted his head and chewed on his thumbnail. "I don't know. I texted him, but he didn't answer."

"Was he supposed to be home tonight?" Matt asked.

"Yeah," Dustin answered. "We were going to play *Call of Duty*."

"Where was he today?" Bree asked.

Dustin dropped his hand. "He had a class this afternoon. It was supposed to end around five thirty. Then he was coming home."

"Where was his class?" She poised her pen over a notepad.

Dustin gave her the name of a building.

Bree wrote it down. "Does he usually walk or take university transportation to class?"

"Depends. His class is across campus. In the summer, he'll ride his bike, but with the snow, he usually walks or takes an Uber."

Bree froze. "An Uber?"

"Yeah." Dustin nodded. "Especially if it's cold."

Bree turned to Todd. "Put out a BOLO and send a couple of deputies over to the university to look for Christian. Call his cellular provider. Tell them it's an emergency and we need to find his phone."

In life-threatening situations, the search warrant requirement could be bypassed to access cellular location data.

With a nod, Todd rose and left the room.

Bree had a sick feeling deep in her belly. "Dustin, is there anything you can tell us about where Christian could be? Friends, girlfriend, family he could have stopped to see . . ."

Dustin shook his head. "Christian's family is in Florida, and he doesn't have a girlfriend right now. Of the four of us, he's the one who's usually at the house." Dustin swallowed. "He should be home."

"Where were you all day?" Bree asked.

"I had two classes, and I had lunch in the student center in between." Dustin wiped a hand across his face. "I got home about a half hour before the deputy came to the house."

"Did you use your meal plan?" Bree asked.

"Yes." Dustin looked around the room. He seemed lost.

Bree had only graduated college thirteen years before, but it felt like much longer. Had she ever been this young? "Do you have a card to swipe?"

He nodded.

"Do your professors take attendance?" she asked.

"Yeah."

Bree ripped a piece of paper from the back of her notepad. "I want you to write down your movements for the whole day. Give us names, places, times, and the numbers of anyone you came into contact with. Also, give me a list of people Christian hangs out with and their phone numbers if you have them. Any information you have about Christian's schedule would also be helpful. No detail is too small at this point."

"Am I in danger?" Dustin shifted his seat on the chair.

"I believe so." Bree was honest. "But you are safe here, and this is where I want you to stay for now. Is that all right?"

With a short exhale of relief, Dustin breathed. "Thank you."

"Do you need anything? Are you hungry?"

"No, ma'am." He picked up a pen and began writing.

Bree and Matt got up and left the room, closing the door behind them.

Todd met her in the hall. Bree jerked a thumb at the closed interview room door and explained Dustin's assignment. "Verify his movements throughout today. Also, see if you can find out from the university if Christian attended his class today or used his meal card."

Todd's gaze drifted to the closed door. "Do you think he killed his friends?"

"Honestly, no," Bree said. "I can't think of a motive, and he seems genuinely shocked and afraid."

"Two of his roommates are dead, and the third is missing. He'd be stupid if he wasn't scared," Matt said.

Bree agreed with a nod. "That's why we're not letting him out of our sight. We don't have any free deputies to babysit him, so he can stay right here."

Logically, Dustin would be next.

"Let's go see Earl Harper," Bree said. "It's always interesting when your next of kin is also your prime suspect."

# CHAPTER TWENTY-EIGHT

Matt stared through the windshield at Earl Harper's place. He needed a shower, fresh clothes, and a toothbrush, but he wasn't going to get any of those things anytime soon.

Bree offered him a mint.

"Thanks." Matt took one and popped it into his mouth.

The property looked ominous in the dark. The only light shone from a window on the side of the bungalow. Earl hadn't left the porch light on for visitors.

"Let's do this." Bree parked her SUV near the house and grabbed her flashlight from the console. Matt took his own out of his pocket. They got out of the vehicle and navigated the icy front walkway. The dog barked behind the house. Bree jumped, then slipped.

Matt reached for her elbow. "You OK?"

"I'm fine," she snapped and shook off his hand. "Sorry. That was rude."

"It's all right." Matt knew it wasn't personal. The dog had her on edge.

They climbed the two concrete steps onto the stoop and flanked the door. Bree knocked.

No one responded for a solid minute. She knocked again, louder this time. Another minute passed, then heavy footsteps approached the door. A curtain next to the window shifted. Finally, the front door opened, and Earl Harper stared down at them from a one-step height advantage. Standing in the middle of the open doorway, he crossed his arms and tucked his hands into his armpits. Was he cold?

Or hiding the backs of his hands?

"May I speak with you, Mr. Harper?" Bree asked.

Earl looked over their heads and scanned the front of his property, as if verifying no other law enforcement was present. "What do you want?"

"I'd like to come inside," Bree said. "I'd rather not do this in public."

"Too fucking bad." Earl shook his head. "Say what you've come to say."

Bree cleared her throat. "The body of your daughter, Sara, was found today in Grey Lake. I'm sorry for your loss."

Earl said nothing. His throat shifted as he swallowed. Matt watched his eyes. Surprise shifted to something else. Shock? Sadness? Fear? The emotion disappeared before Matt could identify it.

After a few minutes, Earl asked, "You're sure?"

"Yes, sir," Bree said. "The medical examiner positively identified Sara. Her fingerprints were on record."

Earl squinted. His head turned in slow, small shakes of disbelief. "I won't believe it until I see her with my own eyes."

"She is at the county medical examiner's office." Bree was treating Earl as gently as she would any other grieving family member, regardless of his difficult nature or criminal record. "You'll need to select a funeral home. Are you sure you wouldn't rather have this discussion inside?"

Earl didn't budge from the doorway, and his hands stayed firmly tucked under his arms. "How did she die?"

"The medical examiner has not made that determination yet." Bree danced around the word *autopsy*. "I will keep you informed."

"She was killed, wasn't she?" Earl's small eyes went smaller, angrier, and his weight shifted forward. His body reminded Matt of a snake coiling to strike.

Matt's body tensed, ready to react.

"I should have that information for you tomorrow," Bree said.

Bree and Earl stared at each other for a couple of long seconds.

Matt jumped in. "Do you know Zachary Baker?"

"The nerd?" Earl seemed taken off guard by the question. "Yeah."

"Had Sara seen him recently?" Matt asked.

"How the fuck would I know?" Earl's face flushed. He jabbed a forefinger a few inches in front of Matt's face. The other hand went to his hip. No red mark on either hand. "I don't need to answer your questions."

Matt ignored the finger in his face. "We're trying to find out what happened to Sara."

"Yeah. Right." Earl stepped back and prepared to shut the door.

"Mr. Harper," Bree called. "I need to ask you some questions about your daughter."

"You know what, Sheriff? Fuck you. I told you earlier today that I didn't know where she was at or what she was doing. That hasn't changed. Come back when you actually know something. And if you want me to answer questions, call ahead so I can have my lawyer present."

"I'd like to see Sara's old room," Bree said. "And I'd like to talk to Rowdy."

"Get a warrant or fuck off." Earl stepped back and slammed the door in their faces.

"That went well," Matt said.

Bree backed off the step. "I notified him. There's nothing else I can do. He is under no obligation to answer questions. I have no right to enter his home without a warrant, and I have no probable cause to get one."

"We need something to tie him to the burglaries or the murders."

"But what?" Bree asked. "He has a record. His fingerprints are on file. But it was Sara's fingerprints on the jewelry, not her father's. He didn't have a mark on either of his hands. He doesn't drive a Dodge Charger. We have nothing on Earl Harper. Maybe we're way off base. He seemed shocked by the news that Sara was dead."

"He did." Had Matt been wrong about him? Just because the man was an ass didn't mean he was guilty.

Or at least not guilty of killing his daughter.

Bree checked the time. "We've fulfilled our obligation here. Let's catch up with Todd and Stella. Maybe one of them had some luck. Todd was working on searches, and forensics should have something for us tonight."

They returned to the sheriff's station. Marge greeted them in Bree's office.

"Thank you for staying." Bree hung up her coat.

"You're welcome. Detective Dane just arrived. I put her in the conference room. The sandwiches are here as well. See that you both eat something." Marge gave Bree and Matt each a hard stare.

"Yes, ma'am," Matt said.

Marge sniffed. "I sent food to Alyssa and the deputy on duty at her motel. I also fed Dustin. He is still in interview room one. He seems content to stay there."

"I don't know what I'd do without you, Marge." Bree rubbed the back of her neck.

"Me either," Marge said on her way out of the room.

Bree collected her notes and files and led Matt from her office. In the main bullpen, Todd looked up from his computer. Bree gestured, and he got up and followed them to the conference room, bringing his laptop with him.

Inside, Stella was taking off her coat. She looked wrecked. Dark semicircles hovered under her eyes, and the rims of her eyelids were red, as if she'd been crying.

Bree sat at the head of the table. Matt dropped into a chair. He grabbed a sandwich and took a bite.

Todd set down his phone and leaned over the platter. "What kind is that?"

"I don't know." Matt looked down. He barely tasted the food. "Looks like ham and cheese." He took another bite.

Bree didn't look hungry either, but she also took a sandwich and ate mechanically.

Stella eased into a chair and grabbed a water bottle. "Your sister was very helpful. Thank you for sending her."

"Cady is the best." Matt pushed the plate of sandwiches toward her. "How was Mrs. Whitney?"

Without taking any food, Stella pushed the platter back to Matt. "Not good. Not good at all." Stella pressed the cold bottle to her forehead. "Your sister said she would make sure she wasn't alone."

"Not much else anyone can do." Matt didn't know how Mrs. Whitney would survive her grandson's death.

"Except find the person responsible," Bree said.

"Yeah. Let's do that." Todd flattened a palm on the table.

Bree brought Stella up to speed. "Earl Harper wasn't quite as reactive when we notified him of his daughter's death. I'm not sure how he took it. He's a cold one. Dustin Lock is in interview room one. Christian Crone is missing. We're still waiting to hear from the ME."

"Stella, have you made any progress on the burglaries?" Matt asked.

Stella shook her head. "No. I've had an officer working the contractor angle since we spoke last. I now have a list of contractors who worked in each of the burglarized homes three months before the burglary. I see one or two companies repeated, but none are listed more than twice." She closed her eyes for a few seconds. When she opened them, she looked angry. "Please tell me *you* have suspects?"

"Sara Harper's father and brother seemed like the most likely two. Neither one of them drives a Dodge Charger. Earl didn't have a mark on his hands, but Rowdy was wearing gloves."

"I could see Earl letting Rowdy do the dirty work," Matt said.

Bree lifted a palm. "Let's prepare a photo array for Alyssa. When we're finished here, I'll take it to her and see if she points out Earl or Rowdy."

Todd ducked out of the room and assigned a deputy to pull mug shots of Earl, Rowdy, and a few other men who met the same basic physical description. He returned in a couple of minutes.

Bree set her sandwich on a napkin. She'd barely eaten any of it. "If Alyssa recognizes Earl or Rowdy, we'll get a search warrant for their property. Simply bringing them in for an interview will be pointless. Earl wouldn't even let us into the house to do the death notification. He won't say a word if we bring him here."

"Sounds like he has something to hide." Stella took a long drink of water.

"But who knows if it has anything to do with the case." Bree let off a sigh of frustration. "We need to stop this killer, and we need physical evidence to do that."

Todd returned. "I have an email from forensics. Evidence logs from the crime scenes."

"Finally." Matt massaged his injured hand. Standing outside at Earl's house in the cold had set off an ache in the scar tissue. "This killer is picking off people faster than forensics can process the evidence."

Bree nodded. "If we get another crime scene, we might have to call the state lab for help."

Todd shook his head. "The state lab is so backed up, we won't get results for months. At least you can pressure the county lab."

"Other suspects?" Stella asked.

"Phil Dunlop?" Todd suggested.

"We have nothing on him except an ACE bandage on his hand." Bree tapped her pen. "We're all in agreement that Christian was most likely kidnapped?"

Everyone agreed with a chorus of "Yes."

Todd's phone rang, and he answered the call. He set down his phone in a few minutes. "The deputies on campus verified Dustin's attendance at his classes today, and his meal plan card was swiped at the student center. Christian did not make it to his four thirty class. Christian's meal card was used in the student center at three o'clock. So, he was likely taken between three and four thirty this afternoon. Dustin was in his own class at that time."

"He's clear," Bree said.

"Yes," Todd continued. "Deputies showed Christian's picture around campus. They walked the route between the cafeteria and his classroom. They are currently with campus security looking for surveillance video footage along the route Christian would have walked to get to class."

"OK. Tell them to keep trying." Bree pushed her hair off her face. "Sara had an ex-boyfriend, Zachary Baker. He lives near Earl and recently had words with him." Bree wrote down the name and address. "He has two prior misdemeanors for pot possession. Other than that, he's clean. He drives a Toyota Camry. Have a deputy track him down and bring him in for questioning."

"Motive?" Todd asked.

"Jealousy," Bree said. "When we talked to him, it seemed he still had feelings for Sara, but she wasn't interested in him. He was also angry at Earl. Maybe killing Sara was his way of hurting him."

Todd took the paper. "We're running out of deputies."

"Call more in," Bree said. "I'll approve the overtime and figure out how to pay for it later."

If they saved Christian, Matt had no doubt the county board of supervisors would find additional money for the sheriff's department. If Christian died, Bree's decisions would be held against her. As a new sheriff, she had little established political goodwill to leverage. But she would never allow potential political ramifications to weigh on her decisions. Her refusal to play politics might come back to bite her in the ass.

Marge walked into the room, a thick bound book in her arms. "Here's a Grey's Hollow High School yearbook for 2016. Who wants it?"

Stella raised her hand. "Pass it here. If Sara was a cheerleader, she should be in a lot of photos." She set it down, then took a folder from her briefcase. "Here's a list of utility and service contractors that worked in the houses that were burglarized. This list needs fresh eyes."

"I'll take it." Matt reached for the folder.

"Who wants to review the evidence logs from the crime scenes?" Bree asked.

"I'll do it," Todd said. "I'm also going to call the cell phone company about Sara's phone records again."

"Where's that list of Dodge Chargers in the area?" Bree asked.

"Got it." Todd passed a list to Bree. "I filtered it by males, ages eighteen to forty."

"There are still dozens of names on this list." Bree's open laptop dinged with an incoming email. "Hallelujah. The trace evidence reports from Monday's crime scenes."

Matt scanned the table full of reports. *There must be a clue in here somewhere.*

And they'd better find it before Christian turned up dead.

# CHAPTER TWENTY-NINE

Bree's eyes were crossing as she read the final page of the forensics report from the boat ramp scene. Exhaustion was hampering her comprehension. She blinked hard to clear her vision. The second paragraph on the page caught her attention. "The techs found traces of spackling paste and PVC solvent cement in the suspect's boot prints. What does that mean?"

"He's been to a construction site or house reno." Stella pushed her chair back. "I need coffee. Anyone else?"

Bree's sour stomach said no, but her brain overrode it with a hard yes. She raised a hand. "Please."

Stella walked out of the room.

"So, maybe he works for a contractor?" Matt asked.

"That's what I was thinking." Bree sorted through the piles of reports on the table for Stella's contractor lists from the burglarized residences. She skimmed the list with her fingertip and stopped on a company. "This name sounds familiar. ABC Plumbing. They did work at two of the homes that were burglarized."

Stella returned with two cups of coffee. She handed one to Bree.

Bree accepted it and took a sip, though the new evidence thread had already perked up her brain. She could feel the pieces of the investigation beginning to come together.

"Which houses?" Stella leaned over the table and skimmed the list.

Todd read the addresses.

"The first one is where the ruby-and-diamond bracelet was stolen," Stella said.

"ABC Plumbing? I've read that name before too." Matt leaned back in his chair and scrubbed both hands down his face. He opened Bree's laptop and turned the screen to face him. "ABC Plumbing is owned by Stanley Hoover, age thirty-eight. Stanley is a master plumber with sixteen years of experience."

"I don't know that name." Bree glanced around the table. No one looked like the name rang any bells. "Let me see the master list of Dodge Chargers in Randolph County."

Matt passed her the list.

Bree scanned for Stanley Hoover. "Damn. He's not here. But wait. Here's a Dodge Charger on the same street that Earl Harper lives on." She slid her finger across to the name. "Guess who it's registered to?"

"Who?" Matt asked.

Bree laid the paper on the table and tapped the name. "Roger Marcus."

"That's the same last name as the neighbor we interviewed." Matt straightened.

"His name was Joe." Bree checked the address listed on Joe's driver's license. "Same address too."

Todd typed on his computer. "A Toyota Corolla is registered to Joe."

"But he said he inherited the house from his father," Bree said. "The Charger could also have belonged to his father. Maybe he inherited the vehicle too."

"Is it possible that Earl used Joe's Charger, with or without Joe's permission?" Todd asked.

Matt's gaze sharpened. "They didn't seem that close, but who knows? All we have is Joe's statement. We didn't ask *Earl* about *Joe*."

"There was a van in Joe's driveway." Bree reached for her phone. "I took pictures of the front of Earl Harper's place." She scrolled. "Here." Bree transferred the images to her laptop.

Matt tapped on the screen to zoom in on the van in the neighbor's driveway. "ABC Plumbing."

Bree pulled up Joe's driver's license info. "This is him." She spun the laptop around so Stella and Todd could see the photo. "How is he related to all this?"

"He went to school with Sara," Matt said. "He's known her all his life."

Stella grabbed for the yearbook. "I saw him in here somewhere. Here." She tapped on a page.

They all leaned across the table to see the yearbook picture. It was Sara Harper, in her cheerleader skirt, pressing her face against Joe's and mugging for the camera. "I marked all the photos in the yearbook that Sara appears in." Stella had used sticky notes. She went from page to page. "There is one picture of Sara with her supposed boyfriend Zachary Baker in the whole yearbook, but Joe is in three with her."

Matt tapped Joe's face. "Maybe it wasn't Zachary who was a sucker for Sara. Maybe it was Joe."

"What did he say?" Bree closed her eyes and tried to recall their conversation. "He said Sara has a way of making a guy do what she wants."

"Maybe she talked Joe into doing something bad," Matt said.

"Did he kill her?" Stella suggested. "Sara was hot. Joe is not. In high school, relationships between individuals from opposite sides of the attraction index don't happen very often."

Bree drummed her fingers on the table. "Joe seemed nervous when we talked to him. At the time, we attributed his nervousness to fear of a reprisal from Earl. But maybe we were wrong."

They'd made assumptions based on Earl's criminal record and general nasty disposition. One of the prime rules in investigation was keeping an open mind. Let the evidence lead you, not the other way around. Bree mentally kicked herself. Earl was an ass. But he could be an innocent ass. Or at least, he might be innocent in these murders.

"So, how do Eli, Brian, and Christian play into this?" Stella chugged her coffee like a frat boy with a beer bong.

"Let's ask Dustin if he recognizes Joe." Bree printed Joe's driver's license photo. To cover her bases, she also printed photos of Earl and Rowdy Harper. "Todd, where is the photo array you prepared for Alyssa?"

Todd pulled a handful of photos from a folder. Bree took them from the conference room and snatched her three pictures off the printer. The squad room was quiet at ten o'clock. The graveyard shift was out on patrol. The deputies at the university were still driving around campus looking for surveillance cameras that might have caught an image of Christian.

Bree went into the interview room. Dustin was sound asleep at the table, his head pillowed on his folded arms. She tapped his shoulder. "Dustin. Wake up. I need to ask you something."

He jumped, then sat up and blinked at her. "Oh. OK."

"Do you know any of these men?" Bree placed the photos on the table in a row, adding pictures of Earl, Rowdy, and Joe to the mix.

Dustin shoved a hand through his hair and rubbed his eyes before focusing on the pictures. "Yeah. I know this guy." He pointed to Joe Marcus's picture. "He's the plumber who drained and disconnected our water heater when it leaked a while back. Our douchebag landlord never replaced it."

"Did anything happen the day he worked at the house?" Bree asked.

Dustin flushed and looked away.

Bree nudged his arm. "What happened?"

Dustin sighed. "Eli was making fun of him. The guy was an idiot. He even burned his hand on the hot water heater element. His pants wouldn't stay up. His butt crack was hanging out." Dustin studied the table. "The guy was a loser. Eli took his picture and posted it on Twitter." One side of Dustin's mouth twitched, as if he still thought it was funny. "Eli has a series of pics he calls—called—the Phil McCracken Files, where he posted butt-crack pics." Dustin sobered. Was he remembering his friend was dead?

The red mark wasn't a tattoo or birthmark. It was a burn.

"Eli was the only one mocking him?" Bree asked.

Dustin's shoulder jerked. Then he shook his head. "No, we were all giving him a hard time."

"So, this man came to repair your water heater, and the four of you tormented him?" Bree asked.

"Yeah," Dustin admitted. Regret seemed to subdue him. "Have you found Christian?"

Did Joe kill Eli and Brian for revenge because they made fun of him?

"Not yet. You hang tight in here, OK?" Bree closed the door and went back to the conference room. She repeated what Dustin told her. "Let's get all the information we can on Joe Marcus."

"What do we have so far?" Stella asked.

Bree ticked the facts off on her fingers. "One, we know he was long-time friends with Sara Harper. Two, he has access to a Dodge Charger, the same model vehicle used in Eli's abduction. Three, the plumbing contractor who employs him worked at two of the houses that were recently burglarized in Scarlet Falls." Bree sighed, frustrated. "This is all circumstantial. If we want a search warrant for his house, we need something more direct to establish probable cause."

"We also need to verify that *Joe* actually worked at those houses that were burglarized, not just the company he works for," Stella pointed out.

"I'll call the owner of ABC Plumbing." Matt left the room, phone in hand.

"This all started with a man shooting Sara Harper at the Grey Lake Campground. How would he know where she was?" Bree thought out loud.

"If Sara was killed by her burglary accomplice, then maybe she told him where she was staying," Todd said.

"If they were partners, they would have been in communication with each other," Bree agreed. "Do we have the records for Sara Harper's prepaid phone?"

"Let me check again." Todd pulled his laptop out from under a folder and opened it. "Yes. It's in."

Bree moved around the table to look over his shoulder. She'd taken Joe Marcus's contact information after speaking with him, so she had his phone number. She opened her phone for the notes she'd made on the interview, then compared the number Joe had given her with the list on Sara's phone. No matches. "There's a number in her contact list under the initial *J*. Sara called this number on Sunday at eleven p.m. It's the last call she made."

"There's no personal information attached to this number. Maybe it's a burner phone." Todd scrolled through the list.

"Maybe." Bree closed her eyes and turned the development over in her head. "*J* could still stand for Joe. Maybe he has another phone. It would be pretty stupid to use his regular cell phone."

*Too many maybes.*

"Todd, you write up the affidavit for the search warrant with our evidence as it stands. I'll call you if Alyssa IDs Joe, and you can add her statement. Make sure to include the garage, other outbuildings, the dock, the woods, and any vehicles on the premises. I want to compare tire treads with the impressions we made at the boat ramp. We'll want footwear, to compare those treads as well, trace evidence, computer and electronic equipment, biological evidence." Bree listed specific language she wanted on the search warrant. If she didn't cover all the possibilities, their search would be limited, or evidence collected could be challenged in court later. "We need to be able to execute the warrant tonight, so detail the exigent circumstances for the judge. This is a life-or-death matter. We need to find Christian now, before he becomes the next victim."

Normally, search warrants could only be served during reasonable hours. Bree would take no chances that evidence found would be thrown out by a judge because she hadn't served her search warrant properly.

She collected the six photos she'd shown Dustin. "I'm going to take these to Alyssa and see if she recognizes Joe as the man who shot Sara Harper."

She'd been a wishy-washy witness, but Alyssa's ID of Joe would strengthen the affidavit. Otherwise, Bree would have to convince a judge she'd never met to have faith in her.

Matt returned. "I called the owner of ABC Plumbing. He confirmed Joe worked on the burglarized houses. He also said Joe didn't show up for work today."

"That helps." Bree made her own notes as she spelled out the details for Todd. "Let me know when the warrant application is ready. I'll call the judge and ask if he'll sign electronically. That'll save time." Bree turned to Stella. "Would you be willing to stay and help execute the warrant?"

"Just try and stop me." Stella stood and picked up her coffee cup. "I'll caffeinate."

"I'll go with you, Bree." Matt followed her from the room.

She stopped in her office for her coat. Then they hurried through the back door to the SUV.

Nerves hummed in Bree's blood as she prayed she was right. A young man's life depended on it. She knew in her gut that if they didn't find him, he'd be dead by morning.

"We're close." Matt fastened his seat belt. "I can feel it."

"We have to find Christian tonight." Bree sped out of the parking lot. "We have no indication that this killer holds his victims long before he kills them."

"He won't take Christian to the inn where he killed Eli and dumped Sara."

"No. We ruined that location for him. I also doubt he'll return to the boat ramp where he dumped Brian," Bree agreed. "Joe had a garage behind his house. Maybe he took him there."

The drive to the motel was less than ten minutes. Bree lifted her foot off the gas pedal as they approached the entrance.

Matt leaned forward and squinted through the windshield. "Is that smoke?" He cracked his window.

The smell of smoke hit Bree's nose. She took the turn into the parking lot too fast. The SUV lurched. Tires squealed. Matt grabbed for the armrest.

Smoke billowed from the two-story structure. An alarm blared. People were emerging from motel rooms.

"Shit." Bree grabbed her radio mic and reported the fire to dispatch as she slammed the gearshift into park and jumped from the SUV. She sprinted toward the sheriff's deputy vehicle parked in front of Alyssa's room. Bree raised a hand to knock on the window, but froze, her hand in the air. A hole had been punched through the glass. The deputy was pitched forward. Blood covered the back of his head. "He's been shot!"

Was he dead?

Where was Alyssa?

Fear for the girl bubbled into Bree's throat. She unholstered her weapon and used the butt of her gun to smash the window. She reached through the broken glass and pressed two fingers to the deputy's neck.

"It's Wallace. He's alive." But his wound was bleeding heavily. "He's lost a lot of blood."

She and Matt dragged the deputy from his car.

A man ran from the office toward Bree. He stopped, panting. "I'm the manager. What's happening, Sheriff?"

"This deputy has been shot!" Bree yelled. "Do you know which rooms are occupied?"

"Yes." The man glanced around, his expression stunned.

Bree pointed toward the small group gathering on the other side of the parking lot. "Try to account for all your guests."

He headed for the cluster of people.

Matt was on the radio, reporting an officer down and requesting an ambulance and backup.

A woman in a bathrobe ran barefoot across the parking lot. She carried a short stack of towels. She dropped to her knees beside Wallace's still body. "I'm a nurse." She pressed a folded towel to the back of the deputy's head and applied pressure.

"Thank you." Bree turned toward the building. Was Alyssa still inside?

Smoke poured from the windows below her room. *Is she alive?* Bree couldn't see any flames, but most fire fatalities didn't burn to death. They died of smoke inhalation.

Swallowing her anger, Bree raced for the concrete steps that led to the second-story landing, gun in hand. Matt was at her side.

"Careful!" Matt touched the door lightly with his fingertips, clearly checking for heat. "Feels OK."

The door was locked. Matt stepped back and kicked the door. It held. He kicked the door twice more until the frame gave. Wood splintered. The door flew inward, bouncing off the wall.

Bree went in first, leading with her weapon. She swept the room with her gun until she was sure it was clear. Smoke filled the top half of the room and burned her eyes. Her vision blurred as they watered. She wiped a forearm across her face and blinked to clear her eyes. The beds were stripped of their sheets. Smoke clogged Bree's nose. She coughed and ducked low, trying to stay beneath the thickest cloud.

"Alyssa?" she yelled, choking.

Matt rushed by. Coughing, he pulled the collar of his jacket over his mouth and nose. He pushed the bathroom door open. Bree peered around his shoulder. A rope of sheets was tied around the base of the toilet and threaded through the tiny window. Not many people could have squeezed out the small opening. Alyssa was very thin, but getting out the window must have required some gymnastics—and desperation. But then, the motel was on fire. So, yeah. She'd been desperate.

She'd also been prepared. It wasn't likely that she'd made that rope at the last minute. She'd probably had it ready.

Bree didn't know whether to be relieved or panicked.

"Alyssa's gone." Matt coughed and pulled Bree back toward the door. "We need to get out of here."

Bree yanked her arm free of his grip. She stepped into the tub and looked out the window. The rope of sheets led almost to the ground below the window.

How had she gotten out? The girl must be as flexible as Gumby. But then, when Bree had chosen the room, she'd been more worried about a man getting *in* than Alyssa getting *out*.

The smoke thickened and tears poured from her eyes.

"Bree!" Matt grabbed her arm and dragged her out of the room.

On the walkway, Bree ran down the cement steps and around the building.

Most of the snow had melted in the sun earlier that day, leaving mud in low-lying areas. Fifty feet of weedy ground separated the motel from the woods. Bree pulled her flashlight from her pocket and shone it on the ground. A set of footsteps in the mud led from Alyssa's landing point at the base of the wall into the trees.

Bree took off running, but her smoke-filled lungs protested, and she had to stop when she reached the tree line. She leaned on her thighs and coughed, the taste of smoke thick in her mouth and throat.

*Damn it!*

Matt was right at her side, also coughing. "Just breathe for a minute, then we'll chase her down."

Bree straightened and wiped her mouth with her sleeve. Worry for Alyssa drove her forward. Bree stumbled along the trail. The cold night air soothed her lungs. In a few strides, she recovered her wind and broke into a slow jog. In two hundred yards, the trail ended at a narrow, unlined paved road.

Bree turned in a circle. "Where is she?"

"She couldn't have gotten far." Matt pointed his own flashlight on the ground and walked along the shoulder of the road.

Bree took the other side, looking for a spot where Alyssa left the pavement. "What road is this?"

Matt had his phone in his hand. "Rural Route 31. It runs parallel to the interstate. There's not much on it but a couple of farms. It cuts through miles of nothing and intersects with several other country roads."

"I can't track her on pavement." Bree stared down. "I wish Brody wasn't hurt. My department needs a K-9."

"It does."

Brody's injury had convinced her. She couldn't rely on a borrowed, retired dog, no matter how good he was. He was not a young animal. She had to put her own fears aside and figure out a way to acquire a dog.

She called the state police and requested a K-9 unit, but she didn't have time to wait for it to arrive.

Matt and Bree returned to the motel parking lot. Two fire trucks were hosing down the motel. Guests clustered in small groups in the parking lot.

Bree grabbed Matt's sleeve. "Would you take my SUV and drive a couple of miles down that road to see if you spot Alyssa?"

"Of course." Matt took the keys she offered. Bree watched him drive away in her vehicle. Then she turned toward the chaos. The motel fire alarm blared. A siren sounded the arrival of another fire truck.

It seemed impossible that Alyssa had run away on foot that quickly. The fire had just started. *Had* she escaped?

Or had Alyssa also been taken?

If Joe had her, he would certainly kill her.

# Chapter Thirty

The electric trimmers buzzed in his hand, and the asshole squirmed. But he was securely zip-tied to the chair. He wasn't going anywhere. A drop of blood fell from his wrist to the concrete floor. The plastic was digging into his skin.

"Stop it." He grabbed a handful of blond hair and ran the clippers along the scalp. "You'll just make it hurt more."

Handful by handful, the hair piled up on the tarp. The hair, he decided, was a big part of the image. Without it, the guy looked pathetic and weak. The clippers slipped a couple of times. The target flinched every time his scalp was nicked.

What a pussy.

The man moaned behind his gag. His blue-and-red-striped rugby shirt and jeans that cost a week's pay were folded in the corner. He shivered.

These assholes pretended to be so tough, but they were actually just facades of straight teeth, expensive clothes, and haircuts that cost as much as most people's rent. Underneath, they were nothing. Their whole world was superficial. What did they know about being a man?

He was self-made. He didn't have parents to pave the way for him. Unlike this privileged jerk, who was handed his life and his looks. Didn't work mean anything anymore? Why did women fling themselves at rich douchebags when they could have real men?

His victim shuddered hard. Goose bumps covered his skin. The garage was cold, but it wouldn't matter. Soon, he wouldn't care about the cold.

When the head was completely shaved, he admired his work. Without the pretty hair and clothes, the guy was nothing special.

He pulled the gag away from the mouth. "Convince me not to kill you."

"What is wrong with you, man?" The target's voice broke. He was going to cry.

Glee filled him. He'd broken the jerk already. "You're not helping your case."

"What do you want?" The man sniffed. His eyes were watery, and his lips were turning blue.

"I don't know. Maybe I just want to know that you're not a total asshole."

"Look, man. I'm sorry if we offended you. We were just joking around." The asshole tried to blow him off.

"You aren't funny." He walked in a circle around the chair.

The target's neck swiveled, trying to keep him in sight. He stood directly behind him, just to freak him out.

"What are you doing?" Panic raised the pitch of the man's voice.

Fear.

He could smell it. Taste it. Enjoy it.

It was about time someone feared him for a change. He'd spent his whole life being second to these so-called alpha males. Well, that wasn't how it was going to be from now on. He was alpha tonight. He was calling all the shots.

"I'll give you anything. Just let me go," the target begged.

"Your friends begged too." He leaned close to his victim's ear. "Do you want to know what happened to them?"

The target's breathing sped up, until he was almost hyperventilating. Which was more fun, freaking them out or killing them? It was hard to decide.

He remembered his second victim. Killing them. Definitely.

The torture was like foreplay.

"Let me tell you exactly how your friends died." He closed his eyes and pictured the second killing. The memory rolled in his mind, clear as a video. He leaned close to the man's ear and whispered. When he'd finished describing every detail, he opened his eyes. "That's exactly what I'm going to do to you."

His victim was breathing hard too, and his entire body shook with tremors. He inhaled the scent of terror. It made him hungry for more.

He wanted this night to last forever.

# CHAPTER THIRTY-ONE

Matt leaned on Bree's SUV. A few yards away, Bree was talking with the fire chief. She shook his hand, then turned and walked back toward Matt.

The motel parking lot was a sea of first responders. An ambulance waited to take Deputy Wallace away. Two EMTs wheeled his gurney toward the open rear doors. Bree stopped to check on him. Now conscious, Wallace reached toward her. Bree gave his hand a squeeze, then backed away from the gurney. The deputy was loaded into the vehicle.

The nurse who had administered emergency first aid stood and brushed rock salt and dirty slush from her bathrobe. Blood stained the pale blue terry cloth. Bree stopped to shake her hand as well.

Bree might complain about the politics her job required, but she was actually damned good at it. She was a natural leader. She appreciated people and let them know why. Her praise felt genuine, not like bullshit.

"I drove three miles up the road." He handed Bree her keys. "No sign of Alyssa, but there are plenty of places she could have gone off the road without leaving tracks."

"Thank you." Bree rubbed her forehead, leaving a smudge of soot.

"She could have heard the gunshot and escaped before the fire was started." Possibilities spun in Matt's head. "Or he used the fire to flush her out. It's even possible she left earlier. You said she was pretty spooked when you talked to her."

"This is true. Deputy Wallace was only watching the front of her room." Bree nodded. "Todd called. One of the deputies at the university found a surveillance tape at a building near Christian's class. The tape shows Christian being forced into a Dodge Charger at gunpoint. The license plate is covered with mud, but Todd did confirm that Roger is the deceased father of Joe Marcus and that Roger had a 9mm Glock registered in his name. The bullets used to kill Brian were 9mm."

"How was the fire started?" Matt asked.

"Someone broke into the unit below Alyssa's, poured gasoline all over the beds, and set them on fire." Bree gritted her teeth. "He did this after shooting Wallace. The motel security camera recorded the entire incident. The image is grainy, but the shooter-slash-arsonist was driving a Dodge Charger. Again, we can't see the license plate, and his face is covered by a ski mask."

"No one heard the shot?" Matt asked.

"Actually, several people did. But the motel's proximity to the highway made them think it was a vehicle backfire."

"He's not being as careful or clever as he was with the first victims. This fire was bound to draw more attention than the other kidnappings. They were slick and quick. Is he losing control or getting overconfident?"

"Either way, we'd better hurry. Cross your fingers I can convince the judge." Bree climbed into the driver's seat of her SUV and dialed her phone. Matt stood next to the open vehicle door. He was thankful for the digital age as he listened to her lay out her case with the judge. With nerves on edge, Matt's toe tapped on the asphalt. Bree didn't fidget. Her entire body was still as she focused.

"Thank you, Your Honor." She lowered her phone and pressed "End." "He agreed. He'll sign the warrant electronically."

A process that used to take hours was reduced to thirty minutes. Progress.

"Congratulations," he said.

Bree exhaled. The relief in her voice made it sound as if she'd been holding her breath. "Though the judge did say I'd better be right."

"You are," Matt said.

"Let's hope so. If I'm wrong, Christian is the one who will pay." Exhaustion lines bracketed her mouth. "Time to serve that warrant."

Matt checked his watch. It was after midnight. "Let's roll."

Forty-five minutes later, Matt secured the strap on a Kevlar vest with the word SHERIFF printed on the front and back. His body hummed with nerves as he remembered being shot on a similar nighttime operation three years before. He swallowed the memory and focused on the present. Serving warrants was dangerous. He couldn't afford to be distracted.

Bree, Stella, and Todd stood in the street in front of Joe Marcus's house. The driveway was empty. No plumber's van. No Corolla.

*Where is Joe?*

They were not sneaking up on him. At the Harper house next door, Earl's dog launched into another barking frenzy. Everyone within a square mile knew they were there.

The dog barked again, and Bree startled. Beads of sweat dotted her forehead. She wiped her sleeve across her face.

Two patrol vehicles parked on the shoulder of the road. Deputies Rogers and Oscar joined the group in the street. Bree brought them up to speed with a few sentences. "Joe Marcus is armed and dangerous.

He's already killed three people. This afternoon, he kidnapped a fourth victim at gunpoint."

"Doesn't look like he's home," Matt said.

"Get the battering ram." Bree checked her own vest. "Deputy Oscar and Detective Dane, cover the back door. We don't want him getting away."

The two disappeared around the side of the house.

Rogers pulled the black metal ram, nicknamed the Enforcer, from his trunk. They moved down the driveway in the dark. Bree and Todd went to the front door and stood on opposite sides. Bree knocked hard. "Sheriff! Open the door. We have a search warrant!"

Silence ticked by for a full minute.

Bree knocked again and yelled louder. "This is the sheriff's department. I need you to open the door now or we will force entry."

When no one responded in several more minutes, she stood aside and waved Rogers forward. He swung the battering ram and breached the door in one practiced blow. They entered the dark house, flashlights and weapons pointed forward.

Bree flipped on the wall switch. Light flooded the foyer. The furniture was dark pine. The only modern element in the living room was the flat-screen TV and video game system.

The house was a three-bedroom, one-story. It didn't take long to make sure Joe wasn't home. Stella and Oscar came in the back door. Donning gloves, they split up and began their search.

"His Corolla is in the garage," Stella said. "So, he's probably driving the Charger."

"Where is he?" Bree scanned the empty kitchen. Her face was strained. "There must be some sign of where he took Christian."

"Sheriff?" Todd called from a doorway. "You need to see this."

Bree walked down the short hall that led to the bedrooms. Matt followed close behind her.

"It looks like Joe is still living in his childhood bedroom." Todd pointed into the largest bedroom. "The master is still full of his father's stuff, like a shrine or something." He led the way into a smaller bedroom. "But that's not even the creepy part."

The furniture looked like a teen's bedroom set, with a matching twin bed, dresser, and desk. An office chair had been pulled up to the desk.

"First of all," Todd said. "We found a prepaid cell phone in the drawer. It's a super cheap model with no passcode protection. It's the number on Sara's phone labeled *J*. The last call on her call log. The second bit is probably the worst thing I've ever seen."

Matt braced himself, and Bree stiffened.

Todd tapped the keyboard and woke the computer. The screen brightened to show a video of a young man tied to a chair. Brian. His hair was roughly shorn, and he'd been stripped down to his boxers. Off to the side, his clothes were folded in a pile on the floor of what looked like the Grey Lake Inn's garage. The concrete was clean.

Grim-faced, Todd clicked "Play."

Bree widened her stance, visibly bracing herself for what they all knew was coming.

Matt wanted to look away, but he didn't.

On the screen, Joe Marcus strode into view. He stood in front of Brian, leaning his face close. "Not so pretty now, are you?"

"What are you doing, man?" Brian cried. Tears ran down his face. "We weren't being serious. We didn't mean anything."

"You're a prick." Joe pulled a gun from his waistband. "An entitled little prick. You don't care about anyone except yourself. I bet you don't even know Sariah's real name is Sara. You don't really care about her, but you fucked her anyway, didn't you?"

"I care about her." Brian's voice trembled with cold and fear. His skin was pale and puckered with goose bumps. Tears flowed from his red-rimmed eyes.

"It's OK. She doesn't care about you either. You fucked her because that's what you do. She fucked you so she could steal your mother's jewelry."

Brian's spine stiffened.

"You didn't know that?" Joe shook his head. "You're fucking stupid. You thought you were using her, but she was using you. Do you know how I know? Because the little bitch turned on me first. Really, you two are perfect for each other. Not that it matters. I'm going to kill her next." Joe leveled the gun at Brian's face. "Then I'm going to kill your three asshole friends."

"No." Brian recoiled, but he could only move his head.

"I've been thinking about killing pricks like you for ages." Joe's breathing quickened. His face flushed. "Guys like you have been treating me like shit my whole life." He licked his lips. His eyes widened with excitement.

"No—" Brian cried.

Joe pulled the trigger. Brian's head snapped back as the bullet hit him in the cheek. A mist of blood hit the wall, and Brian slumped sideways. Joe's brows dropped. He looked disappointed. He pulled the trigger again. The second bullet struck Brian's forehead, but he was already dead. Not much happened beyond a spurt of blood.

Joe walked forward. With a disappointed frown, he nudged Brian's foot with the toe of a boot. Brian was clearly dead. Joe took a knife from his pocket and cut his binds. Brian's body collapsed onto the floor on its side. Joe rolled him onto his back. He paced next to the body, kicking it every couple of steps, as if the killing hadn't been satisfying.

Setting the gun aside, he grabbed a hammer from the workbench. Rage lit his face as he raised it high and brought it down on Brian's face. The result seemed to please him. He struck Brian's face again and again. When he was finished, he and the room were covered in blood and gore, but his face was oddly calm.

He sat back on his heels. A satisfied smile split his face. He faced the camera. "Now that was payback."

The video stopped. The room was silent. Matt's stomach did a queasy roll. He'd seen some sick shit in his life, but that might be the worst yet.

"Look at this, Sheriff." Stella stood in the open closet, with two open cardboard boxes at her feet. The boxes were labeled BRIAN and ELI. Inside each was a plastic bag of hair clippings. Under each bag of hair was a folded set of clothes.

"Why did he keep the clothes?" Matt asked. "Souvenirs?"

"Here's why," Todd said and pointed to the computer. In the middle of the screen was a picture of Joe wearing Brian's clothes. "He killed them, but he also wanted to *be* them."

The blood had drained from Bree's face. She opened her mouth to speak, but only a dry croak came out. She swallowed hard and cleared her throat. "We need to figure out where he took Christian. Have a couple of deputies run by the Grey Lake Inn and check the garage, but I seriously doubt he'll go back there. The whole place is still covered in crime scene tape. Any ideas?"

Matt looked out the window. Behind the house, the ice on Grey Lake shimmered in the moonlight. "Every place he's chosen so far has been on the lake."

"Let's go look at a map." Bree turned on her heel and left the room. Matt followed her outside. She strode down the driveway to her SUV and climbed behind the wheel.

Earl's dog exploded into more barking, and Bree jumped. She pressed a hand to her chest and breathed.

Matt stepped into the passenger seat. "You OK?"

"Yeah." In the light of the dashboard computer, Bree's face was colorless. She called up a map of Grey Lake. "Here's the campground." She pointed to the computer screen. "The boat ramp is here, and the Grey Lake Inn is over here."

"And Joe's house is all the way on the end of the lake. Miles from the other three locations."

"Yes," Bree said. "What's in between?"

Matt scanned the map. "Not much."

"Looks like acres and acres of wilderness."

"Can you switch to a satellite image?" Matt asked.

Bree clicked an icon, and the screen changed to an aerial view. She scrolled along the edge of the lake. "There are some buildings on the waterfront, but I can't tell what they are."

"I know this property. It's a farm." Matt pointed.

"It's too much acreage," Bree said. "There has to be a way to narrow down the territory."

Matt pulled his phone from his pocket and dialed the owner of ABC Plumbing. A groggy voice answered the call. "Mr. Hoover?"

"Who the hell is this?" Hoover asked.

"Matt Flynn, sheriff's investigator. We spoke earlier. I'm sorry to wake you, sir, but this is a matter of life or death. Has Joe Marcus worked on any jobs on Grey Lake? A place that would be empty but provide privacy, maybe some kind of vacant building."

"We've been working on the Grey Lake Estates project. Everyone in the company worked there at some point last month. But some permit issues came up, so construction has halted, and the project has been delayed. Two model homes are built. We did the rough-in work, but none of the fixtures are in yet." Mr. Hoover gave Matt an address.

"Thank you, sir." Matt ended the call and plugged the address into the GPS on his phone. "A few miles from here, there are two empty, unfinished model houses where Joe has worked recently."

Two more sheriff's cars arrived as Bree jumped out of her SUV. She assigned the two new deputies to secure Joe Marcus's house as a crime scene. "There's going to be too much evidence to rush a search of the premises. We'll find Christian, then worry about collecting evidence."

Then she called her original team outside. "We have a lead on two possible places Joe might have taken Christian." She gave everyone the addresses. "Todd, you take Oscar and Stella to the first house. Matt, Rogers, and I will check out house number two. We go in dark and silent. I don't want to spook him into doing anything."

Oscar and Rogers turned toward their patrol cars. Rogers tripped. His gait was unsteady. He was sweating and pale, looking almost feverish. Oscar grabbed his arm and asked, "You all right?"

"Fine. Leave me alone." Rogers shook off his hand. The two deputies slid into their cars.

Stella and Todd did the same.

Matt walked to Bree's SUV. Rounding the vehicle, he reached for the passenger door. Bree stood in the driveway, giving instructions for the two deputies remaining at Joe Marcus's house.

She turned away from them and headed toward Matt. Something jingled, and the sound of heavy breathing approached. Behind her, Earl's big dog raced up the driveway, aiming right for Bree. Matt's heart lurched. He started around the vehicle, knowing he'd be too late. He could not outrun a dog. The animal would reach her before Matt, and she was a good fifteen feet from her SUV.

She'd never make it.

# Chapter Thirty-Two

Bree saw the dog approach in the corner of her eye. Her heartbeat sprinted, but her body froze.

"Don't run!" Matt yelled.

But Bree couldn't run. She couldn't move. She couldn't even draw a breath. Her throat locked. Even screaming was impossible. Her feet were rooted to the ground as terror short-circuited her brain. All thought was blocked out by the dog's breath, the jingle of its collar, the muscular rush of its lean body toward her. Time slowed.

It was barely thirty feet away.

Her own pulse muffled her hearing. Her vision tunneled.

Twenty feet.

Her eyes focused on the big dog's head. Its mouth was open, its teeth shining.

"Shoot it!" someone yelled.

"I can't!" another voice shouted.

But Bree could not respond. Her body tensed, bracing itself for the impact, for the pain, for the gush of hot blood.

The dog slowed, coming to a stop about ten feet away. The beast growled, lowered its head, and side-eyed Bree. The body was stiff. The ears had been cut. The remaining triangles of cartilage were pinned back to the animal's head.

Bree still couldn't move.

Someone jumped between Bree and the dog.

*Matt.*

The minute his big body was in front of her, Bree inhaled. Oxygen hit her lungs and kick-started her brain. Even though the dog was still loose and growling, she knew she was safe. Matt would handle the animal. Humiliation washed over her, mixing with the fear in a queasy cocktail of negativity.

Crouching, Matt turned sideways to the dog. He looked at the ground in front of him and talked to the dog in a high-pitched voice. "There's a good boy."

The dog's posture softened, and it stopped growling and gave a whole-body shake.

"That's it," Matt said. "Shake off that tension."

Stiff-legged and low-bodied, the dog craned its neck toward Matt and sniffed the air.

"Who's a good boy?" Matt crooned.

The tip of the dog's docked tail quivered. Matt slowly extended a hand, and the dog sniffed it. A minute later, Matt turned his hand over and scratched the dog behind the ears. The dog shifted its body and leaned on him.

Bree's vision and hearing slowly returned to normal. A movement on the other side of the driveway caught her attention. Earl stood a few feet away from Matt. Earl's arms were crossed over his chest, and his lips were twisted into an angry scowl. He was disappointed the dog hadn't attacked her. Bree could see it in his face.

"Sorry about that. Don't know how he got loose." The lie glinted in Earl's eyes. "Rufus! Gitcha ass over here."

The dog cowered as Earl stalked closer and grabbed its collar. As he led it back toward his property, Rufus glanced at Matt over his shoulder, the dog's expression defeated.

Bree's knees were shaking so hard, she was afraid she'd fall down if she tried to walk. She gritted her teeth and forced her body to turn around.

Todd was a dozen feet away, his gun drawn, a *what the hell?* look on his face. He'd done what Bree should have done: prepared to eliminate a threat. No one wants to shoot a dog, but sometimes you didn't have a choice.

Too embarrassed—and too shaken—to respond to Todd's questioning expression, she walked toward her vehicle. She had a killer to catch. She'd better shake off this weak-kneed crap.

She was grateful that Oscar, Rogers, and Stella were in their vehicles at the time. Maybe they hadn't seen. But Todd definitely had. Bree slid behind the wheel. Her hands trembled. It took her three tries to get the key in the ignition.

Matt climbed into the passenger seat. "Take a deep breath."

"I don't have time to take a deep breath. We're trying to save someone tonight."

"Earl let that dog loose on purpose."

"I know." She started the engine and pulled away from the curb.

"The dog isn't vicious. It's afraid."

"My actions—or lack thereof—weren't rational." Tasting bitterness, she punched the gas pedal. "Thank you. If you hadn't intervened, I don't know what would have happened."

"Todd was almost in position to shoot the dog," Matt said. "You would have been all right."

"Not because of anything I did." Bree was disgusted with herself. She had a perfectly good firearm on her hip. Her Glock was enough to stop a pit bull. Yet she'd just stood there, useless.

"You held your ground. If you had run, you might have engaged its prey instinct, and the situation could have turned out much worse."

Bree's voice was a rasp. "I didn't *hold my ground*. I froze. I was not functional."

Matt sighed. "No one is perfect, Bree. Not even you."

The dog had upended every nerve in Bree's body. Her stomach roiled. Under her body armor, sweat soaked her shirt.

"Are you all right to drive?" Matt asked.

"Yes." Bree had better be. She gathered her willpower and shoved the dog encounter to the back of her mind. She'd deal with it tomorrow.

The three-mile drive took ten minutes. Bree stopped the vehicle on the side of the road. The rest of the team had already parked their cars on the shoulder of the road near the construction entrance of the development. A hundred yards away, the shells of two large houses squatted on waterfront lots. Oscar, Rogers, Stella, and Todd stood in a circle next to Todd's cruiser.

*They're waiting for you. Get your act together.*

Bree got out of the car and approached the group. "We'll walk from here. No flashlights unless absolutely necessary. I don't want to alert him to our presence."

"Yes, ma'am," Todd said.

Bree grabbed a pair of binoculars and a small tool kit from her vehicle. Blocking every thought that didn't relate to the job at hand, Bree checked her armor and weapon. Rogers and Oscar pulled their AR-15s from their trunks. Stella drew her Glock from its holster.

The team split up. Bree veered right, Matt and Rogers close behind her. Todd, Stella, and Oscar turned left and headed for the other house. Sunshine earlier in the day had melted the snow, leaving mud that was refreezing in the cold night air. A thin layer of ice crunched under their boots. They approached the house. White house wrap covered the exteriors, and the windows had been installed. Would that be enough to muffle the sounds of her team's approach?

The house was huge, at least six thousand square feet, with a two-story open foyer and a three-car attached garage. The windows were dark. Bree led the way. She stopped when the house was in sight and looked through her binoculars. "I can't see inside. The windows are too high."

Matt scanned the surroundings. "There's no high ground."

"We'll make a circuit around the house." Bree made a circling motion in the air with her forefinger. "Let's see if we can locate Joe and Christian inside the house before we go in."

The under-construction neighborhood was wide open with little available cover. Bree held her breath as her team jogged across the open lots, moonlight guiding their way. They stopped at the front of the house. Behind it, she could see the moon reflecting on the frozen lake.

Matt and Rogers crouched on either side of the concrete stoop. Bree went up the steps and glanced in the narrow window next to the door. The house was dark inside. If Joe was in there, he'd need some sort of light. She made a circular motion in the air with her right forefinger. Weapon in hand, she jogged around the side of the house. Rogers and Matt stayed close. The windows were over their heads. Bree gestured for Matt to give her a boost. While Rogers covered them with his AR, Matt laced his fingers, and Bree stepped into them. He boosted her so she could see in the window. They repeated the process at each window. But Bree saw no one. At the last window, she grabbed the windowsill with both hands and peered over the top. Moonlight streamed in through a rear window. The room was empty.

Was this not the right house?

She glanced at the other house, but she couldn't see the rest of her team.

Bree felt the first chills of panic as she jumped down and whispered, "There's no one there."

Matt motioned for her to keep moving toward the back of the house. They passed a pile of construction materials: pallets of shingles, a roll of orange safety fencing, lumber, and bags of ready-to-mix con-crete encased in clear plastic. They rounded the corner. A light at Bree's feet caught her attention. She motioned toward it with her weapon. Someone had nailed plywood over the narrow basement window, but light leaked around the edges of the wood.

Bree crouched and listened. She heard the murmur of voices. Someone was down there.

# Chapter Thirty-Three

Matt listened. He couldn't identify the voice or the words, but the tone sounded male.

They needed to get into the basement, and they couldn't go through the window. It would take too long to kick the board out and shimmy through the tight opening one at a time. Joe was armed. He would shoot whoever went first. They'd be dead before their feet hit the floor. They needed to find a door.

Matt motioned for them to continue around the back of the house. Matt spotted a set of french doors, but the threshold was five feet in the air, clearly designed to open onto a deck that hadn't been built yet. They stopped at the opposite corner, at a regular exterior door. Moonlight shone through the panes on the top half of the door. Matt shielded his eyes and peered through the glass. The shape of the room and placement of pipes in the wall suggested this would be a laundry room.

Bree gestured for them to lean closer. She whispered, "We need to get inside and find the stairs. I'm going to pick the lock. Cover me."

Rogers adjusted the grip on his rifle. Bree holstered her gun and reached into her pocket for her small tool kit. She pulled out two slim metal tools and inserted them into the lock. The mechanism clicked softly. Returning the tool kit to her pocket, she drew her weapon again and eased the door open. Bree slipped inside. Matt let Rogers, who was carrying the AR-15, go next. Unarmed, Matt felt less than useful. He pulled his knife out of his pocket and unfolded it. The knife didn't require as much finesse as pulling a trigger.

The inside rooms were roughed out with drywall but no doors had yet been hung. Particleboard covered the floor. Matt walked near the edge of the wall to minimize the chance of the subfloor squeaking. They eased through the laundry room and emerged into a short hallway. His heart thudded, and under the body armor, sweat dripped down his back.

They moved slowly, trying to be quiet. The hallway opened into a large room. Pipes protruding from the wall indicated this would be the kitchen. Construction materials littered the floor. Faint light shone through an open doorway. Bree went to the opening and cocked her head.

Matt stepped over a spool of electrical wire, moved closer, and listened.

Joe's voice floated up the stairs. "You're going to die." He sounded gleeful.

Matt thought of the video of Joe killing Brian. Murdering three people had bolstered his confidence.

"Why?" In contrast, Christian's words quaked with terror. If Joe had stayed true to his MO, Christian was probably also freezing. There was no heat in this unfinished house.

Bree eased down another step.

"Because you're an entitled little prick," Joe said. "A rich, useless shithead who girls want to fuck just because he's privileged enough to be born rich and good-looking. You won a genetic lottery. Instead of using your advantage for real benefit, you chose to be a douchebag."

"I don't understand," Christian cried. "What does that have to do with you? I'm sorry we treated you like shit. Sometimes we're assholes. But that's no reason to kill people."

"Sure, it is. Killing your friends made me feel a whole lot better about myself. I'm excited to kill you. I'm making the world a better place. If all of you privileged assholes are gone, women will have to consider guys like me. Guys who work for a living and earn their own place in the world."

Christian didn't respond, but then what could he say? Joe was a nutter. An armed and angry nutter.

"Please, don't do this," a female voice cried.

*Alyssa?*

"I'll do whatever the fuck I want!" Joe shouted. "You're hardly innocent, sweetheart."

"No one was supposed to die!" Alyssa yelled. "You killed Harper."

"That's what happens when you blackmail someone." Joe's voice was condescending. "Why do you care, anyway? Sara played you. She dragged you into her stealing scheme too. She was going to double-cross you just like she did me. She was running with all the stuff *you* helped her steal. Now the police have the jewelry, and we're screwed. All that work for nothing."

"I made some mistakes," Alyssa admitted. "But killing him won't get the jewelry back."

"Killing him has nothing to do with the stuff we stole," Joe said. "Burglary was work. This is pure pleasure."

"So, I guess you're going to kill me too?" Alyssa said, her voice shifting from fear to bitter resignation.

"You didn't leave me a choice. You called the sheriff!" Joe screamed.

"Because you shot Harper!" Alyssa screamed back.

Joe lowered his voice. "Shut up or I'll shoot you right now. I should have killed you already. I shouldn't have brought you here, but I thought maybe I could talk you into being on my side." Joe's voice slid from angry to lonely to sullen. "But you're just like the rest of them. You don't understand me either."

Bree eased down a step. Rogers didn't move, and Matt nearly ran into him. Sweat shone on the deputy's forehead, and his face looked pasty in the moonlight coming through the bare windows. His fingers opened and closed on the rifle in his hands. His eyes were open wide enough to show the whites.

Matt felt the nerves swirling in his gut, but Rogers looked more than nervous. He looked terrified. But there was no time to reassure him or take stock of his condition.

Bree crouched low and craned her neck as if she was trying to see more of the basement. Rogers should have gone next, but he seemed to be frozen in place. His eyes had gone wide with fear, like Bree's earlier, when the dog had rushed her. Matt jostled him with an elbow, but the deputy didn't react.

Bree looked back. Her face was alarmed as she scanned Rogers. She jerked her chin toward the rifle and then inclined her head at Matt. Rogers plastered his back to the wall and trembled.

Matt's pulse hammered as he pulled the AR-15 out of Rogers's hands. He was grateful that it was a long gun. Someone had to cover Bree, and he could shoot a rifle much better than a handgun with his left hand. Bree eased down another step. Matt passed Rogers and started down the steps, moving swiftly to catch up with Bree. She shouldn't have to face Joe alone.

The next step squeaked under Bree's boot. A shot rang out, and wood splintered near her foot.

# CHAPTER THIRTY-FOUR

A chunk of wood struck Bree's cheek, but the pain of the sting faded almost instantly as adrenaline roared through her bloodstream. She jumped off the steps, ducking for cover behind the wooden staircase. Glancing up, she saw Matt rushing down the steps.

Across the basement, Christian was seated, his wrists bound together behind the back of the chair. His ankles were tied to the chair legs. His hair had been shorn so closely that the shears had left bloody tracks on his scalp. Dressed only in boxer shorts, he shivered so hard Bree could see the movement from more than twenty feet away.

Alyssa was bound to a support beam on the other side of the room. Her face was streaked with soot and tears. She cringed behind the metal pole, and she looked unsteady. Joe stood behind Christian, aiming a handgun at Matt. But Matt was at least twenty feet away and moving fast. Joe's second shot also missed. Joe crouched, peering over Christian's shoulder and using him as a shield. He was dressed in a thick gray sweatshirt and jeans. A coat was tossed on the concrete nearby.

Bree had no clear shot at Joe.

Matt jumped off the steps, landing next to Bree in a crouch. Dropping to one knee, he rested the rifle across the third step and took aim, his left index finger on the trigger.

"This is the sheriff, Joe," Bree called. "Put down the gun. You don't have to die here tonight."

Joe pressed the gun to Christian's head. "I'm not the one who's going to die tonight. If you don't let me go, I'm going to kill him."

"He's the only thing keeping you alive," Bree called.

"No shit." Joe shifted his gun to his left hand. He pulled a knife from his pocket and cut the binds around Christian's ankles. Pocketing his knife, he yanked Christian to his feet. He kicked the chair to its side, clearing Christian's arms, which were still bound behind his back. "Move back, Sheriff, or I'm going to kill him."

"Why should I let you out of here?" Bree asked. "You're going to kill him anyway."

"That's the chance you'll just have to take." Joe advanced. He chicken-winged Christian's arm behind his back and forced him to walk forward. "Drop the gun, or he's dead."

Tears streamed down Christian's face, and his eyes pleaded.

Joe dug the muzzle of the gun into the back of Christian's head until he cried out in pain.

Next to Bree, Matt's body was rigid with frustrated tension. Bree knew he didn't have a shot either. Joe was keeping Christian's body in front of his. Bree couldn't risk the young man's life. She hoped Joe saw Christian as his ticket out of that basement and kept him alive.

Bree lowered her gun and set it on the floor. "OK, Joe. You win. Don't hurt him."

Triumph glowed in Joe's eyes. "Tell your man to put his gun down too. And both of you back up."

Matt set the rifle on the floor and took two steps back. "He's the only reason you're not dead."

"Keep backing up, all the way to the wall," Joe said. "I'm not going to let you jump me."

Bree and Matt continued to move until their backs were pressed against the cinder blocks. Shuffling awkwardly, Joe pulled his victim up the staircase. He kept the muzzle of his gun pressed to Christian's head. Christian's movements were stiff, and he was trembling. He was barefoot, and his feet were probably numb from the cold. He tripped on the fourth step. Joe held his arm at a ruthless angle, and all Christian's weight fell onto his twisted arm. Bree heard a pop as Christian's shoulder dislocated. His face contorted in agony. He looked as if he'd pass out.

Joe transferred his grip to the other arm. "Keep going or I'll do the other one."

Christian stumbled backward up the stairs.

Bree crossed her fingers that Rogers had recovered from what had appeared to be a panic attack, but she doubted it. The one she'd suffered earlier hadn't ended until the threat was gone. Joe and Christian hit the top of the stairwell and stepped through the open doorway onto the first floor. A body launched at Joe, hitting him midbody. A scuffle sounded.

*Rogers!*

Matt grabbed the AR-15 off the floor and ran up the stairs. Bree scooped up her Glock and raced after him. They reached the top of the steps. On the plywood subfloor, Rogers and Joe struggled for possession of the gun. Christian had fallen to his knees, frozen in shock. A gunshot boomed. Joe stepped away from Rogers, immediately yanking Christian in front of him again. Rogers dropped to the floor and clutched at his leg. Bree aimed for Joe, but the little bastard excelled at keeping his human shield in place. He dragged Christian to his feet, across the floor, and toward the hallway that led to the laundry room. He backed out of the room. A door slammed.

Blood had already pooled on the floor under Rogers. Bree pulled the combat tourniquet off her belt and tossed it at Matt. "Stop the bleeding and call an ambulance."

Without waiting for him to agree, she raced after the killer and his victim.

At the laundry room door, she skidded to a stop and looked for Joe. Through the open door, she could see him running through the backyard. No doubt he was headed for his car parked in the trees out front. But sirens approached from that direction. Joe stopped and looked around. Then he pulled Christian toward the frozen lake. Bree went through the door and sprinted after them. Her thighs burned as she dug her feet into the ground and reached for more speed.

On the ice, Joe and Christian slid the first few steps, then adjusted to the slippery footing. But their progress was slow. Christian was barefoot and injured. No matter how hard he tried to keep up, he couldn't. Thirty feet from the edge of the lake, he stumbled. Joe was half dragging him now.

Bree leaped from the bank. Her boots hit the ice with a cracking sound. Sliding, she kept her balance and forward momentum as she sorted out her stride on the frozen lake. She was gaining on them. She prayed that Joe would realize he had to let go of Christian or she would overtake him.

Then she would run his ass down.

Ahead, Christian stumbled again and fell to his knees. The ice cracked, the sound traveling across the lake and echoing. *No!* Bree's lungs locked up as the ice opened up beneath them and both men fell through into the freezing water.

Bree slid to a stop, her feet and arms spread for balance, holding her breath as she waited. Would the ice underneath *her* break? Nothing happened. She breathed, then took three steps forward, toward the men in the water.

A loud crack stopped her cold. She lowered her body to her belly, lying facedown and sprawling to distribute her weight across as much of the ice's surface as possible.

The ice held, and she began belly crawling to the edge of the hole in the ice. Neither man was visible. They'd both gone under.

# CHAPTER THIRTY-FIVE

Cursing, Matt applied the tourniquet to Rogers's leg. The bullet must have hit something vital. Rogers was bleeding like a slaughtered deer. He groaned as Matt tightened the strap of the tourniquet. Then he pulled out his phone. Sirens sounded in the distance as he requested an ambulance, then he called Todd.

Todd responded in a breathless voice. "We heard the shots. We're on our way."

"Rogers is in the back of the house," Matt said. "He's bleeding badly. I'm going after Bree."

Rogers's eyes rolled into the back of his head. Matt pulled the tourniquet tighter. He couldn't leave Rogers alone.

"Help!" Alyssa shouted from the basement. "Help me!"

Matt raced back down the stairs. He used his knife to cut the zip ties binding Alyssa's wrists behind the metal support pole. "I'm trusting you to not run. I need you to help him."

Matt ran back up the steps.

"OK." Rubbing her wrists, Alyssa followed Matt.

He stripped off his jacket and pressed it to Rogers's leg. "Keep pressure on this."

She didn't hesitate but put both hands on the jacket and leaned her body weight into her arms. Her eyes were traumatized, but her jaw was set in determination.

"I can count on you to stay here, right?" he asked. "I need to help the sheriff."

She nodded. "Please, stop him."

Matt looked out the french door. He scanned the back of the property and spotted Bree's dark form facedown and spread-eagle on the pale, frozen lake. A few feet ahead of her, a hole in the ice told Matt exactly what had happened. Something moved in the hole. A head, bobbing.

Everything inside Matt went bone-cold.

Joe and Christian had fallen through, and Bree was on the ice. Despite the danger of the lake swallowing her too, she would try to save them.

Matt turned and looked around the room. This was a construction site. There had to be something here he could use as a rope. He spotted a spool of electrical cord. It would have to do. He grabbed the spool and the AR-15 from the floor. He slung the rifle over his back by the strap. He opened the french door and jumped out. He flexed his knees to absorb the landing, then sprinted for the lake. He stopped at the edge. He weighed more than Bree. He might make the situation worse.

He cupped his hands around his mouth and shouted, "Bree!"

She glanced over her shoulder and saw him. "Stop!" she yelled as she pulled her body forward by her elbows. "The ice won't hold you."

"Wait!" He began unraveling the electrical cord.

The ice cracked, the sound rippling across the lake. Bree barely paused for a second before continuing to slither across the ice. Christian had been bound. When he went through the ice, he must have sunk like a brick. Matt knew what Bree was going to do.

"Wait!" He let out the cord as fast as he could. Then he tied a slip-knot at the end and quickly coiled the cord.

She was going into the water after Christian.

# CHAPTER THIRTY-SIX

Bree dragged her body toward the hole. Her heart rammed against her rib cage as if it no longer wanted to be inside her body. She didn't blame it. She didn't want to be here either.

But she couldn't find Christian just in time, then let him die. Ten feet ahead, a hand clawed at the edge of the ice. The large red mark on the back of the hand was bright red. The arm that followed wore a sleeve.

*Joe.*

He hoisted himself out of the ice on his belly and dragged his legs out of the water. As soon as his feet were clear, he rolled away from the hole. Bree crawled faster, her gaze darting from Joe to the water, where there was no sign of Christian.

"Bree!" Matt called.

She glanced back. Matt held a coil of what looked like electrical cord in his hand. He heaved the coil at Bree underhand, like he was bowling. The coil slid across the ice. She caught it. Matt had tied a loop in the end of the cord, which she appreciated. Her fingers were too cold to have managed it. She shimmied into the loop and tightened it around her waist.

She pushed visions of Kayla and Luke from her mind. Christian was someone's kid too. Bree couldn't not risk her life to save him because she was afraid of leaving her niece and nephew without a guardian. Christian could be alive in the water. She imagined his terror. Under the ice in the dark, unable to swim with his hands bound.

Helpless.

Then she continued to inch forward. Back on the shore, Matt was tying the cord to a tree near the edge of the lake. At least if she drowned, Matt could recover her body.

Joe saw her. His gaze locked on hers. Anger and resentment passed through his eyes, then he looked at the hole in the ice and an insane smile spread across his face. "Fuck you, Sheriff." He climbed to his feet and took a few shaky steps away. After scooping his gun off the ice where he must have dropped it, he staggered away.

Bree had no time to worry about him. She'd reached the hole. The water shimmered darkly as she plunged both hands into it. The cold-shock stole her breath. She reached as far down as she could, but she felt no body.

Where was Christian?

*No.*

Panic scrambled in her chest.

*He can't die.*

She did the last thing she wanted to do. She stripped off the outer layers that would weigh her down in the water: jacket, body armor, and boots. Then she slid into the hole feetfirst. Even though she'd expected the deep freeze, the intensity of the cold stunned her. Hypothermia would set in quickly. She didn't have much time. She had to find Christian now. She moved her feet around, stretching them as far as possible, but she felt nothing.

After taking a huge breath, she let herself go under. The water closed over her head. Even with her eyes closed, the cold froze her eyeballs. She was barely submerged when her feet touched the bottom.

The lake was about six feet deep here. She felt around with her toes. Nothing. She surfaced again and gasped. Her body was quickly going painfully numb.

Christian's hands were tied behind his back. He would have been helpless, unable to keep himself afloat. He would have sunk to the bottom, but he should be close to the hole.

*Please, let him be here.*

She filled her lungs, went under again, and opened her eyes. The water was too dark and murky to see anything. She closed them again and felt her way along the bottom with her toes. Her feet encountered nothing but mud and weeds. She pushed toward the surface. But her head hit solid ice. She was no longer below the hole. She opened her eyes, the cold blinding her. The solid ice above her was barely lighter than the darkness below.

Her mouth opened, and water rushed in, choking her. Panic nearly shut down her brain and body, but she felt for the electrical cord around her waist and followed it, hand over hand, to the hole. She'd only been three feet away, and she'd nearly drowned in panic.

Her head broke the surface, and she sucked in air. She could not stay in the water much longer and survive. Her heart was stuttering, beating wildly, erratically, panicking inside her chest as if it knew her system would shut down soon. Her hands were losing strength, and her fingers were wooden. She could barely hold on to the cord. Fighting her own instincts, she went under again, fanning out both legs.

Something brushed her knee. She grabbed it. An arm?

Summoning strength she didn't have, she pulled the dead weight to the surface. Christian was dressed only in boxers, and his skin was slippery. She pulled his head clear of the water. He bobbed and almost went under again. Bree threw one arm over the edge of the ice and wrapped the other under his chin, but she could not haul him out of the water. She didn't have the leverage of her feet on the bottom or the strength to get him out of the lake with just her arms. She tried to untie the electrical cord from her own waist, intending to secure Christian instead, but her fingers wouldn't cooperate. She'd lost her dexterity.

"Christian," she croaked. "I'm sorry."

He didn't answer. His skin was gray and his body lifeless. He wasn't breathing.

# CHAPTER THIRTY-SEVEN

Matt grabbed the roll of orange safety fencing and ran for the lake. He spotted Bree's head above water. She was holding Christian up as well, but just barely. Even from the shore, Matt could see her grip slipping. She went under again for a brief second but managed to slap her arm back up on the ice. Her grip on Christian never faltered.

She would die before she would let go.

Matt wrapped the orange fencing around the tree a couple of times. Then he unrolled it across the ice like a horizonal rope ladder. Lowering himself to his belly, he army-crawled out onto the lake.

"Hold on, Bree," he shouted. "I'm coming."

She didn't answer.

He moved as fast as possible. The ice groaned under his body, but it held as long as he kept his weight spread out. He reached the hole just as Bree's arm slipped off the ice. She and Christian went under. Matt plunged his arms into the water. The cold hit his injured hand like a knife. He grabbed Bree and pulled her up. Her eyes were closed. Her grip on Christian loosened. Matt reached for the young man and managed to get ahold of his arm.

Bree opened her eyes. "Get him out first."

She was tied to the tree, but if Christian went under, Matt might not find him again. As much as he didn't want to let go of her, he needed to release her to pull Christian out of the water.

Matt pushed the orange mesh into the water. Bree shoved her hands through the holes and locked her arms in at the elbows. Matt used both hands to haul Christian out onto the ice. He was cold and unmoving. His skin was as pale as the ice he lay upon.

Matt turned to Bree. She was trying to climb the mesh, but her movements were clumsy with cold. Matt grabbed her by the belt and pulled her onto the ice.

Teeth chattering, she rolled away from the hole. "Take. Him."

Matt slid Christian along, using the safety fence as leverage. Bree grabbed her jacket, vest, and boots, then moved toward shore. When they reached land, Matt dragged Christian onto the bank. Bree crawled onto the ground and collapsed, coughing.

Todd and Stella ran to meet them. Stella had brought blankets and a first aid kit from her vehicle. She covered Christian while Todd began CPR. Stella dropped to her knees beside Christian, pinched his nose, and covered his mouth with her own. She gave him rescue breaths, then waited as Todd counted chest compressions.

"Ambulances will be here in a few minutes," Todd said. "I called the state police for assistance. Oscar is with Rogers. The girl is still there too."

Christian coughed up a lungful of water. Stella rolled him to his side and rubbed his back.

Bree shoved her feet into her boots, then put on her vest and jacket. She checked her weapon and looked at Matt. Her lips were blue, she was shivering almost uncontrollably, and blood ran from a cut on her cheek. "I'm going after Joe," she said between the chattering of her teeth.

Matt didn't bother trying to stop her, but he wouldn't let her go alone. He swung the rifle around to his hands. "I'm with you."

They set off jogging along the shoreline. Bree must have been operating on sheer stubbornness.

Matt flexed and released his grip on the butt of the AR-15. "I doubt he got far, not after being submerged in the lake."

"He's wet. He has to be developing hypothermia if he's still outside." Bree barely kept pace next to him. Her strides were uneven, and her breathing was ragged. How was she still on her feet?

Five minutes later, they ran behind a cedar-sided lakefront house. Matt heard music and laughing. He glanced over his shoulder to see people gathered around a firepit in the backyard. A party.

He turned back to the lake and spotted a figure stumbling on the ice toward the dock. "There he is!"

But Joe saw them too. He changed course and moved unsteadily toward the center of the lake.

Bree cupped her hand around her mouth and yelled, "Joe, the ice is weak. You can't get away!"

Joe wobbled, but he kept going. He looked like he could barely stay upright. The ice groaned and cracked again, the sound reverberating across the lake, and he veered toward the shore again. Matt pressed forward. He drew ahead of Bree.

Matt intercepted Joe at the shore. Joe pulled out his handgun. The hand that held the gun trembled. Behind him, Matt heard more laughter. He couldn't let Joe take a shot and risk the partygoers being hit by stray bullets.

He turned the AR-15 at Joe. "Drop the gun."

"No. I won't go in." Joe's voice was surprisingly strong. His words trembled from cold but not fear. He'd made a decision. "I can't go to prison."

Matt knew what he'd chosen before it played out. His gut twisted. Matt didn't want to kill him. He wanted him to pay for what he'd done.

"You don't have to die, Joe." Matt looked down the barrel and took aim.

But Joe's eyes were defeated, his jaw clenched, and his posture went rigid. "Fuck you."

The scene seemed to slide into slow motion. Joe met Matt's gaze. He raised the gun to point it at Matt. Training took over, and Matt pulled the trigger twice.

Joe didn't move for a few seconds. He looked down at his chest, then up at the night sky. Finally, he fell backward onto his ass, his arms outspread. His head bounced twice on the ice. He dropped his gun, and it skittered toward the shoreline.

Panting, Bree reached the edge of the lake and stopped next to Matt. "You had to do it. If he had fired, he could have hit those kids."

"I know." Matt eased a few feet out onto the lake, careful of his footing, his weapon still pointing at Joe. Adrenaline flooded his system. His vision narrowed to view only the threat, and his hearing was muffled by the sound of his own pulse. The ice cracked. A long line cleaved across the lake.

"Stop." Bree had her phone out. "The ice is breaking up."

"He could still be alive." Matt stared at Joe. The moonlight was bright, and Matt could see a dark stain had spread across Joe's sweatshirt.

Bree met his eyes for a second.

They both knew the odds that Joe was alive were slim. But she understood. She scanned the area. She pointed to the house in front of them. "There's a kayak under that deck. We'll use that to get to him."

Matt ran back to the house and untied the kayak and paddle from its winter storage place under the deck. He dragged it down to the water and pushed it onto the lake. The boat broke through, but it was slow going. Five full minutes passed before Matt reached Joe. Joe's eyes were open and unfocused. Matt touched the side of his neck. No pulse. He was dead.

Matt pulled his body across the front of the kayak and paddled back to shore. The return trip was easier, with the ice already broken.

Bree helped him drag the boat ashore. They both stared at the body for a few seconds.

"You couldn't have saved him," Bree said, apparently reading his mind. "You hit him dead center in the chest with two shots." Her voice was grim, but matter-of-fact. "We both know the damage an AR-15 does."

Normal bullet wounds caused lacerations. Even a handgun shot to the heart could be survivable with prompt medical treatment. But an AR-15 fires a bullet at high speed. The velocity causes a huge swath of damage. It explodes bone and shatters organs. The bullets had likely shredded Joe's heart. Matt swallowed a wave of nausea.

"Joe aimed his gun at you knowing exactly what would happen," Bree said, her voice low. "He made you shoot him. It was suicide by cop—or almost cop."

"I know." Matt had fired at center body mass, exactly the way he'd been trained. He wished he hadn't been forced to pull the trigger. He couldn't regret stopping Joe before he killed another person, but Matt would have one more traumatic memory to live with for the rest of his life. "He was a murderer. I don't know why I care."

"The fact that you didn't want him to die has nothing to do with who he was and everything to do with who you are," Bree said. "You're a good man, Matt Flynn."

# CHAPTER THIRTY-EIGHT

After a state trooper arrived and took control of Joe's body, Bree made her way back to the construction site on rubbery legs. She was frozen, inside and out.

Matt walked at her side. "Hard to believe it's over."

Under her jacket, her clothes were wet. Every minute or so, she was gripped in a bout of insane shivering. Her teeth rattled in her head. Her emotions were as numb as her body. Too much had happened that night to process.

Two ambulances were parked in front of the house where Joe had kept Christian and Alyssa hostage. Christian was already loaded into the back of the first ambulance. The EMT at his side was grim-faced. One glance reassured Bree that Christian was breathing, and his heart was beating. That was more than she had hoped for earlier. She didn't waste time with questions. The ambulance driver closed the rear doors and jumped behind the wheel. Lights flashed and the siren wailed as the vehicle drove away.

She watched it disappear. "How long do you think he was submerged?"

Matt lifted a palm. "I have no idea. Five minutes? Maybe ten. I lost track of time."

"Me too." To Bree, it had felt like ages. "He could still die."

Matt reached over, gave her hand a squeeze, then released it.

She continued to the second ambulance. Rogers was being loaded into the back. His eyes were closed. He wore an oxygen mask, and an IV line snaked out from under a pile of blankets.

Bree touched her deputy's forearm. "How is he?" she asked the EMT.

"We've controlled the bleeding, but he lost a lot of blood." The EMT fastened a strap over Rogers's blanketed body.

Bree worried about his emotional state as well, but his mental health would have to be addressed later. She went looking for Alyssa. Everyone except Joe had survived, and Bree could accept those results.

In front of the house, Stella handcuffed Alyssa and put her in the back of her SFPD cruiser. The sight depressed Bree.

"She was involved in a string of burglaries that ended in three—nearly four—murders," Matt said, as if he could read Bree's mind.

"I know. She's not innocent."

"Maybe Sara Harper took advantage of her," Matt suggested.

"Doesn't excuse her from withholding information. She knew more than she would admit from the very beginning. She wanted our protection, but she wasn't honest with us. If she'd been up-front, she might have prevented Christian's kidnapping and this entire nightmare." Bree waved a hand in the air. "So, why do I even care what happens to her?"

"But it's more complicated than that," Matt said. "To echo your statement to me earlier, you care because that's who you are."

"Maybe," Bree said. *Complicated* didn't even begin to describe this case. "The burglary case belongs to the Scarlet Falls PD. It's out of my hands, which is probably for the best." Bree was too emotionally involved. She'd seen Luke's grief in Alyssa's loss of her father. From the very beginning, Bree had drawn personal parallels. "I don't feel as if I was completely objective."

"Stella seems to be a good cop. I don't see her railroading Alyssa with charges she didn't earn."

"No," Bree said.

"But you'd feel better if she had a good attorney looking out for her."

Bree snorted. "Not something that's ever happened to me before."

"Sometimes you have to do what's right, not what's expected."

"Know any good defense attorneys?" Bree asked.

"Ironically, the best in the area is Stella's sister, Morgan Dane."

"That *is* ironic," Bree said. "But Alyssa has no money. She can't afford the best."

"Morgan Dane has a reputation for taking pro bono cases. I know her husband. I'll see if I can get to Morgan in a roundabout way."

"That would be best. A sheriff's department employee can't interfere with a different department's case."

"Of course not," Matt said. "Now can I drive you to the ER to get your face stitched?"

Bree touched her cheek. Her fingers came away red. Blood was dripping down her face. "I guess. I'd like to keep tabs on Christian and Rogers anyway. Todd can handle things here."

But she spent a half hour issuing instructions before she climbed into the passenger seat of her SUV. Normally, she liked to drive. Yes, she had control issues. But tonight, she was content to hand over the keys to Matt.

An hour later, Bree sat on a gurney in the triage area of the ER, diagnosed with mild hypothermia. She felt like she'd never be warm again. The cold pack on her cheek wasn't helping. She was chilled from the inside out. Adrenaline letdown had left her shaky, with a steady low-level anxiety that made her slightly ill. Under the heated blanket, her foot tapped on the gurney.

The curtain was whisked aside. Bree startled as a nurse came into her cubicle to take her vital signs.

"How do you feel?" the nurse asked.

"I'm fine," Bree said. "Where's the doctor?"

"He'll be along soon, Sheriff." The nurse sighed.

Bree might have asked the same question a dozen times. She would have gone looking for him herself—if she had pants. But there was no way she was putting on her cold, wet uniform.

"Do you have an update on Christian Crone?" Bree asked.

"No, ma'am. HIPAA regulations." The nurse left.

"Of course."

"Knock knock," Matt called from the other side of the curtain.

"Come in," Bree said.

Matt came into the room. He set a duffel bag on the end of the gurney. He'd driven to the station to pick up a dry uniform for her. "How's the face?"

"Doesn't hurt too much." Bree looked for signs of trauma in his eyes. Two months ago, she'd killed a man. The fact that he'd deserved it hadn't made it easier. Matt would suffer for what Joe had made him do as well.

"Are you all right?" she asked.

"I will be," he said. "Eventually."

Ironically, that he didn't deny the difficulty was reassuring.

"Did you call Dana?" he asked.

"Yes. Thankfully, the kids slept through all the breaking news reports, and I should be home in time for breakfast." Bree grabbed the bag and pushed him on the other side of the curtain to change into the dry uniform. She tugged on wool socks. Her boots were under the plastic chair in the corner. She shoved her feet into them, then put the plastic bag of wet clothes in the duffel bag and tossed her body armor on top. After securing her duty belt and weapon around her waist, she opened the curtain.

"You still need your face stitched." Matt stepped closer. "Where are you going?"

"I don't know." But Bree felt like she had to keep moving, as if stopping would allow her nerves to catch up with her.

Matt pulled the curtain closed again and wrapped his arms around her.

"What are you doing?" Bree stiffened.

"Just give me a damned minute. We're alone."

Bree leaned into him. At first, the embrace felt like indulgence. But some of the tension eased from her muscles, and the physical contact shifted into something Bree couldn't quite identify. Something she had never experienced. He smoothed out her pulse and soothed her nerves. She closed her eyes and breathed in the scents of smoke, lake water, and sweat that clung to him. They could have died tonight, but they hadn't. Their physical contact was affirmation of their survival, though that wasn't all this hug was about.

But she was too tired to analyze it. For now, she was just going to experience it. Whatever it was, she felt ten times better when he released her a minute later.

He stepped back. "Thank you."

"I feel like I should say that back." The post-adrenaline anxiety spinning through Bree's gut had calmed.

Footsteps approached in the hallway. Matt opened the curtain, and Bree spotted the doctor heading in her direction.

"I called a plastic surgeon in to stitch your face," he said, inspecting the wound.

"How long will that take?" Bree asked.

He checked the time on a wall clock. "He'll be here in an hour."

"OK." Call her superficial, but Bree didn't want a big scar on her face. Plus, she wasn't leaving the hospital until Rogers was out of danger.

"I'll be back. I need to check on my deputy down the hall. He's going into surgery."

The doctor checked her chart. "Your body temperature is still low."

"I'll get some hot coffee," she promised.

The doctor nodded. "See that you do."

"Thank you." Bree stopped at the other end of the same ER hallway, where Christian was being treated for near-drowning and hypothermia. Outside a curtained-off cubicle, a middle-aged couple huddled on plastic chairs in the hallway.

"Sheriff!" The woman reached for Bree with both hands, enfolding her into an embrace. "I'm Christian's mother."

Bree missed her first name.

Christian's father was next with a bear hug. "We don't know how to thank you."

Bree returned his fierce hug, then held him at arm's length. "You're welcome. Just take care of him."

His mother wiped tears from her cheeks. "We will. Don't worry."

"He's going to be all right?" Bree asked.

"They're keeping him for a day or so in case he has complications, but he's awake and alert," she said. "We're grateful."

"Good luck," Bree said. "We will eventually need a statement from Christian, but we can wait until he's feeling up to it."

His parents hugged her again before they let her walk away.

Bree scanned the hall and saw Deputy Oscar standing next to a glass-walled room in the trauma area. Through the glass, she could see Rogers lying in the bed. IV lines ran into both arms, and a heart monitor beeped in a steady rhythm. Bree hurried toward the room.

Matt put his back to the wall next to Oscar. "I'll wait out here."

Bree stepped up next to the bed.

Rogers's eyes opened. They were bloodshot, and his skin was the color of a corpse.

"How's the leg?" she asked.

"Clean wound." Rogers frowned. "But I'll probably be out of work for a few months."

"I'm not worried about your physical recovery." Bree had heard a report from the doctor when she'd first arrived in the ER.

Rogers's face reddened. "I'm sorry for what happened."

"We don't have to talk about this now."

"I do." His voice rose.

"OK."

"I froze. I panicked. If Matt hadn't been there, I could have gotten you killed." Rogers turned his face away from her.

Bree pulled a plastic chair to the side of the bed, so she was eye level with him. "Did you see the dog charge me at Joe Marcus's house?"

He frowned. "I was in my car. I saw the dog, but I didn't see what happened with it."

"I froze because I'm afraid of dogs."

Rogers's head turned back to her. She'd surprised him with the admission.

She continued. "I was mauled as a child. I'm trying to overcome it, but I haven't been successful. Matt had to step in and take control of the situation."

Rogers met her gaze.

"Clearly, I have a major issue I need to work on," Bree said. "How long have you been struggling?"

He studied the folded sheet at his waist. "Since the shooting."

"Which shooting?" she asked.

He hadn't been part of the active shooter Bree and Matt had handled back in January.

"When I shot Matt Flynn and Brody." Rogers raised a hand and covered his eyes.

"That was over three years ago."

Rogers lowered his hand and closed his eyes for a few seconds. When he opened them, his expression looked bleak. "I was able to mostly suppress it until January, when I saw Matt again."

"And it's been building since then?" Bree had seen his stress level rising just over the three weeks since she'd been appointed.

"Yeah." He swallowed. "I know. I let it go. I thought . . ." He breathed. "I thought I should just get over it, that admitting I couldn't handle it was weak. It sounds stupid now."

"Not at all. I let my trauma fester for thirty years, so I understand. Do you want help?" Bree didn't assume, nor did she tell him he wouldn't go back on duty until he'd been cleared by a psychiatrist.

His voice dropped to a raspy whisper. "Yeah. I don't know if I'll ever get past it."

"You'll get help, and we'll see how it goes." She pointed to his leg, encased in bandages under the sheet. "You're going to have some time."

"I guess I will." He sighed, the sound long and full of pain. "I need to talk to Matt."

"You'll be out of surgery in a couple of hours," Bree said.

"No." Rogers grabbed her arm. "I need to talk to him now. I have something I need to say, in case . . ."

"Rogers—Jim." Bree squeezed his hand. "You're going to be OK."

"Please."

"OK. I'll get him. Can you keep the dog thing to yourself? I'd rather that not be general knowledge."

Rogers took a finger and drew a cross over his heart. "I won't tell a soul."

"Thank you." Bree ducked out of the room and called for Matt.

He peered through the doorway.

Bree said, "Rogers wants to talk to you."

# CHAPTER THIRTY-NINE

Apprehensive, Matt walked into Rogers's room. Rogers looked rough, all tubes and wires and pasty skin.

"You stay too, Sheriff. Please." Rogers licked his chapped lips. His voice was hoarse. He was heading into surgery, so no water.

Matt approached the side of the bed. "This can wait until tomorrow. You look like hell."

Rogers responded with a small shake of his head. "Just in case. I want you to know. It wasn't intentional. Me shooting you and Brody. It was dark, and the sheriff told me you were in the other side of the building. I thought you were one of the drug dealers."

Matt opened his mouth to respond.

"Let me get this out before I run out of air." Rogers held up a weak hand. "I won't presume to know the sheriff's intentions. I can only speak to mine, and I am sorry. You'll never know how much."

"Thanks for that." Matt touched his shoulder. "I think I do."

Rogers closed his eyes. His body relaxed, as if he'd just rid himself of a great weight.

"I'll be back later to check on you," Bree said.

Matt and Bree returned to the hallway. His step felt lighter, as if he'd made the confession instead of Rogers.

"You believe him?" Bree asked. "I know you had concerns that the sheriff targeted you."

"Yeah. I believe him." Matt and Rogers had both suffered at the hands of the old sheriff. Maybe Matt could put his past behind him now. He hoped Rogers could do the same.

"Me too."

They walked back to the ER triage area. The plastic surgeon used five tiny stitches to close the gap in Bree's cheek and covered the cut with a small bandage. Then she and Matt found the surgical waiting room and drank coffee until Rogers came out of surgery. Once she was satisfied her deputy was recovering, Bree was ready to go home.

It was four in the morning before they headed for the exit. The glare of camera lights greeted her at the emergency room glass door.

"Do you want to sneak out a different exit?" Matt asked.

"No. This is part of the job." She pushed through the doors.

Matt stepped aside and let her do her thing. She gave a brief statement about her deputy's condition, the condition of the rescued victim, and the unfortunate death of the suspect. She did it without grandstanding and credited her deputies and the Scarlet Falls PD. But the exhaustion in her eyes and the bandage on her cheek spoke of her involvement.

She looked badass.

When a reporter asked her a question, she raised a hand. "You'll have to wait for questions until I've had time to consult with investigators." She excused herself. The crowd of reporters parted as she walked toward her vehicle.

He climbed into the passenger seat, and Bree drove to the station, dropping him off at his SUV.

He reached for the door handle. "Good night."

"More like good morning." Bree reached over and took his hand in hers. "Thank you for having my back."

Matt squeezed her fingers. "You're welcome."

She held on for a few seconds. The connection formed by their joined hands was deeper than any Matt could remember.

"Get some sleep." She let go.

He missed the physical contact immediately. "Are you heading home?"

Bree glanced at the dashboard clock. "I'll write up some notes first. I have some time before the kids wake up. I want to get some of the details down while they're still fresh in my mind. I'll need a statement from you as well, but I can wait until you've slept."

"I'll see you later, then." Matt had something to do first as well, while he still had an hour of darkness.

He drove his Suburban out to Grey Lake and parked a half mile from Joe Marcus's house. Then he climbed out, filled his pockets with Brody's kibble and an extra leash, and walked into the woods. He followed a game trail parallel to the lake until he reached the back of Earl Harper's property. Several law enforcement vehicles and a forensic unit were parked at Joe Marcus's house next door. The dog had no doubt barked all night. Hopefully, Earl was ignoring him by now.

But the big dog didn't bark as Matt crept through the trees. Instead, Rufus whined.

"Shhh." Matt tossed a handful of kibble toward him.

Rufus paced the length of his chain a few times, then he lowered his head and approached the kibble. Hungry, he inhaled it.

Matt tossed him another handful and moved a few steps closer. "Remember me, buddy? I'm not going to hurt you."

Rufus continued to eat as Matt stepped up to him and rubbed his ears. The dog's collar was loose. Matt slid it off and dropped it in the mud. Then he threaded his leash through its own handle and slipped the loop over the dog's head. He hand-fed him the dog kibble and led him away. Matt backtracked to his SUV and put the dog in the back seat. As he drove away, he reached over the seat and scratched the dog's head. Then he dialed his sister's number, talking to the dog while the phone rang. "Your life just changed, my friend."

It was nearly six in the morning when Matt turned into his own driveway. His sister was in the kennel, feeding her rescues. She whipped her ponytail over her shoulder. "I saw the news. You're all right?"

"Yes."

She hugged him, then looked down at Rufus. "Is that the dog?"

"Yes. He's going to have some trust issues."

"Where did you get him?"

"Just call him a rural stray," Matt said. "But it would be best if you could send him to a foster out of town and maybe keep his picture off the internet."

Cady raised a brow.

Matt patted her shoulder. "Tell you what. You don't ask where he came from, and I won't ask where you send him. Trust me on this."

"OK." Cady finished feeding the dogs, then took Rufus's leash. He sniffed her hand and leaned in for a scratch. "Does he have a name?"

"No. Rural stray, remember?"

Rufus was going to have a new life. He deserved a new name.

Cady rolled her eyes. "If he has a microchip . . ."

"He won't." Matt pictured the muddy yard he'd been chained in. "I doubt he's ever been to a vet."

Matt watched Cady load the dog into a crate in the back of her minivan.

She closed the rear hatch. "I didn't feed Brody or Greta yet."

"I'll take care of them." Matt was still too wired to sleep.

"Are you completely besotted with Greta? Is our gorgeous black shepherd going to be a foster fail?" Cady's voice was hopeful. "There aren't many people who can handle a young dog like her."

Matt shook his head. "I have an idea. Let me think on it awhile before we talk, OK?"

"OK." Cady kissed him on the cheek. "Get some sleep. You look terrible."

"I love you too." Matt went into the house, expecting Greta to be wild when he let her out of her crate. But she greeted him in the kitchen. The crate was open. Matt stroked his beard. She'd figured out how to open the metal door. *Wonderful.*

Life was going to get interesting. Brody looked less than thrilled.

"How did you do that?" Matt asked her.

She wagged her tail.

"You are too smart," he said.

Matt fed both dogs and took them out in the yard. Back inside, he closed the bedroom door to keep both dogs confined. Then he showered and fell into bed face-first. Greta surprised him by curling up on the floor and closing her eyes.

He pointed at Brody, stretched out next to the bed. "You're in charge."

Brody groaned.

Matt hoped she didn't eat the bedroom while he slept, but he was too tired to care.

# CHAPTER FORTY

Bree walked into the Scarlet Falls Police Station that afternoon. She'd already stopped at the hospital. Christian would be released that evening if he showed no signs of complications. Rogers's surgery had gone well. He would stay in the hospital for a couple of days, but the prognosis was good for his injury. His willingness to address his probable PTSD was the first step toward emotional recovery.

She stopped at the front desk and asked for Detective Dane. Stella appeared a minute later, looking as ragged as Bree felt.

Frowning, Stella escorted Bree to the interview room. "Overnight, Alyssa magically retained the best defense attorney in the area."

"Who is that?" Bree asked.

"My sister, Morgan." Stella studied Bree's face. "You didn't call her, did you?"

"No." Bree didn't blink. Technically, that was not a lie.

Stella turned. "I thought you and I would conduct the interview, since we're the most familiar with the case."

"Fine."

They walked into the interview room. Alyssa sat in a chair, her shoulders hunched, her head bowed. A woman rose from the chair next to her. She was tall, with long black hair and blue eyes. She wore a well-fitted suit, a silk blouse, and heels.

She held out a hand to Bree. "I'm Morgan Dane. I'll be representing Ms. Vincent."

The family resemblance between Morgan and Stella was clear. But Stella dressed like Bree. No jewelry, no makeup, simple hair, utilitarian clothes. Morgan was the sort of woman who made Bree wish she had a clue about accessorizing. She was wearing pearls. Actual freaking pearls.

Stella and Bree settled on the opposite side of the table. Stella announced everyone's name for the recording, then read Alyssa her rights and had her sign a standard form. Then she began. "Alyssa, I'd like to start by asking you how you knew Joe Marcus."

Morgan leaned forward. "Before my client answers a single question, let's clarify her position." The attorney consulted a notepad. "At this point, you have no physical evidence tying my client to any of the burglaries. Nor is she implicated in any way to the murders of Sara Harper, Brian O'Neil, or Eli Whitney. In fact, my client was nearly a murder victim herself."

"Before he died, Joe Marcus stated that Alyssa was complicit in burglaries committed by Sara Harper," Stella said. "It's in Sheriff Taggert's report, and so is your client's confession."

Morgan looked up from her notes. "Your only evidence linking my client to a potential burglary charge is the word of a dead serial killer?"

Three heartbeats of silence passed.

Morgan continued. "In the sheriff's report, Alyssa admitted to making some mistakes, and even that statement could be attributed to trying to placate Joe Marcus in order to stay alive. My client did not confess to any crime. Sara Harper's fingerprints were on the recovered jewelry, not Ms. Vincent's."

"We have videos showing your client's vehicle being used during the burglaries," Stella said.

Morgan shuffled papers. "In one of Sheriff Taggert's interviews, my client already explained that Sara Harper used the vehicle without permission," she replied, holding up a copy of Bree's notes.

Marge had texted Bree early that morning to let her know the defense attorney was requesting copies. Bree wasn't obligated to provide them, since Alyssa hadn't formally been charged, but Bree saw no reason to withhold her reports. She still had to complete and close her investigation into the murders, but with Joe Marcus dead, there was no trial on the horizon.

"While she was sleeping?" Stella asked in a disbelieving tone.

Morgan answered with a bland expression. "That's what we assume."

Which was lawyer code for *can you prove otherwise?*

Bree sat back. Morgan had summed up the situation nicely. They might all know that Alyssa was involved in the burglaries, but they couldn't prove it. Maybe evidence would arise later, but that didn't matter today.

*Morgan has been busy this morning.*

Bree was impressed. Morgan Dane was a damned good lawyer, advocating for her client with the letter of the law and no theatrics. Bree had been worried about Alyssa being charged in Stella's burglary case, but she hadn't had time to thoroughly evaluate the evidence, or lack of it. Morgan had sliced through it like a human machete.

Morgan stacked her papers. "I would like to request you release my client immediately. We would also request her vehicle and personal possessions be returned to her. When do you think that might happen, Sheriff?"

"That's up to Detective Dane," Bree said. "As far as the murder cases go, forensics is finished with the 4Runner and Alyssa's backpack. Her wallet was found in Sara Harper's bag, which is part of the burglary investigation."

Morgan lifted a brow at her sister.

"Fine," Stella huffed.

"Excellent." Morgan tucked her notes into her briefcase.

"We're not finished," Bree said. "Ms. Vincent can still be charged with criminal trespass for entering and remaining in the campground without permission."

Morgan sat back. "Which is a misdemeanor."

"But is still punishable with up to one year in prison." Bree felt like a jerk, but Alyssa had information no one else could provide.

"What do you want, Sheriff?" Morgan asked.

"Answers," Bree said. "The victims' families deserve to know what happened."

Morgan paused for a few seconds. "My client will only answer questions in exchange for immunity from any and all charges. Otherwise, she will invoke her fifth amendment right to remain silent."

"Agreed," Bree said. The trespassing charge was lame anyway. There were no damages to the property. The typical sentence was a fine and community service, which they all knew. She'd deal with the prosecutor later, but she doubted he'd want to muddy a very complicated serial murderer investigation by charging the only witness with a minor crime. Besides, it was Bree's case, and without her cooperation, it would be impossible to make the charge stick.

"Fine." Stella tossed a frustrated hand in the air.

Bree turned to Alyssa. "Tell us how you know Joe Marcus."

Alyssa swallowed. "I didn't *meet* him at all until he forced me into his car after he set the motel on fire, but Harper had told me about him. She said he was her former partner. She didn't want to work with him anymore because he was going scary crazy. She said he wanted to kill some guys because they'd made fun of him."

"Did she say how he became her partner?" Bree asked.

Alyssa nodded. "They already knew each other. He was a plumber. Sometimes, when he was on a job, he'd be alone in a house. He'd go through the place looking for valuables. Nothing that could be traced, just small, easy-to-steal things like jewelry and cash." She breathed. "Joe would make lists of houses he thought would be easy to break into. No alarms, et cetera. He wrote down where the valuables were kept and other notes that helped Harper get in and out fast. Harper was supposed to wait three months before hitting the houses, but a couple of times she jumped the gun."

"But she didn't want to work with him anymore," Bree prompted.

"Yeah. He didn't take it well." Alyssa took a deep breath. "When I saw him shoot her, I didn't know for sure it was him, but I guessed it might have been."

"But you did see him clearly?" Bree asked.

Alyssa lifted the end of her hair and chewed on it. "Yes."

"You recognized him in Walmart," Bree said.

"Yes." Alyssa's voice was barely audible.

Bree had been right about the incident. She had no doubt it had been a test by Joe to see if Alyssa could identify him. She'd failed, and he'd decided she needed to die.

"Which houses did you help Sara Harper burglarize?" Stella asked.

Morgan interrupted. "I'll need that immunity deal in writing from the DA before I allow my client to answer that question."

Alyssa put her hand flat on the table. "Look, I know I was wrong. But I was broke and depressed and sorry afterward. I'm not a bad person."

"It's what you do going forward that matters," Bree said.

A bad person would have run instead of helping Rogers. Alyssa had stayed, even though that decision had gotten her arrested.

Alyssa's eyes opened wide. "It won't be something stupid like that again. I learned my lesson."

Bree pushed back her chair.

"That's it?" Alyssa glanced back and forth between Morgan, Bree, and Stella.

"That's it." Morgan smiled. "You're free to go."

"Do you have a place to stay?" Bree asked Alyssa.

"Yeah. Marge called the manager of the campground. He's going to give me a job as caretaker for the next two months. If I do an OK job, we'll talk about making it full-time."

"That's great." Relief flooded Bree. The girl had committed crimes. But she'd been desperate and easily manipulated by Sara Harper. Bree could not excuse her criminal behavior, but Alyssa had done the right thing when it had mattered. People weren't perfect. Going to prison wouldn't improve her chances of becoming a functioning member of society, but a little help might.

Bree drove back to the sheriff's station. Her butt had barely hit her office chair when Todd knocked on her doorframe.

"Come in," she said. "Did you get any sleep?"

He stretched his neck. "I went home for a couple of hours."

"Good." Bree had eaten breakfast with the kids and napped for three hours before returning to work. "Where do we stand on wrapping up our investigation?"

Todd sighed. "Ballistics matched Joe Marcus's gun with the bullets used to kill Brian O'Neil."

"Good," Bree said. "The ME hasn't completed the autopsies on Sara Harper or Eli Whitney yet, but I spoke to Dr. Jones briefly about the lack of blood on the ice behind the cabins. She won't commit, of course, but she speculates from an external exam that the bullets that killed Sara struck her in the liver. Most of the bleeding would have been internal."

"That makes sense," Todd said. "Forensics is still processing Joe's house. But his computer was a jackpot. He kept an online journal, starting back in high school, where he was bullied. He was pretty much a social outcast since graduating. His posts escalated from loneliness and isolation to anger over the next couple of years. Everyone at the plumbing company thought he was weird. He had no friends there. He mentioned Sara in a number of posts, and he became resentful that she wasn't interested in him. After the four roommates picked on him, he wrote about his rage, with lots of details on how he wanted to kill them. Also, he had a whole computer folder full of pictures of Sara Harper, going all the way back to high school. He was clearly obsessed with her, but she had no interest in him. The only reason he helped her with her burglary scheme was because he wanted to please her."

"And she used him."

"Seems like it," Todd agreed. "He was convinced Sara had slept with both Eli Whitney and Brian O'Neil."

"Maybe she did. There were pictures of her with both Eli and Brian," Bree said. "Joe's company regularly serviced the house Eli, Brian, Christian, and Dustin lived in. Joe had already worked on Brian's mother's house. So, he was probably the one who put Brian in Sara's sights. Sara targeted both Eli and Brian, but likely dropped Eli when she figured out his family didn't have any money."

"Yes," Todd agreed. "According to his journal, Joe was already jealous when he went to work on their water heater. Eli and his roommates picked on Joe, and that sent him over the edge."

"At least there's no doubt that we got the right man."

"No doubt at all," Todd said and left the office.

Marge popped her head in. "There's an Earl Harper in the lobby to see you. He insists on speaking only with you."

Bree sighed. She couldn't refuse. His daughter had been killed. He was an ass, but he was also a victim. "OK. Bring him in."

A minute later, Marge ushered Earl in.

"Have a seat." Bree gestured toward the chairs that faced her desk.

"I don't want to sit." Earl planted his fists on the desk and loomed, his anger palpable in the small room.

"How can I help you?"

"You killed Joe Marcus?" Earl asked.

"He was shot by the sheriff's department," Bree said. She hadn't given out Matt's name.

Earl straightened and crossed his arms. "Someone stole my dog."

The abrupt change in topic confused Bree. "What?"

"My dog. Someone stole it." A vein throbbed on Earl's temple.

The memory of the dog charging her raised goose bumps on her arms, and a slight wave of nausea passed over her. She swallowed it. Earl Harper was the last person she wanted to see her weakness. "Do you want to fill out a report?"

"Maybe." His eyes narrowed. He'd seen her reaction.

*Damn.*

Bree didn't like him knowing about her fear. "Is the dog microchipped?"

"No." His jaw sawed. "Did you steal it?"

"Why would I do that?"

He didn't answer. But then, what could he say? *Because I let it loose to bite you?*

"I haven't been anywhere near your dog," Bree said. "Do you have vet records? Ownership papers? Photos?"

"No. I knew you wouldn't help."

"Mr. Harper. You are welcome to fill out a report, and one of my deputies will investigate, but it would be helpful to have ownership records and pictures of the dog." Bree stood. "I'm truly sorry for the loss of your daughter."

Earl's face reddened. "Would have been great if someone had figured out Marcus was a murderer *before* he killed Sara." He stormed out of her office.

Marge came in. "What was up with him?"

Bree explained. "I suspect he doesn't know how to process his daughter's death, and he needs somewhere to focus his anger."

Bree had a bad feeling she hadn't seen the last of Earl's misplaced rage.

"Who do you think stole his dog?" Marge stared at Bree. They both knew.

*Matt.*

Bree stood. "I'm going home."

# CHAPTER FORTY-ONE

Bree left her paperwork incomplete and arrived home in time to have dinner with her family. She parked next to her brother's ancient Bronco. Wanting fresh clothes before she saw the family, she went in the little-used front door. Bree headed for the bedroom and changed into jeans and a sweater.

She didn't want to be the sheriff tonight. She just wanted to be with her family.

Bree joined Dana in the kitchen, which smelled of garlic and lemon. Vader perched on the counter, watching Dana cook. Out the back window, Bree spotted Kayla grooming her pony, Pumpkin, in the fading sunlight. Adam perched on the top of the fence, a sketch pad on his lap. Ladybug napped in the grass at Adam's feet. The barn door stood open. The day had warmed above freezing, and the waning sun shone on the grass.

"Where's Luke?" Bree wandered to the fridge.

"In the barn." Dana stood at the stove, stirring something in a saucepan. "They were all stir-crazy, including your brother. I sent them outside."

Chuckling, Bree opened a can of seltzer. "What are you making?"

"Chicken piccata with a side of penne. There's tiramisu for dessert."

"Homemade?" Bree checked the fridge. She hadn't eaten a real meal in days.

"Of course it's homemade. My Italian grandmother would rise from her grave and swat me with a wooden spoon if I served store-bought." Dana shook her head. "Matt called and invited himself to dinner."

"Matt called you?" Bree was suspicious.

Dana lifted a shoulder.

Bree checked her phone. Matt hadn't called her. The last time he'd gone directly to Dana, Bree had ended up with a rescue dog she hadn't wanted. "What is he up to?"

"He didn't say." Dana paused to catch Bree's gaze. "I thought maybe he just wanted to see you."

Warmth flushed Bree's face.

Dana shook her head. "I was going to invite him anyway. That is one fine man."

"I know."

Dana glanced up, her face surprised. "So, why are you not pursuing that fine man?"

"Because I'm an idiot?" Bree sipped some seltzer. "I was all bogged down with making time for a relationship, but that's ridiculous. Matt fits right in with the family. The kids like him. I like him."

She thought about the moment they'd shared in the hospital and knew the potential existed for more than *liking* him.

Dana tapped her spoon on the edge of the pan. "I'm glad you finally got some sense."

"But I just hired Matt as an investigator." Bree frowned. "I'm not sure if that complicates things."

Dana waved off her concern. "He's a civilian contractor."

"Money flows from the sheriff's office to Matt. It doesn't look good if I have a romantic relationship with him. What will people think?"

"Fuck 'em," Dana said.

Bree choked on her seltzer. "What?"

"Since when do you care what people think?" Dana pointed at Bree with her wooden spoon.

"Since I became an elected official, who wasn't even really elected." Bree coughed and wiped seltzer off her chin.

"That doesn't mean you don't get to have a life. Whether or not you are dating one of your criminal investigators won't be the reason people don't support you. Besides, you have like three years until your current term is over. I wouldn't worry about an election just yet. Your predecessor was crooked as shit, and he was hugely popular. People will see what they want to see. So far, you're looking like a damned good sheriff. Don't worry about anything else. Just do the job to the best of your ability. Be fair. Be honest. In short, be you."

"I need the job."

"You need *a* job." Dana set down her spoon, then moved to the cutting board and began slicing bread. "If you don't get reelected in three years, you'll find another one. Or Adam will write you a giant check. Hell, I have my pension. You and the kids will never starve."

"I like to be independent."

"You like to control everything." Dana paused to make eye contact. "But it isn't possible, and you'll make yourself crazy trying."

Dana was probably right.

Outside, a vehicle door slammed.

Dana glanced out the window and grinned. "Speak of the handsome devil. Oh, he shaved. I don't know how I like him best."

Bree couldn't decide either.

Dana whistled. "He's fine any which way."

Bree agreed.

Matt lifted Brody out of the vehicle and set him gently on the ground. The big dog moved toward the house. His gait was stiff, but he seemed better. Ladybug rose and greeted Brody with a wag of her tail stump and a feminine arch of her neck. *Flirt.*

Bree knew how the dog felt.

"I think your dog is sweet on Brody." Dana laughed.

Matt went into the barn while Brody and Ladybug sniffed each other. Bree relaxed and set the table. When dinner was ready, she called everyone in. Dinner with her family—and Matt—was just the tonic Bree needed. Adam showed her the sketch he'd done of Kayla. Luke and Matt talked about the latest video game. Kayla chattered nonstop. It was loud and chaotic and perfect.

After dinner, Adam went home, the kids settled in with homework, and Dana cleaned up the kitchen.

"I'll do barn check." Bree put on her coat and boots.

"I'll help." Matt followed her outside. They walked in silence to the barn. The night was cold and clear, the black sky dotted with stars.

The barn smelled like warm animals and fresh straw. Bree checked water buckets and tossed hay.

Inside Pumpkin's stall, she looked over the pony's rump at Matt. "You wouldn't know where Earl Harper's dog is, would you?"

"I have no idea where Earl Harper's dog is," Matt answered. His deadpan expression reminded Bree of the way she'd answered Stella's question about calling Morgan Dane.

He wasn't lying, but Bree could sense he knew something. Matt had stood between her and Earl's dog. He'd risked taking a bite so she wouldn't—probably because he also hadn't wanted Todd to shoot the dog. Earl had risked getting his dog shot. He didn't deserve to own an animal.

She let it go. "Never mind. I don't want to know."

Matt leaned on the half door. "I talked to Luke tonight before dinner."

"Thank you. What do you think?"

"He's having a hard time, but he doesn't want you to worry. He sees himself as the man of the house. He wants to help you carry the burden, not add to it."

"He's just a boy."

"But that's just it. He's not." Matt moved backward so Bree could exit the pony's stall.

"You're right." Bree had been seeing him all wrong. Luke was on the brink of manhood. "What do you think I should do?"

"He wants to feel useful right now. Let him do the heavy work on the farm. Ask him for his help. Contributing to the family makes him feel part of it. He needs to be needed, if that makes sense."

"It does." Bree ducked into Cowboy's stall to adjust the paint gelding's blanket. "I'll just have to be patient."

"Try not to worry. I'll keep checking in with him."

"Thank you. He needed a man to talk to. I can't be that for him." Bree patted the horse and left the stall. "Adam is trying really hard, but he can't read people."

"Anytime." Matt closed the door for her. "I have a proposal for you."

Bree turned.

"You want a K-9."

"For the department, yes."

"I'm working with a young German shepherd. She needs another four months or so to mature before she can start training, but I think she would be an excellent police K-9. She has the drive, the confidence, and the intelligence."

"I have no money in my budget for a K-9. I'm going to have to raise the funds. It'll take me a few months."

"This dog is a rescue. She'd be free. You'd only need to raise money for training and equipment, and I'm sure Cady would help with that. She's great with fundraisers. People like dogs. They'll give."

"And you think this dog will work? Because I'd rather invest in the right dog than cut corners." Bree saw no point in saving a few bucks only to have a subpar K-9.

"I do. She's the whole package, very much like Brody when I first started working with him."

Bree stopped him. "I trust your judgment on all things canine."

"You trust me." He grinned and walked her backward until she was pressed against the wall.

"I do."

His face sobered. "The last time I tried to kiss you, you shut me down."

"Did I?" She rested her palms on his chest.

"You did." He pressed his big body against hers. "It was a huge blow to my fragile male ego."

She snorted and patted his pecs. "There is nothing fragile about you or your ego."

"Why do I have the urge to flex?"

She laughed. "I'm sorry I shut you down."

She was. Very. At this moment, she couldn't think of anything she'd like more than to kiss him.

He leaned close. His breath was warm on her cheek. "So, you're saying if I try to kiss you now, you'll let me?"

She tilted her head back and looked up at him. His blue eyes had gone dark. His intense focus felt like a touch. Her toes curled. If she was going to give up some of the tight control she held on her life, she may as well enjoy the ride. "I'd say it's a sure thing."

He lowered his head a few inches, then paused. "But you also have to promise me we're going to spend time together when we're not standing over a dead body."

"Deal."

# ACKNOWLEDGMENTS

It truly takes a team to publish a book. As always, credit goes to my agent, Jill Marsal, for ten years of unwavering support and great advice. I'm thankful for the entire team at Montlake, especially my managing editor, Anh Schluep, and my developmental editor, Charlotte Herscher. Special thanks to Rayna Vause and Kendra Elliot for help with various technical details, moral support, and plot advice.

# ABOUT THE AUTHOR

*Photo © 2016 Jared Gruenwald Photography*

#1 Amazon Charts and #1 *Wall Street Journal* bestselling author Melinda Leigh is a fully recovered banker. Melinda's debut novel, *She Can Run*, was nominated for Best First Novel by the International Thriller Writers. She's garnered numerous writing awards, including two RITA nominations. Her other novels include *She Can Tell, She Can Scream, She Can Hide, She Can Kill, Midnight Exposure, Midnight Sacrifice, Midnight Betrayal, Midnight Obsession, Hour of Need, Minutes to Kill, Seconds to Live, Say You're Sorry, Her Last Goodbye, Bones Don't Lie, What I've Done, Secrets Never Die, Save Your Breath*, and *Cross Her Heart*. She holds a second-degree black belt in Kenpo karate, has taught women's self-defense, and lives in a messy house with her family and a small herd of rescue pets. For more information, visit www.melindaleigh.com.